T0146490

"When I knock a woman out, I like to make sure she survives the experience."

Heat ticked down her spine and uncoiled in her abdomen. Why the hell did everything he say sound sexual? She narrowed her gaze. "You assaulted a police officer, buddy."

"Kellach. Kellach Dunne." He smiled, revealing perfectly white teeth in stunning symmetry. "I didn't mean ta hurt you, Alexandra, and you know it."

True. He had been busy shielding her from careening fire when his shoulder had connected with her still aching face. "Detective Monzelle to you. How about you come down to the station with me and answer some questions?" She carefully slid from the bed, her bare feet touching cold concrete.

"No."

She glanced around the pristine room again, wondering if she could take him down. "This isn't what I expected," she mused to herself.

"This is your first time in a bed at Fire?"

She stilled and turned to face him, hiding her vulnerability. "I try not to fuck motorcycle gang members, especially those involved in the local drug trade."

His grin was slow—dangerous—and amused. "Club. Motorcycle *club* members. Titans of Fire Motorcycle Club, to be exact." He stood and leaned against the door, blocking the only exit. "We need ta discuss that allegation before we get to the fucking."

THE DARK PROTECTORS SERIES
BY REBECCA ZANETTI

Wicked Ride

Realm Enforcers, Book 1

REBECCA
ZANETTI

LYRICAL PRESS
Kensington Publishing Corp.
www.kensingtonbooks.com

LYRICAL PRESS BOOKS are published by

Kensington Publishing Corp.
119 West 40th Street
New York, NY 10018

All Kensington titles, imprints, and distributed lines are available at special quantity discounts for bulk purchases for sales promotions, premiums, fund-raising, educational, or institutional use.

Special book excerpts or customized printings can also be created to fit specific needs. For details, write or phone the office of the Kensington special sales manager: Kensington Publishing Corp., 119 West 40th Street, New York, NY 10018, attn: Special Sales Department; phone 1-800-221-2647.

LYRICAL PRESS and the Lyrical logo are trademarks of Kensington Publishing Corp.

First electronic edition: June 2015

ISBN-13: 978-1-60183-413-3
ISBN-10: 1-60183-413-6

First print edition: June 2015

ISBN-13: 978-1-60183-557-4
ISBN-10: 1-60183-557-4

This book is dedicated to all of the energetic Dark Protector fans who asked for more of those wild immortals and their mates. Thank you for your support, for the reviews, for the fan emails, for the tweets, and for the Facebook posts through the years! I very much hope you like this spinoff series, The Realm Enforcers.

ACKNOWLEDGMENTS

I have many people to thank for help in getting this new series to readers, and I sincerely apologize to anyone I've forgotten.

Thank you to Big Tone for giving me tons to write about and for being supportive from the very first time I sat down to write. Thanks also to Gabe and Karlina for being such awesome kids and for making life so much fun.

Thank you to my talented agents, Caitlin Blasdell and Liza Dawson, who have been with me from the first book and who have supported, guided, and protected me in this wild industry.

Thank you to my amazing editor, Alicia Condon, who is brilliant, willing to take a risk, and has absolutely fantastic taste in shoes. She also has the knack of finding the coolest restaurants in any city.

Thank you Alexandra Nicolajsen, who has been known to tear up while making guacamole upon finding out one of her authors has hit the *Times*; and thank you to Vida Engstrand, who throws the best parties in the universe, because they make shy and introverted authors feel comfortable. Thanks to Arthur Maisel for the excellent production. I can't remember in which book I learned that *pistoning* wasn't a verb, but I've never forgotten it; and thank you to Fiona Jayde for creating just the right cover.

Thanks also to Steven Zacharius and Adam Zacharius for taking a family company and including everyone, especially authors, in that family.

Thank you to Romance Writers of America for all the great classes, contacts, and conferences. Thanks to my RWA chapters and friends: IECRWA, KOD, FF&P, and PASIC.

And thanks also to my constant support system: Gail and Jim English, Debbie and Travis Smith, Stephanie and Don West, Brandie and Mike Chapman, Jessica and Jonah Namson, and Kathy and Herb Zanetti. Thanks to Augustina Van Hoven for such skill in naming books.

Chapter 1

Kellach Dunne held his fire and turned the corner, keeping his prey in sight. Rain smattered the concrete sidewalk in a weary Seattle fashion, while garish lights from bars and massage parlors marred the comforting darkness of the midnight hour. He stepped over the legs of a bum and ignored the stench of piss, absently wishing for his bed and a good night's sleep.

He'd left his Harley parked in a side alley to follow the bastard who stalked a woman through the city's underbelly.

The woman scurried ahead, glancing over her shoulder, her instincts obviously kicking in. Her tight neon blue mini-dress hampered her movements, but he could appreciate the outfit—the kind that curved in just under the ass. The woman had a hell of an ass. Too bad she tottered in five-inch heels and from what smelled like Fireball whiskey.

He opened his senses to the night and the universe, scenting what humans couldn't even imagine. Yep. Fireball and tequila. Dangerous combination. Although a lingering smell, just under the surface, sped up his blood.

Woman. Fresh and clean . . . all woman.

The man ahead of him stank of body odor, dime store cologne, and cigarette smoke. And something else, something that made Kellach's temples pound.

Damn it, hells fire, and motherfucker. The bastard had taken the drug. The human had somehow ingested the drug right under Kell's nose.

Kell had hung out in the Seattle underground bar for nearly a week, and somehow, the dealer had gotten past him. No wonder the foul smelling human was hunting the woman. He wouldn't be able to help himself.

She broke into a run, surprisingly agile on the heels. As she reacted to the imminent danger, she leaped over a mud puddle and turned down a barely lit alley.

Why the fuck did they always run down an alley? Shaking his head, Kellach increased his strides while the human male in front of him did the same. Idiot didn't even know Kellach tracked him.

Dim light from the upper apartments filtered down through the fog to barely light the way, although Kell could see fine in the dark.

The woman ran by two overflowing dumpsters, a couple garbage cans, a cardboard box housing a vagrant smelling like marijuana, and an odd arrangement of yellow flower pots perched on the back stoop of a porn shop. She reached the end of the alley blocked by a brick building and whirled around.

Gorgeous. Meager light shone down, highlighting a stunning face. Even with a ridiculous amount of blue eye shadow, pink blush, and bright red lipstick, she was a looker. Deep blue eyes, the color of the witching hour, stared out from a fine-boned face.

A woman like that not only didn't belong in a fucking alley . . . she didn't belong in the bar she'd just left.

The human male slowed and let out a low chuckle that sounded slightly manic. He towered over the woman, even in her heels, and before Kell's eyes, his shoulders seem to broaden in his flannel shirt. "Looks like you're at a dead end," the guy said.

The woman sucked in air, her chest moving nicely with the effort. "W-what is wrong with your eyes?"

The human shrugged.

Kell gave a slight nod. Yep. His eyes should be all sorts of crazy at this point.

The skin down Kell's arm sprang to life and the hair rose in warning. The atmosphere changed.

Flames, an unhealthy dark blue and morphing, danced down the human male's right arm. He gasped and shook out his wrist. Then he threw back his head and laughed. "Did you see that?"

The woman gaped and then slowly shook her head. "Did you just set your arm on fire?"

"No. I *am* fire." He held out his arm again, and flames licked down.

The woman inched to the side of the alley and stumbled over a loose brick. "What drug are you on?" Her focus narrowed as she regained her footing.

"Who cares? I'm invincible. I can create fire." More flames danced. The guy formed a ball in one hand. "Take off the dress, or I'll burn it off."

"That's not garing ta happen," Kell said, moving to the side, opposite of the woman.

The guy whirled around, fire whipping. "What the hell?"

"Been following you." Kell kept his hands loosely at his sides while fighting back the urge to alter matter with quantum physics and create his own fire. Just being in the same vicinity of another fire starter, one who didn't have a clue what to do, made him itchy. "Get lost, lady. I have business with the gent here."

The guy squinted. "You Australian?"

"No." Kell drew himself up. *Australian?* Fucking moron. "Move. Now," he ordered the woman, who'd frozen in place.

The guy shook his head. "If she moves, I'll burn her. Even through the rain, I'm all powerful."

"W-what's your business?" asked the woman as she took a tentative step along the building. Water sloshed up her shapely leg, and she had to shove short wet hair away from her face.

"Doesn't concern you." Kell angled deeper into the alley so the guy would have to partially turn to keep him in sight, thus giving the woman a chance for freedom. Rain splattered into his eyes. "Just get moving, would you?"

"No." The guy shook out both hands, and fire flickered. Blue and yellow stripes cut paths through his brown eyes, and red bloomed in the white parts. "I'll kill you both."

Kellach sighed. "How much of the drug did you take?" If the guy had only taken half a dose, he might live.

"The whole damn thing." The guy spun around, and plasma fire sailed into a dumpster, ripping a hole in the metal. "They said I'd be a god. I'm a fucking god."

The woman cringed against the brick building. "I don't understand. What kind of a weapon throws fire?"

Kell shot forward and slid an arm around the guy's neck, spinning him into a headlock, their backs to the woman. Fire burst along the guy's arms, burning Kell. Pain dug under his skin. With a low growl, Kell allowed his own fire free. Deep and green, it crackled along his body, shielding him from harm. With a puff of smoke, Kell's fire quelled the human's.

The human convulsed. Hard and fast, he shook against Kell, who held him upright. It was too late to help the guy—he had taken too much. Way too much. A wretched scream spilled from the human's throat.

Kell released him and stepped back.

The guy fell to the wet ground, still convulsing. Red poured from his ears, his eyes, and then his nose. The rancid stench of burned flesh filled the alley. He hit hard, shook, and then went still. His eyes retained the bizarre colors, and he looked sightlessly up at the cloudy night. The rain mingled with blood across his face.

Kell sighed and pushed wet hair out of his eyes. Another dead end, and he'd wasted more time, which he absolutely did not have right now. He needed to get rid of the body and then somehow convince the woman she hadn't just seen what she'd just seen. Plastering on his most charming smile, he turned around and froze.

"Seattle PD. Freeze, asshole," she whispered, her stance set, a Sig Subcompact in her hands and pointed at his head.

Detective Alexandra Monzelle kept her balance on the ridiculous heels and her gun pointed at the definite threat.

Well over six feet tall, muscled, graceful as hell . . . the guy facing her showed no fear. No emotion, really. Black hair fell to his broad shoulders, the darkness a perfect match for his eyes. Chiseled face, huge-ass hands, and feet big enough to waterski on. Yet he moved with the smoothness of a trained soldier.

He lifted one dark eyebrow. "Seattle Police Department?"

She nodded and tried to stop shaking from the chill in the air on her bare skin. Way too much bare skin, but she'd been undercover. "Get on your knees."

Intrigue leaped into his glittering eyes. "Not garing ta happen."

Was that a true Irish brogue? It fit him somehow. "I will shoot you."

He shrugged a massive shoulder beneath a leather duster. "That's your choice, lass."

Did he just fucking call her lass like some lady from a century ago? "Oh no, Irish boy. Get on your knees. Now." She put every ounce of command she possessed into her voice.

"Well now. At least you knew I was from Ireland." He glanced down at the dead man and his foot slid forward as if to kick. Then, apparently changing his mind, he focused on her again and smiled. "As opposed to Australia."

Okay. She really didn't want another body on her hands, but in the dress and heels, she was at a physical disadvantage. The last thing she needed was to spend all night filling out more paperwork than had already been created. "Down. Now."

He cocked his head to one side. "I can't help but ask where you were keeping your weapon." His gaze, dark and intense, roved over her entire body.

Tingles. Damn weird and very unwelcome, tingles cascaded wherever his gaze landed. She might just have to shoot the bastard and fill out the paperwork anyway. "I don't want to shoot you, but I can live with the decision. Get on your knees or say a quick prayer to your maker."

He glanced over his shoulder. "I don't suppose you have backup coming?"

No. Her backup had followed the dealer. She shook her head to provide warning and lowered her aim to his right leg. "I guess losing one leg won't kill you."

His focus returned to her. "You shoot me, and we're going to have a problem." He spoke slowly and clearly, without a hint of distress.

A chill wandered down her back. The man was damn serious . . . and damn scary. Yet she couldn't let any fear show. She sighed and tightened her arms to shoot. "If you'd just get on your knees, this night would go so much more smoothly."

"Say *please.*"

She blinked. Seriously? Hell, if it got him to cooperate, she'd chirp a Haiku. "Please."

"As you wish." Graceful as any dancer, he dropped to his knees. Water splashed up.

Funny, but the guy didn't seem any less dangerous. She cleared her throat. "Cross your ankles."

He sighed and crossed huge boots behind him. "Why were you trying to entrap this guy?"

Her handcuffs were in her purse in the bar, and she hadn't had a chance to grab it before rushing out so the junkie would take the bait and follow her. Her gun, on the other hand, had been strapped to her inner thigh. "Clasp your hands together on the back of your head."

He kept her gaze and clasped his hands on that thick black hair. His shirt pulled tight over defined muscles in his chest, and he seemed more in control of the situation than ever. "You don't have cuffs."

Yep. Might just have to shoot him. "My partner will be here soon." She hoped Bernie would be there soon.

"Aye, I'm sure." The man glanced at the body. "Do you know how he died?"

Duh. "Overdose. What's your name?"

"Kellach." He lifted both eyebrows. "What's yours?"

"Detective Alexandra Monzelle." Everyone called her Lex. Between the disappearance of her adrenaline rush, the chilly rain, and her aching arms, the gun became heavy. Yet she didn't twitch. "What do you know about the drug?"

"What drug?" The man's eyelids half-closed as if she were boring him to sleep.

Heck, she'd like to plug him one in the leg just to get his attention. "You asked about the drug. It's too late to play dumb."

He shrugged.

"Okay, then how about explaining all that fire. Did you douse yourself with some weird accelerant?" She couldn't quite come up with a reasonable explanation for the strange glow over his skin and the corpse's, so he'd better damn well explain, because she hadn't gotten a good look with their backs turned to her. "Where's the weapon?"

"No weapon. It's a chemical that looks like fire but obviously isn't."

True—no burn marks marred his skin or the dead guy. Who was

Kellach? Was he a rival dealer or something else? He wore a leather duster, flack boots, and faded jeans. Motorcycle gang member?

His head lifted, and his nostrils flared just like a German shepherd she'd seen scouting for drugs once.

Long shadows mingled on the alley floor, and two men drew nearer. Deep blue flames morphed along the arm of one of them. More of the damn weapons?

"Ballocks," Kellach muttered before launching himself off the asphalt and right at her. He cleared the dead body, wrapped himself around her, and tackled her to the ground. One hand cushioned her head, while a rock-hard arm banded around her waist and kept her from injuring, well, anything. He rolled, released her, and jumped to his feet in front of her.

The scent of salt, ocean, and pine surrounded her.

No way. No way should he have been able to move so quickly when she'd had him contained on his knees. Shock made her hands tremble. She shoved herself up and kicked off the heels. Shit. She still held her gun in her hand but was acting like a rookie.

"Gentlemen?" Kell asked, his stance casual. "Can I help you?"

The guy with the blue arm glanced down at the corpse and hissed. "We came to help Chuck." His face contorted and turned an ugly red. "You killed him."

"No. The drug he took killed him." Kellach's stance widened. "How much of it did you take?"

Lex peered around the solid brick of the man toward the two guys. The light illuminated them from behind, so she couldn't see their eyes. What was Kell seeing?

"Enough to be a god." The first guy lifted his hand and threw what looked like a ball of fire at Kellach.

A massive fireball instantly crackled from Kellach, and he threw it toward the other ball. They smashed into each other with an unholy bellow of steam, fire, and energy. Kellach's ball encircled the other ball and snuffed it out before disappearing.

What the holy fuck? The damn criminals did have some new weapon that threw fire. She hadn't had a chance to frisk anybody to see what her assailants might be carrying.

Lex slid to the side to keep every man in sight while lifting her weapon. "Everyone get down on your knees."

Kellach shook his head. "Not again. Just stay out of the way, darlin."

Oh. He. Did. Not. She focused the gun on him.

The first guy raised his arm again, and fire slammed her way. She pivoted, turning and catching her foot in a pothole. As she started to go down, another ball flew toward her head.

"Enough." Kellach jumped in front of her, his right shoulder slamming into her cheekbone.

Stars exploded behind her eyes, and she hit the ground.

He groaned, and the scent of burning flesh filled the rainy evening.

She blinked, her brain fuzzing and her body going numb. He'd saved her. Unconsciousness tried to claim her, and she fought against the darkness with her remaining strength.

Kellach straightened to his full height, and balls of what truly looked like green fire shot out, but with his back to her, she couldn't see the weapon. The fire hit each of the men dead center. They both flew back about three yards and crashed to the ground.

Lex groaned as rain continued to beat down on her face. She couldn't pass out. If she passed out, she'd be dead. Her hand trembled on the asphalt. Where was her gun?

Kellach turned and started toward her—a massive hunter in a darkened alley.

"No," she whispered just as the darkness won. Drugs had nearly ruined her childhood, and now, the search to destroy the new drug on the street was going to end her. The last thought she had as she succumbed to oblivion was that she was about to be killed by a predator with the face of a fallen angel.

Chapter 2

Lex groaned and blinked, instantly awake. Silk sheets, pleasant lemon cleanser, pine scent surrounded her, and the sound of rumbling motorcycle pipes came from outside her widow. Holy shit. She sat up, reaching for the weapon at her thigh.

Nothing.

Her gaze slowly focused on the man sitting quietly in a chair at the end of the bed, twirling her Sig around one large finger. The scent of male overtook the lemon. Early dawn light peeked between half-drawn shades, illustrating the masculine features and darkened shadows on his face. "Looking for this?" He'd ditched the leather duster to reveal a black Metallica T-shirt, ragged jeans, and motorcycle boots. Even in a relaxed pose, the man looked like a wolf about to lunge . . . at his leisure.

A Titans of Fire motorcycle cut hung on a hook by the door.

Damn it, she was at Fire. She quickly took stock, relief coursing through her that the shiny blue dress remained on her—between the thousand thread count sheets.

He lifted one dark eyebrow set in a brutally angled face. "I wouldn't have taken your clothing." Those incredibly dark eyes somehow darkened further. "Unless you'd asked nicely, of course."

That Irish brogue should be bottled and sold to lonely women everywhere. The guy had to be early thirties, with a wealth of experience in those glimmering eyes.

"Give me my gun," she said evenly.

"Of course." He tossed the weapon onto the bedspread next to her.

The ultra-posh, smooth, expensive bedspread. She glanced around the clean-to-the-point-of-sparse room, fully aware of her current location, and her heart sped up as adrenaline flooded her veins. "Somehow I imagined the personal rooms at Fire to be a bit more, ah, disgusting." An undercover operative had reported back the previous year on the stinky and dirty bachelor haven used by the motorcycle club members.

"I like clean." The man's lips twitched as she gingerly reached for the weapon. "I took the liberty of removing the bullets. You may have them back when you leave."

So he wasn't going to kill her. She met his gaze evenly, at a definite disadvantage still sitting in the bed, but she liked being partially covered, considering the slutty dress she'd worn earlier to hunt. "This is kidnapping."

He shrugged one massive shoulder. "When I knock a woman out, I like to make sure she survives the experience."

Heat ticked down her spine and uncoiled in her abdomen. Why the hell did everything he say sound sexual? She narrowed her gaze. "You assaulted a police officer, buddy."

"Kellach. Kellach Dunne." He smiled, revealing perfectly white teeth in stunning symmetry. "I didn't mean ta hurt you, Alexandra, and you know it."

True. He had been busy shielding her from careening fire when his shoulder had connected with her still aching face. "Detective Monzelle to you. How about you come down to the station with me and answer some questions?" She carefully slid from the bed, her bare feet touching cold concrete.

"No."

She glanced around the pristine room again, wondering if she could take him down. "This isn't what I expected," she mused to herself.

"This is your first time in a bed at Fire?"

She stilled and turned to face him, hiding her vulnerability. "I try not to fuck motorcycle gang members, especially those involved in the local drug trade."

His grin was slow—dangerous—and amused. "Club. Motorcycle *club* members. Titans of Fire Motorcycle Club, to be exact." He stood and leaned against the door, blocking the only exit. "We need ta discuss that allegation before we get to the fucking."

He was laughing at her. The criminal, the one who'd held some new fire-shooting weapon, dared laugh at her.

Temper tickled up the back of her neck. "Listen, asshole. You assaulted and kidnapped a police officer, and now you're committing false imprisonment by barricading that door. Move your butt, now." She put every ounce of power she owned into her voice.

Muscles flexed when he crossed his arms. His gaze swept her barely-there outfit, head to toe, leaving sparking tingles along her skin. "You don't look like any *garda* I've ever seen."

Garda. Cop in Irish. She eyed the leather cut hanging on a hook by the door with the full club emblem across the back and an enforcer's patch across one shoulder. Then she looked up—way up—into his implacable face. "Your cut says you're a full member here in Seattle."

"Aye."

She frowned. "How?" Sure, he could be part of a different chapter, but not this one. The cops kept files on all members and recruits, and this man wasn't in a Seattle file.

He sighed. "It was a merger of two affiliate clubs, and I was assigned here."

She put both hands on her hips, facts clicking into place. Resignation and anger swirled through her chest. "I see. What would a Seattle based motorcycle club want with an Irish based motorcycle club?" This new drug killing people on her streets—did it somehow originate in Ireland?

He shrugged. "Seemed like a good idea at the time."

She exhaled slowly. "What part of Ireland you from, Kellach?"

He smiled. "I like how you say my name. Smooth, with a feminine hint of sass."

She was too damn tough to feel feminine and fragile, but this guy? Yeah, he knocked her off her game with such blatant masculinity. Shoving down any awareness of him as a man, as if she could, she concentrated on solving the puzzle in front of her. Guns. The Seattle club was known to run guns, and didn't they seriously need those in Northern Ireland? "What are your ties to the IRA?"

His gaze hardened. "None. My only ties are to my club."

Ah ha. "So, let me get this straight. Ireland merges with Seattle, providing drugs, and Seattle merges with Ireland, providing weapons. A win-win for the streets."

The air in the room changed slightly as tension built. "You leap ta conclusions faster than a Blue Hare during mating season."

The emphasis on the word *mating* skittered awareness down her spine. "What kind of weapon do you have that throws green fire?" she asked evenly.

"No weapon. You hit your head and ended up out cold. It was your imagination," he said just as evenly. A whistle echoed outside, and he inclined his head. "Your taxi is here."

She blinked. "You called a cab?"

"Aye. I didn't think you'd like me to drop you at the station on my bike." He slid to the side, all male grace, and opened the door.

She faltered and glanced down at her pink-polished toes. "Where are my shoes?"

He reached out a hand and enveloped hers. "They fell off your feet when I brought you back here."

She paused, her mouth almost dropping open. "You rode your bike back here with me unconscious?"

"Yes." He gently tugged her from the room, the size of his hand overwhelming hers in a way that tightened her girly parts.

She stumbled and quickly regained her footing, her breath heating. Even with her knocked out, he'd ridden a motorcycle and had managed to control the bike and her. Just how strong was Kellach Dunne? "You're crazy."

"You're not the first to say so." He ushered her down a long hallway to the main bar area of the club and toward the double door. The stench of old beer filled her nostrils. A guy snored on a far couch with a scantily dressed woman on top of him, also out cold.

She pulled on her hand. "Those were good shoes, and they weren't mine, damn it." She'd borrowed them from another cop, and she didn't have the money to replace them. "Any idea where we lost them?"

He tightened his hold and shoved open the door. "Nope."

Darn it. She stumbled across the entryway. The clubhouse was one of three buildings forming a square with two massive garages. The yellow taxicab had parked in the center. Several bikes were lined up in front of a half-opened garage door. Pyro, the president of the club, slowly wiped down his Harley, his hard gaze on her.

She fought a shiver. He had a rap sheet longer than the line of bikes, and he'd done time more than once, being well known for a hot temper, hence the nickname. He'd been the president of the club for the last ten years, leading it into more drug and firearm running, and who knew what else. If he was creating or distributing the new drug on the streets, she was going to take him down. She met his gaze levelly, trying to appear in control, even biting back a wince as her bare toe scraped a rock.

Kellach glanced down at the asphalt and then at her bare feet. "Hold on." Ducking, he lifted her, tucking her against a chest harder than steel and chiseled like granite.

She swallowed, once again struck by the sense of being delicate. Fragile. Intrigue flashed through her. "Put me down."

"No." He strode across the square toward the taxi as if not taking note of her weight. Finally, he opened the back door of the cab and set her town. Small rocks rolled across the bottom of her feet.

Pyro strolled over with a greasy lug wrench in his left hand. "Detective Monzelle. I've pictured you in a dress like that, leaving Fire just like this."

Lex met his gaze evenly, noting the beer belly protruding over his greasy jeans. If she had a file on him, it figured he had a file on her. "I've pictured you in orange with shackles around your ankles."

He smiled, showing a cracked front tooth. "Kinky. I like that."

She had to regain control and now. "I'm sure you'll see *kinky* in the joint. All sorts of kink."

Red fused over Pyro's cheek. He moved toward her, and her legs tensed in anticipation.

Without warning, Kell shoved her into the taxi. She landed on her side, fury rippling through her. Son of a bitch. He'd moved to intercept Pyro, damn it. If Pyro had made contact, she could've arrested him finally, and Kellach had thought to save her? Idiot.

Planting her hand on the torn seat, she jumped from the taxi. "Kellach Dunne, you're under arrest for kidnapping, battery, and assault." She glared up into his calm face. The battery charge could actually be made, considering he'd shoved her, and he certainly deserved it, trying to get her out of Pyro's way. "Come with me to the station to answer some questions, and maybe we can forget about actually booking you."

"Fuck it, Dunne," Pyro hissed. "I told you not to bring a cop here, and you said you'd handle it." He stepped closer, the wrench handle clenched in one beefy fist.

Kellach held up a hand. "You're not serious," he muttered.

"I am." She lifted her chin. "In fact, if you don't come with me, I'll have SWAT here in an hour to do a full sweep." She'd have to fudge some facts, but to raid the Fire facilities? Yeah. She'd do it. "Your choice."

Fire flashed in Kellach's eyes in the first real show of emotion he'd allowed to slip free. "You sure you wanna take me on, little blond woman?"

Oh, fuck that. She'd dealt with dangerous drug dealers while still playing with Barbies. "Get your ass in the cab." She jumped in and scooted over. The man would learn she could fight her own battles, and maybe by taking him in, she could finally get some answers.

Bringing him to the station in a cab wasn't her first choice, but she had to do something before he disappeared back to Ireland. At the moment, he was the only lead she had for the drugs and the new weapons. "Or back away so I can go suit up with SWAT."

"Ballocks." Kellach nodded at Pyro. "Call Simone and have her meet me at the station." He sat next to Lex and slammed the door, his bulk taking up most of the back seat. He turned toward her. "I thought we could be friends. You'll regret this, Detective Alexandra Monzelle, as you don't want me for an enemy."

A chill swept down her back, although she kept her face calm and serene. She'd taken down some of the worst criminals in the northwest. Even so, instinct whispered she'd never come up against a force like this man. "That's your choice." She turned and leveled her gaze at him. "You want me for an enemy? You've got it."

Chapter 3

Kell sat back on the cheap plastic chair, his hands resting lightly on the scarred wooden table. The smell of sweat and despair filtered through the small interrogation room, going nicely with the dingy yellow walls and faded tile that might have been white at one time. He'd been read his rights by a bored junior detective who had a barely-there mustache, making Kell wonder if the kid was older than twenty.

He waited. Had been waiting for nearly three hours, damn it.

High heels clicked down the hallway, and soon the door was shoved open. "Simone," he said, half-rising from his chair.

His cousin raked him with a black look as she shoved dark curly hair off her slim shoulders. "I told you I had a spa week planned, Kellach. What the hell are you doing dragging me away from my seaweed wrap? I had to fly back here on the double." She clicked around the table and sat when he'd drawn out her chair. "For the love of the Liffey, why are we here?"

Shite. He'd forgotten about her plans that week. "I apologize for cutting short your spa trip." Why would anybody want to be wrapped up in seaweed, anyway? "I shouldn't have called you." He glanced down at her dangerously red designer suit, black patent heels, and silver jewelry—including the Celtic Knot pendant he'd given her for her birthday decades ago—and his heart warmed that she always wore it. Sentimental little witch, even if she acted like such a mean girl. "Although you look stunning, cousin."

She turned and fluttered naturally long eyelashes. "Do no' even try to humor me, Kellach Gideon Dunne."

Her slip to the brogue proved she'd been touched, and her deliberate use of the middle name he hated showed he'd truly pissed her off. "Can't help it. You are beautiful." True statement, and buttering her up wouldn't hurt anything.

She tapped long nails on the table. "You're paying for another spa week for me, and you know I won't have time for a while because you keep getting into trouble. So you're buying me a new car for this."

"All right."

"I want a Porsche 458 Spyder," she purred.

His wallet took the hit and vibrated. "Done."

The woman had just as much money as he did, yet she hated to spend it.

"Now get me out of this," he said.

"Of course," she said smoothly. Her main job was as a council member on the Coven Nine, the ruling body for the entire witch species, but she'd multi-tasked through the years. She'd attended law school for fun years ago, and they'd made use of her knowledge more than once during the many years she'd spent in the United States. "Then I'd like to go home."

"Seattle is home now, sweetheart." He'd never understand why she preferred New York over the west coast. Too many humans in the cities in the east.

She sighed and then glanced at the face of her phone. "Interesting. Your Detective Monzelle became a cop because her daddy was a drug dealer who was arrested when she was a little girl. He's still incarcerated."

Kell's chest heated. "You ordered a background check on Alexandra?"

"Of course, and these are just the highlights. Alexandra has a younger sister who's, ah, in a band?" Simone pursed her lips.

The door opened, and Alexandra strode inside, followed by a middle-aged detective wearing a hang-dog expression. Kellach swept his gaze over Alexandra. Black flats, pressed black pants, crisp white shirt, badge and gun at her waist. Her blond hair reached her shoulders, barely, and her blue eyes glimmered with intelligence. She was too fragile to be a garda, and he wondered if there were males in her family other than her incarcerated father, and if so why they were failing to protect her. No wonder she was a crusader. The slight bruise on her cheekbone still pissed Kell off.

She slapped a file on the table and sat as her partner took the other chair. "I'm Detective Monzelle, and this is Detective Phillips."

Simone nodded, setting down her phone. "Simone Brightston, counsel for Mr. Dunne."

"You clean up nice, Alexandra," Kellach drawled, fighting the absurd need to protect her.

A pretty pink climbed into her face, while her gaze focused directly on Kell. "Do you understand the rights as they've been read to you?"

"I do," he murmured.

She glanced at the very expensive suit covering Simone and raised an eyebrow, then studied Simone's face before turning to Kellach. "You and your attorney share a resemblance. Family?"

Simone shifted her weight. "Our situation is none of your concern, Detective. My client saved your life last night, took you to safety, and now you drag him down here under the pretense of a fishing expedition? Shame on you."

Alexandra smiled pretty lips. "Definitely family. Here to protect you, huh, Dunne?"

Actually, as a Coven Nine Enforcer, it was Kell's job to protect Simone——with his life if necessary. "She's pretty, but she's fierce." He leaned back and slid an arm across the back of Simone's chair just in case she lost her temper and lunged. While brilliant, the spirited witch might very well say *fuck it* and attack, even if she was acting as his attorney.

A slight lift of Simone's shoulder acknowledged his warning.

Alexandra flipped open her file. "What do you know about the drug that killed this man last night?" She spun a picture around and slid it in front of him. It was a picture of the junkie who'd died the previous night in the alley.

Kell shrugged. "I don't know anything about the drug. What do you know?" He kept his voice level and measured her heart rate by studying the faint vein in her neck. Man, he'd love to lick his way to where that pretty vein went.

"You asked him about the drug, and you followed him into the alley," Alexandra persisted. "Tell me what you know."

"I followed *you* into the alley," he said silkily. "Sexy blue dress, high heels . . . I thought you were a lady of the evening."

Her eyes flashed. "Bullshit."

Simone coughed delicately, her lips twitching. "Detective, please watch your language."

"You were looking for a hooker, Mr. Dunne?" Detective Phillips muttered.

"No," Kell said smoothly, studying the older man. Phillips seemed relaxed and almost lazy, but sharp intelligence glimmered deep in his gaze, and his posture remained turned slightly toward Alexandra, as if ready to defend. Kell liked him immediately. "But I saw Alexandra in that dress, and I was intrigued. Long legs, smoothly toned, and I wanted more than anything to have them wrapped around me." Yeah, he was being an ass, but prodding her was suddenly so much fun.

Simone dug an elbow into his gut, and he bit back a grunt.

"All right. How about we exchange information?" Alexandra rolled her eyes. "I know this drug is something new, and it gives junkies temporary strength before killing them. It's taken in liquid form and via injection, and it's flooding my streets. Informants tell me your motorcycle gang is the middle man, distributing this killer to the public."

Aye, her intel was spot on. "Have your labs broken down the components?"

"Not yet." A veil dropped down over her eyes. "Why don't you tell me what it is?"

Because the main ingredient in Apollo was a mineral that was deadly to witches. "I don't know what it is, but I'm trying to find out." He gave her a little information, just to keep her talking.

She rubbed the bruise on her cheekbone. "About that. You asked the junkie last night where he'd gotten the drug, and how much he'd taken. Why?"

"Don't speak," Simone said quietly. "My client followed you into the alley, saw this poor man overdosing, and naturally asked how much of a drug he'd taken. A good Samaritan, if you ask me."

"Right." Fury blazed into Alexandra's stunning eyes.

Kell's entire body reacted with heat, a low growl getting trapped in his chest. Such passion, such raw female power—and all human. There was no enhancement to her like human psychics or empaths, so she couldn't mate an immortal. Only enhanced humans could mate a witch, vampire, demon, or shifter. Yet even knowing they had no future, his groin hardened, and he shifted on the uncomfortable chair. What would she look like, desire in her eyes, candlelight flickering across her delicate skin while he kissed every inch? He had a feeling once her control unraveled, she'd be wilder than any storm he'd ever ridden through. "I would've helped the lad."

Simone stiffened as he let his brogue loose. She turned and eyed him before glancing back at the detective. "Give me a break," she muttered under her breath.

He smiled. Though he'd never reacted to a female human so fiercely, he could do nothing but explore the overwhelming sensation.

Alexandra leaned forward. "I'm thinking the only reason you'd ask where he acquired the drugs is because there's a rival distributor somewhere in Seattle, and you're looking to take it out. Right, Enforcer?"

The woman added two plus two quickly. Smart girl.

"I just wanted to help him, and then I realized you were in danger, too," he said. The cops might be adding things up, but they didn't have any concrete information. It was well worth the trip to the interrogation room, even if he did have to buy Simone a new car. "I'm sorry I can't help you other than that." He flattened his hands on the table, heating his hands so he wouldn't leave prints.

"What about the weapon?" Alexandra asked, a snap in her voice.

What would it take to get her to lose that edge? To make her tone husky? Needy? He shifted his weight again, trying to force down his suddenly raging cock. "I didn't have a weapon."

"You did." She lowered her chin. "The other two men threw balls of fire, and I saw you return fire. You had a weapon, something new, that I haven't discovered as of yet."

He leaned back. "I don't know of any weapon that throws fireballs." He rubbed his chin, wondering what color bra she wore. Probably tan or white, considering he couldn't even catch a glimpse. "You hit your head, and you went down, so I'm afraid your mind is messing with you."

She reached in the file and shoved another set of pictures toward him. "Burn marks on the brick building, the garbage dumpsters, and even the flower pots. *Burn marks.*"

He shook his head, careful not to touch the pictures. "One of the men who came into the alley did have some sort of road flares, and he tried to ignite everything. That's when I got you out of there."

"Where is that man now?" Detective Phillips asked quietly.

"I truly don't know." Dead and buried where he'd never be found. "I'm sorry I didn't get his name."

Kell had had to take him out quickly in order to get Alexandra to safety. He'd called in a cleanup crew for the extra two bodies, while leaving the first junkie. So far the human medical examiners had failed to find a trace of the drug in any corpses the drug left behind. Somehow, the thing evaporated after incinerating all the internal organs. Sometimes they couldn't even find a centimeter of the spleen.

Simone's phone buzzed, and she reached into a five-thousand-dollar briefcase to draw it out. Reading the face, she shoved her chair back from the table. "This interview is over. Get up, Kellach."

Kell stretched to his feet, his focus narrowing at the smile twitching Alexandra's lips. "What's happened?"

Simone grasped his arm. "The garages, the clubhouse, and the club apartment complex are being raided at Titans of Fire Motorcycle Club."

Alexandra smiled, triumph sliding across her face. "The burn marks gave me probable cause for a warrant. Enemies, right?"

Chapter 4

Kell leaned back in the leather chair, his gaze focusing across the banged up oak table in the club's main conference room. The smell of sweat, motor oil, and tequila danced around.

Pyro sat at the head, gaze somber. His nephew and vice president, Duck, sat at his side.

Three more heavy-set, rough, angry Fire members lounged around the table, while Kell's brother, Daire, leaned against the door, his gaze inscrutable, his eyes a blazing green.

"How bad?" Kell asked quietly.

"Two caught with a little meth, three with unregistered weapons," Pyro noted. "Could've been helluva lot worse, if we hadn't had those three hours to clear the place."

Daire nodded. "We should keep headquarters clean at all times, because I'm sure the police will be back."

"I say we take out that bitch of a detective," Duck muttered in a gratingly nasal tone.

Fire lashed through Kell, but he didn't move. "You want to take out a policewoman? Are you fucking crazy?" He focused on Duck's bloodshot eyes and fidgety fingers. "Or are you sampling the meth?"

Duck hissed. "We all sample the meth, and now I want to take a try of Apollo."

Fucking stupid name. The drug was rumored to make the taker feel like a god by somehow giving humans witch-like powers before killing them. "The last two who tried Apollo ended up bleeding out in alleys," Kell said.

"Pussies," Duck returned. He turned toward his uncle. "Have you sampled it yet?"

"No. Wanted to flood the streets and make some money first, but next batch that arrives, we'll sample." Pyro shot a hard look Kell's way. "All of us will take a hit, right?"

"Of course," Kell said smoothly. "When will that be, anyway?" He was running out of patience and time to get answers.

Pyro's lips stretched back in a parody of a smile. "Soon enough. Did you bang that bitch last night or what?"

"Or what." Kell kept his voice level and his expression nearly bored, when all he wanted to do was punch through Pyro's face to the wall behind his head. "The police think we're supplying the drug, and you're supplying guns for our brethren back in Northern Ireland."

Duck chuckled. "So they have it exactly backward."

Stupid little fucktard had to state the obvious. Kell nodded. "Exactly."

"When will our next shipment of guns be arriving? We have an order from the Alaskan Crips I'd like to fill," Pyro said.

"Soon enough," Kell repeated.

Duck sneered. "What are these weapons that throw fire I keep hearing about?"

"No such thing," Kell said. "Must be a hallucination from Apollo."

Duck squinted, his beady eyes nearly bugging out. "Why do I think you're not telling me the truth?" His nearly concave chest puffed out somewhat, and he glared.

Kell lifted one shoulder. "Dunno."

Pyro frowned. "When we agreed to a merger, we agreed to full disclosure except for sources of drugs and guns. You need us for the drugs."

Daire shifted off the door. "You need us more."

"He fucking *can* speak," Duck muttered.

Daire turned his focus from Pyro to Duck, his gaze veiled, power all but cascading off his massive form.

Duck swallowed, and red climbed into his face. Finally, his gaze dropped to his fingers, which twitched on the table. "Whatever," he muttered. While the moron had no clue witches existed, even his dulled instincts could probably sense a predator in the room.

Kell measured Daire's mood, wondering at what point his oldest brother would decide to decimate the humans. Daire had a short temper, was fucking fine with that, and would have no problem erasing the problem and starting over.

Daire focused on Kell once again and lifted an eyebrow. For Daire, that amounted to a full blown conversation.

Kell nodded and focused back on Duck now that he'd been castrated by a Daire glare. "We're in agreement that we do not kill police officers?"

Duck snorted. "I say we make a statement with that bitch, if you're done with her."

Actually, something whispered that Kell was nowhere done with the sexy Detective Alexandra Monzelle, human or not. "Bringing the full force of the police down on us right now would be a colossal mistake." He aimed his statement at Pyro.

Pyro rubbed the silver goatee on his chin. "Agreed. For now."

Duck sighed heavily. "Fine, but before we kill her, I want a shot at her."

Kell barely kept his lips from twitching. Alexandra would probably quite easily cut off Duck's dick and feed it to him if he made a move on her. "We just agreed we're not killing her."

"For now," Duck said, his too thin upper lip curling. "I think you have a hard-on for the cop."

"Are we done?" Daire asked, his tone strongly suggesting that they were, in fact, done.

Duck didn't meet Daire's gaze, but he did shift slightly toward his uncle. "We need to talk about the Grizzlies. They're cutting into our gun trade, and rumor has it they have a hit out on you."

"Your suggestion?" Pyro asked.

"War. Let's make a statement," Duck said, rubbing bony hands together.

Pyro eyed his other men. "Anybody agree with making a statement?"

Nobody moved.

Finally, Pyro shook his head. "We're flooding the streets with new product and shouldn't split our attention or our time right now by going to war with another club."

Smart. Kell nodded.

While Pyro sampled the meth and drank more tequila than a liver could handle, there was no doubt the man had risen to power with sharp intelligence and the willingness to spill blood with no remorse. Did the man know his nephew would never lead? Not smart enough.

Sometimes family blinded a man.

Kell cut his gaze to Daire. Yep. About to incinerate the humans. They were getting nowhere with the conversation. So Kell stood. "I'm out."

"Meeting adjourned," Pyro said and shoved back from the table.

Kell pushed open the door and wound through the clubhouse to his bike waiting outside. Daire's Ducati waited silently next to it, dark and somehow deadly. The Ducati had taken a bit of ribbing from the other club members, but as usual, Daire didn't give a shit. He blended in by not trying to blend in, and always had.

Daire reached him. "Wanna ride?"

"Aye." Kell straddled his bike, wanting nothing more than to feel the wind against his face.

"Is yer cop gonna be a problem?" Daire asked.

"Aye." The pretty Alexandra was definitely going to be a problem, but how much of one, he wasn't sure.

Daire's face split in a rare—very rare—grin. "To you or to our mission?"

Kell paused and lifted his head. "Both."

"This is a shitty idea, Lex," Bernie muttered for the seventh time, his knuckles white on the steering wheel. They'd turned off the interstate long ago, and quiet forestland surrounded them.

She nodded. "I know." Then she grinned at the man who was more father to her than the bastard who'd deserted her. "You trained me, buddy. What do you expect?"

Bernie shook his head. "I got four girls at home, women now, and you in my life. Pretty much five daughters. What the hell did I ever do to God?"

Lex laughed. "You must've been somebody really bad in a past life." When she'd been assigned as Bernie's partner years ago, as a rookie, he'd instantly taken a serious approach to teaching her how to survive. After many close scrapes, tons of arrests, and way too many stakeouts, she couldn't love him any more than she did. "But I agree, this is a little crazy."

"Then let's turn around and head back to the station." Bernie twisted his neck to look up at the sky through the front window of his nondescript Cutlass. "There's a hell of a storm moving in, and we can get that paperwork done." Thunder bellowed high above as if in agreement.

She wiped her damp palms on her faded jeans as the trees flew by outside. Pine and the smell of oncoming rain filled her senses. While she understood Bernie's reluctance to getting shot so close to his retirement, she had a feeling about this case. "We have to get those drugs off the streets, and while this is risky, I think it's worth a chance."

"You're gonna get us both fired. Or dead." Bernie was six months from retirement, and he was, in a word, *done*. Grumbling under his breath about missing breakfast, he turned down the long, asphalted private road leading to the Grizzlies' clubhouse. "We're trespassing, we don't have no warrant, and the brass is already looking at us for the botched mission the other night. You know? When our mark ended up dead in an alley, and my partner ended up at Fire?"

She rolled her eyes and straightened her black leather jacket, which nicely covered the gun holstered near her ribs. "The gang task force has investigated the Grizzlies for a decade, and not once has anything illegal popped up. The majority of motorcycle clubs in the country are clean and made up of good guys, Bern."

"Titans of Fire ain't clean." Bernie rolled down his window and spit out his gum. "Even if the Grizzlies are clean, they ain't gonna help the cops against another gang."

"*Club.* They're clubs."

The narrow road led to a two-story garage with three sprawling garage doors straight ahead and a clubhouse to the right. The clubhouse wasn't nearly as large as Fire's and probably didn't have private rooms.

Interesting. "Just relax and back me up." Lex opened her door and stepped into the rapidly cooling day.

Quiet. Compared to Fire's territory, the Grizzlies' headquarters was peaceful. A bird chirped in the surrounding trees, and in the distance, a wolf mourned. The breeze picked up, and she shivered.

A normal sized door opened next to one of the massive garage doors, and a man strode out, wiping grease off his hands with a torn rag. "Help you?"

Lex paused, recognizing the president of the motorcycle club from files she'd pored over the previous week. According to the file, he'd started the club ten years ago, but before that, the man was a mystery. Shifting slightly, she allowed her jacket to slide away from the badge clipped at her belt. "I'm Detective Monzelle, and I'd like to talk to you, Mr. McDunphy."

"Bear." His gaze dropped to her badge, he lifted one dark eyebrow, and then his eyes traveled every inch of her from her boots to her blond hair. He finished wiping his hands and shoved the rag in his back pocket, his jaw a solid block in a square face. "Pretty girls call me Bear."

He looked like a bear. Well over six-feet tall, broad as a barn, shaggy brown hair, and honey-warm chocolate eyes. A solid hint of danger cascaded off him, and he moved with the grace of a wild predator. Not one almost tamed by civilization that would eye a human warily from the side of a country road. One that would instantly pounce and eat, no friend to humanity. He strolled closer, cutting his gaze to Bernie in the car.

Lex fought the urge to step back. She was a cop, damn it. An *armed* cop. What was up with the wild men she kept running into lately? She glanced around at the so very quiet area. "Where is everybody?"

"Out on a ride," Bear said, turning his focus back to her and stopping his advance near the car as if accustomed to people backing away. "What can I do for you, Detective?" No expression touched his handsome face, and his body remained relaxed.

Her heart beat faster, and her breath sped up. Instinct? "I was hoping you'd be kind enough to answer some questions."

"About?" he asked softly, his voice still a low rumble.

"Titans of Fire, drugs, and guns," she answered just as softly.

He rubbed his whiskered chin. "We're at peace with Fire, we don't do drugs, and we don't run guns. Anything else?"

She tilted her head. "There's a new drug on the streets called Apollo, and it's killing people. Fire is distributing it."

"So?"

"Rumor has it your club protects this northern territory. Tell me you don't want a drug like that killing people." She eyed him.

The wind picked up and slammed pine cones against his motorcycle boots. "If people are dumb enough to do drugs, they deserve what they get." He glanced up at the billowing black clouds. "Better get your sweet butt back in your car before the rain starts, Detective."

"Did you know that Fire merged with an Irish club?" she asked.

His smile was slow and a dimple winked alive in his right cheek. "There isn't anything that happens in this town I don't know about."

"Who are the men from Ireland? More important, where are they getting the drugs?"

He rolled a shoulder. "Considering you spent the night in Dunne's bed, I figure you know more about that than I do."

She lowered her chin. The man really did know everything that happened in town, now didn't he? "Say I don't. What do you know?"

He sighed. "Kellach Dunne is an enforcer, and he's dangerous as hell. While I'm sure your very pretty face distracted him, he lives for his job and for his brothers. He's not here to cause problems, and he's on your side about the new drug. Wants it off the streets."

"Why?"

Bear shrugged. "For as long as I've known Kellach, he's been a crusader. Doesn't like criminals and doesn't like drugs. He's here for one reason, one I don't know, but it has to do with getting that drug off the streets. While he has a noble purpose, he's ruthless when determined, and you should stay out of his way, pretty detective."

As warnings went, it seemed heartfelt and serious. She shivered and covered up by leaning against the door. "What about the fire-throwing new weapons? Do you really want those on your streets? Possibly turned against your brothers?"

He studied her for a moment. "My brothers can handle any weapons pointed their way."

She had to get through to him since he obviously knew something. "You could help the police get a handle on the drugs and guns, if you wanted."

"I have no interest in assisting the police." Three large steps brought him within touching distance. He smelled like the wild outdoors, earthy and fresh. "However, you? *You* I'd help."

Bernie shoved open his door and stepped outside of the car. "Back away, Bear."

Bear kept his focus on Lex, and she had to tilt her head to meet his gaze. "Then help me," she said.

The roar of pipes echoed down the lane, and Bear cocked his head to the side. "Two riders. Ducati and Harley."

She blinked and turned as two riders dressed in black leather pulled up. Kellach and another huge man with black hair, green eyes, and similar bone structure. *Brothers?* They cut their engines right next to her.

What in the hell were they doing at the Grizzlies' club? She looked Kell over and then concentrated on the other man, who swung his leg over the Ducati. "We haven't met."

The hulking guy glanced at Bear, Kell, and then back to her. "Daire."

She blinked. That was it?

Kellach shot a hard look at Bear. "Back away."

Bear smiled a full set of teeth. "It's like that, is it?"

"Aye." Kellach didn't look at her.

Bear met her gaze and pushed a strand of hair off her forehead, his smile widening when Kellach growled. "You're welcome here any time, Detective Monzelle. I hope you come back." Turning on a large boot, he nodded at Daire. "Let's meet inside before it starts to rain. Join us when you can, Kellach."

Daire nodded and fell into step with Bear, both massive men striding toward the quiet clubhouse, their shoulders wide beneath the leather.

Lex focused on Kellach. "What in the world is going on here, Mr. Dunne?"

"Just a friendly get-together among mates," Kellach said, his hand cupping her jaw, his dark eyes flashing ten kinds of fire. "Did he frighten you?"

She blinked. "Bear? No." Warmth spread from Kell's hand, while her nerves jumped alive from his obvious anger. "Why are you here in the enemy's camp?"

"Not enemies." He released her and backed away. "Yet." Reaching around her, he yanked open the car door. "Get in."

"No." If she entered the clubhouse, would they give her any information? How completely odd for the Irishmen to be meeting with Bear. "Back off, Dunne."

He moved faster than she could track, lifting her and setting her in the seat. A quick snap of the seatbelt had her secured, and Kell's face in hers. "Stay away from Bear, stay away from Fire, and keep your sweet ass off the streets. For now." The door shut, and he turned on his heel, long strides eating up the distance to the clubhouse, where he disappeared inside.

Fury rippled through her, and she struggled with the seatbelt.

Bernie dropped his bulk onto the seat and shut his door. "We can charge him with a battery, but since we're here without a warrant or any probable cause, it'll just be a pain in the butt. Right now, we're done here, partner. Should definitely report back to the task force about Fire members aligning with Bear. God knows what this could mean."

She nodded, her gaze on the silent building. Oh. They were nowhere done here. "We have to cut off the supply of that drug."

Bernie sighed. "One thing I hope to accomplish before I retire?"

"Getting rid of Apollo?" Lex mused, watching the silent clubhouse.

"No. Finally convincing you that you've got nothin' to prove any longer."

She blinked and turned toward her partner. "Huh?"

He rubbed his belly. "You've proven yourself as an excellent cop, Lex. The fact that your dad is in prison for selling drugs doesn't matter, and you have to let it go."

She swallowed, her body chilling. "I'm not obtuse as to my motivations in life and know I became a cop to right my father's wrongs. But I've seen firsthand what drugs do to people, to kids, when one of my friends overdosed in my backyard, and my dad went to prison. I'm not trying to prove myself." Hell, she was trying to save lives from a drug worse than any she'd ever seen.

"If you say so." He patted the dash. "Let's go."

She nodded, looking for one more glimpse of leather through the door. "Why in the hell does everyone think I have a 'sweet ass?'" she muttered.

Bernie threw back his head and laughed. "If they only knew what a complete badass you really are."

"They're about to find out." She grinned at her partner and quite possibly her best friend. "Let's get back to work."

Chapter 5

Lex leaned back at her kitchen table with a dinner of frozen macaroni and cheese, and too many bills. She paid the most important ones first, those that dealt with her mother and her care at the facility until her Relapsing-Remitting Multiple Sclerosis died down again. If it died down again.

She'd visited her mother right after work, and her mom was doing better. Thank goodness. Every once in a while, the disease really flared up, and each time, Lex was afraid her mother wouldn't improve.

Lex wandered over to the fire escape to check on her spice collection. She'd recently taken a cooking class with a couple of buddies from work and had quickly figured out that fresh spices made all the difference.

The phone rang, and Lex grasped it, reading the front. "Tori," she answered.

"Hey, sis." In the background, drums and a flute tuned up. "Just wanted to check in."

"Where are you?" Lex kicked back in the chair.

"Right outside of Los Angeles in a bar near the ocean. Wish you were here." Tori raised her voice to be heard over what sounded like drums falling down stairs. "How's mom?"

"Doing better," Lex lied. Why bother Tori with the truth when she was so far from home?

Tori sighed. "Bullshit. I have some money to send you and will do so tomorrow."

Lex shook her head. "Absolutely not. I've got it." She'd protected her baby sister since day one, and there was no reason to stop now.

"Um, I had another reason for calling," Tori whispered.

Lex straightened, her chest tightening. "What?"

"Somehow dad got a letter to me."

Anger roared through Lex. "How the hell would he even find you?"

"I don't know, but a guy slipped me a letter during our second set last night near Vegas, and it was from dad, asking me to testify for him at his next parole hearing."

How in the fuck had their dad even found Tori, much less on the road? "He's got to have pretty good contacts out here," Lex said, standing. "Toss the letter, and forget about it. I'm testifying, and no way will that prick get out of prison."

Somebody in the background called Tori's name. "That's what I figured, but I thought I should let you know. If he found me, he might've found mom."

Yeah, Lex had already hit that conclusion. "I'll find out. For now, go sing your heart out."

"I will. Bye." Tori clicked off.

Lex rubbed her lip and looked around her piece of shit apartment. The smell of oil and grease rose from the restaurant below, and a chill wandered around from the shoddy insulation. The fear in Tori's voice tightened Lex's fingers into a fist. The man had told them they were useless from day one, and it had taken years of working on self-esteem for Lex to help Tori realize the problem had been with their father and not with them.

For now, it was time to don another slutty dress and get back to work.

One drug dealer at a time.

Several hours after her run-in with Bear, and after her alarming phone call with Tori, the hard thrum of brutal music ripped through Lex's legs, pounding against bruises from the other night. The smell of vomit combined with the stink of piss and made her want to puke. She was in another low-end underbelly of a bar, although this time, she'd opted for sexy boots with her whore-like outfit.

The makeup coating her face itched, and a demanding pain hammered in her temples.

Sometimes she fucking hated her job.

Bernie sat at the far end of the bar, pretending to size up hookers.

They'd had to switch bars because of Kellach Dunne, but at least she wouldn't run into him. Fire members were select in the dive bars they frequented, and she was currently in Grizzlies territory. She idly wondered if Bear would show up.

When Kellach stalked inside the front door, all leather bound, dark and dangerously sexy, she should have been surprised.

Yet she wasn't. Who the hell was this guy? Bear had pretty much vouched for him, saying he was on a mission to end the drug and was not a bad guy. Considering Bear was completely clean, record-wise, and had a reputation of protecting his territory, maybe he'd been telling the truth. He had no reason to lie.

Kell's gaze cut through throngs of gyrating drunks, zeroing right in on her in what felt like a claiming. Hot, wet, and physical. Her body thrummed alive for the first time that night, once again reminding her that she was more than a cop, more than a weapon. She could be all woman.

Going on instinct, she gave him a look, slid off her stool, and headed for the twisty path to the bathrooms.

He reached her in an odd alcove, as she'd planned.

Turning, she grabbed his arm and used a spin move to put his face against the wall. He turned easily and with a suffering male sigh. If he was holding a weapon, she'd take him downtown and start questioning him again.

Bending, she started at his ankles and patted up, frisking every inch of hard muscled male. Could he freakin' be real? Not an ounce of fat. Nothing but pure solid steel filled her palms. She had to stretch up on her tiptoes to finish, finding neither weapons nor contraband. But did a man his size need weapons? Probably not.

Finally, she stepped back.

"All done?" he asked, amusement dark in his voice.

"Yes," she said, a bit too breathlessly.

Then he moved.

She knew he moved because she ended up face-first against the wall, but she didn't see him move. He held her at least a foot off the ground with one arm wrapped around her waist.

A foot off the ground.

Her breath whooshed out of her lungs and tingles exploded in her abdomen. Her mind fuzzed.

He held her easily, his breath fanning the side of her neck. "My turn," he rumbled.

A slow shiver wandered down her spine, and he chuckled.

Why did she react this way to him? "Let me go," she murmured. "I'm a cop."

"Turnabout's fair play." He set her down on her feet as if she weighed nothing and then crouched, his large hands easily encircling her ankles. He tugged. "Spread your legs, baby."

A low groan escaped her as she widened her stance. This was wrong. This was so fucking wrong.

Yet desire flushed through her with the speed and heat of pure, red, unadulterated lava.

Warm palms ran above her boots, over her bare skin, to her inner thighs. She stiffened as he reached the small Sig strapped to her right leg.

"There it is," he whispered, his voice hoarse.

Enough. She twisted, and he slapped one firm hand against her rear, holding her in place.

"Not finished," he rumbled, straightening and stepping into her, his solid form holding her in place. His thighs pressed against her butt, and his chest cradled her head. God, he was big.

He skimmed her waist, caressing across her abdomen and up her ribs, pausing just under her breasts.

She stopped breathing. Her nipples pebbled harder than any diamond she'd ever touched.

A group of giggling women tripped by on the way to the bathroom, and neither she nor Kell gave them a glance, although Kell shoved her deeper into the alcove and out of the hall. Too much was happening, and Lex shook her head, even as her body trembled head to toe. What was happening to her?

"Fuck it," he muttered, both hands cupping her breasts.

Her knees gave out, and only his unreal body kept her upright. Electrical sparks zipped from her chest to her clit, and she arched into his hands.

His head dropped to the nape of her neck, his warm lips enclosing the sensitive flesh. His fingers found her nipple.

Heat uncoiled inside her, spiraling into an explosion. *God.* She was going to orgasm.

Shit, no. Her eyes flashed open and she shoved back as hard as she could. He released her, and she spun around to face him, her breath panting out. She slapped a hand against his chest in utter panic. Never in her life had she reacted to a man like that.

His dark eyes glowed in the dim light, and a dark red flush spun across his high, angled cheekbones. Perfectly symmetrical nostrils flared like a predator on the hunt.

"That wasn't proper frisking," she gasped, trying to slow her heart rate.

"Fuck proper." He grabbed her hand on his chest and shoved it down over a definite bulge in his jeans.

She locked her knees so she wouldn't fall. Heated and pulsing, his well-endowed, hard as iron cock warmed her palm, even through the worn denim.

His palm flattened over hers and pressed.

His groan mingled with hers, and he leaned over her, his lips connecting with her forehead. "Do no' stop," he ground out, the Irish brogue escaping in full force.

She could make him come right then and there, but she pressed back against the wall, which pounded with the hard rock being played, and fought to free her hand. The guy was a badass, really bad biker gang member dealing in drugs. "No. Not going to happen."

He released her, only to plant both hands on the wall on either side of her head, bracketing her. The scent of male and ocean caressed her senses. "Come home with me."

"Are you joking?" She coughed. Her body bellowed a *hell yes* and actually bowed toward him, while her mind moved to shut down all sensation. "Yeah, me at Fire doing the walk of shame tomorrow. Step back, asshole."

"I have a flat across town." He leaned down until his breath brushed her lips. "It'll be our secret."

She met his gaze directly, even as her mouth tingled with need. She thought she'd gotten rid of her penchant for bad boys. "I don't have secrets."

His gaze warmed. "Sure you do, baby. I promise."

"I'm nobody's baby," she said, finally getting her body under control.

"Now that's a true pity." He brushed hair back from her face. "A girl like you is made to be cosseted, protected, and loved until the world is a safe oasis of pleasure."

She blinked. "Jesus. What century are you from?"

Amusement tilted his lips. "You wouldn't believe me if I told you."

She shook her head. "You're a bad guy, Kellach. Your gang sells drugs and guns . . . which lead to violence and death. There's no safe oasis in your life."

"No." His lips curved in almost a gentle smile. "My job as an enforcer means no oasis for me. But I was talking about you. I could give you that."

"I've never wanted safety." She noted, almost sadly, that he didn't dispute her statement about guns or drugs. "Who's the distributor of Apollo?"

His head lifted at her use of the drug's name. "You've been doing your research."

"That's my job." She flattened both hands on his hard pecs. "Tell me what you know, and I'll get you a deal. Away from here and somewhere safe."

He grinned, a flash of white through the darkness. "You're offering me immunity and a new identity?"

"Yes." She tried to press her advantage.

"How about I take you out of here, get *you* somewhere safe until things quiet down with this drug?" He leaned in, his lips hovering above hers. "I'll get it off the streets for you."

"Bull." She shoved him, and he stepped back. "Don't lie to me."

"Never." He brushed hair from her face, his hands cupping her head. "You need to stay away from Bear, darlin'."

"Why?" she breathed, going on instinct. "You jealous, Kell?"

He blinked. Slowly. It was an oddly curious sight, a foreshadowing of a dangerous temper. "You like to play with fire, Alexandra?"

The way he said her name, all Irish brogue and lilting consonants, caused desire to burn in her abdomen. "Lex. It's Lex."

"No." He shook he head, his hold tightening. "You're all Alexandra— each and every syllable." He leaned down, his lips nuzzling hers, his big hands tethering her in place. "Want me to be jealous? Give me something to protect."

A definite dare. She'd never been able to turn from a dare, and being challenged by a guy like Kell? Yeah. She could meet his challenge and raise him one. Screw it. They'd just see who won this battle of wills. She pressed her lips against his, her eyes fluttering shut. Heat and male—all spice.

With a low growl, he tugged her into him, his mouth overtaking hers. He overwhelmed her in power and strength, kissing her hard, half-lifting her against the wall to settle his groin at the apex of her legs. Her thighs trembled and tightened against his hips, her hands shooting into his thick mass of hair. He shoved up her dress and pressed his cock against her panties, gyrating against her swollen clit. One firm hand dragged back her hair, while the other palmed her breast.

A mini-orgasm rippled through her, making her gasp into his mouth. Then another uncoiled, sparking flashes of electricity through her. She shook her head, trying to regain control of her body. She couldn't climax there. No way. No way could she let him know he had that much power over her.

He leaned back, one hand tethered in her hair, the other on her breast. "Problem?"

She gasped and tried to remain perfectly still. "Put me down and back away. Now." Her breathy voice didn't sound like her. At all.

He eyed her, awareness dawning in those deadly eyes. "How close are you?"

Too close. Way too fucking close. She swallowed. "Nowhere near. Now put me down."

"Aw, darlin'," he breathed, his gaze hardening. "If you wouldn't have lied, I woulda put you down." The Irish brogue licked along her skin, and she shivered. "Now? Now you're gonna come." He released her breast and tapped her lips with his fingers.

She opened her mouth in surprise, and he dipped in one finger. "Hey——" she started.

His head lifted, while his eyelids lowered to half-mast. Then his moistened finger wandered down her front, between her breasts, over her abdomen, and slid inside her panties.

"No——" she hissed, just as he pressed his wet finger against her clit. Sparks lit through her. She shoved her head back against the wall and shut her eyes, arching into his palm. "Please," she breathed, truly not knowing what she was asking for.

He pressed his thumb against her clit and slid the finger inside her. "Now, baby." He pinched, nearly forming a circle with his fingers.

She exploded into a million pieces, her mouth opening on a scream only to be covered by his. He kissed her deep, even as his fingers worked her, drawing out the waves until she sagged against him, allowing him to take all of her weight. Her mind fuzzed, and her body turned boneless.

He removed his hand and slowed his kiss, gently setting her on her feet. Two seconds later, and he'd set her dress to rights. "You're a keeper, Alexandra Monzelle," he whispered, stepping back.

She shoved hair away from her face, blinking up at him. What in the hell had just happened?

As she watched, he slowly licked his hand. "You taste like heaven."

Bernie rounded the corner. "Lex? You all right?"

"Fine." She slid toward Bernie, grateful for the escape, her face blushing fiercely enough it hurt. Her heart thundered hard enough, everyone had to be able to hear it. "Just talking to a Fire member here in Grizzly territory. Weird, huh?"

Bernie eyed Kellach, his hand perched precariously close to the weapon secured beneath his jacket. "Yeah. Weird."

She hustled toward her partner and away from the heat. Either Fire was making a move on Grizzly territory, or Kellach was up to something else. Her instincts hummed that there was a hell of a lot more to the Irish enforcer than she'd initially thought.

What the hell had just happened?

It was as if her body had taken over, giving in to him, knowing something her brain didn't. She had to get away from him and now.

"Detective," Kellach said from behind her.

She turned to meet his gaze, not saying a word.

"Those secrets of yours?"

Her knees trembled, so she held her stance.

"You'd better run wide and fast, or I'll unravel each and every one." With that, he turned and headed in the opposite direction.

Chapter 6

Kell dropped his leather jacket over a table in Simone's entryway and stalked toward the spacious living room, his body still rioting after making Alexandra come. The taste of her still lingered in his mouth.

"Hang up your damn jacket," Simone said without heat, her gaze on a pile of papers in her hand, a wide wall of windows behind her. The witch lounged in a yoga outfit that probably cost as much as a car, the darkness of the Puget Sound behind her appearing vast and mysterious.

Daire strode in from the wide kitchen and tossed him a beer.

"Thanks." Kell dropped onto the leather sofa and put his boots on the coffee table until she glanced up from the papers and lifted an eyebrow. He paused. With a sigh, he settled his boots back onto the wooden floor. He could take the feisty witch in a fight, but she fought dirty. As he'd taught her. He twisted off the cap and drank deeply, allowing the brew to cool his throat.

He'd been fucking combustible since tasting Alexandra.

Daire sat in an overstuffed chair and slammed his boots onto the coffee table.

Kell bit back a grin. His older brother had lived in Russia on his own for much too long. "Your cousin is going to kick your ass."

Daire lifted his head and looked toward Simone. "Why?" He was truly perplexed.

Kell shook his head.

Simone huffed out air, looked at Daire's boots, and then his face. Her expression softened. "Nothing."

Once again, Kellach wondered what had happened centuries ago in Russia when Daire had rescued Simone from something. Or someone. The two cousins had always been close. She remained vigilantly protective of Daire, and he her. Not that he needed protection, considering the power the witch held.

Kellach studied the two. While their dark hair was similar, Simone had nearly black eyes, and Daire's were a mixture of different greens, and always alert. Simone was tall for a woman at just under six feet, but Daire was at least six-six—an inch taller than Kell. The family resemblance was obvious in the classic features, which on Simone were feminine and beautiful, and on Daire deadly.

Daire focused on Kell. "Did you find anything at the bar?"

Yeah, a sexier than hell detective he wanted naked and screaming under him. "No, and it appears Bear has his people locked down under fear of death for anybody going near Apollo. Nobody is dealing in Bear's territory." Kell stretched his neck.

The front door opened again, and Adam Dunne loped inside, his phone to his ear. He shut the door and shrugged his leather jacket onto the floor.

"Damn it," Simone muttered, shooting Adam a glare.

The witch enforcer finished his conversation. "I agree. Bye, King." He crossed into the room and sat next to Kell on the couch.

Daire lifted an eyebrow at their middle brother. "King?"

Adam sighed and ran his hands through his shaggy brown hair. "Kayrs wanted an update on the phenakite situation."

"Planekite," Simone said absently. "I'm sick of the different names for the dumb mineral. Let's just call it PK from now on."

Kell shrugged. "Fine with me." The mineral was mainly mined in Russia and could be used to negate a witch's power or even cause death, so it didn't really matter that different species had used different spellings with the name. It was dangerous no matter how one spelled it. He glanced at Adam. "The king's mood?"

"Pissed and worried about the drug, considering two of his sisters-in-law are witches, one with new twins and the other pregnant." Adam eyed Kell's beer.

Kell nodded. Dage Kayrs was a vampire and the king of the Realm, a coalition of immortals aligned with the witches. "Does the king have any clue who's importing the mineral or melting it down into the drug?"

"No, but he's working on it," Adam said. "He has the same question we do. Why is the manufacturer trying out the drug in Seattle? Why here?"

Kell shrugged. "Seattle has a larger witch population than most cities in the USA, and if the goal is ultimately to harm witches, it's a good place to start before hitting Ireland." Yet something, a tickle at the base of his neck, hinted he was missing something.

Adam nodded and focused on Simone. "I'm tired of being the liaison. You do it."

She rolled her eyes. "I'm a lawyer these days, apparently." She cut her eyes to Daire. "Although, I could take over the liaising if I headed back home to New York."

"No. Until we figure out what's going on with PK, you need to stay close and protected as a member of the Coven Nine." Daire was always dedicated to protecting the members of the Council of the Coven Nine, who ruled the witch nation. "I can't afford a security detail in New York with the Apollo distribution happening here in Seattle."

She slammed the papers down next to his feet. "I'm a centuries old witch, Daire. I do not need a security detail."

Daire slowly raised one eyebrow. "I said no."

Blue fire crackled down Simone's arms and irritation spiraled through her eyes.

Daire waited patiently.

Adam shot Kell a grin, and they both tensed in case they needed to jump away from the fire. Simone served on the council that ruled the witches, but Daire was an enforcer, and when security was at issue, the enforcers trumped coven members. So Daire would win, even if they burned down Simone's penthouse during the debate.

Kellach grew bored of the silent struggle of wills. "Any deaths tonight?"

Simone slowly turned to face him. "Not that we've heard. Were you distracted with your cop again?"

Daire jerked his head. "Distracted?"

Simone smiled slowly like a cat playing with a mouse. "Aye. Your brother has the hots for the vice cop working the drug case. She's also quite concerned about new weapons that throw fire hitting the streets."

Daire focused on Kell. "She saw you throw plasma?"

"No. She saw a junkie throw fire and then die," Kell said slowly. "She thinks it's a weapon and has no clue about the distortion of molecules or application of quantum physics." Witches used quantum physics to take a state of matter and create a different state of matter in a skill humans could not possess or understand. Ever. He kept his voice level while unease bubbled up in his stomach.

"Do we need to take her out?" Adam asked quietly, amusement in his eyes.

Kell lifted a shoulder. "Not at this point." If his brother thought he'd rise to that bait, he was delusional. "If we need to contain her, we will." Not one inch of her pretty head would be harmed; he'd make damn sure of her safety.

"Is she an enhanced human?" Daire asked. "A possible mate to an immortal?"

"No." The reality of that statement cut a little deeper than it should. Kell took another drink of his beer. "We may have an issue with Duck wanting to harm the police."

"That fucking moron," Adam muttered. "So far, our merging with that club hasn't gleaned any results. We're no closer to finding the manufacturer of the drug. Let's just blow them all up and start over."

Kell grinned. He could always count on Adam to go to the extreme. "That gets my vote." Although, then they might not find the drug creator, and that was their goal. "You haven't had to spend much time at the club, now have you?"

"Hell, no." Adam shuddered. As the most scientific of the three brothers, he'd taken a break from enforcing to study the drug's components in a lab set up in the warehouse district. "I liked our club at home, and I like Bear's club here. Good men, good riders all around. Not like Fire."

"Aye." Kell finished his beer. There were good clubs and bad clubs, just like anything else. He studied his older brother. Lines of red fanned out from Adam's dark brown eyes. "You look like you need a break, brother."

"We all do." Adam let his head fall back onto the sofa and shut his eyes.

Simone reached for her phone. "Pizza. We need pizza." She viewed them. "I think this is the first time in a century I've had all three Dunne brothers in one place."

Kellach grinned. "And you're going to feed us pizza?"

"Damn straight," she said.

His phone buzzed, and he eyed the screen. "Got a body." He stood and nodded at Daire. "Save me a slice, would ya?"

Lex triple-locked her apartment door and kicked off her boots. Her feet ached and her head pounded. But her body? Man. Loose and satiated after an incredible orgasm induced by Kellach Dunne.

What in the fucking hell had she been thinking?

She pressed a hand to her head and flicked on the light to illuminate her quiet studio apartment. The smell of burned noodles filtered up from the Thai restaurant below, easing through the cracks in the yellow linoleum. Though she hadn't eaten in hours, the dingy kitchen with dented avocado appliances didn't inspire hunger. Maybe she should get a cat to make the place feel homey. Or a goldfish to brighten the room.

A car alarm went off down the block, and in the distance, sirens trilled.

Limping, she crossed into the tiny bathroom to wash the pound of makeup off her face. Wriggling out of the tight dress, she sighed as it hit the floor.

Her phone rang.

She turned and glanced with longing at her small, unmade bed before answering. "Yeah?"

"We got another one," Bernie said without preamble. After giving her directions, he hung up.

She eyed the dress on the floor and quickly hurried to the tiny closet to snatch jeans and a long-sleeved shirt before dragging on flat boots. *Better. Much better.* Tucking her gun and badge at her belt, she hurried through the door and down the cracked steps to her car, thinking all the way. Kellach Dunne had been with her for part of the night, and why was that exactly? What the hell did the Fire enforcer want with Bear's crew? It was almost as if Kell shared a secret or some type of mission with Bear. What was going on?

She drove through rain and dingy streets to reach an alley across town. Blue and red lights swirled around while cops moved, doing their jobs. She pulled to the curb.

Bernie opened her door before she could. "This way." He lifted crime scene tape and led her around a building to a quiet alley. "It looks like he crawled back here, bleeding all the way, to die in the corner and out of the rain."

Like a wild animal. Didn't animals go off on their own and find a quiet place to die?

The guy lay on his back under an awning, one arm thrown over his chest.

She reached the body, careful not to step in blood. "Male, early twenties." She crouched down and used the flashlight on her phone to run a light over the corpse's bare arms. Track marks. Many track marks. "Junkie for years." She looked around and spotted a crime tech she knew. "Daisy? Got gloves?"

Daisy reached into her pack and handed over two black gloves. "Yep."

Donning them, Lex gingerly lifted the corpse's eyelids. Red, blue, and green striations shot out from sightless blue eyes. Blood pooled beneath his eyes, in his ears, and dripped out of his nose. She released him and stood. "Definitely an Apollo overdose. Do we know where he got the drugs?"

"No." Bernie pointed back to the main street. "Known drug neighborhood. Can buy on any corner. We're canvasing right now, but in this area? Nobody saw nothin'."

She shucked the gloves and then rubbed her eye. "Do we have an ID?"

"Fingerprint scanner shows the vic as Jon Flank. He's done time for dealing, possession, and minor B and E. DMV says he lives alone around the corner. We had patrol knock on the door. Nobody answered."

Sounded like a normal junkie. Sad but true.

A chill swept down her back, and she looked around. Nothing. Lifting her head, she peered at the tops of the nearby buildings.

"What?" Bernie asked, glancing up.

"Nothing. Just somebody walking on my grave." A car door slammed, and she turned around. "Great," she muttered as two homicide cops strode her way.

Bernie snorted. "Dumbass and Dickhead in the flesh."

She smiled. Most cops, she liked. Hell, she liked them a lot. These two? Not so much. She lifted her head. "Masterson? What are you doing here?"

Detective Donny Masterson slicked back his already slicked back hair and peered down at her with light blue eyes. "The brass wants results, and even in those very nice dresses you've been wearing lately, you're not getting anywhere. We're here to help." His navy blue suit probably cost more than she made in a month, and he wore it pressed to within an inch of its life.

"Don't need your help," Bernie growled.

"Right." Masterson's partner, a blond surfer type named Bud Bundt, sighed and eyed Daisy's ass as she bent over to examine the asphalt. "Too bad you're not wearing one of those dresses right now, Lex." He turned and focused on her tits.

"You're both such dicks," Lex sighed, turning to her partner. Unfortunately, they were dicks with an impressive arrest record.

Bernie nodded. "Obviously compensating for something."

Lex snorted and nodded at Daisy. "Let's get out of here, Bernie." Her mind ran as they exited the alley. "We can't do much until we receive the ME's report." Reaching the main street, she glanced down both sides of the darkened road. Empty. Everyone out had scampered the second the police lights showed up. "We're not gonna find his dealer tonight."

"No. How about we hit known associates tomorrow?" Bernie opened her door. "Get some grub, get some sleep, and we'll go hard tomorrow."

She frowned. "I might head to the station and start a search."

"No. We've been on for almost twenty-four hours, and you need a little shut-eye. And makeup." He grinned and slammed her door, ambling away toward his car.

She chuckled. Oh yeah. She'd washed her face and had forgotten to even apply lip-gloss. Her eyes felt gritty and her temples ached.

Maybe a little sleep wouldn't hurt. She ignited her engine and drove slowly through emergency vehicles, stopping at the corner.

Her passenger door flew open, and Kellach Dunne dropped into the front seat. She reached for her gun, and he placed a hard-boned hand over hers.

He smiled, dark eyes unfathomable in the moonlight. "Evening, Detective."

Chapter 7

Kell kept his hand over Alexandra's as she decided whether or not to fight for the gun. He didn't much want to get shot, even though he'd survive any normal bullet. He peered closer at her pale skin. Sans the makeup, the woman looked about eighteen. A fine blue vein pulsed at her temple, and her hand trembled under his. The detective needed sleep and probably a good meal.

"When was the last time you ate something?" he asked quietly.

She blinked those stunning blue eyes at him. "None of your business."

"That's what I thought." Blast but the woman needed a bloody keeper. He sat back, figuring if she shot him, she'd have to deal with more paperwork than she wanted so near to dawn. "You choose the place, and I'll buy you an early breakfast." *Or later dinner.* Either way, the sexy cop wasn't going to waste away on his watch.

Not that he was watching.

Of course he was watching. Alexandra was beautiful and didn't know it. Add in a stubborn chin, sharp intellect, and what appeared to be a nearly obsessive drive to solve crime? Yeah. He was hooked. Even without the feminine pull drawing him like never before, the woman intrigued him.

"I'm not hungry," she ground out, her hand moving from her weapon to the steering wheel.

Irritation lifted his chin. "Ah, darlin'. Last time you lied to me, you orgasmed. Are you going for another one?"

If he'd expected to shock her, he failed. She slowly turned toward him and lifted a shoulder. "Wasn't good enough to do again."

He smiled, amusement filtering through him. God, she was some-thing. He'd felt the power of a good orgasm move through her, and then she'd been weak as a kitten for a few moments after she'd come. He knew it was good. "Breakfast, and I'll tell you everything I know about Apollo."

Her lips tightened into a line, and she hit the gas pedal.

Yeah. He'd figured out she wouldn't be able to pass on such an offer.

A small smile hovered around her mouth, and he gazed, curious. Just what was she up to? Good thing he was a patient man and had no problem waiting to find out. He settled into the seat, allowing the scent of woman to tease his senses. He rolled her scent around his tongue. Violets. Sweet and wild, just like they grew along the hillsides he'd roamed as a boy.

Her eyes were so blue as to be nearly violet as well. Should've been her name. But, no. She'd been named Alexandra; a warrior's name. How could somebody so delicate be a warrior?

It was a true pity she wasn't an enhanced human. What would she be like mated to a witch and therefore immortal? Powerful and sexy as hell. His jeans tightened, and he shifted to ease the sudden pressure in his groin. While he might be attracted to her, he wasn't looking for a mate, anyway. Especially one who wore a gun and appeared all right with shooting him.

He cleared his throat to stop his rioting thoughts. "My cousin ran a background check on you, and she shared a little bit of it with me. About your father."

Alexandra stiffened. "Your cousin needs to be punched."

"Simone was doing her job as my attorney, and believe me, you don't want to punch her." Kell bit back a smile. He'd taught Simone to fight dirty centuries ago, and even a trained cop wouldn't stand a chance. "Is your father still in prison?"

"Yes."

"Are you in contact?" More than anything, Kell wanted to tuck her close and hold her tight.

"Of course not." She sighed and cut him a sideways look. "My dad was a bad guy, he hurt my mom, and he's dead to me. Enough said."

Yeah, that told him more than enough. "Who protects you?" he murmured.

Her head jerked to the side. "I protect myself, dumbass."

He shook his head, not having meant to speak out loud. "And you protect your sister?" It was just a guess.

"Yes." Alexandra pulled the battered car into a parking lot near an all-night diner. A fluorescent sign proclaimed the place as BETTY'S, but one of the T's was burned out. Rain fell over the sign and splattered the sidewalk. Kell figured Alexandra wouldn't wait for him to open her door, so once she'd shut off the engine, he grasped her arm and tugged her out his side. She struggled, and he gentled his hold so as not to bruise her, safely depositing her outside the car and under a ripped awning.

"I'm stronger than you," he said mildly.

"I have a gun," she returned before pivoting and heading into the dismal restaurant.

God, she was stubborn. He shut the car door and followed her inside to a cracked and ripped somewhat peach-colored booth in the back. When she would've sat facing the door, he quickly took her arm and assisted her to sit across the booth, so he could face the entrance.

She scowled as he sat across from her. "I prefer to face the door."

As did he. Considering he was a hell of a lot more dangerous than she was, he would keep watch. "Oh, sorry. This side is ripped, and I didn't want you to be uncomfortable."

She narrowed her gaze. "Are you being a snob?"

"By saving your sweet ass from a dangerous booth?" He grinned, truly enjoying the color sliding across her too-pale face. "You don't know me, darlin'."

"No, but you definitely have money." She eyed his leather jacket. "I've seen your bike."

"Aye." Money was just money—unless one didn't have any. "I work hard."

She lifted her chin. "As an enforcer for a motorcycle club that runs drugs and guns? Blood money."

An enforcer for the Coven Nine made excellent wages, and it was rarely tinged with blood, although that was a distinct possibility sometimes. "I do what I have to do." He paused as an elderly waitress in bright pink shuffled up in geriatric shoes to plunk down two sweating water glasses.

She smiled cracked teeth. "Lexi, you sweetheart. How have you been?"

"Great, Frankie." A genuine smile lifted Alexandra's lips.

Kell paused, intrigued. Gentleness filled Alexandra's eyes, and he wanted that look. For him.

Frankie turned faded eyes on Kell. "You're a handsome one, now aren't you?"

He smiled and fought the urge to scoot over and ask the lady to sit. "You're a looker, yourself."

She twittered and patted him with a gnarled hand on his shoulder. "Charmer." She glanced at Alexandra. "How's your mama?"

Alexandra stilled, her smile seeming more forced. "Wonderful. Having a marvelous time."

"That's good, but we sure miss her around here." Frankie nodded, her gaze softening. "You're a good girl, Lexi. Want the usual?"

"Yep. For both of us," Alexandra said.

Frankie nodded and lumbered away.

"Come here often?" Kell asked.

"Yes." She cupped her water glass with both hands.

"Where's your mama?" he asked, trying to read her expression, wishing those slender hands were on him instead.

She leaned back, hands going to her lap as she met his gaze. "Tell me about Apollo."

"Tell you what"——he drummed his fingers on the table——"we'll take turns answering questions. That's only fair. *Lexi.*"

She blinked. "You first."

Did she play chess? He'd have to find out. "Apollo is a drug reduced to liquid form and injected. A quarter to a half dose gives the taker feelings of euphoria verging on godlike. A full dose does the same and then melts the user's internal organs."

"What is in it? We've never found a sample, and the drug is absorbed into the body upon death, so even autopsies don't help," she said.

He shrugged. "We don't know yet, either."

She narrowed her gaze but didn't challenge his lie. "Where is it from?" she asked.

"Where's your mother?" he returned evenly.

Her chin lifted. "Bakerston's Rehabilitation Home in western Seattle. Now, where's the drug from?"

"Initially? I think Russia, but I don't have confirmation of that yet." He could afford to give her that much.

She tilted her head to the side. "Why not?"

"We just merged with Fire, and we aren't privy to all the information." He sat back.

"But I thought you supplied the drugs, and they supply the guns." She twirled her water glass around.

He smiled. "You jumped to conclusions."

She squinted, disbelief filling her eyes. "I don't trust you."

"Nor should you. Why is your mother in a home?"

Alexandra sighed. "She has Multiple Sclerosis, and right now is having a difficult time. She usually gets better and then can live either with me or on her own until the next flare up. Right now, she requires extra care, and she's getting it."

Ah, what a sweetheart. "That type of home is costly."

"Yes. Yes, it is." Alexandra shook her head. "Who's making Apollo?"

"Dunno." Kell gave in to temptation and reached for her hand. Small boned, slender, very smooth skin. "Why are you a cop, darlin'? Is it because your father dealt drugs?" She couldn't atone for the sins of her father.

She shook her head and then leaned back when Frankie deposited large plates in front of them.

Kell glanced down at eggs, bacon, and hash browns, cooked perfectly into a heart attack on a plate. The delicious aroma made his stomach growl. He glanced up at Alexandra to catch her quick smile.

"You figured oatmeal?" she asked.

He nodded. "Something like that." Reaching for utensils, he happily dug in. Much better than pizza. They ate in silence for quite a while with a temporary peace easing around them. "So, why a cop?" he asked finally.

"You didn't answer about the origin of Apollo," she returned, sitting back with a sigh.

"Because I don't know." God, if he never ate again, he'd be content. "That was delicious."

She reached for her back pocket.

"No." His voice rumbled out harsher than he'd intended.

She paused. "Excuse me?"

"I'm paying." Cop or no, he wouldn't allow her to buy. Slipping a credit card from his wallet, he handed it to Frankie as she passed. Apparently the waitress agreed with him because she ignored Alexandra's attempt to hand over a card.

Alexandra sat back and frowned. "I can't let a known criminal buy me breakfast."

"How known?" He leaned toward her. "You've surely run me as well as contacted the garda in Ireland. I have no record."

She pursed her lips. "The Irish authorities haven't responded as of yet."

He wanted more than anything to kiss those full lips back into surrender. "I'll give them a call and tell them to hurry it up." He grinned.

She chuckled. "You are so full of it."

Actually, he could have Interpol vouch for him if he just asked. Of course, that'd break his cover. "Trust me a little, Alexandra."

"Absolutely not. You definitely don't add up." She crossed her arms. "Why did you meet with Bear the other day?"

"Bear is a good guy," Kellach said, choosing his words carefully. "My family and his go way back."

"Bear is from Ireland?" Alexandra leaned in. "Seriously?"

Kell shook his head. "No, Bear is from here. But he does have distant cousins across the ocean." Well, kind of.

"So it was personal and not business?" She narrowed her gaze and studied him.

"Yes." He captured her hand and tugged her toward him.

"Does Pyro know you're meeting with Bear?" she asked.

He shook his head. "Hell no. When you look at me like that, I want nothing more than to strip you naked and kiss you senseless. You screaming my name would please me greatly."

Her lips formed a perfect O of surprise, while a blush filled her high cheekbones. "You're terrible."

"I bet I could change your mind on that score." He rubbed his thumb across her knuckles. The woman was sexy and sweet and certainly didn't belong undercover in seedy Seattle bars. "Are you continuing your undercover operations?"

"Why?" She yanked her hand away. "Am I cramping your organization?"

Feisty little temper she had. He wanted to turn that passion in another direction.

"Obviously not." He accepted the receipt from Frankie and quickly dashed off his signature with a generous tip. His curiosity wasn't quite appeased with Alexandra, however, and he wondered if he could get her to stay awhile.

The door opened, and three men walked inside. His head pounded. "Bloody hell," he muttered.

Chapter 8

Lex blinked as Kellach's expression went from heated to stone-cold. A shiver slithered down her back, and she turned to see who had caught his frosty attention.

Three men stared back at Kellach. One appeared to be in his thirties with black hair, light eyes, and a true fighting shape. An odd streak of gray cut a swath through his hair.

The other two men were about twenty, both tall and broad and with dark hair. The nearest one grinned what could only be a smart-ass smile.

Kell rose from the booth and went straight for the men. Oddly enough, the younger two instantly flanked the older one in a protective move. The older one shoved them both back with a low growl.

A real growl?

She scooted out of the booth.

"Stay there, Alexandra," Kell ordered, his back to her.

Oh, hell no. She shoved free and walked up behind him, her hand resting near her gun. If something was happening, she couldn't let Frankie or the other few patrons get hurt. "Kellach? Who are your friends?" As she neared the four hulking men, she was reminded of her smaller stature. These guys were all huge and cut hard. Who were they?

The older one glanced down at her hand and then back up with a smooth smile. "Detective Monzelle? I'm Dage."

How did he know her name?

Kell stepped in front of her. "King, now isn't the time."

King? Was he a member of a motorcycle club? That would explain the nickname.

Dage sidestepped Kell and held out a hand. "It is a pleasure."

She shook his hand while eying the other two men.

Dage nodded. "My nephews Garrett and Logan. They're prospects for Titans of Fire." He gestured first to the smiling young man. Square features, way too handsome, intelligent eyes behind what appeared to be light-refracting glasses. The second kid was just as big, with ancient-looking green eyes. The kid had definitely seen some shit.

"Oh, hell no," Kell said, his powerful shoulders shooting back. "I have enough going on without worrying about Kayrs and Kyllwood progeny. Take your boys and go home, King."

Garrett's smart-ass grin slid from his face, and he stepped forward. "Watch how you talk to the king, enforcer."

The king?

Kellach dropped his gaze to the kid and stepped in. "Wanna burn, kid?"

Burn? Did he have one of those fire weapons? Lex slid to the side. "What exactly is going on here, gentlemen?" She put every ounce of authority she could into her voice.

Kellach exhaled slowly, his nostrils flaring. He turned, manacled her arm, and all but dragged her past the hulking group. At the door, he turned back. "Meet me at Simone's in thirty minutes." Without waiting for an answer, he opened the door and escorted her to the car.

She jerked free and slapped his chest with both hands. "You're manhandling a cop, asshole. Right now, I'm heading back inside to see who the hell those people are." Whoever they were, they'd pissed Kell off just by walking into the diner. Every instinct she had told her to pursue the lead she'd just been given.

Kellach stepped into her, pressing her butt against the wet car. "Get your arse in the car or I'll put you there. This is way above your pay grade, Alexandra." His jaw clenched and pure fire lit his dark eyes. For the first time, he completely lost his customary charm. Deadly danger all but cascaded off him in tension and warning. "I'm stronger, and whether you like it or not, I'm a hell of a lot meaner than you are. You won't win if you fight me."

Her temper caught in her chest and then exploded. "Forget you." She reached for her weapon, only to have him grab it first. She gaped. Who the hell moved that fast?

He lifted her, opened her car door, and shoved her inside.

Quick strides had him around the car and in the driver's seat before she could even gasp. He had even somehow grabbed the keys!

"Who in the hell are you?" she breathed.

He engaged the engine and shot into the road, driving easily with one hand. "Someone you really don't want to mess with right now." With a snap of his fingers, he yanked out his cell phone and put it to his ear. "Daire? The fucking king is here with Garrett and Logan." Kell winced and held the phone away from his ear before slowly pressing it back. "I take it you didn't know? Well, apparently the boys are new *prospects* at Fire."

Even across the car, Alexandra could hear the *"hell no"* bellowed across the line.

Kellach smiled. "That's what I thought. Call the council and have this taken care of. It's our business, not theirs." He clicked off with a grim smile.

Lex tried to think rationally and not kill the son of a bitch driving her car. "Who are Dage, Garrett, and Logan?"

"Nobody." Kellach took a corner way too fast and yet managed to keep the car on the ground. "Forget you met them, because they are not staying in town. Period." His voice lowered to a tone darker than raw gravel being spun.

She shivered. If he talked to her like that, she'd probably leave town, too. "What's going on?"

He sighed and turned toward her, his impossibly hard face softening. "I'm sorry if I scared you."

"I'm not scared," she lied.

"Okay." He rubbed a hand through his thick hair. "Here's the deal, and you're not going to understand it. But from now on, you're under my protection. If anybody threatens you, if anybody comes after you, you use my name. Promise me."

She coughed, her mind spinning. "I'm. A. Cop." Why the hell did he keep forgetting that? "I protect you, badass biker buddy." Just how dangerous were King and those two boys?

Kellach pulled the car up to the curb in front of her apartment in record time.

She gaped. "How did you know where I live?" As a cop, her address was unlisted.

"I have my sources." He jumped into the rain and hustled around to assist her from the car.

For the briefest of moments, she was tempted to wrestle him to the ground and arrest him. But for what? Sure, he'd taken her gun, but she really didn't want to admit that one, did she?

He frowned at the closed Thai restaurant and then looked around at the dingy, dangerous neighborhood. "You live here?"

Her spine stiffened. "I do now." She'd sold her house to pay her mother's medical bills, and so far just kept going deeper and deeper into debt. That was none of his business. She held out her hand. "My gun."

He finished perusing the neighborhood and looked up at her apartment. His body stilled. Then, slowly, he pressed the gun into her hands. "Stay here, darlin'. There's somebody in your apartment."

Kell ran up the stairs toward Alexandra's apartment, his senses on high alert. Three heartbeats. Tuning in, he could make out their locations. Spread out, waiting to strike.

Fucking bastards.

He reached the door, and Alexandra shoved him aside.

Damn it. He'd told her to remain downstairs.

She gingerly slid a key into the lock, her gun out, total focus on her stunning face. He paused to give her a signal, and the woman darted inside. She yelped and jumped to the side.

Electrodes pierced his chest, and voltage zipped into him.

His breath caught and he staggered, reaching out an arm to the wall.

Alexandra leaped in front of him, hitting a moving man dead center in a hard tackle. They went down, crashing a wooden coffee table into splinters. Then the woman fought. She scored two sharp punches to the guy's nose, and then scissored both legs around his neck, quickly incapacitating him even though he was twice her size. A closer look revealed the prick to be Duck.

Holy fucking damn it.

A second man, one Kell didn't recognize, tried to jump into the fray.

Kell shook his head to clear the electricity and leaped over the grappling duo and rammed the second guy into a wall. The human fought back, and well, punching Kell in the gut and then the face. Kell twisted, wedging his elbow beneath the man's jaw, jerking his head up and against a print of a tranquil lake. Another quick punch to the nose, and the man went down, spraying blood.

"Freeze," Alexandra yelled from behind him.

He turned just in time to see her jump up and run out the front door, gun out. Kicking free of the tangle of limbs at his feet, he hurried after her, taking the stairs four at a time. At the street level, he ran into her.

She turned around, her gaze sweeping the street. "See anybody?"

A car flared to life two blocks away and spun out. Kell's shoulders relaxed. "No." His heart finally slowed, and he curled both hands over her shoulders to turn her around. "Are you all right?" Beneath his palms, her pulse beat wildly.

"Yes." She panted out air. "Ticked we lost the third guy." Lifting her head, she winced and then tugged electrodes from his chest. "How are you even standing?"

"Not enough juice in the stun gun, I guess," he lied. He brushed the hair from her face, irritation filling him when he spotted a bruise near her temple. "How's your head?"

"Good." She tugged a phone from her back pocket. "I need to call this in."

Yeah. And he needed to go fight with the King of the Realm.

"I'll wait for your backup to arrive." Turning her, he headed back inside. "Next time we face danger, how about you let me go first?"

"Why?" She flashed him a grin. "You took the charge instead of me."

He rubbed his smarting chest. "Good point."

"Did you see the third guy?" she asked, nudging her door open with one foot.

"No. He was off to the side and slid away while we were fighting with the other two." Kell nodded toward the two men who lay unconscious still, and smiled. "Where'd you learn to fight, sweetheart?"

She'd been a pleasure to watch, however briefly.

She shrugged. "Junior High. Where else?"

Where else, indeed. He eyed her ruffled hair and bright eyes. There was a lot more to Detective Alexandra Monzelle than he'd initially thought. "How about you let me question these two guys for you—

just until your backup arrives?" He could awaken them easily and with minimal burning, considering they were just human, as was the guy who'd escaped.

Temptation glimmered in her eyes. "I wish I could"—she looked at the man she'd knocked out and kicked him in the leg—"but I have to follow procedure." She cranked her neck to check out Duck. "I take it you didn't know your brother would be here?"

"That's no brother of mine, club or no," Kell ground out. He'd have to explain to Pyro why he'd knocked out Duck in a police detective's home. Of course, at first glance, it appeared Duck had violated orders. "How long will you be at the station?"

She rocked back on her heels, her face thoughtful. "Dunno. Long enough to question these jerks."

"I'll come back later and help you put your home to rights." Hell, he'd love to move her somewhere nicer.

"That's all right. Unless you want to tell me all you know about Apollo and new guns, we're done." Her blue eyes were clear and way too serious. "Thank you for breakfast, however."

Fire danced down his spine at her ultimatum. He'd never responded well to those. Almost without thought, his arm snaked out and tugged her against him. "Do you really think it'll be that easy to forget me?"

"Yes," she breathed, meeting his gaze.

Sirens sounded in the distance. He pressed a hard kiss against her lips, satisfied by her sharp intake of breath. His mouth twitched with the need to take her deeper, but he had to go. Releasing her, he headed for the door. "We're nowhere near done here, Detective. I'll see you soon."

Chapter 9

Lex tossed the file on the scarred table and drew out a chair to sit across from Duck. The chilly air smelled of sweat and desperation, and even though the heater clunked somewhere in the building, the warmth failed to enter the interrogation room. She'd thrown on a sweater before entering, well accustomed to the shitty system.

After several hours in the tank, no doubt detoxing, the club member slouched. She studied him. At one time, he had probably been handsome with angular features and a nice build. Now, after what she suspected was years of alcohol and drugs, red lines colored not only the whites of his eyes but the skin along his neck. His nose was nearly bulbous, and youthful muscles had gone to fat.

She eyed the file. "You're only thirty-two."

"So?" He leaned back and patted a wide belly.

He looked over forty. "You've lived a hard life, Duck."

"I like hard. Don't you?"

Quick. Even burned out, the guy was quick.

She grinned. "It's nice to see you haven't killed all your brain cells."

The door opened and Bernie stomped in to sit. "He gonna talk or what?"

"We hadn't gotten to that part." Lex settled back in her seat. While Duck hadn't asked for a lawyer yet, she didn't want to spook him. "You're in deep shit, Duck."

He shrugged. "Bullshit."

Bernie snorted. "You broke into a cop's apartment and committed a battery. Dumbass."

Duck rubbed the unruly whiskers lining his weak chin. "Maybe I was waiting for my good buddy, Kellach, who I knew was dating a cop. He gave me the go-ahead to wait inside for him."

Shit. Lex hadn't had a chance to talk to Bernie and somehow explain how Kellach had ended up in her car and then outside her apartment door.

Her partner's expression didn't change. "You didn't have an invite, and you know it, which makes it trespassing. And assault. And battery. And, oh, um . . . resisting arrest?" He lifted an eyebrow and turned toward Lex.

She nodded solemnly. "Yep. Definitely resisting arrest. Considering you're a suspect in an ongoing investigation, it truly does mean you're screwed."

Duck's smile flashed yellow teeth. "I'm not sure about that. You positive you want it officially on the record that you were coming home early morning with a known Fire club member, a possible suspect in your drug case, hot on your heels? To your apartment?" He patted his big belly again. "That might be a career breaker, you know? I can see the headline now. SLUT COP LOSES DRUG CASE."

She had enough problems at work with Masterson and Bundt breathing down her damn neck, so she settled back into her seat. "I've been called worse, and who knows? *Slut Cop* has a good ring to it."

Bernie snorted. "Could be one of them reality shows. Make you totally famous, you know?"

She smiled. "I do have a face for television, right?"

"Definitely." Bernie tapped meaty fingers on the damaged table. "Stop fuckin' around, Duck. Tell us why you were at the apartment, who the other two guys are, and where the hell you're getting the drugs."

Duck wiped off his lips. "I was in the apartment waiting for my club brother, and I'm sure he'll testify to the same facts. The guy you've arrested is a new prospect named Rock, because he's about as solid as one. As for the drugs? I have no idea what you're talking about."

"Is that a fact?" Bernie shook his head. "So you'll take the fall for these guys?"

"Nope, no fall." Duck sighed and focused his gaze on Lex's tits. "How long you been fuckin' Kell?"

She rolled her eyes. "Don't be silly. Give us the info we need, and we'll get you a deal, Duck. A good one."

"Don't need a deal. It's my first arrest, and you got nothin', especially after your boyfriend backs up my story." Duck's beady eyes gleamed. "You might be a nice piece of ass, but he's a brother now, and he'll have my back."

Bernie stiffened at the insult and jumped to his feet.

Lex quickly pressed both hands on the table. "Who was the third guy at the apartment?"

"I figured another one of your boyfriends," Duck sneered.

Lex sighed. "You know, I think it's time to book you." The bastard wasn't going to break, and he wasn't going to tell them anything about the drugs. Yet. Maybe some time in a cell would help.

Bernie grabbed Duck and hauled him across the table. His knees hit hard, and he flopped onto the other side.

"What the fuck, man?" Duck bellowed.

"You're a piece of shit," Bernie growled, shoving Duck hard against the wall. "Stop with the bull and give us something. Where are the drugs coming from?"

Duck's face reddened. "Ask her boyfriend. You think he just showed up from Ireland right when the good stuff hit the streets? Jesus. Use your fuckin' brains."

Bernie stepped closer into Duck's face. "I will. While I'm at it, all you Fire guys have nicknames. Why doesn't Kellach?"

"He does." Triumph curled Duck's upper lip. "It's Lasair."

Bernie twisted his head and wrinkled his forehead.

Lex shrugged. "Never heard of it."

Bernie shoved Duck toward the door. "It's probably bullshit."

"Nope." Duck grimaced as his face hit the door frame before Bernie yanked open the door. "It's Irish."

Bernie propelled him into the hallway where a uniform was waiting to take him to booking.

Lex stepped into the hallway. "What does it mean?"

Duck tripped as the uniformed patrol officer hauled him down the hallway. He turned, and a hard smile twitched his lips. "Means *flame*. Apparently your boy has always had a thing for fire." Duck's high-pitched chuckle echoed down the hallway and around the corner.

Lex heaved out a breath. "Fire?"

Bernie rubbed his chin. "That's interesting, right?"

Yeah. "Everything about this case involves fire. Apollo burns the organs of victims, and somehow new weapons throw balls of flame." And Kell's nickname was all about fire. Just who the hell was he? "The key is Kellach Dunne."

Bernie leaned against a hard block wall. "Speaking of Dunne."

Heat rose into Lex's face. "It's not what you think."

"I already know that." Bernie shuffled his loafers. "It doesn't look good, anyway."

"I know." She leaned back against the wall and shut her eyes. "We're missing something. I don't know what, but it's right in front of us."

"It's Dunne," Bernie muttered.

Heavy footsteps sounded, and Detective Bundt sauntered down the hallway. "So, Lex. Fucking suspects now?"

Bernie instantly jumped forward and slammed Bundt into a wall. Bundt swung out, connecting a solid right to Bernie's cheek.

Damn it. Pivoting, Lex nailed Bundt in the balls. With a hoarse "*oof*," he doubled over. She grabbed his chin and threw him back into the cinder blocks. "I'm not fucking Dunne, and you know it. Watch your mouth, asshole." She released him and grabbed Bernie's arm to drag him down the hallway to the bullpen. "What the hell?"

Bernie wiped his cheek. "Sorry. Lost my temper." He jerked his arm free. "You need to get your house in order, partner. Now." Without another glance, he turned and headed toward the break room.

Lex exhaled several times, her mind whirling. Yeah. She did need to get things in order, and the idea that she'd disappointed Bernie made her nauseated. But first? She had to figure out who the hell Kellach Dunne was and how involved he was in the current case. Something told her she'd have to arrest him and soon.

Then all hell, and probably her career, would go up in smoke.

Kell stormed into Simone's penthouse apartment, his gut churning, his head aching, and his temper fraying. Two steps inside the door, a wave of power nearly set him off. *Jesus.* He strode into the living room where Daire faced off with the king. Two powerful immortals, both cascading energy, and neither one particularly pleased to see Kell.

Sounds banged from the kitchen, and Kell tuned in. Garrett and Logan—a young vampire and a young demon—no doubt eating everything in sight.

Kell paused at the entryway. "Where are Adam and Simone?"

"Lab," Daire said, lounging in nowhere near a deceptive pose by the large wall of windows, his gaze remaining on the king, who stood near the fireplace wearing a bored expression, a grape energy drink in his hand. "Want to explain why you were caught in a police-woman's house tonight?"

"No." Kell glanced from his brother to the king. "You two about to fight?"

"No." Dage winced as something broke in the kitchen. "I hope Simone is insured. When those two start cooking, something usually blows up."

Speaking of which . . . "When did a young demon soldier become your nephew?" Kell asked slowly. While Garrett really was Dage's nephew, Logan was anything but.

Dage shrugged. "Logan's brother married my niece, which makes him my nephew-in-law. So Logan might as well be a nephew, and it's a simpler label."

Plus, considering Logan's older brother was the leader of the entire demon nation, why not make friends? Vampires and demons claiming each other for family. Where the hell had reality gone?

Kell lifted an eyebrow at Daire, who just matched his shrug.

"As I was saying," Dage said, "I'd like to ask a favor from you. Basically for Logan and Garrett to work this case with you."

Well, shit. Kell sighed. When the king of the Realm told you what to do, you hit him in the face and started throwing fire. But if the king nicely asked for a favor? Yeah. You gave the vampire king a fucking favor. "Shit."

Dage smiled. "Yep."

And when the king was actually the brother-in-law of two of your cousins, you did a good job with the favor.

"You're an asshole," Daire said without heat.

"I've been called worse." Dage crossed over and dropped onto the couch, crossing one knee over black pants. "I do appreciate your assistance."

Kell grinned and took a seat. "What did they do?"

Dage scowled. "Let's just say that those two on their own, without a war going on, and too many human girls out there . . . cause problems."

It always came down to girls, didn't it? "You're punishing them by making them work a case where they're not needed?" Kell asked.

"Yes, and plus, it's a case where they'll be kept safe. I trust you to involve them, get them some undercover training, but keep them from getting their heads cut off." Dage eyed Daire. "Surely there's something they can do to help. As prospects."

It would keep the king in the loop, where he always fucking wanted to be.

Daire loped over to sit in the overstuffed chair, instantly plopping his boots on the table. "Well . . . as prospects, they can get closer to the other prospects. Maybe get some info we can't without appearing obvious."

"Plus, they can party pretty hard in town." Kell rubbed his chin. "If one or both of them can pretend to be on the lookout for drugs, especially if they're not wearing their cuts, we might actually get a break." The more he thought about it, the better he liked the idea. "This might actually work." Of course, he'd have to make sure neither kid got hurt on his watch. Talk about a disaster.

Dage nodded. "I would certainly owe you one." He stood and stretched his neck. "Thank you."

Kell stood. "How is your mate?"

"Pregnant and beautiful and a bit cranky." Dage's face relaxed in a way it only did when speaking of Emma. "She's four months along now, and the kid kicks. A lot."

Sounded like Dage's child. "Well, congrats," Kell said. The Kayrs ruling family seemed to be multiplying exponentially now that the war had finally ended.

"Thanks." Dage reached into his back pocket and drew out a thick, folded envelope. "About your cop. Everything."

Kell took the envelope, his head lifting. "How . . ."

Dage rolled his eyes and moved toward the kitchen. "I'm the fucking king. Everybody seems to forget that." He turned and smiled. "I'll say good-bye to the boys and then be on my way. Good luck with them."

Chapter 10

Lex spread the file out on her bed, looking at pictures of Titans of Fire, Grizzlies, and corpses. She knew it all fit together somehow, but she was missing the link. Glancing toward the clock, she sighed. Two in the morning.

When had sleep become impossible?

After returning home from work, she'd thrown away the demolished coffee table and repaired the rest of her crappy apartment. A stack of bills lay in a nice pile next to her dinosaur of a computer, and she tried to avoid those. How she was going to pay for the next few months of her mother's care was beyond her. Even with her sister, Tori, chipping in, they didn't have enough money. If she could just solve this case, she'd have more time to figure things out. To maybe work a second job and make some extra cash.

The smell from the Thai food place below gurgled up again, and she reached over to open the window so the scent of rain would banish the oily smell.

Her phone dinged.

Instantly, her heart leaped to life, forcing her to take several deep breaths to glance at the face. Bernie. Shit. "Yeah," she answered.

"Duck's dead." A cacophony of action could be heard melding with the outside rain. "Happy Maple Subdivision, fifth house on the left from the entrance."

She jerked her head. "How the hell is Duck out?"

"Made bail," Bernie muttered. "This is bad, Lex. Really bad."

"How so?" She leaned down and grabbed discarded jeans to shimmy into.

Voices lifted in the background. "Just get here. You need to see this." Bernie clicked off.

She hustled into clothes and out into the rain to make the quick drive across town to the crime scene in a subdivision. The stench of burned flesh assaulted Lex's nostrils the second she stepped out of the car. She faltered for the briefest of seconds and then straightened her shoulders, striding past the crime scene tape, the milling officers, and even the gawkers out late to see the commotion. Unlike the last crime scene, the nicely treed street held freshly painted houses with perfectly manicured lawns.

Through the swirling red and blue lights, she caught sight of Bernie up a long driveway next to a white colonial. Small but quaint.

Stepping over a couple puddles, she skirted an overgrown hydrangea bush and reached her partner. She glanced down and breathed out. "Holy shit."

Bernie nodded. "Yep."

Duck lay on his back, one hand thrown over his forehead. Scorch marks and what appeared to be burned blood covered his mouth and jaw, and even his neck. Lex covered her mouth and nose while crouching down.

Bernie shoved a pair of gloves into her hand. "Check out his fingernails."

She donned the gloves and gingerly lifted Duck's free hand, which had turned red and crusty. Blood seemed to have pooled at the nail beds and even burned a path toward his wrists. "What the hell?"

"His eyeballs are burned out, and I'm sure when the ME opens him up, we'll find incinerated organs. This is the worst we've seen from an Apollo overdose. There's bruising around the jaw as if his mouth was held open and the drug shoved down his gullet." Bernie jerked his head toward the quiet home. "Duck's house."

Lex slowly stood. "Duck lived in this nice house?"

"Apparently." Bernie rocked back on his heels. "Just waiting for a warrant to go in, since he was found outside."

Lex glanced at the waiting crowd, many of whom wore hastily thrown on robes over pajamas. "Who found him?"

Bernie pointed to an elderly lady in a flowered housecoat huddling under the eaves of the adjoining home—a blue rancher with pristine white shutters. "Mrs. Lakeland. Retired teacher and neighbor for about three years."

Lex nodded and maneuvered past several crime techs to the white-haired lady. "Mrs. Lakeland, I'm Detective Monzelle. Do you mind if I ask you a couple questions?"

Mrs. Lakeland lifted surprisingly sharp blue eyes. "Not at all."

Lex tried for a reassuring smile. "How long have you known the deceased?"

Mrs. Lakeland took a deep breath that shook her entire eighty-pound or so body. "Albert moved in about three years ago. Such a sweet boy. Brought my trash cans in every week and helped me to find Razzles every time the darn cat decided to take off."

Lex blinked. *Sweet boy?* "Um, are we talking about Duck? The Motorcycle club member?"

"Duck." Mrs. Lakeland chortled. "Yes, that was his little nickname." She sighed and brushed a wiry white curl away from her wrinkled forehead. "I heard him swearing on the phone once to someone, and it was like he turned into somebody else. When he came outside, he saw me tending to my tulips. That boy apologized up and down for the crude language."

"Duck apologized?" Lex asked slowly.

"Of course. We all have more than one persona, young lady. To me? He was Albert, my very nice neighbor."

Well, hells bells. "Yes, ma'am." She cut a look to Bernie, who just shrugged. "How did you find Du—Albert, Mrs. Lakeland?"

"Oh my." Mrs. Lakeland wrung bony hands together in front of her tightly knotted belt. "A ruckus woke me, so I fumbled for my glasses and tried to hurry to the window. At my age, hurrying is more of a slow-motion movement." Her faded pink lips trembled. "I reached the window in time to see a fire on his driveway." Tears gathered in her eyes. "Turned out it was Albert."

Lex reached out and patted the woman's thin arm. "Did you see anybody else in the driveway?"

"Two men." Mrs. Lakeland nodded, shaking the loose skin on her chin. "Big, really big men dressed in long black coats. I think they had dark hair, but that's all I can say. I saw them jump into a black SUV at the curb and speed away. Why would they set Albert on fire?" she asked, a tear slipping out.

"I don't know." Lex rubbed her arm. "Is there anybody we can call to come stay with you tonight, Mrs. Lakeland?"

The elderly lady shook her head. "No. I'm fine." She shivered in the chilly air.

Lex nodded for a female uniformed officer, who hustled over. "This nice officer is going to take you inside and maybe make you some tea, ma'am."

Mrs. Lakeland nodded, pausing as she turned. "You'll find who did this to sweet Albert, won't you?"

"I'm sure going to try. I promise." Lex kept silent until the women disappeared around Mrs. Lakeland's home before turning to Bernie. "Two large men, huh?"

"Interesting." Bernie glanced back down at the corpse, sympathy lightening his eyes. "How much of the drug do you think they gave him to result in this much damage?"

She shook her head. "Way too much. The feeling of it going in must've been excruciating."

"Duck's screaming must've been what woke Mrs. Lakeland." Bernie straightened as a statuesque redhead strode toward them in very nice leather boots. He lifted his chin. "Out for a late night, August?"

August Summerling, Seattle prosecutor, scowled down at the body while slapping a piece of paper into Bernie's hand. "I thought I'd bring down the warrant myself."

Bernie lifted a bushy eyebrow. "We have e-mails on our phones now, you know."

August smiled, showing even white teeth. "I know, but I'd like to take a look at Duck's house, too. When this shithole of a case goes to trial, I want a full picture."

Bernie met her grin. "How much ribbing you get from your name, anyway?"

August sighed. "More than you'll ever know."

Lex hadn't had a case with August yet, but the woman had a stellar reputation, and she was willing to go on a little faith. "Your parents were hippies?"

"No. No father, and Mom is a new-age, crystal-wearing, tarot-reading, one-with-the-universe woman in natural fabrics. Love her, so I could never change the name." August eyed Bernie top to bottom and then wiggled her brows. "What's your last name, Detective? I'm always looking for a new one."

Bernie blushed beet red from his jowls to his hairline. "Knock it off. Geez. I'm old enough to be your father."

Lex elbowed him. "And you're married."

Bernie somehow turned even redder. "Oh yeah. Yeah. I'm married." He held out his left hand to show his gold band. "Forty years. Forty wonderful, excellent, she's gonna kill me if we keep talking, years."

August chuckled. "I'm just messing with you. Sorry."

The prosecutor went up about ten notches in Lex's book, and that meant something. She rubbed her hands together. "Let's go through Duck's white-picket fence of a house."

"You don't suppose we'll get lucky enough that this will be a stash house, do ya?" Bernie muttered, avoiding the hydrangea bush to clomp up the front porch.

Anticipation hurried Lex's movements. "It's entirely possible." What better place to stash drugs and weapons than a pretty subdivision down a nicely treed street? "We've done searches on property owned by Fire and its members, and this didn't come up."

"It's owned by a corporation called NewBerry, Inc.," August said, waiting for Lex to precede her into the house. "My office is doing a deeper search now to find the connection, but a cursory glance shows the company being a front for property owned by Titans of Fire." She shrugged. "Not unusual, actually."

The house smelled like lemon cleanser and featured a quaint living room with matching couch and loveseat, a stark but clean kitchen, and one bedroom off to the side. Small but somehow sweet.

Lex headed instantly for the kitchen and started tapping on walls.

August leaned over her shoulder. "Hidden rooms?"

"Here's hoping," Lex agreed, continuing to tap. In the living room, other cops began the arduous process of searching for contraband.

"Eureka," Bernie bellowed from the bedroom.

Excitement roared through Lex's veins, and she all but ran into the bedroom, where Bernie had opened a false back in the closet to reveal a shitload of weapons. AK-47s, pistols, even sawed-off shotguns. Her shoulders hunched. All known weapons. Nothing that could throw fire.

She turned and yanked the white quilt off the bed. "Let's get going. We have an entire house to search. There have to be more weapons somewhere." She'd tear the entire house down to find the fire-throwing weapons along with the Apollo drug. She was getting closer; she could just feel it.

Who the hell had murdered Duck and why?

Chapter 11

Dawn hadn't yet begun to arrive, and darkness shrouded the area like an omen of things to come. Bad things. The rain had ebbed, but a hint of another storm hung in the damp air, chilling right through cotton and leather. Lex sighed at her empty, stinky apartment, her limbs weary and her gut churning.

Seven foil packets of meth and several more pistols had been found at Duck's, but no fire-throwing weapons, and no Apollo. His home had been a stash house, but not for the right stuff.

She'd headed home for a few hours of sleep, and Bernie had, very annoyingly, insisted upon following her and then checking out her crappy apartment for any more intruders.

"I'm a cop," she had snapped.

"You're my partner," he'd snapped back. Satisfied that no bad guys lurked beneath her bed or in her tiny closet, he'd nicely suggested she hire a maid and stated he'd pick her up the following day to go speak with Kellach Dunne. Only then had he sauntered out.

What a fucking day, or rather, night. Lex washed her face and yanked on a tank top and fresh underwear before falling face-first on her unmade bed. Seconds later, she was dreaming about a fire-throwing Irishman near a half-crumbled castle surrounded by rolling hills.

The smash of glass had her rolling over. A man dressed in all black, wearing a ski mask, landed hard on the floor, spreading glass and rain. Thunder echoed outside, and the wind pummeled rain into the room.

A second later, wood splintered, and a second man dodged inside her apartment.

She reached for the gun on her end table, and a hard kick from the first guy sent the gun spiraling into the wall.

Panic heated her lungs, and she shook her head to gain her bearings. Her heart beat rapidly, and adrenaline pricked up the hair on her arms. Focus. She needed to focus.

"Who are you?" she asked, shuffling back to sit against the headboard and drawing up her knees. Fear and intent rushed through her and narrowed the moment to heartbeats. If one of the men attacked, he'd have to lean over to get to her, and she'd take out his nose with a kick.

"Where is it?" the first guy asked, his voice garbled.

About six-four, solid muscle, narrow waist. Black pants and shirt, some type of boots—looked military. She couldn't get an angle on his facial features behind the thick mask, but his eyes appeared brown. Maybe.

"What?" she asked, eying the other guy at the door. Not as tall but definitely thicker. Slight gut. Brown running shoes, and Beretta in his hands, pointed to the floor.

The first guy, obviously the guy in charge, took out a Glock and pointed it at her face. "Last chance. Where is it?"

She shook her head. If she jumped at him, he'd definitely get off a shot. Her phone lay over on the dresser; she couldn't get to it in time. "Listen, asshole. Tell me what you're looking for, and I'll be happy to find it for you. As things stand, I have no fucking clue what you want."

"He said he gave it to her," the guy by the door whispered. "It has to be here somewhere."

The first guy nodded. "Right." He slipped his gun into the back of his waist. "Let's take care of the detective here, and we'll search." Moving forward, he pressed one knee on the bed.

A gunshot would make too much noise. Made sense. The asshole thought he'd suffocate her.

She pushed back against the wall and tried to whimper.

The lower part of his mask moved as if he smiled. He moved closer.

She kicked up as hard as she could, nailing him under the chin. His head went back, and she landed on top of him, pulling out his gun.

The guy at the door stepped closer, his gun pointing. "Drop it, or I'll shoot."

She was dead anyway—at least if he shot, somebody would hear. Whether or not they called the cops in this neighborhood was iffy, however. Keeping her balance on top of the first guy, she pointed the gun at his nose. "You shoot, and I shoot."

The door slammed open into the first guy, and another body lunged inside, tackling the gunman to the floor.

The guy under her shot out a hand and nailed the gun, sending it flying into the far wall.

Damn it. Lex punched him hard in the nose, satisfied with the loud crunch.

He bellowed and blasted a right cross into her cheek. Pain exploded in her face, and her vision wavered.

Not moving, not gaining any extra leverage, the guy grabbed her waist and threw her over his head.

She crashed through the apartment, her arms flailing, and smashed into the refrigerator. Her right shoulder took most of the impact, and agony ripped down her arm. She landed hard, and glass from the broken window pierced her legs.

Blinking, she used the dented fridge to haul herself to her feet. Shards of glass cut her toes.

The guy by the door went down, and Kellach stood there, fury on his angled face.

The man who'd thrown her stood and faced him. "What the fuck is an enforcer doing here?" he muttered. Fire instantly shot out from him, huge balls of blazing death thrown with a pitcher's aim. His weapon was hidden by his long coat. Kellach ducked and plowed forward in a hard tackle.

The first man rolled to his side, took in the scene, leapfrogged at Lex, and shoved her into the counter. Pain flared along her back.

She yelled and brought both elbows down on his nape.

He roared and straightened up, lifting her into the air. She struggled, kicking and hitting, trying for a good angle at his still covered nose. He jabbed a needle into her arm and depressed the plunger.

Instant sedation slid through her skin, muscles, and maybe bone. Her head swam.

Damn it. What had he given her?

Holding her tight, turning, he charged through the damaged window, boots clanking on the fire escape and scattering her potted plants. Drawing in a breath, he leaped over the railing and landed on the awning of the restaurant below.

She screamed as wind and rain beat her skin. Her elbow connected with his throat, and he yelped. Taking advantage, drawing deep, she shoved two fingers near his eyes.

He dropped her.

She bounced, scrambling across the awning almost in slow motion, trying to find purchase so as not to fall. The drug slowed her movements, and she tried to clear her head.

He turned and fell on his belly, holding on to the ripped material, swung his legs over, and then disappeared from sight. The sound of running footsteps echoed through the storm.

She slid across water and glass to peer over the side, two stories below. Nothing. He was gone.

She blinked water from her eyes as rain soaked her thin tank top. Her gun was inside, as was Kellach and the other gunman. Gingerly, trying not to be cut, she tried to crawl on the awning back toward the building before she passed out.

An oscillating blue ball of fire careened outside and dropped next to her. Fire licked her palm.

She screamed and tried to scramble away from the fire. The ball burned a hole in the awning and kept going right through. Shit. The whole thing would go up. She rolled to the other side, hoping she could grab hold and jump. She'd probably break something in the fall, but that was better than burning to death.

"Alexandra?" Kellach bellowed from the window.

She looked up in time to see him illuminated from behind as fire hit him. Flames cascaded out around him, his eyes widened, and then his body was propelled outside.

If he hit the awning, he'd keep going. She tried to swing her legs over the side and out of the way, but the drugs in her system slowed her down.

Kellach ducked in a summersault, landed next to her, and grabbed her up.

She cried out and shoved against him.

Two more spins in the air, and somehow, they landed safely on the pavement below. She blinked up through the rain at his rough face, cradled in arms harder than granite.

"W-what?" she stuttered.

He gazed at her face. "How badly are you hurt?"

"Dunno." Her mind fuzzed. How were they standing on the street?

He strode over to her car and yanked open the door, shoving her to the passenger side. "Keys?"

"Upstairs." She couldn't catch a thought, or a breath. Liquid dropped into her eyes. Frowning, she wiped her forehead and looked at her hand. Blood. "I'm bleeding."

He grasped her chin and turned her to face him. "Just hold on. You'll be okay."

Those were the last words she heard before darkness grabbed her, took her under, and covered her.

Kellach stood in the doorway, his gaze on the too-quiet woman on his massive bed. It wasn't how he'd dreamed of her sharing a night with him. He'd administered to her cuts, washing each one clean and covering the two largest with a bandage. Her hand had been burned, and he'd placed an ointment on it while she remained out from a sedative.

He'd tasted the remaining drops after recovering the syringe, and it was just a normal sedative. Whoever had broken into her apartment had meant to subdue her and maybe take her.

Her heartbeat had remained steady, and her breathing solid. She'd be fine once she woke from the sedative.

She blinked and her eyes opened.

Finally.

Her entire body stilled, and she stopped breathing.

"Alexandra." He kept his voice smooth and commanding. "You're all right."

She sat up. A couple blinks, and those stunning blue eyes focused on him. "Where the hell am I?"

"My flat."

She looked down at the blue silk shirt he'd gently placed over her head. "You undressed me?"

"Your clothes were wet, and believe me, that shirt covers a lot more of you than I'd like." He kept his stance relaxed and his voice nonthreatening, already sensing the emotions pouring from her. The tension he could handle, but the fear bothered him on a level he didn't quite want to explore yet.

She glanced around carefully.

"I didn't bring your gun." He kept the smile from his face. "Although, after seeing you fight again, I'm not sure you need one."

She reached up and fingered the butterfly bandage over her right eye. "You patched me up?"

"I did."

"Why?" She focused on him again.

Why, indeed.

He couldn't have left her there. No doubt, more witches would return. The one he'd fought had thrown fire like a master, and surely had backup.

Who the hell was that man? Kellach had lost him when trying to rescue Alexandra from falling. The witch wasn't known to Kell, so he was probably just muscle for hire. Whoever wanted Alexandra or whatever she held knew enough about her to know she had enforcer protection, so they'd hired a witch. The guy had seemed shocked to be face to face with an enforcer, so apparently he hadn't been given the full story. "I brought you home to protect you," Kell said.

She growled and shoved the covers off her bare legs. "What did they inject me with?"

"Standard sedative. You should be fine."

"I am." She glanced around again. "I have to get back to my apartment. Bernie will be beside himself."

"Bernie has no clue." Kellach crossed his arms. If she thought she was going back to that war zone to face a species she didn't even know existed, she was fucking crazy.

"Baloney." She stood and wobbled slightly. "You're telling me three men broke into a cop's apartment, started a fire, burned the awning outside, and nobody called the cops?"

He sighed. "I sent my brothers to deal with anybody else who showed up." Once the witch, whoever he was, saw two enforcers there without any humans to protect, the asshole would surely go the other way, no matter how much he'd been paid. "The awning and your apartment will be fixed before dawn arrives."

The storm rolled outside, spattering wind and hard pellets of rain against the glass window. Seattle at its finest.

Alexandra shook her head. "What about the men who broke in?"

Regret slithered through him like a snake. "I couldn't contain them and save you, so I chose you." He'd find the bastards, however. Then they'd regret harming her.

She shoved wet curls off her forehead.

"Why do you cut your hair so short?" he whispered, cocking his head to the side.

The blond mass was stunning, and if that curl was real, she'd look like a goddess with it long. Not that she didn't look stunning and tough with it short.

She faltered, vulnerability darkening her eyes. "It's easier to take care of short, and it's harder to grab in a fight."

"You shouldn't be fighting." He strode toward her to brush a finger over the bruise darkening her cheekbone. "You're too delicate." *Too special.*

She kept still, allowing him to touch her. "I don't understand you."

"Aye." How could she? She didn't know a damn thing about him. "Who were those men at your apartment?"

She shrugged. "I don't know. They were looking for something that somebody left me, but they wouldn't say what or who. If you ask me, they had their wires crossed."

Kell nodded. He'd know soon enough. Daire and Adam were searching her apartment top to bottom while ensuring the proper repairs were made.

"I saw the first guy throw fire at you, but I couldn't see the weapon since I was behind him." She lifted her head to meet his gaze directly in the darkened room. "Tell me about the weapon."

He sighed. By law, he couldn't tell her the truth. But she was too damn smart to keep lying to about a nonexistent weapon.

"I don't know how it works, but the weapon somehow takes plasma, forms a ball, and fires it at the victim." Well, it was kind of true. Throw in a witch species, a thorough understanding of quantum physics and genetic gifts . . . and one could throw plasma balls of fire.

"You had one of the weapons the first night in the alley," she murmured.

"Yes." He'd forgotten he'd thrown fire that night. "I sent the weapon to my people in Ireland to take apart and study." He had to quit lying to her, damn it.

She shook her head. "Are you supplying these weapons?"

"No." His agreement was to supply AK-47s and semiautomatic weapons to Pyro and Fire, but he had yet to give weapons to the criminals.

"What about the drugs?" she asked.

"I'm trying to find out about the drugs the same as you are," Kell said, finally giving her the truth. "I promise you, give you my solid word as a Dunne and an enforcer, I do not know who's making the drug. I will find out."

She blinked. Her nostrils flared. She tried to step back, but the bed held her in place.

He knew the second her fear turned to something else. To awareness. Even desire.

A pretty flush wandered up over her face. "Did you kill Duck?"

"No." His thumb brushed her bottom lip, and he stared, entranced. "Again on my word, I didn't kill Duck, nor do I know who did. Yet."

She breathed out, warming his thumb. "Duck was killed by an Apollo overdose."

"Aye. I heard." Lust blared through him, hardening his muscles, slamming an ache to his groin. "Alexandra." He drew out each syllable, enjoying the feel on his tongue. "In my shirt, and in my bed."

She nudged her head back, and his hand fell away. "I don't know you."

"No." He stepped into her and cupped her face, tilting her head back. "But you have excellent instincts. I can see from your eyes, and I've watched you in the field surrounded by guns and fire. Look into my eyes. Did I kill Duck?"

Her nostrils flared, and her chest moved under his shirt in a sharp inhale. Her stare delved deep; impressively so. Finally, her facial muscles relaxed. "I don't think you'd waste your time killing Duck."

An unerringly true statement. More heat speared through him. The woman was intriguing with a side of deliciousness, and just being near her tingled awareness in his nerves. "You're right."

She held his stare, a brave woman half his size. "But you've killed."

His head lifted. He'd been a warrior for more than three centuries and lived through two immortal wars. Plus, he was an enforcer for the Coven Nine. "Aye. I've killed."

She frowned. "You're a soldier."

"Aye." He didn't have to tell her with whom.

"With whom?" she asked.

He smiled, his fingers extending around to knead her neck. "Not your people, darlin'."

"Why are you here, Kellach?" she breathed, her gaze dropping to his mouth.

He could give her that much. "I'm on assignment to find out about the drugs."

"Why?" she asked.

Regret tightened his hold slightly. "I can no' tell you that, but I can promise we're working to end the drug's production. To take it completely out of existence once I find the source."

"That's not good enough."

Facing him, so brave, she provided a temptation he hadn't felt in decades. Maybe longer than decades.

"It has to be." He gave in to temptation and lowered his head, brushing his mouth across hers. Sweet. So damn fucking sweet. Knowing better, he began to move back, when she grabbed his chest and hauled him closer, her mouth working under his.

A roaring echoed through his head, and he was lost.

Chapter 12

The second his lips touched hers, Lex forgot the case. Hell, she forgot everything.

His mouth overtook hers, firm and hot. He kissed her deep, his large hands holding her head in place, all fire and passion. She moaned deep in her throat, and his chest vibrated against her as if he fought to hold himself back.

He'd saved her life, and that meant something to her. She was so damn tired of fighting and of being alone. For once, she just wanted to *feel*.

One broad hand released her head and caressed down her spine to pull her into that hard body. Flush against him, she could feel every defined ridge, every powerful muscle. Her abdomen flared awake, and her sex softened. Even being held so tightly, she levered up on her wounded toes to kiss him deeper, to rub against him. Her nipples hardened to sharp points, and she rubbed them against his chest.

A growl lumbered up from him.

Heat somehow cascaded off him, hotter than normal.

He angled an arm around her waist and lifted her, his mouth releasing hers to nip along the side of her jaw to her ear. He bit gently, and a mini-explosion rocketed through her, pinpointed right at her sex. She slid her hands through that silky hair and wrapped her legs around his waist.

The hand at her nape turned, cupped her scalp, and drew back her head, firm and controlling in a way that dampened her panties.

His eyes had turned darker than midnight, and desire flushed deep under his cut cheekbones. "Alexandra."

She panted out air. "What?"

"Are you sure?"

She liked that. A lot. Liked that he'd asked the question, when her body was on fire, and it'd be easy to get lost in passion. Unreal, combustible passion. "This is such a mistake." She half-laughed and half-moaned the statement.

"Aye." His eyes glittered, and he held them both still. "If you're gonna make a mistake, make it a good one."

A motto she'd always lived by, actually. She released his hair to slide her hands down over his chest, her fingers digging in. She purred, enjoying the perfection that was Kellach Dunne. "How are you even real?" she murmured.

His gaze softened. "I've lived lifetimes, Alexandra, and I don't think I've ever wanted a woman this much."

Lifetimes? Yeah. Definitely a soldier who'd seen too much— enough to feel old in his thirties.

She smiled. He wasn't exactly wounded, but definitely seasoned. Maybe even cynical, and that feminine part of her, deep down that didn't make much sense, wanted to ease him. To provide a soft place to land and show him *wonder*. How long ago had he lost that?

She'd thought she'd lost it as well . . . until now. Until being held by a man with power and gentleness. If she had a hundred years, she'd probably not be able to plumb the depths of Kell. But they didn't have that time. They had now and now only. Either he was lying and she'd end up shooting or arresting him, or he'd succeed in his mission and return to his home across the globe.

"I hope you're the good guy in this," she whispered. Yeah, she might need a little more reassurance.

He clasped a hand over his heart. "I'm not a good guy, but I'm not the criminal you seek. On my word, I'm working with you to take the drug off the street."

"And the weapons?"

"If I find another man-made weapon that shoots plasma fire, I'll hand it over to you instead of sending it to my people."

Odd wording. What other weapon could there be? But she believed him, or at least, she wanted to. He'd saved her life, not once, but twice. If he was truly working against her, he wouldn't have saved her.

Her body vibrated with so much need, her brain just wanted to shut down so she could feel. "What the hell." She softened against him, her lips tipping.

She expected a grin or some sort of triumph to glimmer in his eyes. What she got was pure intent and male satisfaction. Enough to make her insides quiver.

He gently pushed the shirt off her shoulder, and his lips enclosed her flesh. He bit. Not hard, but with enough snap to send an electric shock zapping to her abdomen. She gasped and writhed against him. His muscles shifted, and she landed on her feet. Their gazes remained connected, and he ripped open her shirt, scattering buttons across the room. The torn material followed.

The air washed over her bare skin, and she shivered. Doubt crept in. The man was perfection and had probably been with a lot of women. She was short, hardly busty, and bruised. It had been at least a year since she'd taken the time to be with a man. And Kellach Dunne was all man.

He cupped her chin. "Second thoughts?"

She swallowed. "No."

"Good." His hands caressed over her shoulders to cover her breasts. "Absolutely exquisite."

The compliment bolstered her, and she reached for the hem of his T-shirt to pull it over his head. He ducked his head to help her. An intricate tattoo wound over his left shoulder and partially down his arm. A myriad of complex, Celtic lines with a barely discernible *C9E* combined in the middle. She fingered the jagged edges. "Beautiful."

"Thank you."

Her hand flattened over the dark ink. "What does it mean?"

He glanced down at the tattoo. "It's a military designation from home. It means, well, everything." His Irish brogue rolled the words into a sound of dedication. Of love.

She swallowed. The design appeared old, and his voice lowered when he spoke of it. What would he sound like with a woman? One who meant as much to him as whatever he'd vowed to protect? "I don't know a thing about you, do I?"

He covered her hand over the tattoo. "You know more than almost anybody who isn't family." His mouth sought hers, instantly possessing her with warmth and passion. His palms burned across her breasts, and he rolled both nipples between his fingers.

Her knees weakened, and she reached for his belt buckle. Trembles weakened her fingers, but she managed to disengage the belt and release his zipper. His mouth continued to overwhelm hers as he kicked out of the worn jeans, leaving them both nude. She blinked twice. He was fully erect, long and thick. No wonder he seemed so confident in everything. She grinned.

Suddenly, both his hands clamped her ass, and he tossed her back on the bed, following to stretch out on top of her. The air whooshed out of her lungs. His mouth didn't release hers once.

How was he so strong? The thought instantly spiraled away as he kissed along her jaw, down her throat, and licked her collarbone.

She gyrated against him, and he groaned as he moved lower and closed his lips over one nipple. Raw heat streaked to her core. She traced his ribcage around to his back, tugging him more solidly against her. He nipped and sucked—sensations exploded through her. Need, want, and even lust combusted as every pull on her nipple rode down and seemed to engulf her clit.

He moved to the other nipple, stimulating to the point of erotic torture. Finally, he freed her. "You're stunning, Alexandra." Tapping long fingers down her torso, he grinned at her sharp intake of breath.

She'd never felt like this. Worshiped and taken all at once. He was completely into the moment, completely into her. The knowledge went to her head, and she caressed down to his truly fine ass.

He pressed his fingers between her thighs, brushing across her clit. "So hot and wet."

She needed him and now. Crossing around his hip, she stroked his cock.

He stilled. "Slow, Alexandra."

"No." She smiled and tightened her grip. "Fast this time. Slow later."

Levering up, he pressed his forehead to hers. "We can go fast to take the edge off, but baby, I'm gonna play my fill afterward."

An electric thrill ran through her, and her entire body shuddered. "If you think you're able."

He grabbed her hip and brushed her mouth with his. "Aye. I'm able."

She smiled and arched against his dick. "Condoms?" Sighing, she glanced at the bedtable.

He stiffened and raised his head. "Ah, no. I won't get you pregnant."

She blinked, her body on fire, her mind awakening. "I'm not worried about pregnancy." She released him to focus on his desire-filled eyes. "You don't have condoms?"

"No. I'm clean, I promise. Just had a physical." He brushed her nose with a kiss.

"I'm clean too, and I'm smart. No condoms, no sex." God, she wanted him. Her entire body thrummed, and wetness, more than ever before, coated her parted thighs. She blinked as vulnerability joined desire. Nude and beneath him probably wasn't the safest place to be. "Without condoms, it isn't going to happen."

He scrutinized her, an unreadable series of expressions crossing his rugged face. Finally, he nodded. "Okay." He kissed her again and moved away, gentleness curving his lips. Regret filtered through his eyes, and his massive chest exhaled slowly. "I'll visit a drugstore first thing in the morning. For now, I guess I get to play." He kissed her throat, nuzzled down her neck, and licked her already sensitive nipples.

His kiss engulfed her, and he chuckled while scorching a path from her breasts, across her abdomen, right to her aching core. All grace, he scooted off the bed and onto his knees. His strong hands spread her legs wider, clamped around her thighs, and yanked her until her legs were over his wide shoulders. He held her exposed and open, his breath heating her inner thighs.

She gasped and tried to hold still. What kind of virile male didn't have condoms? The thought spiraled away as her body took over.

His teeth sank into one thigh, and she gasped, arching toward his mouth. His hum tickled her skin right before he licked right through her folds. Electricity rocketed through her, and she gasped, her eyes closing and her head digging into the pillow. He licked again, his fingers digging into her legs, and within seconds, she began to thrash uncontrollably against him.

He played, setting up rhythms only to change them, inserting one finger and then two inside her. Moving in and out with a new rhythm, and then altering again. Minutes, many minutes later, she began to whisper incoherently, her body gyrating, right on the edge to the point of pain. He paused, and the whole fucking world held its breath.

"Say my name," he murmured, poised right above her clit.

"Kellach," she blurted out, her body undulating.

He closed his lips over her pulsating clit and sucked hard. Her body detonated, and shock waves reverberated through her core, under her abdomen, right to her breasts. She cried out, arching, flashes of light shooting behind her closed eyelids.

He worked her over, prolonging the orgasm until she went boneless with a satisfied mumble.

Gently, he slipped her legs down his arms, grasped her waist, and lifted her to yank aside the bedclothes and tuck her in.

Darkness shrouded his face, and she glanced up at his large form. "What about you?"

He grinned and slid into bed, turning her to spoon against his granite-hard shaft. "Sleep. You can make me happy tomorrow after I buy condoms."

Her eyelids dropped and she snuggled into him, guilt rising. "What kind of guy doesn't have condoms?"

He breathed evenly against her, his chest a hard wall. "I'm still moving in and hadn't thought I'd need them."

Sweet. Definitely sweet. The orgasm had been spectacular, and she couldn't leave him like this. Plus, although she'd climaxed like there was no tomorrow, a hollowness echoed deep within her. If he was feeling even a percentage of that, she couldn't leave him hard and wanting. "I could do the same for you."

"No." He tucked a solid arm around her waist. "The first time I come with you, I want to be looking in those amazing eyes and feeling your entire body on fire around me. Trust me." He kissed the top of her head. "Go to sleep, Alexandra. I'll keep you safe tonight."

His warmth surrounded her, and for the first time in so long, she actually felt safe. She'd figure out the rest tomorrow.

Chapter 13

Lex awoke with a startle, sitting upright in bed . . . in 1600-thread-count sheets, surrounded by the scent of male. Clutching the sheet to her chest, she glanced around the quiet room. A set of woman's clothing lay on an antique chair by the master bathroom. Soft clunks sounded from what were probably pans in the kitchen. Swallowing, her head spinning, her body way too relaxed, she slipped from the bed and padded barefoot to the clothes.

A slim black skirt, red blouse, panty and bra set still in the tissue paper, socks, and black leather boots that actually made her sigh. Then she grinned. The guy saw her as a dominatrix. Chuckling, she took the clothing into the bath to jump into the many nozzled shower, moaning in pure bliss.

But the extravagance of the penthouse, and the designer clothing did beg a question. Just who the hell was Kellach Dunne?

Lex finished her shower and drew on the expensive clothing. The skirt reached to her knees, as did the luxurious boots. The panties fit but the bra didn't come close, as it was at least a cup too large. Whatever woman had left the clothing at Kell's house had been rather well-endowed.

She paused and glanced in the full-length mirror. *Wow.* Dressed in the bold clothing, she looked . . . dangerous.

Ah ha. The clothes belonged to Kell's cousin, the lawyer. Had to be.

Lex shook out her hair and smoothed her fingers through the already curling ends. Enough hedging. She had to go out and face him.

The night before had been amazing, and he'd controlled her every move, which had only made her come harder. Vulnerability washed through her in complete contrast to the tough outfit. Steeling her shoulders, she hustled out of the bathroom and bedroom, strode through the living room and stopped short in the kitchen. Well, shit.

Two young men, the ones from the diner, sat at the table gobbling up what looked like waffles.

She paused. Damn it. She was a big ole slut cop who'd stayed the night with their friend.

Slowly, they turned their heads.

She expected derision or mocking smiles. Instead, the two men nearly tipped over their chairs and jumped to their feet, overwhelming the kitchen with pure male size.

The one with tinted eyeglasses flushed. "Sorry we started without you. The waffles just smelled so good——"

"They are good." The kid with green eyes nodded solemnly and then reached to his side to pull out a chair. "Please have a seat, ma'am."

Ma'am? She squinted to search for any mockery and only saw polite smiles. She was only a decade older than them, but the politeness was sweet. The one with glasses glanced longingly down at his half-full plate before turning and smiling at her again.

Kellach rounded the counter with a full platter of scrambled eggs to slide to the middle of the table. "Grab a plate now, darlin'. They'll eat the placemats if we don't stop them." Moving toward her, like every dangerous predator with grace, he dropped a chaste kiss on her nose.

She blinked, her body frozen and stunned. "Ah——"

Kell drew her forward. "Alexandra, this is Garrett Kayrs"——he pointed to the kid with eyeglasses first, and then turned his attention to the other kid——"and Logan Kyllwood."

"Ma'am," Garrett said, taking her hand in an übergentle grip to shake ever so slightly. "We're sorry to interrupt your breakfast, but we had to talk to Kell, and we, uh, smelled the waffles." He handed her over to Logan, who shook just as gently.

Logan released her and smiled. "We like to eat."

Beautiful. Both boys, although way too young for her, were stunningly beautiful in totally different ways, yet fiercely masculine and tough. Way too tough for their youth. Young badasses who looked like they could bench press a truck or two.

Kell propelled her forward to sit and then scooted her chair closer to the table, placing another kiss on her ear.

A shiver slid through her, and she cleared her throat.

Both boys instantly dropped back into their seats. Logan piled eggs onto her plate while Garrett dished several waffles on next. Such polite kids, and they genuinely seemed to be trying to help her.

She'd never be able to eat so much. Her mind fuzzed as she tried to make sense of an already odd morning. She wanted to ask Kell about the clothes, but she didn't want to make it so obvious to the boys that she'd been naked and needed clothes. Of course, they had to have known she'd stayed the night, but maybe they didn't think she'd been naked.

Of course they'd figure she'd been naked.

She sighed and poured syrup on her waffles. They did smell delicious.

Kellach finally sat across from her, reaching for a plate. "Garrett and Logan are prospects at Fire."

She lifted an eyebrow. The polite, tough-as-nails cuties were prospects? Hmm. "Since when?" She flashed back to the diner scene.

Logan grinned around a mouth of waffles. "Since the other night."

Lex nodded. "I saw you guys at the diner. Who's King?"

Garrett coughed. "You mean, the king?"

"Sure." The guy had seemed seriously in charge, and he'd ticked Kell off, so what the hell was going on? "He's in the club, right?"

Logan pressed his lips together while mirth filled his eyes.

Garrett snorted. "Ah, no. The king has his own club."

Logan grinned. "The king is a club. Right?"

Garrett nodded and chuckled. "He's my uncle. Our uncle."

None of this was making sense. Lex took a bite and nearly hummed as flavor exploded on her tongue. Delicious. She wiped her mouth with a linen napkin. "Who the heck is the king, and why are you here?"

Both boys looked toward Kell.

He dug into his eggs, his black eyes amused. Then he shrugged.

Garrett lifted one dark eyebrow and met the shrug with one of his own. "We like bikes."

Oh, whatever. Lex glanced toward Logan. "Are you related to Garrett or King?"

"*The* king," Logan said slowly. "Garrett is my new brother because his sister married my brother. That means I'm related to the king, too. Family is family."

Garrett nodded solemnly and reached for more waffles. "Damn straight." He flushed and glanced at her. "Begging your pardon, ma'am."

What the hell? "You two are a bit polite to be Fire prospects." She took a sip of orange juice.

"Just around ladies." Garrett leaned back and patted his flat belly. "My mom is fierce, you know? We don't swear around her." He rubbed his already whiskered chin. "Or my aunts. Or, well, any of them."

Logan nodded solemnly. "Yep. My mom's a demon if we swear."

Garrett burst into laughter, his body moving with humor. "Good one."

Lex frowned as the kids continued to laugh way out of proportion to the small insult. She glanced at Kellach. "I think I missed the joke."

Kell sipped on his juice. "Family joke, I'm afraid. Felicity is one hell of a demonness if she's riled."

For some reason, that sent the boys into more gales of rolling laughter.

Finally, Logan wiped his eyes. "We're sorry, Alexandra. Sometimes family jokes are just funny if you were there, you know. We didn't mean to leave you out."

Garrett instantly sobered. "Shoot. Do you feel left out? I'm sorry."

She shook her head, more confusion dawning. They were so damn sweet, how could they be prospects for a club she just knew was running drugs and guns? "Do your mothers know you're here?"

"Yes," the boys said in unison.

"We were on a beach on the other side of the world," Logan said, his gaze forlorn.

Lex shook her head. "Why didn't you stay there?" They had to be safer on a beach with bikini bunnies than in Seattle with the drug war going on.

"Ask Logan," Garrett muttered.

"Me?" Logan shoved back from the table. "You were the one with the blonde. Hell, the two blondes whose dads showed up."

Garrett flushed. "You were with a redhead and a brunette."

Logan grinned. "Yeah, but their daddies didn't show up with shotguns and bust up the hotel."

Kellach cleared his throat. "Enough. Clear your plates."

The boys instantly stood and began clearing the table.

Lex pushed away, and Garrett shook his head. "We've got it, ma'am. Sit and relax."

She instantly shot Kell a hard look. Something weird was going on, and she didn't like it one damn bit. Her foot tapped as the boys quickly cleaned up, obviously having done so before.

Kellach just looked at her, no expression on his hard face.

Oh yeah? Fine. She turned to face the kitchen. "You boys don't know of any weapons that throw fire, do you?" she asked.

Garrett glanced up from wiping down a counter. "Man-made?"

Why the hell did everyone keep making that distinction? "Of course," she said.

"Nope." Logan finished loading the dishwasher and shut the door. "I guess there are flame throwers like in the movies, but I'm sure that's not what you mean."

She shook her head. "Why did you ask if I meant man-made weapons?"

The boys stilled and both faced her, losing all expression.

A shiver trickled down her spine. That quickly, they'd gone from boys to predators. "Gentlemen?"

Kell stood. "You're welcome for breakfast. Now head on over to Simone's and help her put up the shelving system she wants. Don't tick her off."

Sighing in what sounded like relief, the boys launched themselves toward the doorway with mumbled good-byes. As the door closed behind them, a sense of peace filtered through the penthouse. She hadn't realized the energy the kids had added to the very atmosphere until they'd left.

She turned toward Kell and pressed her hands to her hips. "Are you going to tell me what's going on?"

"Family stuff." He lifted her right out of her chair, boots and all, and crossed to sit in an oversized chair. "How are you today?"

"Fine." She smoothed her hands down the skirt and tried to settle herself on his lap. Raised without a father, unmarried, and more comfortable with work than people, she'd never spent much time cuddling on a man's lap. Any man's. Her face heated. "Are these Simone's clothes?"

"Yes. The skirt is a mini on her, but she has small feet, so I figured the boots would fit." He rubbed her back and then his voice rumbled sexy low. "The bra didn't fit, I take it?"

Her nipples flared to life, as did her girly parts. "Those boys aren't prospects, Kell. Please tell me what's going on."

He glanced down at her lips and then nodded. "Fine. They got in some trouble at the beach, and they were sent here as punishment and to help me figure out about Apollo."

"So they're not prospects?"

"They're prospects the same as I'm a club member. Kind of and with an ulterior motive." His head ducked, and he brushed a kiss over her lips.

Flutters cascaded from her mouth down to her abdomen. "Tell me the truth."

"I am." He rubbed a thumb across the bruise on her cheekbone. "I'd like a do-over on last night."

"Why? It was great for me." She smiled, even feeling saucy. "I doubt you could top it."

"Oh, I could top it and you." His eyes glimmered with something undeniably male.

She shook her head. "Last night wasn't smart. I believe that you didn't kill Duck, and I know you're here for some reason other than just joining Fire and selling drugs and guns. But I don't know if it's a law-abiding reason or not." The guy must know more about Apollo and the guns than he'd let on. So did those two kids who'd just left.

The man drew her, and that was just plain and simple deadly. She didn't know him, and for once, she wasn't sure she could trust her instincts. Charm and danger intrigued her and always had.

"I can't tell you any more than that, except you can trust me, Alexandra. I have no interest in breaking your laws or your heart. You have my word."

Sweet words, but the mere cadence reminded her that his laws might be different from hers. His goals might be, as well. She stood, relieved when he released her. "I'm not sure what to do about my break-in the other night." While she had a duty to inform her superiors that somebody had broken in, there would be no evidence left after Kell's cleanup, and she hadn't a clue who it had been.

She shook her head. "You're not gonna like this, but I need to report the break-in, your interference, and your cleaning up of the crime scene." Her loyalty lay with her job as a cop, no matter how much she liked him. If he didn't understand that, they didn't have any sort of chance going forward. *If* he wanted a chance. Well, *if she* wanted a chance.

Did she want a chance?

Her temples began to ache. No way was the man studying her so intently part of some drug running Seattle motorcycle club. He was far more dangerous than that, but one question harassed her: Was he a good guy or a bad? Was he investigating as some part of an international investigation, or was he protecting widespread drug cartels?

He leaned back in his chair. "How are you going to explain your delay in reporting the break-in?"

She blinked.

"In addition, if I'm questioned, I will tell them where I was last night."

Oh, son of a bitch. Anger flared through her so quickly she swayed. "You'd tell them about last night?"

He shrugged. "Wouldn't have much of a choice, now would I? If you report the incident and that I cleaned up a crime scene, I'll be brought in for questioning. If questioned, I always tell the truth."

Her shoulders settled while angry hurt dropped into her gut. Yeah, it figured he was too good to be true. What in the hell had she been thinking? "That's blackmail. So you used me."

He stood and was in her face so quickly she didn't have a second to react. His hands manacled her arms, and he lifted her up, right off the ground, so they could meet eye to eye. "I. Did. Not. Use. You." His grip was firm and controlling, but not bruising. The hint of violence was there, and raw fury burned in his beyond-dark eyes. He held her easily, his strength unbelievable.

"Who are you?" she gasped.

"I'm the man who has saved your life twice, before making you come harder than ever before." He gave her a slight shake. "I'm the man trying to get this blasted drug off your streets, keep you safe, and still do my fuckin' job."

"Which is?" she shot back, seriously thinking about taking him down. From her current position, if she were to subdue him, she'd have to injure him, and she didn't want to do that. Yet.

Slowly, the muscles in his corded arms flexed and he lowered her to her feet. "Trust me."

"Would you?" She stepped away to give herself leg room in case she needed to strike. "If you were me, a cop, would you just randomly trust you in your current situation? As a supposed enforcer for the Titans of Fire Motorcycle Club?"

He exhaled slowly, his anger dissipating. "No."

She crossed her arms and tapped her foot.

He grinned. "God, you're cute."

"Not what I want to hear." She jerked her head, holding his gaze.

He rubbed his whiskered chin. "I know. Here's the deal. I have a job, I take orders, and one of my orders is to keep undercover. I can't tell you who I am or who I work for. As a cop, one who perhaps has been undercover, you understand that, right?"

She lifted her chin. "I do. However, I also know that if you are from law enforcement, and you're conducting an investigation in my town, you need to let my superiors know about it. We can work together."

"No."

Jackass. "What's your angle, Kell? Apollo seems to be specific to Seattle right now. You're from very far away. What the hell do you want with the drug here?" She spoke softly, her mind spinning.

He shook his head. "Fuck. You're smart."

Why did that not exactly sound like a compliment?

"So level with me."

He shoved his hands in his back pockets. "All I can tell you is that we believe Seattle is a test area, and my people are next. There are ties between Seattle and Dublin, and we've been sent to ferret out the manufacturer and distribution chain before the drug is unleashed in Ireland."

"You work for the cops there?"

"No." He shook his head. "We're not affiliated with the garda, and we're bigger than that."

"Interpol?"

He chuckled. "No. Similar, but no."

Was he full of shit? Somehow, she didn't think so. Or maybe she just wanted to believe him. Who knew?

"Have I heard of your organization?" she asked.

"No." He tugged her closer, and she allowed it. Leaning down, he brushed a kiss against her lips, sending sparks flying through her body. "I have work to do, Alexandra. It's Sunday, and I know you don't need to go into the station. But if that's where you want to go, I'll go and make a statement with you. Yer choice."

She stepped back, and he released her.

What the hell was she going to do?

Chapter 14

Kell finished tossing items on the drugstore counter, fighting the urge to hit something. Fucking condoms. He was an immortal witch who couldn't contract a disease, and he'd never worn rubber over his cock. It had taken him precious minutes to figure out what kind to buy, and he'd felt like a dumbass reading the back of the packages. Thank god there were extra-larges.

A chipper teenager popped purple bubblegum behind the counter, humming softly and not seeming to give a shit that he was buying condoms. Her pink nails tapped easily on the old-fashioned cash register as she rang up condoms, gum, shampoo, and a six-pack of beer.

He'd only needed the condoms but felt as if he had to buy something else.

The outside door opened. Hair stood up on the back of his neck, and tension spiraled through the oxygen.

Damn it all to hell.

Bear stopped at the doorway, one eyebrow raised. His bushy hair curled over his shoulders, reaching his battered cut. His ripped jeans were so old as to almost be threadbare, and his dinged boots had seen better days. He glanced around the store, his gaze returning to the counter and Kell's purchases. His bear-like snort echoed against a rack of potato chips.

Kell kept his gaze on Bear while the cashier bagged his purchases. He slid a hundred across the counter. "Keep it." Without looking back, he grabbed his bag and sauntered toward Bear. "You lookin' for me?"

Amusement still lit Bear's brown eyes. "No."

Kell brushed by him and shoved open the door, his boots echoing hollowly on the worn wooden steps.

Bear followed Kell outside into the windy day. "Saw your bike and wondered why you were in my territory."

Kell paused and turned around to face Bear completely. Mild irritation filtered through him, and he settled his stance, banishing any embarrassment in the hope of a good brawl. He'd never gone head to head with a bear shifter, so maybe it was time. "Thought we were welcome here."

"You are, but some warning would be, ah, polite." A rare grin split Bear's rugged face, and he tipped his head toward the brown bag. "Although, considering I own the store, I do appreciate the sale. I hope you bought the ribbed ones for her pleasure."

"You're about to get hit in the face, Bear," Kell said slowly, anticipation lighting his veins.

Bear pursed his lips. "Might be fun. Wanna go a round?"

Kell lifted a shoulder. "We could. You ever fought a witch?"

Bear rubbed his scruffy chin. "Hmm. No, I don't believe I have. You ever grappled with a shifter?"

"Wolf and cat, yes. Bear . . . no." Kell eyed the massive shifter. "Could be fun."

"Yes." Bear sighed and relaxed his stance. "I'm kinda busy right now, though."

Kell nodded. "Me too. Maybe next time?"

"Sure." Bear lost his smile. "Wanna tell me why the king's nephew and the demon ruler's brother are in my neck of the woods?"

Kell didn't question Bear's intel. It had to be good for him to have risen to leader of all bears, a subspecies of Multi-shifters. Of course, only bears seemed to exist any longer. Kell sighed. "Fucking king."

"Yeah. That's what I figured." Bear shook his shaggy head. "I don't like it."

"You don't?" Kell kicked a rock out of his way. "What about me? I'm supposed to keep those kids safe while trying to find out about the drug, and so far, all they've done is eat me out of house and home. I'd forgotten how much kids their age fucking eat."

"Why are they here?" Bear's irritation sizzled on the breeze.

"They got in trouble and needed an assignment. I figured the king thought they'd be safe enough with me, and well, you—you being in the vicinity—and maybe they can help. As prospects, perhaps more people will talk to them."

"I don't like it," Bear repeated.

Well, no shit. If anything happened to Garrett Kayrs, the entire world would descend on Kell and Bear's heads. Vampires were never good-natured, and the king had one hell of a wrath when riled. "They're both trained, and Logan has seen combat." Shit. A hell of a lot of combat. "Garrett has been in war, nearly losing everybody and almost stepping up as leader of the Realm."

Bear lifted one eyebrow. "You think he could do it?"

Kell paused, his mind focusing. "Yeah. If needed, the kid could do it." Thank god it hadn't been needed. "Why else you seek me out, Bear?"

"The cop." Bear poked the paper bag. "Your cop."

Kell's shoulders went back. "What about her?"

"There's a reward for capturing her. One of my club members was approached late last night."

Fire lashed through Kell so quickly, blue flames wavered between his fingers. "Who?"

"Don't know yet. The second I do, I'll send the name your way. Apparently they think she has some kind of information."

"She doesn't."

"I figured." Bear glanced at the flames, his eyes lightening. "How serious are you?"

"I like her. She stays safe." Kell's life consisted of missions, hunting, wounds, and killing. Although Alexandra was a cop, she was female and delicate. "That's it." A voice whispered deep in his head that she was more than that, and he was fooling himself.

"Fair enough." Bear hadn't reached his position in life by arguing about personal matters, even if amusement did lift his upper lip again. "Why is there a bounty?"

"I don't know." But Kell would damn well find out. "Her apartment has been searched a couple times, too. Somebody thinks she knows something."

"Maybe she does." Bear angled to the side and clomped down the steps. "Perhaps you don't know her as well as you think."

Kell followed him and turned toward his bike. Dust billowed up from a gust of wind, and he tuned in to the quiet surroundings. "I know her well enough, and she is unaware of her importance. We have to figure out what's going on." He hadn't wanted to read the file on her given to him by the king, but it appeared as if he'd have to break the seal. "Thank you for the information."

Bear shrugged. "I have a good relationship with the Coven Nine."

Kell swung a leg over his bike and paused. "You agreed to our investigation in your territory, but you haven't asked any questions."

"I know why you're here, Kellach." Bear straddled his Harley. "Planekite isn't the big secret you witches believe."

Well, double shit. "Phenakite. Hell, we're calling it PK now."

"Whatever." Bear grinned.

Kell frowned. "Why do I think there's a third reason you sought me out today?"

"There was, but you answered my question." Bear gunned his motor.

Kell raised an eyebrow. "How?"

"By buying condoms for a sexy cop." Bear turned his bike and rode west without another word.

Kell blinked. The idea of Bear wanting to date Alexandra didn't surprise him as much as it should. The woman was exquisite and intriguing. A rush of energy rolled through him, unusual and difficult to identify. But the one word that escaped his lips said it all. *"Mine."*

Lex patiently handed her mother a handkerchief, one of her favorites. "And then, it looks like Kate Middleton decided to play a jumping game in wedge heels."

"Oh, my." Her mom's eyes lit up, and she sat back in the plush floral chair. "How did she do?"

"She was the epitome of grace and fun." Lex smiled. "As always."

"I do love that girl." Jennie clapped her hands together. "She's so refreshing and good for the monarchy, you know?"

"I know." For some reason, her mother had always been nearly obsessed with the royal family, and it felt good to bring her some news. Or at least information. "How are you feeling?"

"So much better." Jennie squinted and glanced around the cheerful room. The color had returned to her face, although physical therapy seemed to zap her energy. "Although I should go soon. This is costing way too much."

Yeah, it was. "No, it's no problem. I get a good deal since I'm a police officer and a state employee." *Not.* Nowhere near, but she couldn't allow her mother to worry. "This is a nice place, and you're doing so much better." If Lex had to find another job, she'd do it. But considering her schedule was sporadic, basically based on murders, it was difficult to find another job with such flexible hours.

"Oh, honey. I know that's not true." Jennie frowned. "I wish I had more savings. It's my fault you're struggling right now."

Lex shook her head. "Are you kidding me? You raised me and Tori all by yourself, and you worked your butt off to do it." For years, her mother had worked as a waitress, giving her daughters everything. "I love you, Mom."

Her mom smiled, new wrinkles moving near her eyes. "I love you, too. Soon Tori will be home, and we can have some good family time together. Where is she, again?"

"On tour in California." Pride filled Lex's voice. Her baby sister was the lead singer in a pretty damn good band.

Jennie smiled. "My family is the best." She cleared her throat, her gaze dropping to her hands.

Awareness pricked through Lex. "What is it?"

"Nothing." Her mom's lips trembled.

Heat flushed down Lex's chest. "Mom?"

Her mom bit her lip and then slowly drew an envelope out from behind her back. "I, ah, got this yesterday."

Lex froze. *Damn it.* Her hands somehow remaining steady, she reached for the envelope, clearly stamped with WASHINGTON STATE PENITENTIARY on the outside. "How does he know your address?" she asked, turning over the envelope, which had already been opened.

"I don't know," Jennie whispered. "He's always been able to find me."

Lex nodded and drew out the college-ruled sheet of paper. The scent of smoke wafted around. Taking a deep breath, she began to read.

Dear Jennie,

I'm sorry to hear you've had a flare up and are having trouble walking. I loved those hips. Just kidding. Well, not really. But I am sorry you've had problems. I really must get in touch with Alexandra. She's in trouble, and I have to speak with her. Please try to talk her into a visit. Just one. Her life depends on it.

I'll always love you and my baby girls.

Love,
Parker

Lex managed to keep her expression serene as she folded up the paper and inserted it in the envelope. "I'm sorry he found you."

Jennie shrugged. "It's okay. I did love him, you know, even after I discovered who he was and what he did. All that money didn't matter."

"I know." Lex rubbed her eyes. She'd been twelve years old when the cops had taken her daddy away in handcuffs for being one of the biggest cocaine dealers on the west coast. That moment had scarred her for life. To the point that the only career choice she could make was to get drug dealers and bad guys off the streets. "But he was a bad guy."

Jennie drew a deep breath. "He's up for parole again."

"He killed three people." Lex tried not to let concern enter her voice. "He won't get out." She'd make damn sure of it. Again.

"He might." Jennie's dark brown eyes sobered. "Would it be so bad? I mean, he's definitely done his time."

Lex's mouth dropped open. "Are you kidding? Do you still want to see him?"

"I loved him, Lexi." Jennie shook her head. "You haven't felt that yet, so it's hard to describe. I think he's done his time, and it'd be nice for him to be able to start over." She cleared her throat. "He's changed in prison, and he regrets how he treated me. People do change."

A chill swept over Lex's arms. The only reason her father wanted her to visit was so he could talk her into either advocating for him at his hearing or ask her not to show up and testify against him. She wasn't in any danger. "You can't seriously be thinking of helping him?"

Jennie clasped thin hands together in her lap. "Everyone deserves a second chance. He was a good husband and a good father."

"He was a drug dealer who supplied to anybody, even kids, including my friend who died in our backyard." Taylor had been a sweet kid from a crappy home, and he'd spent all the earnings from his fast-food job buying drugs from Parker Monzelle. Finally, one day, he'd OD'd in the back yard, the police had been called, and then the world had changed for her family.

Lex shook her head. "Dad killed at least three rival drug dealers that we know about. In addition, don't you remember how badly he used to talk down to you?" The words exploded from Lex, and she drew herself up short with a hard inhale.

"He's been in prison for more than two decades, and I think he's changed." Jennie held her hand out for the envelope.

Lex glanced at the envelope and then slowly handed it over. "He knows how to find you because you tell him," she said slowly, realization dawning.

A light pink filtered under Jennie's still smooth skin. "Yes."

"God." Lex jumped to her feet and began to pace. No way did Tori know about this. "Mom. How could you?"

"I made a vow, Lexie." Jennie carefully placed the envelope on the table. "Even though I did get divorced, I've never felt divorced. And I wouldn't normally tell you, but I believe his letter. I believe you're in danger, and I think you should go speak with him."

Betrayal coated Lex's throat. Her mother had been communicating with her father for years, and she'd had no clue. "Oh, I'll go see him, all right." She'd let the bastard know exactly what would happen if he ever bothered Jennie again.

"Be nice, Lexie." Jennie brushed thick curls over her shoulder. "Try to remember the good times. He read to you every night."

"Before he sold poison on our streets." Before he'd been taken away, and they'd lost their home. Even her new stereo had been confiscated and probably sold at auction. "We ended up penniless." And scared. More important, they'd ended up alone.

"I know." Jennie leaned forward. "Please say you'll go talk to him. Just in case."

"I promise." The talk wouldn't go nearly as well as Jennie hoped, however. "Did you tell him how to find Tori?" Lex asked.

"No." Jennie's mouth pursed. "I'd never do that."

Yeah, Lex didn't figure she would, but that just meant their dad had good connections in the outside.

A physical therapist in light blue scrubs turned around the corner and moved their way, his eyes bright, and his movements graceful. "Jennie? It's time for therapy. Whoo-hoo."

Jennie giggled and gestured toward Lex. "John, this is my daughter, Lexie. She's a homicide cop."

John wiggled dark eyebrows under dark hair. Handsome and clean-cut, he appeared to be in his early twenties. "I've heard. So nice to meet you."

"You, too." Lex leaned over and dropped a kiss on her mom's forehead. "I'll be back tomorrow night. And don't worry—I'll take care of the other issue." Reaching under Jennie's arm, she helped her to her feet, while John positioned her walker.

Jennie smiled. "My strength is coming back, and I feel like I'm going into remission again. Yay."

Thank goodness. Lex waited until John had escorted her mother from the room before heading for the door. Her phone rang just as she reached her car. Seeing it was Bernie, she answered, "Hi, Sexy."

He chortled. "You're funny. But I have news that ain't gonna make you laugh."

She sighed and rested her head on the car. "God. What?"

"Got the info on Duck. Guess who bailed him out and picked him up personally the other night. Two hours before he ended up dead?"

Lex swallowed, her heart leaping into fast-paced action. "Who?"

"None other than smooth Irish boy, himself. Kellach Dunne."

Son of a bitch. "I'll call you later." She hung up and jumped into the car. She'd kill the bastard.

Chapter 15

An eerie silence enveloped the large garage and surrounding buildings at Titans of Fire, and even the black asphalt seemed harsher than usual. Lex shuddered. The line of bikes under the garage's eves showed that at least a few of the thirty or so Fire members were on site at the compound.

Bernie had found Pyro at a local watering hole to make the notification of Duck's death. Was it only the previous night that Lex had stood over Duck's burned body? Apparently Pyro had turned to tequila instantly, his eyes wet.

Lex was supposed to be getting some sleep before reaching out to Kellach, but she knew he wouldn't talk to Bernie, and there was no way she could sleep right now. It was her one chance to find out what was going on and get Kell to tell the truth about his bailing out Duck. "This is such a fucking bad idea," she muttered while stepping up to the heavy steel door.

But if she had to arrest him, she would. She was trained, she was fast, and she was pissed.

Even so, if he fought back, it'd be a hell of a fight. Could she take him? Chills cascaded down her back in direct contrast to the fury spiraling heat through her every nerve.

Would he fight her, or would he call Simone? If Lex approached him just right, perhaps he'd be too confident to call his lawyer. The second that woman got involved, the investigation would stall again.

She lifted her hand to knock, hoping Pyro didn't answer, and the door opened.

Kellach blinked, obviously on his way out. "Detective?"

She swallowed. He'd thrown on faded jeans, badass boots, a T-shirt that stretched over powerful muscles, and his cut . . . tough black leather. His dark hair was ruffled around his shoulders, and he'd neglected to shave, leaving his jaw stubbled and making him look even more like a bad boy created just for sin.

"I need you to come down to the station for a few questions." No way could she handle him one on one. She had to keep it professional and forget the amazing night of almost sex she'd just had.

What the hell had she been thinking?

He looked over her head toward her car. "No backup?"

"No. I thought I could get the truth from you better alone." She took a step back. How had she forgotten how large he was? How solidly formed?

He rubbed his whiskers, and something heated deep in her core. "I'll talk to you, but not at the station."

She frowned. "You'll talk to me where I damn well want to talk."

He paused and his gaze swept her head to toe. "You wanna be in charge?"

"I am in charge." Her cuffs hung heavily in her back pocket.

"Hmmm. Well, I bought condoms. Wanna come in and we'll wrestle for control?" Low and soft, his voice rumbled between them to lick right through her skin. Even so, a hint of anger wafted on the breeze.

She blinked and shoved desire away with temper. "You posted bail for Duck and took him from the station."

Kell's jaw clenched, but no expression lightened those too-dark eyes. "After last night, you think I actually killed Duck?"

After last night? "I think you're a liar."

"I didn't lie to you, Alexandra."

The way he said her name, with possession and patience, dark male inflection, inched her hand toward the cuffs.

He stilled her by covering her hand with his at her hip. Drawing her near, he reached around and grabbed the handcuffs, twirling them around one finger. "If we're playing bondage games, you're the one tied up, darlin'."

Heat flared into her cheeks. How was it possible to be so pissed off and turned on at the same time? "You're messing with the wrong cop."

"You're the only cop I want to mess with." He turned and threw the cuffs. The silver spun through the air, went high, and landed on top of the garage with a loud clamor. "I'd prefer you in leather restraints, or at least feather-lined cuffs. No hard iron for such delicate skin."

Even though he was being a total smartass, the image aroused by his words slid under her skin to find desire and uncurl it.

"Answer my question, or I'm going to arrest you."

"Can't. Don't have probable cause." His lips curved, but the amusement failed to reach his darkened eyes. "Tell you what. How about you take a ride with me, and then I'll answer any question you have. Honestly."

A ride behind that body on a powerful machine? God.

The spit dried up in her mouth, and her legs actually tingled. Sounded like a dream come true . . . one of those sexy ones where reality spins away. But she was a cop, and her brain ruled her movements. "Not a chance."

He shrugged. "Your choice." Stepping to the side, he began to walk toward the line of bikes.

She hesitated. No way could she drag him downtown. "Wait."

He paused but didn't turn around. A massive man, a dangerous one, without question. Standing in the early dawn, after a storm and right before the next one arrived.

She took a step toward him. The investigation was heating up, and she needed him to talk. Even more, she wanted a ride. Behind him, on that bike. Just for a moment of craziness. Plus, she was armed. "You'll tell me everything?"

"No. I'll answer every question you have, but you have to ask the right questions." His voice echoed off the garage doors and back at her, powerful and low timbered.

The right questions? She'd just keep asking until she found the right one. "Fine." It was a mistake of colossal proportions, but she needed answers. She had to get those drugs off the street. "Before I decide, answer one question."

He still didn't turn around to face her. "One question."

"Did you kill Duck?"

His head lifted, and his shoulders squared. "Accept the answer this time, because it isn't going to change. I did not kill Duck."

Was he lying?

If she left with him, what kind of danger would she be in? "Fine. One ride." She took her cell phone and quickly typed a text to Bernie that her car was at Fire and she was going for a ride with Kellach. Sure, Bernie would kill her, but at least he'd know where she was, just in case. "I've let the police know I'm with you."

Kellach finally turned at that, his flash of teeth white against a bronzed face. "You scared I'll hurt you, Alexandra?"

She lifted her chin. "Maybe I'm worried I'll hurt you, Lasair."

His chuckle filled the damp morning. "Fair enough." Turning, he strode toward a Ducati.

She gingerly stepped over a large mud puddle. "I thought you rode a Harley."

"My bikes vary." He swung a leg over the side and ignited the engine, holding out a helmet. "Pretty police detectives wear protective gear, baby."

Her brain mattered to her, too. "What about you?"

"My head is way too hard. Trust me." He waited, gaze patient, lips slightly curved.

Her breath heated, and she double-checked the weight at her ankle. Yep. Gun there and ready to be used if necessary. The cop inside her told her she was taking such a risk to make her case, while the woman inside laughed her ass off. This was all about attraction, sex, and intrigue.

She didn't think he'd killed Duck. Her instincts as a cop, as a woman, whispered that truth. Her brain wondered if the attraction was messing with her judgment.

Entirely possible.

Yet she reached for his shoulders and swung her leg over the bike behind him. If she had to, she'd shoot him. Well, if she could get her gun free before he was on her. Hand-to-hand, she could usually hold her own. With this guy? Maybe.

The rumble of power between her thighs sent tingles directly up and under her skin to her chest.

"Hold on." Kell grabbed her hands and drew them around his waist. "Tight."

She leaned into him, her hands clasped.

He angled the bike down the driveway and opened the throttle.

The wind whipped against them, fresh and pure, and she snuggled her cheek into his back, allowing him to shield her. As he made the first turn, she softened against him, holding tight, letting him direct their weight.

A rumble echoed through him in response, and a tension she could feel surrounded them. Her breath sped up, and her heart thumped.

He took them through back roads and through wild forest, all on asphalt and smooth. The air cooled, and the scent of pine soon competed with the scent of male.

Even on alert, even partially breathless, her body relaxed from the sheer enjoyment of flying free.

Finally, Kell turned down a barely there entrance between two trees, still asphalted, and meandered next to a bubbling spring to a log cabin sporting a huge front porch.

He cut the engine.

The energy still tingled through her legs, and she took a moment to settle. Then, grasping his arms for balance, she swung off the bike and handed him the helmet.

He hooked the helmet on a bar and followed her, his movements graceful and relaxed.

A bird chirped high up while the stream rushed along, faster than earlier.

She glanced around. "Where are we?"

"It's our cabin. I come here when I wanna get out of the city." He grinned. "You're safe here. I'm sure your phone has GPS. If I hold you hostage, your garda compatriots will be breaking down my door in no time." He clomped those big boots up the three stairs and nudged open the door.

"Wasn't locked?" Lex asked.

Kellach shrugged. "Who's going to break into my place?"

Good point. Really good point.

She followed him inside and gasped at the luxurious yet rustic furnishings of the living room with a massive fireplace and well-appointed kitchen. Two closed doors took up a wall, probably a bedroom and a bathroom. Nothing beat the exquisite view of the river and surrounding mountains. Finally, she turned toward him, hands on hips. "Just who the hell are you, Kellach Dunne?"

He closed the door just as thunder rumbled high above. "Just a bloke with exceptional timing. We don't want to get caught in what's coming."

As if on cue, lightning illuminated the entire world. Fat drops of water rained down.

Kell crossed the living area and leaned down to start a fire.

She moved closer to the window as the sky darkened and the river reflected the storm. "Aren't we in Grizzly territory?"

"Aye. I rent the place from Bear, actually." Kellach turned and dusted off his hands, a small grin playing on his face. "Don't tell anybody."

She aimed for a shot in the dark. "Does Bear also work for Interpol?"

"Neither of us work for Interpol." Kell eyed the gathering storm outside. "For the record, Bear doesn't work for anybody. What you see is pretty much what you get."

"Why don't I believe you?" she asked slowly.

Kell shrugged. "You're suspicious, I gather." Thunder cracked again, and he frowned. "I need to put the bike on the porch, darlin'. Feel free to make yourself at home." He brushed her arm as he passed. A gentle touch——natural. As if they were together, and he had every right to touch.

She stepped away and waited until he'd closed the door before eyeing the rooms. It had been a long ride, and she definitely could make use of the facilities. Pushing open the door on the right, she grinned. Yep. Very nice bathroom with a sunken tub. Another door set in the far wall—probably storage. She hadn't seen much throughout the cabin.

Her heart kicked it up a notch. Okay. She knew why she'd agreed to the ride, and so did Kell. Yeah, she wanted to interview him, but finishing what they'd started the previous night consumed her thoughts. "Please don't be a bad guy," she whispered, washing her hands.

No towels. She smiled. Even as put together as Kellach seemed to be, he was still a bachelor.

Glancing around, she shrugged. Two steps had her at the other door, and she nudged it open.

Holy fucking shit.

A small table sat in the middle. A myriad of weapons, green and different from any she'd ever seen, took up much of the shelves that lined all three walls of the storage room. She'd bet her ass they threw fire.

Three vials of amber colored liquid perched on the top eastern shelf. Apollo? Had to be.

Her hand shook, and she reached out to grab one of the handguns. Heavy. Much heavier than it looked, and no brand name or caliber on it. Just an odd green color.

The betrayal coated down her torso, followed by a burst of fury. At herself for being so stupid.

She'd test the confiscated weapon outside when she got the chance, just to watch it shoot balls of fire. For now, she'd trust her own weapon. She shoved Kell's gun into the back of her waistband and whirled around to quickly shut the door, wiping her hands down the back of her jeans. The blood rushed through her head, roaring past her eardrums. She'd miscalculated dangerously. Her hands stabilized when she grasped her cell phone.

Shit. No service.

Had he planned to take her out of range? If so, why? And why would he allow her to find the weapons and drugs?

She'd texted Bernie she'd gone with Kell. If anything happened to her, it'd be a start. But she was trained, and once again, she was seriously pissed. Leaning down, she drew her weapon and slowly opened the door.

Kell stood near the fireplace, another log in his hand.

"You fucking prick." She stepped out, gun pointed, aim steady.

He slid the log into place and turned toward her, one eyebrow rising. "Excuse me?"

"Down, now." She gestured with her gun. *Damn it, no cuffs.* "On your face."

"No." Red darkened his cheeks. "I've had about enough of this waffling. One second you trust me enough to ride on my bike, and the next second you're pointing a gun at me. Put down the weapon, and we'll talk."

"No." She settled her stance and lowered her aim. "I'll take out your knee, Kell. I really will."

He moved then. She knew he moved, because she found herself flat on her back, his hard body pressing her into the worn floorboards. But she hadn't seen him move. Not even a twitch. Her gun spun out of her hand, twirling round and round before hitting the far wall with a loud thunk.

Training took over, and she shot her feet to his hips, kicking up. He flew over her head, and she followed, landing on his chest, her forearm against his neck.

His eyes widened.

She'd surprised him. Moving fluidly, she grasped his arm, levered up, and began to roll him over to his face.

The plan was good, and the execution flawless. Yet he countered, one hand gripping her thigh and the other wrapping around her ribs. He pivoted, and she landed face-first on the floor with him straddling her back.

Rapid-fire words ripped from him, the sound angry and magical. Gaelic? His knees hit the floor on either side of her, he levered up, and tossed her onto her back. She struggled, and he lowered his weight, both hands pressing down on her shoulders.

"You're under arrest," she managed to gasp.

Frowning, he grabbed her belt and partially pulled her up off the floor to reach around and confiscate his weapon. "Blast it."

She took advantage of his movement to punch him square in the gut. Pain ricocheted through her fist and up her entire arm. The guy had iron in his ripped abs.

He sighed. "I'd forgotten the weapons were in the storage area." Regret darkened his eyes.

She blinked. Perhaps he'd also forgotten about the drugs. If so, she had one chance to get out of there. "Are you going to try and kill me?"

Both his brows lifted. "Of course not."

"Good. Then get off me."

He nodded. "Fine. But no more pointing weapons at me." Graceful as any jungle cat, he stretched to his feet and pulled her up.

"No problem." She had one chance, and she needed to get free to call for backup. "Shall we sit and talk?"

"Yes."

"Good." Turning, she made to move toward the sofa. At the last second, she pivoted, jumped, and kicked high. Her boot caught him under the chin, and he went down.

She turned and ran for the door.

Chapter 16

Lex shoved outside and leaped across the porch into the swirling storm. Her heart beat hard against her ribs and her lungs compressed to contain oxygen. Fight or flight kicked in, and she barreled away.

Kell shouted her name behind her, crashing through the door.

She lowered her head against the wind, tucked close, and ran as hard as she could for the tree line. Pinecones whipped around her and pine needles slammed down. The rain pummeled her, matting her hair to her head.

She dodged between two cottonwoods and headed closer to the river. Mud coated her boots, and she angled away, wanting the shelter of trees to hide her.

A stick cracked behind her, and she pushed herself harder into the forest. Once she lost Kell, she'd find her way to cell service. Unarmed and becoming winded, she needed to get free before he found her.

The man could fight, and he'd kept his gun.

She ran around a century old spruce and smacked hard into his broad chest. She bounced off, and only Kell's hands manacling her biceps kept her from falling on her ass. He turned, lifted her, and shoved her back into the trunk of a pine.

Not hard enough to hurt, but definitely not gentle.

Rain dripped from his thick hair, running in a rivulet down his cut face. He lowered his head toward hers. "What in the blazes are you doing?"

She gasped, struggling to breathe, trying to keep focused. "The guns. You have the ones that shoot fire." Her breath panting out, she tried not to notice how easily he held her a foot off the ground. "I saw the drugs, Kellach. The vials. You bastard."

He frowned. "Damn it, Alexandra." Slowly, as if to show her how much control he was exerting, he lowered her to the ground and drew out his weapon.

She gasped, the tree to her back, death to her front.

He turned and fired at a cottonwood. A green laser shot from the gun and impacted with the tree, blowing out the middle. Bark disintegrated, and the tree toppled down, hitting several others on the way.

She gaped and shoved water from her eyes. "What the hell?"

"Laser not fire." Kellach grabbed her hand and slammed the gun into it. "It's treason for me to even show you this." Lifting her arm, he aimed the weapon at another cottonwood. "Go for it."

She lowered her chin, curiosity tingling her hand, and gently squeezed the trigger. A green beam shot out, exploded against the tree, and took out about a foot of trunk. Leaves and branches rained down as the tree toppled.

She swallowed. "I don't understand."

"Proprietary weaponry that turns lasers into bullets. No fire, you feisty pain in the ass." Putting his hand over hers, he retook his weapon. "Not what you've been searching for, but apparently what you found."

Oops. She lifted her head, her heart rate slowing. "What about the vials?"

He tucked the gun in the back of his jeans and took a step back. "My guess? Apollo."

She straightened. "Guess?"

He wiped water off his forehead. "Aye. My brothers and I all use the cabin. Adam has been conducting research to figure the crap out. My guess is that he did some out here and left the vials, since he couldn't keep them in our known residences."

"Oh."

Kell turned and gripped her lapels, pushing her against the tree. "We are not manufacturing, distributing, or selling Apollo, and we definitely want it off the street more than you do."

Well, since he put it that way.

"What about Duck? You bailed him out," she said.

Kell's jaw hardened in a way that revealed a vein in his neck, making him appear more than a little pissed off. "Pyro told me to bail out his useless nephew, and as part of Fire, I did it. But I dropped the prick at home and moved on."

She swallowed. "Oh."

"Believe me, I wouldn't waste time killing someone like him." Kell's voice lowered, and his gaze wandered her face. "You're all wet."

That quickly, with three words, her system shot from red alert to inferno. Every ounce of adrenaline coursing through her veins heated, turning from action to passion. He hadn't lied to her, and his weapon definitely wasn't the one she sought. "So are you," she replied thickly, relief flushing through her that he wasn't the bad guy.

Thunder rolled high above, rain splattered dirt into mud, and the river rushed furiously, but the boughs protected their heads.

She shivered.

He wiped water from her cheek, tracing down to her jaw, her neck, and the center of her chest, his fingers warm. His eyes, already so dark, deepened. His chin lifted, and the power of Kell overcame the energy of the storm.

"Kell—"

"Here and now, Alexandra." He grasped the bottom of her shirt. "Aye?"

The fury of the moment gripped her, and after her mad dash, all she could do was feel. "Yes," she whispered.

He tugged off her shirt and tossed it, following up with her bra. The sound he made upon revealing her breasts rumbled through the storm and right under her skin. Demanding and pleased.

He pressed her back and then frowned. "Damn." He let her slide down his body, feeling every hard angle and impressive muscle. When she'd regained her feet, he removed the rest of her clothing, leaving her nude and him fully clothed.

Vulnerability flushed through her on the heels of need.

He grinned. Shrugging out of his jacket, he gently placed her arms through.

She shook her head. "Ah——"

Quick as a whip, he lifted her and shoved her against the tree again. The leather protected her back, while the open jacket left her bare to him. His head dropped, and his lava-hot mouth engulfed one nipple.

She cried out and arched into him, her fingers curling over his shoulders. Almost frantic, she reached down and tugged his shirt over his head, forcing him up.

Perfection. Even ready to combust, she took the time to marvel and caress his sculpted chest and unbelievable abs. "How are you even real?" she murmured, her voice barely discernible in the raging storm.

His mouth possessed hers. All passion, all intent, all male. No questioning, no teasing—he took and took hard.

Fire lashed to her core, and her thighs dampened.

He lifted her higher. "Hold on."

Her legs gripped around his ribs, and he reached to shove down his jeans. Then both hands clamped on her ass, and he lowered her down. "Stand on my boots."

Her toes felt leather, and she regained her balance.

He took her hand and slapped a condom wrapper into her palm. "You wanted condoms—you put it on."

She grinned, desire destroying her mind. A quick bite of her teeth opened the foil and she tossed the wrapper near her shirt. She turned and bit back a moan.

Huge. Fully erect, thick and long, Kellach Dunne had been gifted by the gods. She gingerly placed the condom on him, wondering quickly if it would fit. She unrolled the rubber as far as she could. Good enough.

Then she glanced up and smiled.

His head jerked. A low growl—a real fucking growl—billowed up from his chest. Then he was everywhere. Mouth, lips, tongue, hands . . . he was all over her. Laving her breasts, fingering her clit, pressing against her G-spot. He took her over, showing the storm who was really boss.

She gyrated against him, her hands roaming, her hands massaging muscle and exploring strength. The ache inside her blossomed into an edgy need, desperation increasing her caresses.

His mouth plundered hers, his tongue dueling, his lips overwhelming her. He grabbed her ass and lifted her against the tree, her thighs on either side of his. Finally.

She struggled to get closer, ready to implode.

He held her aloft, kissing her, taking what he wanted. Her moan slid into his mouth, and he increased the pressure.

She shook her head free. "Now, Kell. Now."

He eyed her. Fierce, nearly animalistic, the expression on his face would follow her into forever. Slowly, with amazing strength, he lowered her onto him.

She gasped as just the head of his cock stretched her. Erotic pain buzzed her nerves, and she tried to go faster. To take more of him in.

He kept hold, moving her at his leisure, rendering her powerless in a way too erotic to define. Or admit. She gripped the strong cords of his neck, feeling the veins between her fingers, enjoying the pounding of his blood. Fierce. For her. She smiled and then bit his lip.

The sizzle of blood trickled on her mouth. Empowering.

"Alexandra," he growled, yanking down and thrusting up in one smooth motion.

She cried out, throwing back her head, pain and pleasure mixing into a craving powerful enough to destroy.

Oh God, Oh God, Oh God.

He was too much. Way too much. Yet her body took over, her hands gripping him, her hips tilting. Taking even more of him, pumping against him, as much as he'd allow.

He held still, his chest panting, his muscles a rigid line of control.

Going on instinct, she rolled her hips.

His head shot up. One arm slammed against the tree above her head, while his free hand manacled her hip.

She held on, the jacket protecting her back, his body keeping her aloft.

His shoulders undulated. A wild animal barely tamed, trying so hard to stay contained.

She met his gaze and deliberately clenched her internal walls around his pulsing shaft.

He snapped.

His fingers tightened hard enough to leave bruises. Leaning heavily on his arm, he thrust to the hilt.

She gasped, electricity careening through her, overwhelming all thought.

Hard, powerful, fully free, he pounded into her, the hand at her hip protecting her from the rough bark, the one above her head allowing him to thrust harder, using the tree for balance.

She bit back another cry and held on, powerless to do anything but feel.

Raw and feral, he hammered into her, filling parts of her she hadn't known existed, taking her beyond the moment, beyond herself. Beyond them both.

Energy uncoiled inside her, dangerous and hot, too much to keep. She detonated on a silent scream, her body going rigid, her nails digging into his skin.

He pounded harder, faster, deeper into her, holding her tight, prolonging the waves battering her into a world of pleasure. His mouth enclosed her neck, his teeth sinking into tender flesh.

Another orgasm slammed through her, lighting her with so much heat, she could swear she saw fire. The air crackled and lava burned her hip, sinking deep and taking hold.

He growled her name, his teeth still embedded as he came, his cock jerking inside her.

Finally, he stilled.

Her chest panted against his, her heart thundered, her body lax. They stood like that for several moments, safe in the eye of the storm as nature bellowed all around them.

Suddenly, small pains made themselves known.

He licked her shoulder, his own stiffening as he leaned back. She had one moment to appreciate the lazy satiation crossing his face before awareness lightened his eyes. "I bit you," he murmured.

She made a sound of agreement, words beyond her abilities.

His mouth opened and then closed. One broad hand swept across her ribs and down over her hip.

Pain lashed out. She winced.

He ducked his head, his breath whispering across her hip, right where he'd held her. "I burned you." Slowly, he rose back up.

"What?" she asked, her amazing post-orgasmic glow starting to fade. "Huh?"

He wiped a hand over his wet brow. "Your hip."

Her feet safely on the outside of the boots he still wore, she twisted her torso to glance at her hip. A perfect Celtic knot reddened and then, under her very gaze, turned white, like an old scar.

She blinked. "I don't understand."

He zipped up the jacket engulfing her and reached for her jeans, helping her into the wet cotton. Then he yanked up his own jeans, failing to button the top. A ragged sound emerged from him as he raked a hand through his hair. "I burned you." His gaze slashed to her smarting shoulder. "And I bit you."

The bite she could understand, but not the burn. "I don't understand."

He stepped away, bare chested, shaking his head. Emotion swirled through his dark eyes and tension choked the oxygen around them. "But how? You're not enhanced. I woulda given you a choice. You have to believe that. If I'd known, if I'd even suspected, I woulda given you the choice."

She shook her head, her focus narrowing. What the hell was going on?

Wait a second. He hadn't stopped to remove the condom.

"Did the condom break?"

"No," he choked out. "The condom burned away. That's not the issue here."

Had the man just experienced a mental break?

She reached out, tentatively, trying to understand. "What's going on, Kell?"

"You must be enhanced, but I can't sense it. Why can't I sense it?" He took a deep breath. "I bit and burned you, darlin'. That means something. Forever, actually."

He'd lost it. The man had lost his mind.

She dropped her hand. "Ah, okay."

"Watch." His chin dropped while he held his hands out from his bare chest and drew in a deep breath. Blue and then green danced along his arms and over his torso, morphing and cascading, finally licking into flames. Real flames.

Her mouth dropped open and her breath whooshed out. She shook her head against the illusion. "No." Surely, the man was not on fire in front of her.

"The weapon that throws fire?" he rumbled.

"Y-yeah?" she asked

He flipped over his hand, and a ball of electricity danced on his palm. With a flick of his wrist, the ball slammed into a nearby spruce, igniting the bark. The rain quickly quenched the fire, steam billowing around. "It's me."

Her mouth opened again and then closed. How? Why? "I don't understand."

"Well darlin', there are a couple facts you need to come to terms with right now." The surprise left his expression, leaving a determination that gave her pause. "First, and this is a tough one, I'm a witch. From Ireland. One of the Dunnes, an enforcer for the Coven Nine."

She shook her head. *A witch? God.* There had to be a rational explanation. She just needed some time to figure things out. Figure out how he'd made fire, and why he was messing with her. Was that accelerant on him? If so, was it now on her, too? She didn't smell anything.

Her voice wavered. "The second?"

"The second?" He stood in the rain, a powerful man, one she couldn't figure out. "With the bite and the burn? I've mated you, baby. Welcome to immortality."

Chapter 17

Kell kept his gaze set on the pale woman, hiding the turmoil boiling his blood beneath his skin. He'd actually mated her. As in *mated, mated.* For witches, hell, for most immortals, one didn't just accidentally mate. Some believed in fate, some believed in love—even at first sight. But Kell? He believed in intellect, plans, and passion. In that order. Plus, and this was a big fucking plus, he hadn't sensed one bit of enhancement in the sexy cop. Only enhanced humans, thought to be distant cousins to witches, could mate an immortal.

He hadn't even given the idea a thought. She was not enhanced. But she had to be. He relaxed his body, tuning in his senses, and still couldn't feel any vibrations of enhancement from her.

"You're crazy," she whispered.

Actually, he did feel the edge of insanity tottering nearer than usual. "I don't believe in fate, Alexandra." He sighed. "I also don't believe in coincidence." Was it possible? Was the feisty garda his perfect match? He'd been drawn to her from the beginning, not just intellectually or physically. Somehow deeper. Of course, he'd jumped right into exploring that by fucking her up against a tree. He had to figure out why she didn't seem enhanced.

Her hands trembled and clenched together in front of the engulfing leather jacket. "Witches are women." She shook her head almost violently. "I mean, there's no such thing as witches. Not magical ones. Sure, there's the religion and all of that . . . but not bewitched witches. Not—"

He barked out a laugh. "Witches are male and female—just another race on earth. We employ quantum physics, as humans partially understand it, to alter matter when necessary. Like to create fire and throw plasma." Vibrations of fear cascaded toward him, and he paused, scrutinizing her. No fear showed in her expression, but he was scaring the hell out of her. While he appreciated her ability to conceal her feelings, he didn't want her afraid. "I won't hurt you."

She shoved wet hair off her forehead. "You need help. I can find you help."

Ah. Denial. Okay, he could deal with that. Again, he held his bare arms out and slowly pivoted all around. "I don't have any weapons. A lighter. Even a match, Alexandra." He waited until she gulped and nodded before concentrating to alter particles and create an undulating blue ball of plasma on his right hand. "You should be able to do the same in not too much time. Maybe fifty years or so."

She studied the ball of fire, his torso, and then finally his face. Her shoulders somehow moved even farther back. "Fine. I agree you can do something rare. Something new. So why is a triangle knot burned into my hip? That fireball is round, and so far I've only seen fire or round balls thrown by you." Her voice remained soft and rational, even though complete denial glowed in her eyes.

He snuffed out the flames. "It's a marking from the mating—a simple Celtic knot symbolizing our union. The symbol of my people, actually."

She leaned back against the tree. "So you're saying you, ah, witches mark your mates?" Disbelief echoed in her tones. She *so* was not believing him right now.

The rain continued to slash down and into pine boughs above them, which weakened and began to allow small drips through.

He nodded. "Yes. Well, human mates are marked. I do have a couple cousins who mated vampires, and you can't scar a vampire unless he's inches from death and somehow survives. I'm sure they burn their mates, but no scars."

She coughed, and her head lifted. "Vampires?"

"Aye. More species roam this earth than you humans believe, sweetheart." Should he tell her everything or ease her into reality? Judging by the widening of her pupils, she'd had enough of a shock. He rubbed the back of his neck, where tension gathered. "This complicates things." The understatement nearly made him laugh out loud, but too much heat roared through him to be truly amused.

He. Had. Mated. Her.

The idea didn't bring nearly as much panic as he would've thought. He eyed her and allowed the feelings coursing through him to take hold. Protectiveness. Possessiveness. Satisfaction. Maybe love. He'd known those who'd fallen in love immediately, and many were still together after centuries. "Do you believe in love at first sight?"

Wrong question. Way wrong question.

She paled further, her eyes widened, and she held both hands out as if to ward him off. "This is bullshit."

He forced a gentle smile. "Forget it." His left hand felt like it was on fire, and he shook it out, glancing down. Oh yeah. He held it out to show the mark on his lower palm. "We match."

She slowly, really slowly, shook her head. "No."

"Yes." Man, there was a lot she didn't know. "When a witch mates a human, the witch ends up with the brand on the hand and the human wherever the hand is during the bite."

She squinted. "What if a witch mates a witch?"

Yeah, she was humoring him, but he couldn't blame her. "They mark each other."

"Ah." She took a discrete step away from him. "Do vampires mark their mates?"

"Most vampires mate with a good bite to the neck, but there are other species out there who do brand and mate. I'll give you the low-down later." He only wanted to hit her with so much at one time.

Her brows furrowed. "Wait a minute." She glanced at the ground, her thoughts ticking so fast he could almost hear them. "The fire weapon. Holy shit."

Yeah, he figured she'd get to that once her mind calmed down. "Aye."

Her head snapped up. "You all think you're witches? Everyone throwing fire?"

"No." He glanced around for his shirt and frowned at the wet, crumpled up mess on the ground. "Apollo, the damn drug, is created by melting down planekite, a mineral that harms witches and temporarily takes away our powers. It also gives humans a great high as well as witch-like powers before incinerating their organs."

"Planekite?" she asked.

"Or phenakite . . . or a few other names. It's mainly mined in Russia, although the mineral is found other places. The damn thing weakens witches and can eventually kill us." He had to get her out of the rain before her lips turned any bluer. "Why don't we go back inside to discuss this?"

She shoved her hands in the jacket pockets. "Fine."

Good. He grabbed his shirt and turned toward the barely there trail. "Follow me, and if you need help, let me know."

She mumbled something.

He kept to even footing, making sure to move branches and bushes out of her way. The rain continued to punish them, but he didn't feel the sting. He had a mate. He was so preoccupied with the startling fact that he'd bitten and burned the woman trudging along behind him, he didn't notice the SUV by the cabin until they were almost at the door. *Well, hell.*

He shoved his way inside to find Simone at the table in front of a laptop, the fire crackling merrily behind her.

She glanced up. "Well, I'd wondered—" Her mouth snapped closed when Alexandra moved in behind him. Her dark gaze swept Alexandra's muddy shoes, wet jeans, and his leather jacket before her shoulders moved back. "You have got to be kidding me." Her smile flashed perfectly white teeth. "It's a bit of a conflict of interest to shag a suspect, isn't it?"

"Shut up, Simone," Kell muttered, turning and closing the door behind Alexandra. "Why are you here?"

Simone sighed. "Daire is in one of his moods, and I thought to use the cabin for peace and quiet."

Kell lifted his head. "Why is Daire in a mood?"

"When isn't he?" Simone rolled her eyes.

Good point. He needed to talk to Daire, anyway. "We'll get out of your hair."

Simone smiled and then stilled. She frowned, eyeing the desk, then the fireplace, and then Kell. "There's a tingle."

Oh shit. "Nope. No tingle." He tossed his ruined shirt in the trash.

She stood up, her head lifted, her gaze sweeping the room. A witch on the hunt. "I *feel* something." Almost as if responding to a homing beacon, she wandered around, ending up in front of Alexandra. Then she gasped.

Kell pressed the palm of his hand against the bridge of his nose. Well, hell. "Simone—"

"You mated her?" Simone asked, her voice a soft whisper. She turned to eye Kell, a witch usually full of fire and piss, but now quiet, her expression shocked. "I, ah——"

"I know." Kell slipped an arm over Alexandra's shoulder. "It wasn't planned."

Alexandra shoved away from him, her head slightly to the side, her gaze squarely on Simone. "Who the hell are you people?"

"I didn't sense she was enhanced." Simone pursed her lips, her gaze thoughtful.

"Me either," Kell admitted.

Simone snorted. "Ask Garrett Kayrs if he can feel any enhancement."

Kell stilled. "Garrett?"

"Aye." Simone shrugged. "He's known for having an odd ability there."

Alexandra cleared her throat. "You think you're a witch, too? What the hell is going on here?"

Simone shook her head. "He hasn't told you?"

"Oh, yeah. A complete bullshit story about you all being a different species of witch." A veil dropped over Alexandra's eyes, giving her that *cop look.* "You claiming to be a witch, too?"

That quickly, Simone stopped staring and started laughing. "Kellach Gideon Dunne mated a garda." She laughed hard, her statuesque body shaking, tears gathering in her eyes. "The cousin who tried to chaperone every date I went on in my early centuries mates a cop. That quickly and without planning."

Alexandra stiffened. "Psycho or not, you either stop laughing, or I'm going to plant your face on the floor."

Simone quieted, glee filling her eyes. "Cop or not, I'm really starting to like you."

"Enough. Both of you." Kell put formidable command into his voice, not really surprised when neither woman paid heed. "Simone, keep this under your hat for now. Alexandra, we need to go."

Simone sidled back to her seat. "At least you can become unmated if you decide this was a mistake."

"No." The word burst forcefully from his chest, surprising him more than the two females facing him.

Alexandra focused on Simone. "What is this mating bit you're both talking about, and why the hell do I really have a burn on my hip?"

Simone sighed. "The males just don't explain it, do they? For centuries, whenever a member of a nearly immortal species mated, it was for eternity. One mate only, even if one died by beheading, which is the only way to go, really. If a mated person tried to get physical with anybody else but their mate, they'd develop a horrible, painful rash."

Alexandra snorted. "You're kidding."

"Nope. On the bright side, you're about to be immortal. As a cop, that's good, right?" Simone leaned back in her chair.

"Seriously. How in the hell am I now immortal?" Alexandra hissed.

Simone shrugged. "You're not yet. It does take time. We're different species with different chromosomal pairs. Humans have twenty-three pairs. Witches have twenty-seven pairs. So, the difference between witches and humans is similar to the chromosomal difference between humans and, say, a potted plant."

"Simone——" Kell warned. He was about to burn his cousin with a hard plasma ball if she didn't knock it off.

"So, when a witch mates a human, the human develops more chromosomal pairs until they're at twenty-seven."

"This is bullshit," Alexandra muttered.

Fire crackled down Simone's arms, bright and a deep pink, to morph into an undulating ball in her delicate hands.

"Fuck." Alexandra's eyes grew wide as she stared at the ball of fire. Slowly, she moved forward, her hand outstretched.

"No." Kell yanked her back. "You'll just burn yourself."

Alexandra swallowed. "This is unbelievable."

Simone sighed and snuffed out her flame.

Alexandra immediately moved toward her and grabbed her hand, twisting it back and forth, looking up her sleeve. "Crazy."

Simone, rather gently really, removed her hand. "Don't worry, cop. You don't have to stay mated for eternity any longer. If you want to negate a mating, you can these days."

"No." Kell shook his head.

"How?" Alexandra asked, her expression still skeptical.

Simone sighed and eyed her laptop as if wanting nothing more than to stop messing with Kell's life and get back to work, but she wasn't fooling him. She loved interfering. "There's a virus that can attack the mating bond. At first, it attacked mates and witches, and we thought we'd die. Long story." She waved her hands as if waving the history away. "Short story? We can use a manufactured strain of that virus to negate the mating bond. We have it narrowed down so the immortal doesn't lose immortality with the synthetic virus."

Alexandra backed away, putting her butt against the counter. "I'm not immortal."

"You will be," Simone said.

"No. Saying I believe you, which I don't right now, can you get rid of the immortality as well as the mating bond?" Alexandra asked.

A sharp blade pierced Kell's gut. "No."

"Probably," Simone said, lifting one eyebrow. "You don't want to be immortal?"

"Why would I?" Alexandra pushed her shoulders back, turning toward Kell. "You said you were an enforcer for the Coven, ah, something."

Simone slowly smiled. "The Council of the Coven Nine is the ruling body for witches, and our enforcers protect us as well as rid the world of our enemies."

"You're on the council?" Alexandra asked.

"Of course," Simone said softly.

Kellach sighed. "I told you the truth about my being here to take out Apollo."

"I have work to do." Without another word, Alexandra turned on her heel and strode toward the door. "Being immortal and all, I'm sure you can drive your bike through a rainstorm, right Kell?" She pulled open the door and stomped across the porch and into the thrashing storm.

Simone chuckled. "You know? I really am starting to like her."

Chapter 18

Lex walked into the station, her mind buzzing, her hip aching, and her heart thumping. Way too hard. Kell had dropped her off at her apartment, saying they'd talk later. He'd seemed a little preoccupied, and the tension in his jawline had made her neck ache. She hadn't argued, glad for the reprieve. She had to focus on anything but witches, vampires, and planekite. . . .

So she spent two hours hunched over her computer studying witches, vampires, and planekite, even digging up an old blog by a woman named Sarah Pringle about white-faced scary vampires, one of whom had killed her friend. A national search for the mysterious Sarah found that she'd been institutionalized for a while before escaping, never to be found again.

Maybe that Sarah had been crazy, although Lex's instincts hummed anyway. What the hell was really going on? Could Kell be a real witch, and if so, what the hell? Or was this some great illusion, and if so, how and why?

She drew out a piece of paper and created two columns.

Bullshit	*Reality*
Witches don't exist	*Kellach created fire with his bare hands*
Maybe she'd been drugged	
Chromosomal pairs couldn't multiply	*She hadn't been drugged*
She'd had great sex, which led to tingles	*She felt weird. Tingly, breathless, odd*
Drugs couldn't incinerate organs	*It was more than tingles*
If there were immortals, she'd know it	*Apollo definitely incinerated organs*
	Says who?

She didn't like the lists. The more she tried to find the bullshit, the more reality intruded. While maybe she could come up with some sort of explanation as to how Kellach had created fire, what about Simone? There hadn't been anything up her sleeve—literally.

Lex turned back to the computer and researched everything she could find on both planekite, phenakite, and the Dunnes. Interpol had sent over information on the family, and it was, well, boring. Basically, Interpol either didn't know shit or wasn't sharing.

A ruckus behind her made her turn around to see Detective Bundt hauling in a short, skinny, dirty guy with stringy black hair and a leather jacket so beat up the black had shredded to gray. He protested, kicking out, but his scuffed boots made little progress.

"You got the wrong guy, man," he muttered, spittle flying from his mouth. "Why you cops always get it wrong, I'll never understand." He shook his greasy hair, protesting until Bundt tossed him into the interrogation room and shut the door.

Lex straightened up and narrowed her focus. Her heart started to pound. She stood just as Detective Masterson strode into the room. "Was that Spike Evertol?" she asked, stepping into line with him toward the interrogation room.

"Yep." Masterson opened the door to the viewing room and stomped inside, not holding open the door.

What a jackass. Lex followed him, ignoring the strong scent of drugstore grade cologne, and stood looking through the one-way mirror. "What's the collar?"

"Snitch." Masterson tapped a manila file folder in his hand. "He's been snitching for Bud almost five years now."

Oh. She hadn't known. "So Evertol isn't dealing any longer?"

"Wasn't. The asshole still uses, as you can see." Masterson jerked his head toward the trembling junkie. "Didn't Evertol run with your old man way back when?"

Lex stilled. "How did you know that?"

"Evertol dropped your name when we picked him up." Masterson looked down at her jeans and sweater. "No slut dress today?"

"Fuck you." She pressed closer to the glass, her gaze on the snitch. Years ago, so long ago, Spike Evertol had been almost handsome. When he'd dealt drugs with her father. She remembered he'd actually had a tea party with her once. *God.* A flush heated up her neck, and she forced her voice to remain low. "Why did Bud bring him in?"

Masterson smiled. "Because you and Bernie have fucked up the case enough that we've been brought in to clean up. Our first step is to hit the streets and snitches."

She stilled. "We're not off the case."

"No, but you should be. Seriously. Hanging out with a member of Fire." Masterson clicked his tongue and shook his head. "Ovaries taking over for brains."

She whirled on him, half-chuckling and half-snarling. "Are you kidding me? Are you fucking kidding me, Masterson?"

He took a step back, his eyebrows going up. "Huh?"

"You're that much of a fucking male-chauvinist of a cliché? Really?" She slammed both hands on her hips, shaking her head. *"Really?"*

He held out a hand. "I—"

"No. Honestly. Slut cop? Ovaries?" She advanced on him, incredulity heating her breath. "If I wanted to create an asshole moron from the seventies, I'd create you. Seriously." She poked him in the chest. "Do you really believe women can't be cops? Really believe that bullshit?"

"Uh, no?" His smooth forehead wrinkled, surprise filling his blue eyes.

"No?" She poked him again, square in his muscular chest. "Then what the hell are you talking about?"

He took another step back, his head tilting to the side. "That's, ah, what we do."

She paused. "Huh?"

He gently grasped her finger to draw it away from his chest. "What we do. You know. Give each other a hard time, especially if we're competing for a case." He released her finger and ran a hand through his thick, black hair. "Geez, Lexi. We harass Bernie for being old and having one foot in the grave, but really? He's the best cop I've ever met. We give Jon Newty trouble for having six kids because the guy can't walk by his wife without knocking her up. Doesn't mean we don't like him or wouldn't take a bullet for him."

She exhaled slowly. "So the slut dress comments?"

Amusement lifted his full lips. "Well, those dresses were slutty."

She coughed. "True. But you can't make such sexist remarks these days."

He rubbed his jaw. "We make fun of what's different, and I'm pretty sure you're the only one on this case with ovaries. Well. Phil Jackson may have ovaries, too."

She rolled her eyes. "How about you just stop being an asshole?"

He studied her. "No."

She couldn't help it and burst out laughing. "Okay, how's this? The next time you make a sexist remark to me, I'm going to kick you square in the balls."

"That seems fair." He turned back toward the mirror. "Not for nothin', but if you relaxed and stopped trying to prove yourself so hard, you'd let insults roll off your back."

She stiffened and moved toward the window again. "Right."

"I mean, being a woman is good, but you don't have to prove yourself all the time."

She relaxed. If she did have a need to prove herself, it had nothing to do with having ovaries and everything to do with having a felon as a father. "I'll think about it."

"Don't hurt yourself. Girls are dumb." He chuckled.

What a moron. But she couldn't help smiling as she tuned into the interview. Spike's greasy hair was plastered against his head, and open sores marred his neck and chin. His fingers tapped restlessly on the counter and his shoulders twitched.

"Meth?" she asked.

"Definitely." Masterson reached over and turned up the volume knob.

"Who's supplying Apollo?" Bundt asked, his back to the mirror.

Spike shrugged, his gaze darting around the room, not seeming to land anywhere. "Dunno. Nobody knows, man."

"Who's dealing it?" Bundt asked.

Spike hunched forward. "There's a couple new dealers, and Mants, Scoracio, and that Drew kid all switched over from meth to dealing Apollo."

Bundt leaned back. "Scoracio and Drew were working for Bruno Mansen. There's no way Mansen let them just switch employment like that."

Spike snorted. "Employment. Right."

Lex frowned and glanced at Masterson, who shrugged. Dealers worked for specific distributors, selling specific drugs, and didn't freelance or cross lines. No way.

Bundt shook his head. "That isn't done, man. Level with me."

Spike sucked in a breath and leaned forward more. "Listen. I know it's weird. But whoever's building Apollo has juice, man. Real juice. Sent a message to four of Mansen's boys locked up in the pen."

Lex gasped.

Masterson glanced down. "You hadn't heard? Four of Mansen's guys were killed in the correctional facility during the last week. We figured part of a gang war."

She hadn't heard. Now she really did have to visit her father in the pen. Maybe he knew something. "Drug war, apparently," she said, keeping her voice even.

In the interview room, Spike seemed on a roll. "Yep. The new guy had them killed. Dead, man. Everyone on the streets is scared, and nobody, I mean fuckin' *nobody*, is messing with Mants, Scoracio or Drew. No way, no how. They're living the high life right now. Whoever the big guy is, he pays good top down. Real good."

Bundt shook his head. "Wait a minute. You're telling me low-life dealers have protection from the fucking manufacturer of the drug? Not just the distributors?"

Spike nodded, his skinny jowls shaking. "Yeah. Top down, man. The distributors to the lowest fucking dealers are protected—way more than, well, ever. It's like the manufacturer has to have this drug on the streets. And nobody touches Titans of Fire. Nobody even *thinks* of touching Fire."

Dread slammed into Lex's gut.

Bundt nodded. "So the Titans of Fire are the distributors?"

"The main one." Spike picked at a scab on his forehead. "Right now, anyway. I heard the Grizzlies want in on the action."

"From whom?" Bundt asked.

Spike shuddered. "I need a fix. Come on."

"I ain't givin you meth, Spike. Who says the Grizzlies want to distribute Apollo?" Bundt snapped.

"Can't remember." Spike's eyes glazed and went cross for a moment. "I heard it on the street somewhere." His head snapped up. "The big news is that Apollo is fuckin' for sale. Really for sale."

Lex frowned and stepped closer to the window. *What the hell?*

Spike flattened his shaking hands on the table. "Cheap right now. Real cheap. Like maybe getting folks hooked, and then prices go up? I don't know. But dealers can't touch. It's a rule. They can't sample."

Masterson huffed next to Lex. "Makes sense, considering the drug kills. If the dealers die . . . no dealers."

"Why no sampling?" Bundt asked quietly inside the interrogation room.

Spike shrugged. "Dunno. That's a new one."

Bundt tapped his fingers on a manila file folder before flipping it open to show death scenes. "Maybe it's because this is what happens when junkies overdose."

Spike gagged, his eyes widening. "Ick."

"That's it? Ick?" Bundt bellowed, slapping his hand on the pictures.

Spike jumped and then sniffed snot up his nose. "Yeah. I mean, it's life on the streets, right? Take a little, slow burn. Take just right, heaven. Take too much"—he pointed to the picture—"hard death." He shrugged. "We all know it. From meth to Apollo to black magic. Take too much"—he snapped his fingers—"die."

"Jesus," Masterson muttered.

Lex nodded. "I've heard enough. Let me know if anything else comes up." She walked back into the squad room.

Sitting heavily at her desk, she turned to her computer again, reading everything about the four deaths at the jail. A cursory glance did make it seem like a gang war, but she knew it was about Apollo. Who the hell was the manufacturer, and why so determined with Seattle? Was Kell telling the truth? Was Seattle just a test drive for Ireland? If so, why? Was Seattle some witch haven or something?

Of course, if witches really existed.

Her still smarting hip notwithstanding, there had to be another explanation.

A shadow crossed her vision, and Bundt dropped onto the folded metal chair near her desk. Lines fanned out from his blue eyes, and his blond hair appeared more ruffled than usual. "Masterson said we have to stop ragging you about being a chick."

She coughed out a laugh. "You have to stop being sexist dicks."

He sighed and rubbed the scrubby whiskers on his surfer-boy face. "It's the only thing we got. You're a good cop, and you don't drink or do drugs. Until now, you've never even dated anybody we could make fun of."

"And now?"

"Now you're putting yourself in such deep shit, it's not funny." Bundt leaned toward her and lowered his voice, his blue eyes serious. "I may be an asshole, but I don't want to see you go down for hanging with the wrong guy. Kellach Dunne is a really wrong guy. Titans of Fire is going down."

She blinked. Bundt was actually trying to help her. The Celtic knot on her hip heated, and she winced. Telling Bundt that hey, Kell was a witch, and guess what, she was almost immortal probably, wasn't a good idea. Especially since it seemed she'd gone crazy and Kell was working her. But something in her, something deep down, didn't *feel* that he was working her. Maybe her ovaries *were* screwing with her mind. She couldn't tell Bundt that Kell was undercover, but she truly hoped that was the truth.

"I appreciate the heads-up," she said.

Bundt sighed and stood, patting her on the back. "Also, Spike asked about you, said he misses you."

She shook her head. "He knew my dad and used to drop by. I haven't talked to him since my father was put away."

Bundt frowned. "All right." He sauntered away toward his desk, tossing his file on top of several others.

Spike had asked about her? *Damn it.* How did he even know she was a cop? She hadn't seen him in years. Standing, she grabbed her coat off her chair. It was time to have a father-daughter reunion and figure some things out.

She stomped down the stairs, glancing out the window, pleased it had stopped raining. One of those days, she really had to buy an umbrella, right after she got some sleep. At some point, she needed shuteye, but not quite yet. She shoved outside and maneuvered through people to the parking lot adjacent to the station.

Spike came out of nowhere and grabbed her sleeve.

She pivoted, released herself, and tensed to attack.

He shook his head, hands out, and backed away. "Sorry. Just wanted to see you."

"Why?" She didn't relax and tried to harden her heart. The guy looked terrible. Age, drugs, and life on the street had been rough on him. "What do you want?"

"Your pops wants to see you. It's urgent."

Her head jerked up. "You've been in touch with my father?"

Spike wiped off his nose. "Kind of. Through people. So that's the message." He shuffled his worn tennis shoes. "You got any money?"

Her heart actually hurt. If she gave him money, he'd buy drugs. "No." Unfortunately, that was the truth.

Spike nodded. "'K. Bye." He turned and shuffled away.

Lexi watched him go, hating drugs, the streets, and her father more than ever before.

One mystery at a time, however. Right now, she needed information about the Dunnes, and only one person in town truly knew them. So it was time to talk to Bear again. While she should call Bernie for backup, she needed to get the scoop not only on the Grizzlies but on Kellach, and Bear was more likely to talk to her alone.

Besides, what could go wrong?

Chapter 19

Kell faced his brothers in Simone's living room, waiting for the explosion after delivering the news that he'd mated Alexandra. Adam stared at him, slack-jawed. Daire had slowly lowered his chin during the retelling and watched him through heavy lids.

Finally, Adam shook his head. "I . . . I mean, I just don't—"

Daire glanced at Adam and then back at Kell before snorting. Then he lifted his head and laughed. Hard and long, chuckles rippled through his massive body.

Kell growled.

"Sorry." Daire wiped a tear from his eye, not looking in the least bit sorry. "You mated a cop without intending to mate a cop?" He snorted again and visibly struggled to get himself under control. "Not in a million years would I have expected this one."

Adam cleared his throat. "Congratulations?"

"Shit." Kellach rubbed his aching eyes.

Daire lost his smile and leaned forward, elbows on his knees. "I had no sense Alexandra was enhanced."

"Me either, but Simone said Garrett had some weird ability to sense enhancements. I need to talk to him." Kell relaxed. Although, now it really didn't matter, did it? They'd mated, so the woman must have some sort of enhancement, even latent.

Daire nodded. "Listen. What do you want to do? We can contact the queen and figure out how to negate the bond, if you want."

"No." Kell sat back, and for the first time, his rioting mind finally calmed. "I don't want to negate the bond."

Adam blinked. "You want to keep her?"

"Aye." Kell rubbed his chin. "I like her. A lot."

"Damn. You more than *like her* if you were able to *mate her*, dumbass." Daire coughed out another laugh. "I know you're a reason-type of guy, but even you know that."

Kell exhaled slowly. Yeah, it was more than *like*, but he certainly didn't have to explore his fucking feelings with his brothers, now did he? "I need to contact the queen, anyway. If Alexandra wants out, I have to know how it works."

Daire's head jerked. "She wants out?"

Kell laughed. "I appreciate your shock that the woman might not want to stay mated to me for eternity, brother."

Daire grinned. "I guess that's true. It's just that, you'd think a human would want immortality. Even if she had to stay bound to your ugly mug."

"I guess we'll have to figure that one out." Kell relaxed back into the sofa. Surely Alexandra had some feelings for him, considering the bond had taken with her body. That had to mean something, right? "I may have to court her."

Adam laughed. "You're going to court a Seattle homicide cop who you've already branded and bitten." He turned to Daire, his smile widening. "I am so fucking glad I'm here in the states working on Apollo and not in Dublin like I'd originally planned. I wouldn't miss this for the world."

A cop. Kell blew out air. "She's in more danger than ever now. Whoever broke into her place was a witch, and he could fight. She won't let go of this investigation, and she's smart. Damn smart. Hell, she might even find the manufacturer before we do."

"We searched her apartment and couldn't find anything a witch or the maker of Apollo would want, so we have no clue what those guys were looking for. Besides, I can't imagine a witch would be behind Apollo," Adam said slowly. "Unless it's yet another chance to take out the Coven Nine."

"I thought we were through with intrigue and war for a while," Daire muttered. "We can't even stop and enjoy the fact that our wild brother just mated a cop. A cop!"

"Any chance she'll back off and let you finish the case?" Adam asked.

Kellach shook his head. "Not a chance in hell."

"We can have her contained back home. She won't like it, but you can make it happen," Daire said.

Truly tempting, but Kell would rather not begin his mating by pissing off his mate enough to shoot him. There was only one solution. "We'll have to work together." All he had to do was gain Alexandra's cooperation.

A blue hue of fire danced on his right arm at the idea.

At the challenge.

The heavy weight of her ankle piece offered almost as much reassurance as the gun tucked into Lex's waistband when she slowly parked her car near one of the garages at the Grizzly Club. Two of the garage doors were open, and several members milled around, working on bikes and a couple cars. In fact, Garrett and Logan worked in unison on a vintage Harley.

Now wasn't that interesting? They were prospects with Titans of Fire, and no way in hell would prospects of one club be hanging out at another club, even an ally.

She got out of her car, and instantly, Bear loped her way from near the garage, once again wiping greasy hands on a towel. "Detective?"

Somehow, he was even larger than she remembered.

"Bear. You did say to come back any time." She shielded her eyes from the waning sun.

He looked at her empty car. "Kell know you're here?"

"Why would he?" she countered.

Bear lifted a shoulder the size of a board. "Dunno." He glanced toward the smaller door he'd emerged from the other day. "Would you like to come into my office?"

She swallowed. "I'm good out here." A quick glance at the cycles showed Garrett and Logan watching intently. "Want to tell me what the Fire prospects are doing here?"

"Not really." Bear finished wiping and shoved the rag into the back pocket of very worn, well-fitting jeans. "Anything else?"

She studied him. Wavy brown hair, wild to his shoulders, honey-mellowed brown eyes. Biker boots, jeans, dark T-shirt. Hulking, smooth, and lazily intent. She grinned. "I heard a rumor about you."

"Is that so?" His eyes remained warm and his posture relaxed.

Even so, her heart rate shifted into gear. "Yes. I heard that the Grizzlies are looking to distribute Apollo."

He smiled, transforming his rugged face into something wildly beautiful. "You heard wrong, Detective Monzelle. We don't do drugs, we don't distribute drugs, and we don't sell drugs. Ever."

"Why do I get the feeling you're more than you seem?" she asked quietly.

"Everybody is more than they seem," he countered easily. "Take you, for instance."

She stilled. "Me?"

"Sure. You're fragile, dainty, and really pretty."

She lifted an eyebrow. "And?"

"You're a cop who wears a gun. Smart, too. You could've been anything, and yet you chose to seek justice. There's a reason for that." He glanced around her. "You drive a piece of crap, which means you put your money somewhere else——and not in clothes or shoes." His gaze raked her head to toe. "Definitely not in clothes."

Her jeans weren't that bad. Her reasons for becoming a cop were none of his business. "What do you know about Kellach Dunne?"

Bear's brown gaze met hers levelly. "Is that a personal or a professional question?"

She tilted her head to the side. "Does it matter?"

"Yes."

"Why?"

He grinned. "Because if you're asking professionally, I don't work with cops. If you're asking personally, I'll tell you everything I know."

She frowned. "Why?"

"Because if you know the truth about that Irish bastard, maybe you'll forget him." Bear kept his gaze level on her.

Heat speared into her cheeks. The badass biker was flirting with her. "How about you tell me everything, anyway?"

Another man, a couple of inches shorter than Bear, jogged out from the office. Longish brown hair, mellow brown eyes, definite fighting shape. "Just got a call you need to take," the guy said, his gaze raking her.

She lifted her chin.

"Detective Monzelle, this is one of my lieutenants, Lucas Clarke," Bear said, apparently not caring much about the phone call.

Clarke nodded and took her hand for a big but gentle shake. "Detective."

"Lieutenant," Lex returned.

Bear grinned. "Tell whoever is on the phone that I'll call them back." His gaze remained warm on her.

Clarke hovered and then shrugged a massive shoulder before turning back for the office.

Bear's nostrils flared, and he studied her closer. "Oh my."

She blinked. "What?"

He shook his head. "You and Kellach Dunne, huh?"

So the gossip mill was turning about her dating Kell. If Bear only knew the full truth. "My personal life is not part of this investigation," she said.

Bear opened his mouth to say something, stilled, and then turned to view the long road, stepping partially in front of her.

She turned, her instincts flaring to life. "What?"

Dented and rusty, a delivery truck rumbled toward them, screeching to a stop.

A guy from the garage called out, "I ordered supplies for the Bentley. That's them."

Bear nodded and kept his gaze on the truck, all semblance of a smile gone. For the first time, Lex saw the club leader whispered about on the streets.

"I don't like a guy who doesn't take care of his truck," Bear murmured, tension vibrating along his arms.

A man jumped out from the passenger side of the van, a clipboard in his hands.

The breeze picked up.

Bear lifted his head and inhaled sharply. "Detective? I'm gonna ask you to get in your car and go now. We can talk later."

She turned to face the delivery truck, her hand inching to her gun. "What's going on?"

Almost in slow motion, the delivery guy dropped his clipboard. Yellow and orange cascaded along his arms, and fiery balls curled in his palms.

Lex smoothly dropped into a crouch, drawing her weapon. The second she hit her haunches, the guy threw. Bear grabbed her and pummeled her to the ground. The ball hit her car, denting metal, bouncing to the front.

"Damn it." Lifting her with one arm, Bear tucked her close and zigzagged toward the garage where several club members had run out, yanking off their shirts.

Lex struggled against Bear's implacable hold, firing toward the fire shooter.

Bear plunked her on a bike and jumped in front of her, igniting the engine. "Fight back the second I get her out of range," he bellowed, gunning the motor and zipping around the garage.

Lex cried out and grabbed hold of Bear's broad ribcage. "Go back. Get your ass back there, Bear." She was a cop. She could fight. What the hell was he doing? Why were those men taking off their shirts? She leaned up, her mouth at his ear. "Get back there. We left Garrett and Logan. They're two kids."

Bear ignored her and drove faster along an asphalt road the size of a golf path.

She looked over his shoulder. Was it just for bikes?

He maneuvered between trees and around overgrown bushes. Behind them, the sound of explosions echoed and fire crackled. Out of nowhere, a bike zoomed close, driven by a man already on fire. He grinned, even while flames danced along his arms and across his torso, somehow not burning his shirt.

Damn fucking witches. She had no other explanation and had to face reality to shoot at it. She did both. Lex pointed her weapon and fired two shots. They hit the guy, but he merely flinched. What the hell?

She looked around. So much fire and no other explanation. These guys could create and throw fire, just like Kellach. They had to be witches. She held tighter to Bear, wondering how the hell to explain it to him. The wind rushed by them as they neared the man on fire.

A second muddy dirt bike roared out of the forest, out numbering them. Its front tire scraped Bear's.

He hit the brakes, and the world slowed to barely moving. Suddenly, everything launched back into fast motion.

Lex cried out, her fingers digging into Bear's waist. They swung to the side. Bear released the handlebars, half turned, grabbed her, and flew off the bike. Somewhere in the air, he tucked himself around her, his shoulders impacting a large pine tree. The shock ricocheted through him to Lex, and she held tighter as they plunged to the ground. She landed on Bear and scrambled to her knees, reaching for her ankle weapon to defend him.

No way would he survive that without several broken bones. Hopefully he wasn't dead. Pivoting, she watched the dirt bike roll end-over-end, tossing its rider into a huckleberry bush.

The first guy stopped his bike and swung off.

She pointed the gun and slowly stood, blocking Bear's prone body. "Get down, asshole," she yelled.

He smiled and held out both hands, creating more flames.

She crouched and squeezed off three shots, aiming for center mass. The guy jerked back three times but remained upright. What the hell? Shit.

She probably needed one of those green laser throwing guns.

With a low growl, Bear lurched to his feet, shaking his head.

She eyed him. A deep gash bled above his right eye and his right arm angled oddly to the side—broken in at least two places. "Run, Bear. I'll hold them off."

The dirt-bike rider shoved free of the bush, aqua-colored flames shooting from his fingers.

Interesting that they all had different colored flames.

She shook her head, her voice low and intense. "It's hard to explain, Bear, but these guys throw fire. They're strong and tough and apparently bullets don't hurt them. Run. Now." She'd aim for the legs and hope Bear got to safety.

A ball of aqua fire slammed into the tree behind them.

Bear jumped in front of Lex, and she tried to shove the back of his waist to propel him away from danger.

He growled. Low and menacing, the sound forced her back a step. He lifted his head and let loose with a series of rumbling growls. His arms spread out, even the broken one, and his shirt ripped down the seams.

Lex's breath caught in her throat. What in holy hell? She tried to move back against the tree, but flaming bark burned her, and she cried out.

Bear turned toward her, his clothes hitting the ground. Fur sprang up along his skin, his nose elongated, and he dropped to all fours as a bear—a huge-ass, larger than possible, grizzly bear.

She blinked, her brain shutting down.

Sharp teeth emerged from his mouth, and he snarled.

A ball of fire hit him, and he yelped. The stench of burning fur clogged the air.

Roaring, Bear pivoted and launched himself across the yards to the dirt-bike rider, enclosing the witch's throat with powerful jaws. A twist of Bear's shoulder, and the guy's head was ripped off his body. Blood squirted up as the headless corpse dropped to the already red asphalt.

Bile rose in Lex's throat, but she swallowed it down. Fear sharpened the day, even through smoke and blood. She pointed her gun toward Bear, who was stalking on all fours toward the other bike rider.

She didn't even know bears got that big, much less human turned grizzly. God. Bear had turned into a fucking *bear*.

The guy smiled and twisted his torso, pummeling Bear with fireball after fireball.

Bear howled in pain, bunched, and lunged at the witch, landing on him and knocking him down.

"Bear, stop!" Lex yelled, her gun out, running toward the duo. They might be immortal, freaky creatures, but murder was murder. "Don't—"

Bear sank his canines into the witch's neck, his incisors scratching like nails on a chalkboard as they reached asphalt. His powerful jaws snapped shut, and he straightened to toss the head into the crackling tree.

Lex backed away, her hands shaking. So much fear lumped in her stomach, she needed to puke.

Bear turned and ambled toward her. Her ankle hit the downed

bike, and she began to fall, pulling the trigger. The bullet hit Bear in the shoulder, and blood sprayed. He jerked back and opened his jaw to howl, the sound angry and wild.

The last sight she had before her head impacted with the asphalt was a pissed off grizzly, teeth bared, lumbering toward her.

Chapter 20

"I'm fuckin' going to kill you, Bear," a low voice echoed as Lex forced herself from dreamland.

She opened her eyes to see Kellach peering down, his black eyes blazing, his hand gentle and wrapped around hers. "What?" she asked, tasting soot.

"I have you, Alexandra," he said, smoothing her hair from her forehead, his soft tone a direct contrast to the fury all but cascading off him.

She shook her head and winced. "Ouch." Slowly, she glanced around a typical office. Desk piled high with papers, computer, copier, guest chairs, and a sofa. The smell of motor oil and smoke was strong.

Smoke.

She shoved herself up to sit. Dizziness attacked her, and she shut her eyes, her free hand pressing against her forehead. Memories flashed behind her eyelids. Holy shit.

She opened her eyes and slowly turned to see Bear leaning against the far wall, his arm in a sling, bruises across his jaw.

"You shot me," he said mildly.

She blinked. "I was falling."

"I know. How's your head?" He fingered a bandage above his right eyebrow.

She gulped and shook her head. "You're a bear."

"Yep." He smiled. "Though it was nice of you to try and protect me."

How in the hell was any of this even possible? She turned toward

Kell, who remained protectively close. "Bear turned into a bear," she said slowly.

Kell slid an arm around her shoulder and tucked her into his side. "He's a bear shifter."

"Shifter? Shifters exist." She shook her head. "Witches and shifters."

"Oh my," Bear said, straight faced.

Kell threw him a look. "We have feline shifters, wolf shifters, and multi-shifters."

She shook her head. Pain clamored between her temples. "But he's a bear shifter."

"Aye." Kell ran gentle fingers over her scalp, touching a bump at the top of her head that might get him shot. "Sorry. Multi-shifters used to be able to shift into anything, mainly bear, but now most bears can't turn into anything but bears. I haven't seen a multi in centuries." He turned toward Bear and lifted an eyebrow.

Bear shook his head and winced, touching his bandage. "I don't know any bear shifter who can shift into anything but bear. If you ask me, multies are extinct, and we've all evolved into bears." He sighed and leaned his head back, shutting his eyes. "We're the next generation, baby."

Kell rolled his eyes. "Why are witches attacking you?"

Bear focused again. "We were approached a week ago, via a burner phone, to distribute Apollo, and we said no. I think this was a second request."

"I knew a witch was behind this," Kell muttered. "Any idea who they work for or who approached you?"

"No clue." Bear slid to the side as the door opened.

Garrett and then Logan, both wearing clean clothes, gingerly strode inside.

"We wanted to check on Alexandra," Garrett said.

She eyed the boys and their innocent expressions. "Did you two fight the witches in the delivery truck?"

"Hells ya," Logan said, high-fiving Garrett.

She gave them her strongest cop expression, and they sobered instantly. "Are you two witches as well?"

"No, ma'am," Garrett said softly.

"Bear shifters?"

"Nope." Logan eyed Kellach.

Kell sighed. "Might as well tell her the truth. She knows almost all of it."

Garrett smiled, and sharp fangs slid from his mouth. "I'm a vampire."

Holy freakin' crap. That sweet boy was a creature of the night? "I've seen you outside and in the sun."

He chuckled. "We can go in the sun and are just a different species from humans."

It was too much. The world as she knew it . . . didn't exist. She swallowed. "I read a blog by a Sarah Pringle."

Garrett nodded, his light-refracting glasses moving on his nose. "Aunt Sarah. She mated my Uncle Max."

Mated. There was that damn word again. Lex's abdomen heated. She was mated to Kell. "Sarah wrote that the vampires were white-faced and afraid of the sun." Lex tried to grasp onto any tendril of reality.

"Those were the Kurjans, our enemies. You don't have to worry about them." Garrett's fangs slid back in.

She had enough to worry about and would figure out Kurjans later. "Do you, ah, drink blood?" she whispered.

"No." Garrett chuckled. "I mean, we do, but only in fights or during sex." Red climbed into his face. "Begging your pardon, ma'am."

What a polite freakin' vampire with deadly fangs.

Lex shook her head and focused on Logan. "Vampire?"

"Half vampire." Logan allowed his fangs to drop and then retract.

Lex stiffened her shoulders, trying so hard not to relax into the safety that was Kell. "The other half?"

"Demon. Half demon." Logan shuffled his feet. "We're the good guys. I promise."

Demons were the good guys, and Kurjans the bad guys. The immortal world seemed rather complex. She shook her head and tried her best to adapt without shooting anybody in the room. Not that her bullets did much good, apparently. "Um, so Dage Kayrs, is the, ah, king of the vampires?"

Garrett nodded. "Uncle Dage is King of the Realm, which is a coalition of vampires, shifters, and witches, but you could say he's also the king of the vampires, since he is a vampire."

"Okay," she whispered.

Kell jerked his head toward Garrett. "Did you know she was enhanced?"

Garrett smiled and then slowly lost his grin. "Wait a minute. Didn't you?"

"No." Kell glanced back at Lex. "Not at all."

Lex glanced from one to the other. "Excuse me?"

Kell rocked back on his heels. "Only enhanced humans such as psychics can mate an immortal, and we usually get a sense of an enhanced female if they're in our vicinity."

Oh. "We mated because I'm enhanced, but you didn't get a sense of the enhancement?" She already knew Kell hadn't intended to mate her.

"Yes." Kell glanced over his shoulder at Garrett. "Why can you sense it but I can't?"

The vampire shrugged. "It's really light, almost indiscernible, but my senses are my extra ability."

"Teleporting is a better one," Logan drawled.

Garrett cut him a hard glare. "You can't teleport, demon."

"Yet. I'm still young." Logan frowned. "Someday I'll be able to teleport, and you'll still just get little tingles from humans who might be enhanced."

Teleport? Lex shook her head. That was an issue for another day. "What do you feel, Garrett?"

He smiled, and his eyes lit up behind the glasses. "You're empathic, most likely at an intuition level, meaning you go with your gut as a cop but really have empathic abilities. For now, anyway. The longer you stay mated to Kell, the stronger your abilities should get."

Kell nodded. "So that's why I couldn't sense her."

"No." Garrett shook his head. "You couldn't sense her because she has the ability tamped down. Strongly."

Kell turned toward her. "Excuse me?"

Garrett nodded. "She muffles her abilities, or at least the broadcasting of her abilities, much like a demon destroyer shields against a demon mind attack."

Lex coughed. "Demon mind attack?" She turned toward Logan.

He lifted a large shoulder. "Demons can attack minds with horrible images and pain, but we only do so in times of battle or war. Other than that, we're harmless as puppies."

Garrett snorted. "I know a feline shifter who has the same ability to tamper as Alexandra does, and the cat does it because she's ultra-sensitive and had to protect herself as a young cub. My guess is that Alexandra had to protect herself from pain from those around her and learned to tamp down on not only her ability but the natural broadcasting of it."

Kell swallowed. "Her mother has a degenerative disease, and her father was a drug dealer who killed people."

"Yep. That would do it." Garrett grinned. "Mystery solved."

"I am not an empath," Lex ground out.

Garrett leaned against the door. "You really are. Sorry."

Sure, she'd always been sensitive and able to pick up on when her mom was in pain, or when something was wrong with a friend, but didn't everybody do that? Lex smoothed a hand down her legs.

Kell stood and helped Lex to her feet. He nodded at the boys. "Get back to Simone's. I'll let Dage know about the fight today and how well you two handled yourselves."

The boys loped out the door.

Kell called after them, "She's mad you ate all her food, so you'd better hit the grocery store on the way there. She's pretty, but she'll burn you both to a crisp if you don't replenish her Chunky Monkey." He helped Lex toward the exit.

Bear opened the door wider. "Your woman is a brave one, Kellach Dunne." He reached out and touched what felt like a bruise on Lex's jaw. "You're always welcome here, Alexandra Monzelle, and the Grizzlies are at your disposal for this investigation. You name it, and we're there." His bourbon colored eyes softened. "You're a very lucky man, Kell."

Kell reached out and shook Bear's hand. "I'm in your debt. Thank you for protecting her."

Bear grinned. "She tried to protect me."

Lex forced a smile, although her world was pretty much blowing up into fantasy land. "I'm sorry I shot you, Bear. It was an accident."

"I know." Bear stepped out behind them and pointed to a crumpled, still smoldering mass of metal. "Sorry about your car."

She halted, her lungs compressing. "Holy crap." No way could she afford a new car right now. Not even close. She nodded. "No worries. It was on its last legs, anyway."

Kell hustled her toward his Harley. "You okay to ride?"

She nodded and accepted the helmet he handed over. "I'm fine. Just a little headache." And dizziness, and perhaps insanity. But all the proof had been in front of her eyes. She'd seen witches, bear shifters, a vampire, and a demon. In fact, demons looked like vampires who looked like humans. But they weren't. She held her breath to keep from crying out as she placed the helmet on her aching head. She might have a bit of a concussion, actually.

Kell straddled the bike and held out an arm to assist her. Once her butt hit the seat, she wrapped her arms around him and leaned in, closing her eyes. *Better. Much better.*

He turned so his mouth was closer to her ear. "We need to talk, Alexandra. I'll get you somewhere safe, and then we have some decisions to make."

She kept her eyes closed, knowing she couldn't keep reality at bay that way. As Kell ignited the engine and started driving down the road, she had a reprieve, and she was taking it.

Kellach nudged open the door to his penthouse and fought the urge to sweep Alexandra up in his arms. The second he'd heard about the attack, he'd nearly gone berserk. God only knew how many traffic laws he had violated getting from the flat to Grizzly territory in order to reach his mate. Night was falling with a gathering of storm clouds, and thunder rumbled in the distance.

If this was love, he didn't like it one fucking bit. If not, the woman was still his mate, and thus his responsibility. Deep down, she'd already burrowed into him, becoming part of him. All he had to do was convince her of that fact.

He'd never, in his life, been so frightened until he'd seen for himself that she was all right. By the time he'd arrived, Bear had carried her safely to the office, and his men had already buried the witches who'd attacked them. In fact, by the time the bears had shifted,

Garrett and Logan had apparently already taken care of business. Bear had wanted to get Alexandra to safety and out of visual before his people shifted, protecting her from a reality that was now her own.

She walked into Kell's flat and instantly kicked off her boots. "I can't believe we've missed the existence of so many other species," she mused.

He shut the door, surprised by how much he wanted to engage the lock and keep her there forever. "Humans see only what they want, and we do try to remain under the radar."

"Why?" she asked, turning around, her gaze direct.

He smiled at his stunning warrior. A bruise marred her jaw, another had almost faded along her cheekbone. She'd apparently stood in front of Bear, facing two known immortals, so brave and determined. It would be his great honor to find her a haven of safety and peace where nobody could bruise her. She'd probably love Ireland.

"I find you stunning, Alexandra Monzelle."

She blinked. Her eyes softened to a lighter blue, and she shook her head. "Why are you a secret, Kellach?"

He shrugged and grasped her hand to lead her into his immaculate kitchen. "If humans found out about us, it'd be war."

"War?" she gasped. "Why?"

He nudged her onto a bar stool at the breakfast counter. "Humans would love to be immortal. We'd be a threat, one they needed to figure out in order to keep themselves from dying. We just don't want to deal with it, and we don't want to eradicate them from the earth. So we live apart."

She rolled her eyes and leaned her elbows on the granite countertop. "That's silly."

"That's our law." He reached for a pan to place on the stove.

She grinned. "You're cooking for me?"

He turned to face her fully. "You're my mate."

A very pretty pink blush wandered up from her spectacular chest and slid over her face. He expected her to roll her eyes or to protest.

Instead, she met his gaze levelly, a new vulnerability framing her face. "I don't know how to be anyone's mate."

That quickly, that smoothly, that unintentionally . . . she stole his heart. Her fierceness aroused him, and her intellect intrigued him.

But that sweetness in such a warrior? Yeah. That owned him. So sweet that she'd had to tamp down on her natural abilities just to live among humans.

He forgot the pan and moved toward her to grasp both hands. "Neither do I, but I'd like to try. There's something between us, Alexandra. Something strong and something real."

She drew in a deep breath and then slowly nodded. "I know."

His chest warmed. "There's a method to getting unmated— it's untried and possibly dangerous—but I need you to know that it's possible. You're not trapped."

"I don't feel trapped." Her fingers danced restlessly beneath his hands. "I'm not making promises here, though."

Nothing was wrong with taking things slow. "I want to stay mated to you and figure this out." Hell, that was the mildest way he could put how he felt, and trying to dampen his natural possessiveness forced him to bite back a growl. His woman was a modern cop who had no problem fighting. Oh, he'd win a fight with her, but forcing her to do anything she didn't want wasn't who he wanted to be. She had to stay with him of her own accord, regardless of his natural inclinations.

For now, anyway. If his people went to war again—it was entirely possible sometime in the future—if he had to lock her down to keep her safe, he'd do it. But she had to decide to be *his* first.

At the moment, peace ruled his world, and they all had freedom.

His phone dinged from the counter, and he lifted it to his ear. "Dunne."

"Hi, Kell. This is Emma." The Queen of the Realm didn't believe in formality, yet he snapped to attention anyway.

"Hello, Queen Kayrs." He ran a hand through his hair. "Your nephews are just fine. I promise. In fact, they took care of two dangerous witches without even breathing hard." Of course, the woman was concerned about the boys. He should've thought about calling her or her sister earlier.

She laughed. "I already had an update from Bear. That's not why I'm calling."

Kell stilled. His gaze caught on Alexandra's curious expression, and his mind cleared. "No. No. Definitely not. No, no, no."

Emma sighed. "Come on, Kell. Just a couple tests."

"Hell, no." When it came to his mate, apparently respect for the monarchy flew out the window. "No tests. You and your needles are not getting anywhere near my mate."

Alexandra's eyebrows went up.

Emma coughed. "Please? I haven't been able to study the beginning changes in a human when she mates a witch, and I just need a couple blood samples. I promise. Just two."

Kell dropped his chin to his chest. The queen had been a geneticist before mating the king, and she was notorious for taking the blood of immortal species in the name of research. Of course, she had recently cured the most dangerous virus ever to plague their people.

"If you show up here, I'm siccing Simone on you," Kell said. At one time, about a billion years ago, Simone and the king had dated.

Emma laughed again. "I already talked to Simone, and she agreed to take the samples and ship them to me. We're best buddies now, Kell."

The vampire queen and a snarky member of the Coven Nine as best buddies? "God help the Realm," he muttered. "I'll talk to Alexandra, and if she's agreeable, Simone may draw blood tomorrow."

The queen nearly squealed. "Excellent! Thank you so much! Congratulations on your mating, by the way. I hope you'll find great happiness."

"That's very kind of you. How are you feeling, anyway?" he asked.

She laughed. "Fat and pregnant with Dage's baby, who's already doing summersaults."

"Stay well, Emma," Kell said softly. "Take some time off and take care of yourself." If anything happened to Emma Kayrs, Dage would blow up the world. "For all of us."

"Of course. Also, give Garrett and Logan smoochie kisses for me, would you?" Emma asked.

"Of course." Yeah. He'd smooch them both and get punched in the face. No problem. "Have a good night, Emma." He clicked off.

Alexandra pursed her lips.

He sighed. "The queen wants your blood to study the process of your chromosomal pairs increasing to immortality."

"Oh. Okay." Alexandra rolled a shoulder.

Well, that was easy. Since she's being so agreeable . . . "And I'd like to get you naked and roll around."

Her eyes darkened, and she began to slide off the stool. "Tell you what. If you can catch me, ack—"

His arm wrapped around her waist just as he leaped over the counter, holding tight and barreling them both over the sofa onto the bear skin rug in front of the fireplace. A click of the remote flashed the fire to life.

She settled beneath him and then frowned. "This isn't a real bear pelt?"

He chuckled. "No. It's man-made, not an ounce of real bear fur in it. I bought it to piss off Bear, but the second he saw it, he started laughing. Apparently he can tell real fur from fake." The moment had been such a downer.

Lex sighed and wiggled her butt, her body relaxing inch by inch against his. She reached up and brushed his hair away from his face. "I pretty much live in the here and now, Kellach."

Yeah. As a cop, she'd have to live here and now, considering people shot at her. Or threw fireballs now. Of course, when they moved to Ireland, she wouldn't be in danger any longer.

He pressed his already hard cock into the vee of her legs. "I get that. I've been an enforcer for three centuries, and during times of war, I've not thought about the future. You put your head down, you fight, do your job, and hope you make it through." Even with his brothers as enforcers, his life had been a lot lonelier than he'd realized.

Her eyes widened. "Oh my god. How old are you?"

Amusement bubbled up his chest, widening it. "About three hundred and fifty years. Why?"

She coughed. "You're kidding."

"No."

Her eyes widened. "You're an old fart. Cradle robber."

Geez. He kind of was robbing the cradle. "Too late to worry about that. How old are you, anyway?"

"Thirty-one." She stretched against him, and his blood started to burn. "Maybe forever. How weird is that?"

A roaring rushed through him, primal and deep. He clasped her hands and pressed them above her head, which pushed her breasts against his chest. She gasped, her eyes widening, arousal expanding her pupils.

He grinned, allowing intent to fill his eyes. "So, mate. What now?"

Chapter 21

Surrounded by fur and overwhelmed by male, Lex caught her breath and put up a half-hearted struggle with her hands. Kell easily held her in place, his hands heating hers, his body covering every inch of hers. So big and strong.

A wicked glimmer glinted in his eyes, and that close, she could see the rim around his pupils. Lighter than the black pupils, but not brown. An edgy green.

Likely, not many people had gotten close enough to Kellach Dunne to see that green.

She pulled on her hands again, not entirely surprised when they remained right where he'd planted them. "Let go of my hands," she murmured, not so much serious as curious about what he'd do.

"No." As if to prove his point, he flattened one hand over both of hers and laid the other one gently around her neck. "Your pulse matches mine in tempo." His lips curved. "Let's see if we can speed that up."

If her heart beat any faster, the little organ might explode. Heat from him spread right through her clothes and swept along her skin in a delicious ache—as if tiny pinpricks of fire licked her head to toe.

She gasped and widened her legs, rubbing against him. The delicious friction forced her eyelids closed so she could just feel the raw electricity.

Not for one second did she understand the chemistry between them; so overpowering was the physical that she didn't concern herself with the emotional. Only the moment mattered. Such need

and lust combusted inside her to create a hunger beyond human—
as if fire was at her very core.

His mouth possessed hers, fierce and deep, the force of him holding her head in place.

She struggled to free her hands and touch him.

He denied her, and his control shot shards of electric desire
through her, peaking her nipples and softening her sex.

She. Couldn't. Get. Free.

The thought should tick her off, but in a fluttery feminine place
she'd later deny existed, desire flared to life. Never had she trusted
a man enough to contain her.

Maybe there hadn't been anyone *man enough* to contain her.

Kellach was all man . . . and more. He pressed hot, open-mouthed
kisses along her jaw to the sweet spot behind her ear.

She gasped and arched up into his hardness only to have him pin
her on the rug again. Liquid shot to her thighs.

His hips gyrated against hers, pushing his heated cock against her
core. So hot, so ready, so damn demanding. His free hand swept
down the front of her shirt, scattering buttons. Cool air brushed her
warm chest, the contrast kissing her skin. She moaned.

"Now that's a pretty sound." He licked a nipple and tweaked the
other one between his thumb and forefinger with enough bite to stop
the breath in her lungs.

The erotic pain cascaded from her nipple to her clit, which began
to pound with need. She moved restlessly against him, powerless in
his hold.

He chuckled against her skin, and the vibrations tickled through
her. A heartbeat later, his mouth took hers again.

He unsnapped her jeans and helped her kick them and her panties
off before shedding his somewhere around their feet along with his
boots. Commando. The man had gone commando. His cock lay heavily against her core.

She pressed up into him, her fingernails curling into his palms.
So badly she needed to touch. "Let me—"

"No," he whispered and then smiled against her mouth as she
shuddered in response.

Being held in place, unable to move, magnified every feeling bombarding her. So much and all at once. She clasped her feet at his back and rubbed against him, the friction nearly sending her over.

"Alexandra," he groaned, his voice a low growl.

She opened her eyes.

He shifted, poised at her entrance.

She blinked. "Wait. Condom."

He grinned, sexy and pained. "Immortal. Witch. Can't get or give diseases."

Oh yeah.

Plus, she was on the pill, so no worries. Excitement gripped her, along with intrigue. He'd be inside her, skin on skin. An internal quake shook her.

He entered her slowly, velvety smooth and steel hard. So big, he stretched her, mercilessly gripping her hands as she instinctively tried to fight against him. His demonstration of control and over-whelming strength shot another surge of heat to her core.

Panic tried to rise up—an awareness that she was out of her element. No longer the hard-ass cop, the protector, but someone feminine. A female counterpart to this truly amazing male. The sen-sations overcame any thought or instinct for self-preservation.

Raw, true, combustible.

He sheathed himself completely, his free hand reaching under her to grip her butt to tilt her pelvis.

She gasped as she took him even deeper. "Oh." The moan es-caped her.

His fingers gripped her ass harder, keeping his pulsing shaft inside her. His lips overtook hers, and his tongue danced inside her mouth. She opened, taking him, giving everything.

He held her tight, not allowing movement.

Frustration welled through her as she tried to pump against him. He held her still, top to bottom, in perfect control. He lifted his head, his gaze on hers, the green glowing brighter around his black pupils. Intense and waiting.

She blinked, and heated air exploded from her lungs. He'd move when he was ready, and she couldn't do anything to push him. *Anything.*

At the thought, at the acceptance, her body softened into the rug. All the tension dissipated, leaving her floating. Needy and floating.

The green glowed brighter, and a matching flame rolled down his arm, across his chest, and over her nipples. Erotic heat licked her, heating but not quite burning, forcing a whimper from deep inside her.

Fire kissed her, threatening to singe.

An orgasm uncoiled deep inside her, pulsating around his cock. Sparks were a prelude to the devastating sensation waiting breathlessly out of reach.

He closed his eyes and groaned low, his biceps visibly vibrating as he held himself in check while her internal walls gripped him relentlessly. When she'd ceased, and only then, he pulled out and shoved back inside.

The second he hit home again, fire crackled along his back, snapping along with his control.

He pounded into her, his hands absolute, his body strong and sure. Harder and faster than possible, he thrust, taking her over. Explosions rocked her, one after another, each climbing to a pinnacle she tried to fight reaching. Too much. Way too much.

But he was relentless. He drove into her again and again, fierce and fast, electrical shocks shutting down her brain. Lava uncoiled inside her, hotter than before, becoming the center of everything.

She splintered, screaming his name, flashes of color cascading behind her closed eyelids. Pleasure enfolded her; lifting her so high she spiraled off a cliff and kept on falling.

Finally, she went limp, her muscles going lax.

He thrust inside her one final time, held himself deep, and shuddered as he came.

Her eyelids flashed open just as the fire was snuffed out. Male satisfaction curved his lips as he brushed them against hers, still connected with her, so deep he might never let her free.

She blinked, seeing him clearly for the first time. Deadly and strong, the Realm Enforcer had powers she'd only glimpsed.

What had she done?

Kellach eyed the sophisticated map illuminated on the wall of Simone's home office, rubbing his chin. He'd dropped Alexandra off at work early that morning, and she'd texted around suppertime that she had to go on a stakeout and they'd talk later.

They'd damn well talk later. He didn't like knowing she was in danger, especially since she wasn't immortal as of yet. His woman seemed to court danger, and he wasn't quite sure how to manage that fact.

Simone sighed loudly. Again. She sat in her leather chair, wearing a glimmering red ball gown and a deep frown.

"Daire said you need to stay in," Kell reminded her, not taking his gaze from the wall.

"Ballocks." She kicked out a four-inch heeled Louboutin. "I'm a witch, damn it. He can't shut me down."

"Enforcers can shut down any member of the Coven Nine in cases of emergency," Adam said from behind her desk as he fiddled with the keyboard of a new computer. "We're in an emergency, and the drug is here in Seattle, so you need to stay safe."

Kell nodded, studying the map. Different colored blotches marred areas across the world, illustrating areas of PK deposits.

Adam walked toward the map, a remote control in his hand, the glow turning his skin an odd green. "I've traced the deposits of the mineral to this region in the former Soviet Union." He pointed to several known mines. "We've had these under surveillance via satellite for almost twenty years."

Kellach frowned. "We missed mining activity?"

"No." Adam shook his head. "I think the mineral we're dealing with was mined years ago. Long ago."

Shit. "So somebody has been planning this?" Kell turned to study his brother. "Why wait so long?"

Adam shrugged a muscled shoulder. "I have no idea. The process of melting it down and combining the hallucinogens that make up Apollo is pretty simple, so it could've been done years ago. Why now? I don't know." He clicked a button, and a new screen came up. "Known enemies of the Coven Nine."

Kell sighed as the list continued on and on. "We have that many enemies?"

"Aye." Adam unrolled the cuffs of his crisp dress shirt. With his pressed black slacks and shoes, he looked like one of those Armani models. "I have the Nine going through the list to see who stands out. Right now, I'm concentrating on anyone with ties to Russia, both witch and demon."

Kellach nodded. Witches and demons had populated Russia for

years, with very few vampires or shifters. "We're allies with the demon nation now."

Adam fastened his cuff links. "We're allies with the demon nation, but that still leaves a lot of rogue demons out there. Demons and witches have always mixed like oil and fire—usually a bad combo. My guess is that a demon is after us."

Kellach shook his head. "I don't know why, but I'm thinking witch. There's something personal about this, and I think it's directed toward the Nine. More so, once the bugs are worked out here in Seattle."

"I concur." Simone frowned. "You have a date, Adam?"

He reached for a silk tie from his briefcase. "I do. With you."

A beautiful smile lightened her already stunning face. "You're taking me to the gallery opening?"

"Of course. You want to go, and since we're at level red, you need an enforcer as an escort." He tried to secure his tie and failed.

Simone gracefully rose and crossed to knot his tie. "You're my favorite enforcer, Adam."

Kell frowned. "Hey. What about me?"

Simone tossed her long, black hair. "You're too preoccupied with a human cop. Adam is the best."

The only reason Adam was going was because he knew Simone would go on her own, and then he'd have to track her down. Efficient as always, Adam hit two birds with one stone.

Kellach rolled his eyes. "'Tis probably a good idea. Adam is getting soft, just doing research on the mineral."

Adam chuckled. "At least I'm not soft on a human cop." He tucked a gun at his waist and another at his ankle before shrugging into a jacket. While Adam might look like a big guy on his way to a formal affair, Kellach knew just what a badass his older brother could be.

Brilliant, cold, and merciless, Adam went for the straight kill and didn't waste time or energy on any other solution. If he found the person or persons responsible for manufacturing Apollo, he'd take them out cleanly and efficiently.

On the other hand, Kell wanted a chance to gain information. To figure out not only how, but who and why, somebody wanted to harm the Coven Nine. His curiosity had helped him in his career and in his life. The envelope from the king still sat on Kell's bed table, unopened and unread. He'd rather his mate just told him everything about herself, but even so, that information tempted him.

"Want to come to the gallery opening?" Simone asked.

"No, but thank you." The nape of his neck itched, and he could almost hear a clock counting down. "I'll get some work done and maybe investigate a few of these names." While Alexandra was at work, he might as well do the same to keep himself from going to look for her.

"Suit yourself," Simone said, sweeping from the room.

"Don't kill anybody, Adam," Kell murmured, his gaze memorizing the compiled list.

"No promises," Adam muttered as he followed Simone. At the door, he stopped. "This test in Seattle, of humans right now?"

"I know," Kell murmured. "As soon as it's perfected, then witches are in danger, and that's going to happen soon."

Adam nodded. "I believe so, too. You think human army with abilities?"

"Yes." Kell had seen the end-game since day one. Create an army, possibly a coalition of motorcycle clubs, with the same abilities as the witches had and then take them down. "We may end up fighting humans with stronger abilities than we have." The ticking clock was getting louder, because soon the next phase of Apollo would be arriving. He just knew it.

Adam nodded. "Soon. It's coming soon." He hurried to catch up with Simone.

Kell didn't bother nodding. Somewhere on the list in front of him was somebody who wanted to harm what was his. Adam had it right. Kell would go hunting, and then he'd go killing. This time, he'd forget curiosity and answers.

This was war.

Chapter 22

Lex strolled into her shitty apartment early morning to find Kellach Dunne sprawled on her bed in a Black Sabbath T-shirt and ripped jeans, his hands behind his head. "What the hell?" she muttered.

He lifted an eyebrow. "How was the stakeout?"

"A waste of time." She glanced at muted light pouring through the window, not looking forward to doing the same thing that coming night. "Why are you on my bed?"

"Because you're not in mine." He watched her, eyes lazy, body at rest. Yet a sense of danger, of barely contained energy, cascaded around him. "I figured you'd probably come back here, so here I am."

She lifted an eyebrow. "I live here."

"Not anymore," he said softly.

She stilled and sucked in a deep breath. "We're dating, Kell." With a side of immortality, but still. "I'm not moving in with you."

"Aye, you are." He pushed off the bed, towering over her. "Until we get Apollo figured out, and until you're fully immortal and not so vulnerable, you are moving to a better secured home."

"Better secured? Meaning wherever you are?" She pressed her hands on her hips.

"Aye."

Aye. Bossy Irish enforcer. "If I become completely immortal, then you'll back off?"

He grinned.

She didn't think so.

"There's no such thing as completely immortal, as we can be beheaded." He ran gentle hands down her arms.

Irritation, not quite temper, but suffocating tension filtered through her, and she shoved out. Flames trembled on her arms, bluish-green, and then snuffed out.

Her eyes widened. "Um."

Kell stepped back. "Very nice." He rubbed her arms again. "You created fire."

Yeah, but she hadn't meant to. "It didn't hurt at all."

"Your own fire shouldn't burn you," he said.

She lifted an eyebrow and stepped back from him, trying to concentrate. Nothing.

He smiled. "Pretend you're a conduit for energy, and you can create light. Imagine you can actually see and control the oxygen molecules around you. Feel them touching you, and then grasp them. Change them from oxygen into fire. Then let your skin expand."

That didn't make sense. But she took a deep breath, imagined energy, and watched fire dance along her arms to whiff out. She laughed. "Awesome."

He nodded. "Want to learn how to make fire balls?"

Oh, hell yeah.

Hours after learning to create fire and then taking a very satisfying nap, Lex handed over the extra-large bag of M&M's to Bernie, allowing the chocolate to explode on her tongue. "We haven't done stake-outs two nights in a row in way too long."

Bernie snorted and shoveled in candy, his gaze out the front of his Buick. "Stakeouts suck. You're getting maudlin." He shifted his bulk on the ripped seat and handed back the candy.

"Yeah." She watched a twenty-something in a pink minidress stumble toward the front door of Slam, an old bar east of Seattle. "I am gonna miss you, Bernie." Truer words she'd never spoken. They'd been partners for five years, had watched each other's backs, and had shared dinners together.

"Me too, kid." Bernie glanced at her, his gaze concerned. "Who do you think will be your new partner?"

"Dunno." Lex sighed as another young gal, a blonde, tripped through the door. "That chick is derunk."

Bernie sighed. "She's probably the age of Janice, my youngest."

He and his wife, Liz, had been married for forty years and had raised four kids. All girls. The youngest was finishing up college.

Lex nodded. "We can still do football Sundays together, right?"

"Of course." Bernie lightly punched her in the arm.

Tears pricked the backs of her eyes, and she quickly blinked them away. *Geez.* She was a badass cop, not some debutante. "Cool."

Bernie leaned forward as Spike Evertol sauntered toward the doorway. "There he is."

Lex nodded. "Yep." She waited until Bernie had passed the information on to Masterson and Bundt, who were in place inside the bar. "Bundt said Spike will bring out his connection."

"Yeah. Hopefully we can take them quietly." Bernie tossed his jacket in the back of the car to leave his weapon free. He cleared his throat. "So, you end things with that Fire member?"

Lex stiffened. She had one partner, and she owed him the truth. "No."

"Damn it, Lex." Bernie shook his head. "You're smarter than that."

"No, I'm not."

Bernie chuckled. "Yes, you are. Give me a break. What the hell you doin'?"

Lex turned toward her partner just as the skies opened up and pummeled rain onto Seattle. "Kellach isn't a member of Fire. He's undercover for a military group from Ireland, and he's working to take Apollo off the streets."

Bernie's bushy eyebrows rose and he pivoted to face her fully. "You're fuckin' kiddin' me. You believe that shit?"

"Yes." God, if she told him all of it, he'd have her committed to the loony bin. "I believe him, Bern."

Bernie flicked on the windshield wipers. "Why the hell would some Irish military group give a shit about the streets of Seattle?"

"They think the drug is being tested here before hitting the streets of Dublin." Okay. That sounded lame. "I know it doesn't make a lot of sense, but you have to trust me. Please."

He studied her, and the tick, tick, tick of the windshield wipers filled the silence. "Lex, I do trust you. But the only reason a guy from Ireland joins a Seattle motorcycle club that is known to distribute drugs is because he either wants drugs or guns or both. Your theory about Dunne supplying Fire with drugs and Fire supplying Dunne with guns for the IRA is the best one we've had yet."

"I know, but I was wrong." *And my lover is a witch who has mated me, and someday I'll be immortal.* "Sometimes life doesn't make sense." She shook her head, feeling more alone than ever. How could she trust a guy she'd just met? Men left, and he had the power to leave for eternity. She hunched into her seat.

"Don't be mad." Bernie sighed. "I just don't want to see you screw up a great career."

Forget her career. Right now she was more worried about her sanity. "Do you think there are things in this world we don't see? I mean, like magic or destiny?"

Bernie coughed, and his eyes widened. "No. Do you?"

She shrugged. "Maybe."

"Jesus, Lex. Don't tell me you're thinking this guy is fated for you or some nonsense like that. You're as bad as my Linda." Bernie shook his head.

Linda was Bernie's second daughter, and she'd earned a college degree in Urban Legends, much to Bernie's dismay. She currently worked as a waitress in a yogurt shop and was loving it.

Lex rubbed her eyes. "Maybe Linda has it right."

"God." Bernie squinted to peer through the storm. "I'll never understand how a perfectly smart woman goes bum ass dumb over a guy. I've seen it. I've seen it dozens of times with my girls. But not you, Lex. What the hell?"

She couldn't explain the truth to him. "I don't know."

Gunshots filled the air, and partygoers poured out of the bar. One girl fell into the alley, while another young man leaped over her and into the street, screaming at the top of his lungs.

"Shit." Bernie shoved open his door while calling, "Shots fired, shots fired," into his radio along with the address.

Adrenaline flooded Lex's senses, and she burst from the car, her gun already out. She swept the area, running into the flood of people barreling from the bar. She edged her hip against the opening and shoved inside with Bernie on her heels.

The scents of smoke and sweat assaulted her first. Rock music beat around a darkened room, while lights glowed from the ceiling in a weird red and blue pattern. A bar, painted black, took up the nearest wall.

"Masterson," she yelled out.

"Back here." Bundt poked his head above the bar. "Call it in. Officer down. Officer down." He disappeared from sight.

Bernie called it in while Lex ran around the bar to where Bundt was pressing his hand around an upper chest wound bleeding from Masterson's too still body. Even in the darkened bar, she could see the blood covering the floor around the cop.

She dropped to her knees and felt his neck. Good pulse.

Bundt shook his head. "Spike shot him. The prick shot my partner."

She leaned down and patted Masterson's cheek. "He's out, but his heart rate is good. Keep pressure on the wound." It looked like the bullet had gone through the upper shoulder.

"Freeze," Bernie bellowed from across the room.

Lex jumped to her feet and grabbed her gun.

Across the bar, Bernie had taken a shooter's stance, his gun aimed at a guy nearly glowing with pink fire.

Lex hustled around the bar, her gun toward the guy. He was tall, probably about six-five, and the fire surrounded him.

He walked toward Bernie, and Bernie pulled off three shots.

The guy jerked and then smiled.

"What the hell?" Bernie yelled.

The guy lifted his hand.

"No," Lex yelled, afraid of the fire about to be thrown. She ran toward the guy.

Silver glinted in the darkened room, and he fired some kind of weapon.

Bernie twisted, his body contorting.

Lex hit the guy in a full tackle, knocking him into the wall. Pain flared along her shoulder and neck. The fire singed her skin but didn't burn, and she grappled for control.

He gasped, his eyes widening before he swung and hit her temple.

She saw stars but kept fighting, hitting him in the eye.

"Lex," Bernie called out, clutching his chest, falling to the floor.

"Bernie?" Lex elbowed her attacker in the nose and struggled to flip him over to cuff.

The guy growled and grabbed her hips, throwing her toward Bernie. She landed hard, the air knocked out of her, her palms smarting as they slapped the dirty floor. Her attacker jumped up and ran for the back door.

Sirens sounded in the distance.

She reached Bernie, who lay with his eyes open, gasping for breath. "Bern?"

"Fire. God, fire and hot. Hurts." He gasped, his eyes filling with pain.

She yanked open his shirt, searching for bullet holes. Darts. Two red darts stuck into the top of his chest. What in the world? Gingerly, she tugged them out.

He began to convulse, his eyes closing.

"Bernie," she yelled, patting his face, trying to hold him down so he didn't hurt himself.

What had been in the darts?

Flames shot from his fingertips. Shit. Apollo. She leaned in, holding his face. "Don't leave, Bernie. Please hold on." She pressed her face to his shuddering chest to listen to his erratic heartbeat. Not good. Way not good.

Flames danced up his chest, burning his skin. The smell of burned flesh filled her nose.

"No," she gasped. A tingle whipped through her. Flames, the color of Kell's, appeared on her hands. Hadn't she seen Kell quell another guy's fire with his own?

Going on instinct, saying a quick prayer, she pushed her fire against the one harming Bernie. Sparks flew, and she ducked her head. Concentrating, she tried to capture the fire hurting him.

She'd practiced creating fire all morning, and she could do this. She had to do this. Her fire encircled his, and she snuffed it out by waving her hands.

He gasped a breath.

"Bernie?" she asked, leaning over his face, her body shaking. Creating fire took a lot of energy, and she was out.

His eyes fluttered shut.

Tears filled her eyes. The sound of Bundt talking to his partner, ordering him to awaken, filtered through the bawdy music.

Talking or applying pressure wouldn't help Bernie. While she could snuff out the fire on him, what was happening inside him? She couldn't force fire into him, could she?

He began to flop like a caught fish.

Sucking in air, she pretended the air around them was on fire. Flames danced on her skin. She pictured fire in her mouth, on her tongue, and suddenly, flames danced out of her mouth.

This was crazy. Definitely risky. Leaning down, she opened Bernie's mouth and breathed in. Hard and fast, she shot those flames down his throat, hoping she wasn't killing him. God, she hoped she wasn't burning him from the inside out.

Her fire continued, snuffing his out, but his convulsions increased in pace and strength.

Finally, she ran out of air. Leaning back, she sucked in oxygen and tried to make more fire. Nothing. She tried again. No fire.

Bernie lay out cold, his body shuddering, the smell of burned skin cascading around them.

The door burst open and paramedics ran inside.

Lex slipped to the side and put Bernie's head on her lap, tears streaking down her face. Her vision hazed. "One here and one behind the bar." She watched as they set an IV in place and then helped them load him onto a stretcher.

Bernie and Masterson, whose color had faded to a light blue, were both loaded into an ambulance. She and Bundt, who was covered in blood, stood in the rain for a sliver of a second, watching the ambulance careen away.

"I'll drive," Bundt said, turning and running for his car.

Lex nodded and followed, wiping tears off her face, her knees weak. What if she'd hurt Bernie? What if her fire hadn't been enough to save him? What if Masterson didn't awaken? They had to be all right.

She shook her head and holstered her weapon, leaping into the passenger seat of Bundt's truck. Her throat hurt like claws had ripped down it.

Patrol officers screeched to a stop, lights swirling, jumping out to take statements.

A witch had attacked Bernie right in front of her, and he'd tried to hurt her. She'd head to the hospital and pray her partner lived then go have a talk with the entire Dunne family.

It was time they told her everything.

Chapter 23

Kell's wet boots squeaked on the polished tiles, but he paid no heed while all but running through the hallway to the emergency waiting room. His heart thundered in his chest. If Alexandra had been harmed, he'd know . . . right? As her mate, he would feel her pain, deep in his gut.

But they'd only been mated a short time, and they hadn't fully connected. So maybe he wouldn't feel anything.

Darkness and fury coursed through him, and it took every ounce of control he had to hold back the flames . . . to keep the fire at bay and not start throwing plasma balls in an effort to shove out some of the fear and pain.

He turned the corner, and the second he saw her, he halted. The world slowed, and the frantic beating of his heart mellowed.

She was all right.

Alexandra huddled next to a middle-aged woman on a set of chairs, her arm around the slender shoulders of the crying woman. Fresh bruises marred Alexandra's too pale face, and one near her temple had already turned an angry purple. Blood covered the front of her shirt.

But she was unharmed.

He growled low. His mate. In danger.

Never fucking again.

Cops milled around, some sitting, some pacing. The level of tension, of fury, clogged the oxygen, even though the sensations came from humans.

He needed to touch her and reassure himself that she was all right.

But as a suspect in a current case, he'd only cause a scene by walking through the ocean of cops.

As if she sensed him, she stilled and then slowly turned her head. Despair filled her pretty eyes, and the lost look had him stepping toward her automatically. He'd do anything to erase that expression.

She whispered something to the woman and stood, heading his way. To avoid being seen, he turned and backtracked into the rainy night, making for his truck, sensing her on his heels.

Reaching the black Chevy, he opened the passenger-side door, and she climbed inside without a word.

He tuned in his senses for a threat, found none besides the raging storm, and crossed the truck to climb inside. The second his ass hit the seat, he reached for her, lifting and settling her on his lap.

She struggled, shaking and moving, finally shoving him hard in the chest.

He kept his hold relentless, letting her fight it out, feeling the stubbornness in her when she stopped moving and perched tightly coiled on his lap.

"Alexandra," he whispered.

The first sob shook her entire body. She bit it back, her muscles somehow tensing further.

"It's all right," he said, gently rubbing from her neck to her tailbone.

Another sob emerged, full of hurt.

His heart shattered in two, and a deadly frustration exploded inside him, along with a vow to disembowel whoever had hurt her. He clasped her neck, unwilling to wait any longer, and pulled her head into his chest.

With a huge intake of breath, she broke.

Her cries were the most pained sounds he'd ever heard, including time he'd spent in battles and true war. She shuddered against him, her small hand curled into his T-shirt, the sobs coming from so deep within her, he feared she'd pass out.

The angry thunder and lightning outside the quiet truck was no match for the storm going on inside. He held her tight, rubbing her back, murmuring soft promises ranging from avenging her pain to buying her a villa in France.

She unleashed it all, finally winding down with a soft series of sniffs.

When she'd settled and her pain no longer made it difficult for him to breathe, he kissed the top of her head. "What happened, baby?"

Between hiccups, she told him of both detectives being harmed.

"Darts?" he asked, his mind calculating the danger. *Hell.* The drug had been bad enough when junkies shot themselves up. The bastards had figured out how to weaponize Apollo. It could be used against witches—which surely had been the plan from the beginning. Forget the human army who could fight like witches.

"Yes," she whispered, her voice so raw it made his throat hurt. "Bernie is in a coma right now, and his liver is shutting down. I tried to save him, but I didn't know how."

It was a miracle she'd already been able to create fire. Only her heightened senses in that crisis had made it possible, and even so, she shouldn't have been able to create fire in her mouth without burning herself severely.

She lifted her head, her eyes like a meadow after a rainstorm. "Will Bernie be all right?"

"I don't know, sweetheart." Kell would give anything to be able to say something else, but he truly hadn't figured out the drug yet. "The fact that Bernie is still breathing is an incredibly good sign. You gave him that chance. You did."

Her eyes filled again. "I should've warned him."

"About what? Darts?" Kell rubbed her neck in circular motions, needing to touch her. To make sure she still breathed. "We didn't know."

"About witches." She shook her head. "I owed him the truth."

"How would that have helped?" Kell asked.

She pushed away and wiped off her cheeks. "I don't know." Sighing, she glanced at the rain splattering off the concrete. "Masterson is already up and flirting with the nurses. The bullet went right through his shoulder, and he'll be fine."

Kell frowned. "So Masterson was shot by Spike with regular bullets, and Bernie was shot with darts containing Apollo."

"Yeah." She shoved hair back from her face. "We think Masterson interrupted a drug deal. After he was shot, the witch came in, so maybe the witch was looking for Spike for whatever reason, maybe to do business. Or maybe the witch knew Spike was snitching, and he needed to stop him. Bundt was casing the rear of the bar and heard the shots. Spike ran out the back while Bundt was trying to keep Masterson from bleeding out." Her voice cracked on the end.

Kell tried to hug her closer and shield her from any more hurt. His tough warrior.

"Maybe the witch you fought with is the manufacturer?" Kell inhaled the scent of his woman. "I need a complete description of him."

"Bright fire, brown hair. Dark eyes, I think. About six-five, two hundred pounds, and really strong." She pushed away from Kell and scooted across the seat. "I need to go back in and sit with Bernie's wife."

Kell rubbed his chin, fighting every instinct in his body to pull her close again and keep her away from blood and death. "I'll make some calls and see if I can get a line on that witch. When you're ready to go home, I'll be here." He'd keep out of sight of the cops, just so she wouldn't have to explain.

She shook her head. "I may be a while."

He grasped her chin. "That doesn't matter. I'll wait right here until you're ready to go."

She frowned. "Whoever the witch was, he liked hurting Bernie, and he liked fighting with me. He's a bastard, and I'm going to take him down."

Kellach didn't answer.

She slid from the car, and he watched her run through the rain, keeping her in sight until she disappeared into the blazing hospital lights.

Then, and only then, did he allow his fury to roar. Fire lit along his arms, and he welcomed the burn. Alexandra wouldn't get a chance to take out the witch because he would find him first and rip his fucking head from his body.

He lifted his phone to his ear and snapped out orders to Adam and Daire, including the description of the witch.

Then he called every contact he had in the witch species before moving on to vampires, shifters, and demons. He hit them all. If anyone had a line on a witch matching Alexandra's very vague description, he'd have it by morning.

* * *

Slowly, through the rain, dawn began to arrive.

Alexandra staggered out of the hospital, her eyes widening upon seeing the truck. Walking as if she'd aged overnight, she skirted mud puddles, allowing the rain to pummel her short hair.

Upon reaching the truck, she opened the door and groaned while jumping inside. "Bernie is out of the coma, and the doctors are cautiously optimistic."

"And Masterson?" Kell asked, igniting the engine.

"He's fine." Alexandra rubbed her nose. "He doesn't have any family. None at all. Not even a girlfriend to call." She sounded so bewildered and lonely that Kell reached out and covered her free hand with his.

"I don't have a line on the witch yet, but I will. I promise." It wasn't the time to discuss her moving to Ireland as his mate and being safe, but that time was nearing. "Any news on the human shooter?"

She shook her head. "Patrol officers are still interviewing witnesses, but it was so dark in there, so far, nobody has been helpful. There's a hotline. Spike is a mid-level dealer, so we should have him in custody soon. Hopefully if we get him in the box, we can make him explain why he shot Donny. We also need to convince him to roll on the witch. I want that bastard."

So did Kell. He drove through nearly empty streets while dawn tried to break through the storm.

Alexandra leaned back against the seat and closed her eyes. "I'm not feeling very warm toward witches right now, Kellach."

"If you hadn't mated a witch, you wouldn't have been able to save your partner," he countered without any heat. And if she hadn't mated him, he'd be facing a future he hadn't realized was lonely and bleak until right that moment.

"That's true," she mumbled.

That was his woman. Even pissed off and exhausted, she was fair. Always fair. He rubbed his thumb along the back of her hand as he drove across town to his flat. She deserved a luxury shower and bed, and she sure as hell wouldn't get that at her crappy apartment. Maybe if he just moved all her clothes over, she wouldn't protest too much. Her days of living in squalor were over, whether she liked it or not.

He drove into the underground garage and cut the engine before stretching out and turning his senses into those of a predator. No threatening sounds or smells nearby.

Quiet pounded as he went around, opened her door, and gathered his mate into his arms. For once, she didn't protest, and snuggled right in to his chest.

His instant grin warmed him throughout. The woman was exhausted.

He carried her up the stairs to his penthouse, opening the door and taking her immediately to the master bath to set her on her feet. "Are you hungry?"

"No." She leaned against him, her eyes still closed.

He twisted the shower on to warm and removed her clothing, surprised when she didn't even make a token protest. The night had not only exhausted her physically but emotionally, it seemed.

Taking off his clothes, he steered her into the steam and under the water.

She groaned, one hand flattening on the stone tiles, her head lowering as the water beat down.

Slowly, showing her she could be cherished, he washed and rinsed her hair before turning to her body.

He flared alive in need but kept his touch gentle and reassuring. When he'd rinsed away the soap, he turned off the water and stepped out into the room. Tucking her in a towel, he dried her hair with another towel and grabbed her a worn T-shirt to wear.

She mumbled something, her hands slicking along his bare chest.

Desire heated through him, deep and beyond the moment. He dragged on some boxers and herded her into his sprawling bed, tucking them both in.

She rolled toward him, and her hand whispered along his unshaven jaw. The gentle touch moved past his skin and between muscles, wrapping around his heart. "Kellach," she whispered.

The tone licked down his spine to caress his balls. "Go to sleep, little warrior. We can talk later today."

She blinked and scooted closer, vulnerability and need darkening her eyes. "Don't want to talk. Want to feel."

His mouth lifted. That, he could give to her. He rolled her over onto her back and kissed her, keeping his touch gentle, and his movements lazy. Showing her again that she meant something to him, that the moment was about her.

She caressed his shoulders, her movements slow.

He kissed along her neck to her breasts, where he suckled. She gasped, arching against him, her heated core caressing his cock.

"Now, Kell," she murmured.

He had no problem helping her get lost in passion to forget the pain of the day, but he was taking his time and ensuring she was ready. He played with her breasts, reverently kissing them, taking their lovemaking slow.

His fingers tapped down over her undulating abdominal muscles to reach her clit.

She gasped and rolled her hips.

He moved lower and fingered her slit. Wet and ready. At the feeling, his balls drew up tight.

"Now," she said again.

He couldn't resist such a plea. Maneuvering above her, holding himself with his arm to keep from crushing her, he slowly shoved inside her. He had to move in and out several times to get her body to accept him, finally burying himself balls deep.

The sensation of her internal walls gripping him nearly stole his control. He breathed out evenly to keep from pounding into her.

She moaned and wrapped both arms around his shoulders. "Take me away. Please."

He kissed her, taking her deep, showing her with his body what he couldn't give in words yet. Slowly, sensually, he moved in and out, enjoying each little catch of her breath and the internal rippling of her muscles pulsing around his shaft.

Her nails dug into his shoulders, and the little bite of pain almost sent him over.

Clasping her hips, he pulled her up every time he shoved into her, moving her with his rhythm. She allowed him full control, her thighs tensing against his hips, her soft cries filling his heart.

He increased his rhythm, the sound of flesh against flesh competing with the headboard hitting the wall.

She held tighter, her body stiffening.

Angling just a little, he brushed over her clit, and she detonated. She cried out his name, waves battering through her and against him, her core tightening around him with a strength that had him thrusting hard and holding her in place. His balls swelled, electricity danced down his spine, and he came hard.

Finally, she went limp beneath him, her arms sliding away.

Turning to his side, he dragged her close and wrapped himself around her. "Go to sleep, baby. I'll keep you safe."

Her breathing evened out, and seconds later, she fell asleep. He allowed himself the luxury of holding her for nearly an hour, making sure she was far into dreamland.

Keeping the covers wrapped snuggly around her, he slid from the bed and stood, surveying her.

In peace, in sleep, her face lost the cop look. The bruises on her fair skin were an insult. Her hands on the blanket were small, delicate, and she barely made a shape under the heavy bedclothes.

Determination straightened his spine as he vowed the bruises would be returned ten-fold. She was his, and it was his duty to keep her safe. Whether she liked it or not. It was time to go hunting for the witch who'd dared to hurt her.

When Kell found him . . . and he would . . . there would be no mercy.

Chapter 24

Lex awoke slowly, stretching in luxurious sheets, aches springing to life along her entire body. She sat up, her head muddled, her face aching. Memories zipped through her mind, and she glanced around Kellach's bedroom.

Her phone had been placed near the bed, and she instantly called the hospital for an update. The on duty nurse informed her that Bernie had improved slightly and that Masterson was about to be discharged.

She clicked off the call and ran a hand through her short hair.

The previous night, she'd meant to dig into Kell and get the full truth about the witches, and instead, she'd cried all over him and then pretty much begged him for sex.

God. She was such a girly wimp all of a sudden. *Enough.* Swinging her legs from the bed, she took inventory of each bruise, nick, and pain. That bastard witch who'd dared harm Bernie was going to pay and pay good.

She eyed a set of clothing on a dresser. Designer jeans, green cashmere sweater, incredibly shiny brown boots that made her sigh. All with tags on.

Her head jerked up. Kellach Dunne did not get to buy her clothes. Dressed only in the threadbare T-shirt, she marched out of the room to give him a piece of her mind. A quick stomp around the penthouse revealed a note left in the kitchen.

Alexandra,

I'm hoping you sleep the day away, but if not, you must eat. There are eggs, bacon, and fruit in the fridge. I have a

*lead on the witch and am tracking it down. You're to stay
here until I return.*

> *Thank you.*
> *Kellach*

She frowned and twirled the note around. It was an order. A very
clear order for her to stay in place. *Wow.* The guy hadn't figured her
out a bit. Turning on her heel, she hurried back to the bedroom and
changed into the borrowed clothes. The cashmere made her groan
at the decadent comfort, which meant she had to figure out a way to
pay him back for the clothes.

Well, one thing at a time. Though she couldn't find her ruined
clothing since he'd probably thrown it away, she did find her gun
and badge resting on the bathroom counter. Tucking the gun into
her waist, she borrowed a toothbrush and hairbrush to make herself
presentable.

Without any makeup, she appeared too pale, and add in the bruises,
she appeared to be a victim of a good beating or a disastrous car
wreck. Either way, she didn't look like a cop—which was unfortunate, considering it was time to visit her father and figure out what
the hell was going on. He had a lot of explaining to do about keeping
in contact with not only her mother but with Spike. Hell, maybe he
even knew where Spike would hole up after shooting a cop.

She called a cab from her cell phone and hustled down to the op-
ulent lobby of the high-end apartment building. Having only entered
through the garage, she hadn't imagined the stunning marble fixtures
or over-the-top crystal chandelier in the center.

The doorman, a guy built like a linebacker, opened the door for
her and asked if she'd like for him to call a cab.

She admitted she'd called one all by her itty-bitty self and then
ignored his shocked look. Apparently rich people were too busy or
important to call for a cab. The guy still held an umbrella over her
head while she walked down the wet steps toward her crappy cab,
and she wondered if she was supposed to tip him. If so, he was
outta luck, considering she didn't have her purse. Or any money in
it, anyway.

Even so, she gave him her best smile and a genuine thank-you as
she slid into the back of the cab.

The doorman waited patiently.

Damn it, she didn't have a tip. She shrugged. "I left my purse in the car at a homicide scene."

His dark eyebrows rose. "I was waiting for the address, ma'am."

Holy crap. Rich people couldn't even talk to a cabbie to give directions? She reached for the door to shut it. "I've got it, pal."

He stepped back and still gave a slight bow.

Her gaze met the amused one of the cabbie as she gave the address for Bernie's car at the scene. "I have my purse in the car and will catch you then." She flashed her badge. "I promise." Of course, she'd have to swipe her credit card and say a quick prayer that she had enough credit left for the ride.

"Cop or hooker," the cab driver snorted.

Lex frowned and scooted closer to the divider. "Excuse me?"

Unapologetic and almost wise eyes met her gaze. "Chicks who don't belong leaving ritzy places like that are usually hookers. But since you got a badge, I guess cops hang there, too."

Heat climbed into her face.

She fought the urge to yank on the cabbie's long gray ponytail. "You're opinionated."

He nodded. "The guy you stay with do that to your face?"

"No. The guy who shot my partner last night did this to my face." Lex rubbed the still pounding bruise at her temple. "You know anything about the firefight at Slam last night?"

"Not personally." The cabbie took a sharp left turn and flipped off a Mercedes that tried to cut him off. "I heard on the news, though. Sorry your partner got shot."

Lex nodded. "Thanks. You heard anything about a new drug on the streets called Apollo?"

"Nope. I stay away from drugs." He pounded his chest. "Work out regular and don't even drink diet colas. That shit will kill you faster than most of the illegal street drugs out there today. Bad stuff."

"Hmm." Lex sat back and thought through the night before until they arrived at Bernie's car. In the daytime, with the rain still pattering down, the scene appeared like any bad street in any bad town. Police tape covered the door of the bar, but other than that, there was no sign that all hell had descended the night before.

She shoved out of the cab, opened Bernie's car door and squared up with the driver. She was on her way south before she could think of a reason not to visit the penitentiary.

Ten years. It had been ten years since she'd seen her father, and she'd gone then only because her mother had begged her to see him on his fortieth birthday. He'd been apologetic, she'd been pissy, and the visit had not gone well.

He wanted to see her and claimed to have information about her case. Why he reached out after so much time was beyond her. She settled into the drive that would take two hours.

About halfway there, her phone buzzed.

"Monzelle," she answered, not looking to see the caller.

"Where the hell are you, mate?" a somewhat pissed off Kell asked.

She flipped on her blinker and switched lanes, spraying water. "Working. Why?"

"I believe I asked you to stay here until we could chat."

She snorted. "You ordered me to stay there. You're crazy if you think I'd obey and just sit on my ass when my partner was shot last night."

Silence reigned for several beats. "Not for a second did I think you'd sit on your very sweet ass, but I do expect you to be safe and to work with me. Now get back here."

Interesting. The possessive and bossy tone was new. Great sex seemed to make Kellach turn into a throwback.

"No."

He exhaled in a sound of pure male frustration. "Alexandra."

"Listen, Kell." She didn't have time to deal with a witch apparently caught in the last century, yet she owed him for last night, so she tried to hold on to her temper. "You took good care of me last night. I was down, so I appreciate it."

"Get back here, and I'll take even better care of you."

The sexy tone zinged through ears, down her chest, and ricocheted to her core. "I have work to do."

"Take me with you."

She chuckled and switched lanes behind a slow moving television satellite truck. "Right. You may be undercover, but right now, you're a suspect of my department. We can't be seen together until you make yourself known to my superiors."

"I can't do that," he snapped.

"So back off and let me do my job."

"Back off?" His voice softened. "That's not how this is going down, Alexandra."

Another damn truck was in her way. She honked and jerked to the side to pass the idiot. "I have no idea what you're talking about, but I don't work for you."

"No, you're my mate. As such, we have a couple things to get straight."

Her head lifted. "Like what?" she asked, her temper really wanting to make an appearance.

"Things are heating up, and the fact that you're my mate will be known soon. In fact, when you grappled with the witch last night, he probably sensed the change. Thus, you're in more danger than usual, especially since the darts will really hurt you."

"I'm a cop. Danger is normal, and the darts are dangerous for everybody, even humans." She pressed down on the accelerator. *Finally.*

Something banged hard across the line. "You're rich now and don't need to work."

Oh, he did not. "Unless I won the lottery and nobody told me, I'm not wealthy." Man, the guy had hidden this side of himself pretty well.

"This is a discussion to have in person. What time can you be here?" His tone hinted at command and impatience, and pretty much pissed her off.

"I'll be there when I damn well get there." She clicked a button and ended the call. Just who exactly did he think he was? For the life of Pete, she was a cop, and she had a gun. One she'd shove up his ass if he didn't knock it off.

She fumed the rest of the drive, finally reaching the correctional facility where she took the necessary steps to go through security. Giving up her gun didn't feel right, yet she understood the precaution since she was there as a visitor and not on business. Sure, she could've argued to keep her gun, but the chance remained that she'd shoot her father.

Keys jangled from the belt of a heavy-set guard who guided her through the maze and down several concrete hallways. Lex dragged her heels, her gaze straight ahead, her shoulders back. Even so, her stomach gurgled.

She sat on a curved yellow chair secured to the floor. In deference to her position, the warden had allowed her in a private room and not in the lineup with glass walls.

Thank God she hadn't brought Tori to such a place. Even the thought of Tori's vibrancy and energy being sucked away by so much gray and the stench of evil seized Lex's lungs.

The chill swept through her, deeper than her skin, and she shivered.

Footsteps plodded toward her, getting louder. A guard escorted her father in and secured the chain between his hands to a ring in the table.

"Alex," her father said.

Nobody had called her *Alex* since her early teenaged years. She sat back and studied him. He'd aged, his dark hair turning gray, his smooth skin heavy with wrinkles. Once vibrant green eyes had faded, and harsh lines cut out from the sides of his mouth. "What do you want?" she asked.

He leaned forward, and the chains clanked. "How is your mother?"

She glanced at the clock on her phone, pleased when her hand didn't shake. "You have one minute to tell me why I'm here, and then I'm gone. Spill it."

He sighed. "Alexandra, please take a moment and talk to me. I haven't seen you in ten years."

"So while you're looking, talk." She kept her expression stoic.

His gaze raked her bruised and battered face. "Who did this to you?"

She sneered. "Why? Remind you of how you treated my mother?" Yeah, she remembered how horribly he'd treated her, acting like she was stupid. After a while, Jennie had seemed to believe him. It had taken years for her to regain her confidence.

Her father blanched. "I never once raised a hand to your mom."

"No, but you might as well have. The way you belittled her and put her down."

He sighed. "I've changed. I really have."

"Men who kill, sell drugs, and belittle their wives don't change." Lex shoved her chair back from the table. "Your time is up."

That quickly, her father dropped the concerned look, and calculation filtered through. "I'd hoped we could talk like rational people, but I can see you inherited your mother's flare for drama over reason."

"Screw you, dickhead." Lex stood.

"Wait. I know about Apollo."

She paused and focused on her father. "What do you know?"

His smile sent a chill down her back. "Oh, you need to sit for this."

"No." She lifted her hand to wave for the guard.

"Wait. I know about the mineral from Russia that gives Apollo its power, and I know about the new assembly lines making Apollo-filled darts. Think nail guns with deadly drugs shooting out. Man, will those cause hell on the Seattle streets."

Taking a deep breath, Lex slowly sat down. "I'm listening."

His upper lip curled in what could only be triumph. "Now that's a nice change."

"Not for long. Speak or I'm out of here." Nausea slid down her throat to coat her stomach. This guy was actually her father. "Who's manufacturing Apollo?"

"Oh, no." Her father shook his head. "I don't give you a name until I'm out of here. If you, a decorated cop, testify at my parole hearing next week, I'll finally get out, and I'll tell you everything. The name of the manufacturer, the location of the factories, and even the top distributors. I know everything—especially how they're bringing the drug into the country."

Lex sat back and studied her father. His eyes remained clear and his manner truthful, but the guy was a killer and a drug dealer. He'd survived decades of prison, and surely he could tell a convincing lie.

"How do you have that information?"

He folded his hands together around the chains. "I still have friends on the outside, as well as on the inside. I hear things."

"Right. Where's Spike?"

Her father shrugged. "I don't know."

"Bullshit." She leaned toward him. "I think you do. You're still a part of the drug trade." How in the hell had she missed that? He'd been a key distributor years ago, and it made sense he'd stayed in the game. "If you're working with whoever is manufacturing Apollo, I'll make sure you never see the outside again."

"I'm not." He met her gaze levelly. "I knew that finding out about this drug was my only way out of here, so I called in every marker I still had and found out the truth. Found out everything I could, which is enough to help you solve your case."

Made sense, but she trusted him as far as she could kick him, and that wasn't far. He might have slimmed out, but he was still a big guy. "I think you're full of shit, and you're wasting my time."

"Trevan Demidov," her father said, his eyes beadier than she'd remembered.

"Who?"

"That's all you're getting for now. A gesture of proof and good-will." He rattled his chains. "Guard? We're done here. For now."

Lex stood. "Who is Demidov?"

"Figure it out, Alex."

The guard entered and released the chains from the ring in the table, lifting her father to his feet. He shuffled toward the door, turning at the last minute, looking thin in his orange jumpsuit. "Say hi to my Jennie for me." The guard shoved him out the door, and he disappeared.

Lex took several deep breaths, her hands shaking. Okay. She could deal with this. Now she had to get back to the station and run Demidov before going to the hospital to check on Bernie and Masterson.

And then? Then she had to deal with a fire throwing, dangerous, probably deadly witch who had a truly mistaken view of her as a mate. That one would probably require a weapons discharge.

Chapter 25

Kellach paced the office, his temper frayed and his control nearly shattered. Pictures of five faces cascaded across the screen—all witches who'd had the wherewithal to mine the mineral during the time in question. "Which one do you think?"

Daire, the only other occupant of Simone's home office, shrugged a massive shoulder. "I'm not sure it's one of them, but all five have expressed dissatisfaction with the Coven Nine, and four have withdrawn from membership."

Three men and two women. "Martin Zanbus, Stan Newly, Grid Johes, Sylvia Pelut, and Tama Vichin." None of them looked like much of a danger. "Are we sure these are the most likely enemies?"

Daire nodded, kicking back in Simone's desk chair. "Aye. They are the ones still alive who had access to the mines years ago. We lost so many in the last war that, unfortunately, it was rather easy to narrow down the results to these five witches."

Kell nodded and began pacing again. "We seek them out, then."

"Would you stop fucking pacing?" Daire growled. "Before we seek them out, we need to launch a full investigation into their past centuries. I've put our computer guys on it, and we should have results by tomorrow."

"I'm not pacing." Kell continued to walk back and forth. "Besides witches, demons have had plenty of time to mine the mineral."

"I know."

"So we need a list of demons, too," Kell growled.

"What the hell is your problem?" Daire straightened up in a clear sign he was about to lunge.

Kell pivoted, more than halfway ready to clash with his older brother and draw blood. "Nothing."

"Jesus. You've been mated less than a week, and she has you this tied up in knots?" Daire relaxed back in the chair and plopped his boots onto the antique desk. "Get your woman in order. I need your mind in this fight."

"Get my woman in order? How the fuck do you propose I do that?" Kell nearly spit fire at his brother.

Daire shrugged. "I don't give a shit. You're an enforcer, she's a human, get her under control."

Kell shook his head. "You outdated bastard. Times have changed, brother. One doesn't just get a mate under control, especially when that mate is a cop, an enforcer of a sort for her own people."

"She's fragile, and now, some of her enemies aren't of her own species. This witch we're hunting will kill her without a thought, just to get to you." Daire twirled a letter opener around his fingers.

"I'm aware of that fact." Kell shook his head to regain some control. "Women can be warriors. Cousin Moira is an enforcer for the Nine, and she's mated to a vampire."

Daire flipped the sharp edged opener into the air and caught it, keeping it twirling. "Moira is a witch whom we trained for a century. Even though she's an enforcer, when was the last time she went out on a job without her soldier of a mate accompanying her?"

"Never," Kell acknowledged.

"Right. Listen. You can't do your job if you're worried about your woman, so you need to find a way not to worry, because I fucking need you to do your job." Daire slammed the opener into the desk, sharp edge first, leaving it standing up.

"Simone is going to kill you," Kell murmured.

"I'll tell her Adam did it." Daire yanked the blade free. "Are we clear?"

Kell shook his head. "Do you really think that when you finally mate, you're going to close her down somewhere safe and away from your job?"

"Of course." Male arrogance lived naturally on Daire's rugged face. "I'm not mating an enforcer or a cop or even a shifter. Fate finds us the perfect counterpart, and mine will be nurturing, like having kids, and won't even consider drawing a weapon."

Kell snorted. "You're a moron." He hoped Daire fell in love with a feline shifter who worked as a soldier. Or maybe a bear shifter that could cut ribbons into his flesh with maniacal claws. "I can't wait to see you mated."

"I'm not getting mated for another few centuries." Daire raised an eyebrow. "Look at the hot mess it has made of your life. Adam is next, then probably Simone, and after you all kick out a bunch of fire-throwing witches, I'll be a favorite uncle for years."

"I bet you get mated before Simone," Kell drawled.

"That's a bet."

Daire's phone buzzed and he glanced at the face. "Mother fucker," he muttered, stretching to his feet. "That's Adam. There's a problem at Fire, and we need to get over there now. I keep forgetting that's our cover, and it's time we found out who the damn manufacturer is of the drug."

Kell nodded and turned to jog through the penthouse. "Where's Simone?"

Daire didn't answer.

At the doorway, Kell stopped to view his brother. "Simone?"

"I sent her on a job." Daire reached around him and shoved open the door.

Kell flew into motion, forgoing the elevator for the stairs. His boots clomped in time with Daire's. "What job?" He shoved open the door to the underground garage.

"She's meeting with the demon liaison right now. If they have any history of who could've mined PK fifty years ago, we need it." Daire strode over and slung a leg over his Ducati.

Kell coughed out air, amusement and irritation combining in his chest. "You sent Simone to meet with a demon? If it was Nick Veis, I'm going to hit you in the face for her." Simone and Nick had a history, a long one, and it wasn't pretty.

Daire shrugged. "Nick is the liaison, and he'll tell Simone the truth."

Kell swung a leg over his bike. "God, you're an asshole."

"I prefer the term *efficient*. I'm tired of Simone nearly disemboweling every man she gets close to, and the reason for that is Nick Veis. They need to figure it out." Daire gunned his engine.

"You're a fucking girl," Kellach yelled over the roar. His brother. The badass leader of the enforcers and also a matchmaker.

"No," Daire yelled back. "Her feelings get in the way of the mission, so they need to be sorted out."

Bullshit. Kellach shook his head. Daire was a big softy for family, even though he came across as a first-rate dick. Kell ignited his own engine and yelled over the noise. "The demon isn't good enough for her."

"Nobody is." Daire turned his bike and roared out of the garage, easily employing evasive maneuvers to keep from hitting a taxi.

Kellach shook his head again, not sure he wanted one of his favorite cousins to end up with a demon. Sure, they were allies now, but that wasn't always so. In the way of the world, they might be enemies again. When had his people become so entangled with demons, vampires, and even shifters?

But Simone flashed sharp teeth every time someone mentioned Nick, so maybe there was no need to worry.

Kell skirted a minivan full of kids and drove through the city, finally opening up the throttle upon reaching clear road. He and Daire rode side-by-side, in sync. They'd been young when their parents had died in one of the battles leading up to the first large war.

Merely teens.

At that time, they'd drawn in, becoming a unit of three. When Simone had come along with no father in sight, they'd enfolded her as one of their own.

No, a demon wasn't good enough for her.

He drove into the triangular compound of the Fire Club; a pall had settled over the place. The hair on the back of his neck rose, and a quick glance toward Daire showed absolute focus. Yeah, he felt it.

They stopped their bikes, and the sudden silence pounded down.

Pyro strode from the main compound, his face pale, lines fanning out from his eyes. He wore dirty jeans, scuffed boots, and greasy hair, but the stench of fear pouring from him covered any other scent.

Kell disembarked and strode toward the club leader. "What's going on?"

"Follow me." Pyro turned and hitched across the main garage and around to the back.

The smell of burned flesh instantly slammed into Kell. He and Daire kept going, not losing stride, even when Pyro's steps slowed.

Pyro squared his shoulders and walked around the back corner of the garage.

"Holy hell," Daire muttered.

Kell halted, his gaze catching on a man burned to nearly a tinder, nailed to a white pine. His head was down, his hair singed off, burns streaking down his naked body.

Gaping holes exposed scalded intestines, partially falling out of the abdomen. Part of the liver remained, but the spleen was gone.

Darts, a myriad of them, lined the cracked skin of the neck and most of the torso.

Kell stepped closer to the body and tilted his head. "Spike Evertol. It's Spike."

Pyro gagged, swallowed, and then nodded. "Yeah. He was dealing for us, while also leading the cops away from us."

Kell turned to eye Pyro. "Spike was a snitch?"

"He doubled as one." Pyro backed away, gagging again. "This is a message from somebody to get out of the trade, and the only one I can think of is Bear. The Grizzlies want to take over the distribution of Apollo."

Kell rubbed his chin and cut Daire a look, who gave a barely perceptible nod. "No, Pyro. This is a message to you since your dealer was messing with the cops." The manufacturer of Apollo would have no problem killing a lowly dealer as a warning to other snitches.

Daire pivoted on his heel to face Kell. "What do you want to do with the body?"

In other words, was there any reason to call in the cops and alert Alexandra?

Kellach shook his head. The farther he kept her from the witch at the helm of this disaster, the better.

Pyro slapped his hand against his thigh. "I'm in charge of the club. It's my call."

Kell had forgotten the guy was even there. "What do you want done with the body?" he asked, not really giving a shit. There was no need to involve Alexandra in this shit storm. As a cop, she'd be truly pissed he hadn't notified the police of the murder.

Right now, all he needed was human cops in the way.

Pyro sniffed, his chest puffing out. "I'll have the prospects bury the body where it'll never be found. We can't have cops around here. There's a meeting in an hour with the board. I want to strike back at Bear."

Garrett and Logan weren't going anywhere near the crispy human. They'd both seen enough war and death. "I'll take care of the body," Kell said slowly.

"Suit yourself." Pyro turned and scrambled around the building again.

Kellach wiped his aching eyes. God, he was tired. Tired of humans, tired of Apollo, tired of duty. "Should we warn Bear?"

Daire snorted. "About what? That a human motorcycle group is gunning for him? I think he'd laugh his furry ass off."

Kell smiled and it felt grim. "Good point." He sighed and turned back to the corpse. "I'll take care of this."

Daire shook his head. "I'll bury him. You find your mate."

Kellach moved toward the body, unwilling to make his brother deal with it alone. "Let's get this done, and then I'll lock her down." Alexandra had no clue what kind of danger existed in the immortal world, and she wasn't immortal yet, so she could die.

The idea of losing her, now that he'd found her, hollowed out his chest. Determination, male and sure, filled that void. Oh, she wouldn't like it.

"I guess it's time she met the real enforcer," he muttered, reaching for a spike shoved through Spike's shoulder. Irony or coincidence? Not that it really mattered.

"Good luck with that." Daire slapped him on the back and reached for the next spike. The burned flesh made a squishy sound as he removed another spike. "They're enjoying this game way too much."

Kell nodded. "I know." There was a sense of joy in the kill, and to think that Alexandra was chasing the bastard responsible heated Kell's blood. Fear for his mate hurried his movements, while intent hardened his shoulders. He'd wanted to slowly introduce her to his world, to draw her in and show her how amazing her life with him could be.

Instead, he'd have to shut her down, because no way would she leave the case voluntarily. Even if she understood the true danger, she'd stay. But she just wasn't strong and tough enough for what was waiting out there.

He'd seen it in wars through the years. Wars and weapons humans couldn't even imagine.

The other night, when he'd cared for her, had been the best of his life. Something told him he was about to face the worst.

Adam loped around the garage with shovels in his hands.

Kell frowned. "When did you get here?"

"Five minutes ago. Pyro filled me in after he'd finished puking." Adam grimaced as Spike fell to the ground and shattered bones split in different directions. "I came to find you."

Shit. How hadn't Kell heard Adam arrive? "You on your bike?"

"No. I borrowed your truck." He paused, his dark brown eyes deepening. "I've been doing research and hacking into databases. Your cop went to the correctional facility holding her father this morning."

Kell's head snapped up. "What?"

"Aye. As you know, her father was a drug dealer, and from what I can gather, still is." Adam handed Daire a shovel, his gaze sympathetic.

"Apollo?" Kell ground out.

"There were several visits between Spike here and Alexandra's father, whose name is Parker. So I'd say, yes. Behind bars, Parker is still in the drug trade." Adam rubbed his chin while surveying the mess on the ground. "I don't think your woman knew that fact."

"Why would Alexandra go see him?" Kell shook his head. "Unless she knows now. She knows about the drugs, and she went to investigate. To meet him by herself."

The woman hadn't asked for his help. She hadn't even told him about her plan, much less of her father's probable connection to Apollo. Talk about lack of trust.

He exhaled the stench of burned testicles. "If her father is involved, maybe she's not in as much danger as I feared."

Adam shook his head. "Sorry, but I don't think so. Her father's a real bastard. Killed his own brother way back when, and according to police reports, dealt with rival dealers by slicing open their torsos."

Kell stilled and then slowly turned to face his brother. "Do you think he's a danger to his own daughters?"

Adam's eyes softened. "Sorry, Kell. I do think she's in danger from him, as well as from several other different directions. We'll keep her safe, though. I promise."

Kell nodded. It was his job to keep her safe, and it was time he stepped up. "I have something to take care of. Talk to you later." Without another glance at the body or his brothers, he stalked around the garage and toward his bike.

Chapter 26

Lex wiped rain off her forehead and walked into the hospital, stopping short as Masterson walked her way. His arm was in a sling, and his color a bit white, but the guy was walking easily.

Joy filled her to such a degree that tears pricked her eyes. Even though he was fine, a few inches down, and the bullet would've pierced his heart.

He grinned, tired and weary. "Detective Lex Monzelle, actually happy to see me."

She couldn't help moving toward him to reach up and plant one on his cheek.

He blushed. He actually blushed. "I knew you had the hots for me," he said, quickly recovering.

She chuckled, feeling loads lighter. "Everyone has the hots for you."

"It's a tough burden to bear." He lifted his head as Bundt strode in the door behind Lex.

"Where the fuck's your wheelchair?" Bundt snapped. "It's hospital policy for discharges."

Masterson snorted. "I don't need a fucking chair from just a freakin flesh wound. Just take me home."

Lex grinned. "Badass cop."

"Amen, sista." Masterson inched toward his partner. "Bernie's out of the coma and doing good. All four of his daughters are there right now. The doc kicked me out. He's kicking them all out soon."

Lex faltered. "I'll just pop in and say hi to everyone." She turned toward Bundt, who still frowned at his partner. "Are you heading to the station after you get tough guy here settled?"

"I am. Why?" Bundt asked.

"Would you run the name Trevan Demidov? I think it might be a lead on Apollo." She kept her voice bland. "I have a source. Maybe."

Bundt nodded. "Absolutely. I'll drop you a line after I get Masterson a milkshake and a comfy blanket." He finally stopped frowning. "You going to my place or yours?"

"Mine will be overrun with worried chicks trying for an engagement ring," Masterson lamented. "Can I stay at yours?"

Bundt rolled his eyes. He came from money, and rumor had it his penthouse beat any other in the area, hands down, but Lex had never visited him. "Fine, but I ain't waiting on you." He smiled at Lex. "Drop by and check on the dumbass later, if you'd like. It's time you came over for a game or something."

Her heart warmed. "I'm not bonding with you two morons just 'cause there was a shooting." She turned and headed toward the long hallway before tossing over her shoulder, "Of course, I've heard you have the biggest flat screen around, so I might come to watch the Seahawks."

"That's not all that's the biggest around," Bundt called back.

She burst out laughing, unable to help herself. When she reached Bernie's room, she crept quietly in and had to hold back a laugh at the resigned look on his weathered face. Four young women hovered around, tucking him in, handing him water, basically babying him.

She earned hugs all around, kissed Bernie on the cheek, and pretty much escaped. Yeah, she'd pay for that one.

For the first time in days, she felt that things would be all right. At least, professionally. Personally, who the hell knew? She liked Kellach . . . hell. She felt more for him than she had for anybody in her entire life.

But he was immortal, and an enforcer, and pretty much made up his own rules.

She was stubborn, set in her ways, and a fucking cop. Could they somehow meet in the middle and make it work?

Deep down, she wanted him. Needed him. But was that enough? Look at her mother. She'd loved a man who broke laws, killed, and emotionally beat the heck out of her. Love could blind a person.

Lex drove through her favorite hamburger joint. Eating on the road, she headed in to the station. About halfway there, her phone buzzed. "Hello," she muttered.

"It's Bundt. I found information."

She frowned and pulled over into a gas station. "That was quick."

"I'm good." He chuckled. "Okay, the search took two seconds. Demidov was easy to find. A financier in New York about a decade or so ago. A big wig money wise."

"Drugs?"

"Maybe, but no true connection. However, I'm sending you a series of society pictures that will definitely tweak your nipples."

"Jesus, Bundt." She took a drag of her milkshake. "Where is Demidov now?"

Keys clacked over the line. "Haven't found him yet. Apparently, he left New York and dropped out of sight. I have Interpol doing a search now. Call me later." Bundt clicked off.

Lex set aside her drink and waited for the images to roll across her phone. The first one heated her breath. Demidov was tall and sexy in a tuxedo, at some ball with glittering lights, blond hair slicked back, black eyes glimmering.

Next to him, smiling widely, was a stunning brunette wearing a sexy red sheath and an adoring smile.

Simone Brightston. Kellach's lawyer and cousin. Her hair was lighter, but it was her.

Son of a bitch.

Lex slammed her phone on the passenger seat and flipped a U-turn, ignoring the angry honks around her. Damn it. The Dunnes were up to their fire throwing, immortal, dickhead asses in this mess, and she was tired of not being clued in.

Her temper simmered, ready to roar, for the entire drive to the penthouse. Not giving a holy shit about assigned parking areas, she shot Bernie's piece of crap car into Daire's motorcycle slot and all but ran for the elevator.

Withholding information from an investigation . . . that's what she'd charge Kellach with. Maybe accessory after the fact. Or before the fact. Or just for being a complete Irish asshole.

There had to be law somewhere about Irish assholes.

Reaching his penthouse, she tried the knob, not surprised to find it unlocked. Why would an immortal badass care about locks? Or the truth?

She stomped inside to find him sitting calmly near the fireplace, lounging in an overstuffed chair. He wore faded jeans and a black, button-down shirt that probably cost more than her apartment. The badass boots on his feet matched the leather jacket tossed over the couch.

He looked up. "Detective."

Something about his voice gave her pause. For a tiny moment. Then she gathered her temper close and plastered on her cop expression. "You've been holding back, Dunne."

"Have I, now?" he asked silkily.

A shiver tickled down her spine. The tone, the very body language . . . was all new. "Yes. Just who exactly is your lawyer, Kellach?"

No expression crossed his face, yet a new tension began to overwhelm the atmosphere of the room. "Why do you ask?"

"Just answer the damn question. Who is Simone Brightston, and what's her connection to Apollo?" Family. Lex understood that. She'd do anything for her mother or sister, and anything for Bernie. Just how far would Kell go to protect Simone?

"Simone is my cousin, and she has no connection to a drug that harms witches. She is a witch." Kellach steepled his fingers beneath his chin, giving him a thoughtfully dangerous pose. "Why do you ask?"

Lex had been trained in interrogation as well as interviewing. Give enough to get more back. "I think she has more connections than you've let on. How long has she lived in Seattle?" Lex had Bundt doing a full workup on Simone while also tracking down Trevan Demidov.

Kellach inhaled slowly. "Simone moved to Seattle when we did— about three months ago as part of our investigation."

"Why Seattle? Why in the world is Apollo hitting the streets here?" She pressed on, already getting answers but needing more.

"Test ground." He shrugged. "Seriously. To see how the drug works on the street. It has also given them, whoever they are, time to weaponize it. There's a decent witch population here, as well, so they might be test subjects and not know it. Soon it'll be unleashed on my streets in Dublin. I have to stop it before then."

"Where did Simone live before Seattle?" Lex asked, wondering if he'd lie.

"Why?"

She lifted a shoulder. "Tell me the truth."

His expression didn't change, but he waited a moment before answering. Thinking it out? Figuring that she'd be able to track Simone anyway? "New York. For about twenty years, Simone lived in New York."

The truth. Interesting. Because he wanted to be truthful, or because that was a fact easily discovered? "Doing what?"

"Whatever she wanted to do." Kellach shrugged. "Many of the Nine members live around the world. They have conference calls and get together a few times during the year—just like most companies."

Time for a bombshell. "How long did she date Trevan Demidov?"

Kell stilled. Slowly, his head lifted.

She fought every instinct in her body not to step back or drop into a fighting stance. She held her ground and kept his gaze. "Kell?"

"What do you know about Demidov?" he rumbled.

She shrugged. "Not enough. Tell me more."

He slowly shook his head and stretched to his feet. "'Tis time you and I came to an understanding. You might not like it right now, or in the near future, but someday, I hope you'll see my reasoning."

Oh, she so didn't like where this was going. "I have no problem shooting you."

He sighed. "Alexandra, just hear me out. Apollo wasn't created as a money-making drug or for humans. It was tested on humans but was created to hurt witches, which soon will include you."

"I am not turning into a witch."

"Of course not. You can't change into another species, but you can become immortal as a mate, and as a witch mate, you'll be susceptible to the mineral."

Fair enough, and a concern for a different day. "Who is Demidov and what's Simone's connection to him?"

"Why?"

Stalemate. They faced each other, holding tight to facts, neither giving an inch.

"Tell me, or I'm out of here," she said.

He lifted one eyebrow. "I don't respond well to ultimatums. You might want to rethink your approach." The inherent threat in the words poked her temper.

"Fine." She settled her stance. "Either tell me about Demidov, or be prepared for another arrest. You're hindering my investigation."

"I'm about to hinder your freedom."

Damn wrong thing to say.

"I will arrest you."

"Try it."

She blinked.

Thus far, Kellach had been rather gentle with her, but his implacable expression hinted that the predator she'd sensed beneath his soft touch and kind treatment had tired of lurking.

"I do not appreciate your visiting your father in the correctional facility all alone."

"We're about to have one huge-assed fight," she murmured.

"I get that." Not one six-foot-five inch of him was backing down.

For the first time, she realized how much he'd held back. How much he'd tempered his nature last week. "Why do I get the feeling you're not who I thought?" she asked, curiosity filling her head, and warning filling her heart.

"I've showed you who I am, but I'd hoped to ease you into being the mate of an enforcer." His hands hung loosely at his sides, and his pose remained relaxed, but the power of him still overwhelmed the atmosphere of the room.

The very essence of Kellach sped up her breath and flushed heat through her. He not only ruled the atmosphere, he changed it with the sense of *male*. "What? There's a special handshake I haven't learned yet?"

"Funny." He didn't appear amused. "For my people, a mate can be either the greatest weakness or the greatest strength."

She'd never been either for anybody. "That's unfortunate."

"How so?" he asked, his voice lowering.

"Too much pressure on both parties," she said levelly.

He slipped his hands into his pockets. "Too much trust, you mean." He cocked his head to the side. "You've never trusted anybody that much, have you?"

"Sure."

"Not a man." No judgment, only thoughtful contemplation rode his tone.

The spit in her mouth dried up. "Sure, I have. I trust Bernie that much."

"Do you, now?" Kell trapped her gaze and kept it. "Did you tell him about me being a witch who'd mated you?"

"Of course not," she snapped.

"Why not? If you trusted him, you would've told him the entire story——opened yourself up to ridicule possibly." Kell's voice gentled.

"Bullshit. There's no need for Bernie to know about witches." Her breath heated on the end at the direct hit, but she'd never admit it. Not to Kell. Not even to herself, if she could avoid it.

"I'd like for you to be my strength, Alexandra." His eyes glittered with an expression she couldn't identify but wasn't sure she liked.

"Not for me," she said slowly, her lungs compressing.

"Too late. If anything happened to you, my heart would be ripped out." He lifted one muscled shoulder. "So I can't let anything happen to you, now can I?"

Pleasure burst through her at the declaration—followed by unease. "I can protect myself, but thank you for the hint that you were about to turn into a Neanderthal. I'm glad we had this discussion." She tried to keep sarcasm at bay and failed miserably.

"I do appreciate that we're on the same wavelength." Sarcasm from Kell still seemed classy. "So I'm going to ask you, very nicely, if you wouldn't mind taking a leave of absence and visiting my home in Dublin for a short time."

"No."

"You can take your mother and sister with you, all expenses paid, and have a lovely vacation," he continued.

"No."

"That way, I can take care of the drug issue here and then join you in my homeland, which I truly believe you'll enjoy." His tone remained level, but he drew his hands free of the pockets.

"No."

"You're in danger here, Alexandra, and it's my fault. You're in danger because you're my mate, and you're in danger from a witch, so this is my responsibility, and I have to take action." His words, no longer warm and calm, emerged clipped.

"No." She ignored his rapidly approaching anger and focused. "Why do you think I'm in danger?"

Kell's gaze remained steady. "Whoever's behind Apollo will discover, at some point, that you're mine. You will be in danger at that point."

She'd ignore the archaic language for the moment. "Good. Let them try to come and get me."

"That's not how I work. I'm sorry."

"Don't be sorry—be pissed." Her blood pumped faster with the thrill of a good hunt. "We can take them down. Bad guys are bad guys regardless of the location or, ah, species."

"My duty is to you and to the Coven Nine. If you're in danger, my focus is split. So you're going to Ireland, Alexandra."

She smiled. "No, I'm not." It wasn't the time to arrest him, and frankly, if they fought hand-to-hand, she'd lose. "I'm going to find out everything about Simone and Trevan Demidov, but I'd rather you just told me the truth."

"I'd rather you told me why."

"According to my sources, Demidov is somebody I need to investigate regarding Apollo. I did and found his connection to your cousin . . . interesting." She waited for his response.

"Your sources? You mean, your father?"

She blinked. It figured Kell would have decent sources of his own. "Yes."

"Demidov is dead." Kellach rubbed a hand through his dark hair. "He and Simone dated, he kidnapped her, and he ultimately died for it. Not a good source."

"There's no record of his death." At least, none she'd found so far.

"My friend ripped off his head, so I can promise you, Demidov isn't around any longer." A veil dropped over Kell's eyes.

She'd check relatives of Demidov. The lead was a good one, or her father wouldn't have tempted her with it. "Thanks for the info. I'll be in touch." She turned to go.

That quickly, without making a sound, Kellach blocked the door in front of her. "You're not going anywhere, Alexandra."

Chapter 27

She paused, her breath catching at his speed. "How did you do that?"

"I moved quickly." He leaned back against the door, the pose casual, the expression he wore anything but.

Close to him, her skin heated, the brand on her hip burned, and arousal danced through her body. She swallowed. "Get out of my way."

"No." His voice roughened.

She planted one hand on his chest—hard. "I'm not some damsel in distress you hide in a country far away. I'm a cop, and a damn good one. Now get the hell out of my way so I can go do my job."

Slowly, deliberately, he lifted his arm and checked his watch. "You're off the clock, Detective."

She shoved, and he didn't move an inch. "I'm trying to be reasonable here, I really am, but if you don't move, I'm arresting you."

So he moved.

One second, she stood, hand on his chest. The next, she found her back against the door, her ass in his hands, and her legs straddling his hips. It should've pissed her off, but shocked humor bubbled through her, and she threw back her head to laugh. "God, you do move fast," she gasped.

"Don't be cute." He leaned in, his mouth an inch away, his gaze keeping hers. "I can't fight *cute* right now."

In her entire life, nobody had ever called her cute. She blinked. "I want to trust you. So badly, I want to trust you." The words were ripped from deep within her, and she couldn't bite them back. Vulnerability swamped her, but she couldn't move. Couldn't retreat and regroup.

He exhaled, his fingers tightening on her butt. "I like all of you,

Alexandra, but this sweetness nearly drops me to my knees." His mouth brushed hers. "It's just for me, isn't it?"

She nodded, seeing no reason to lie. "Don't ask me to be somebody I'm not. Please."

His body shuddered, and he studied her, those deep eyes delving into everything she was. Finally, he lifted his head. "No running and hiding, then."

"No." She knew what it cost him, what a guy like him had to fight within himself not to shove her into a safe cocoon while he slayed dragons. An enforcer for centuries? Yeah, she got that. "We can fight together, though."

"Absolutely not."

She lifted her head so quickly, she knocked into the door. "What?"

"No fighting. Not together, and not at all." He kept her in place. "You can do your job as a cop, with humans. But witches? They're mine and you stay clear."

Criminals were criminals, as far as she was concerned. "I protect Seattle."

"From human criminals. This is a compromise, and you'd better take it while it's offered."

That quickly, desire slid to anger. "The second I think you're not a moron, the very moment I think we're on the same page, you fuck it up." She struggled against him, shoving him, trying to push back against the door enough to get some leverage. "Let me go."

"Never."

She folded her hand into a fist and punched him in the throat.

He didn't blink.

Awareness zapped through her, and she opened her mouth, but no sound emerged.

A knock behind the door shocked her.

"Kell? Let me in. We have a problem," a female voice barked.

Kellach gave Lex a warning glance, turned and set her on her feet before opening the door.

Simone swept in, high-heeled black boots clicking on the marble tiles. Her glorious hair had been piled high on her head in a casual clasp. "You're not gonna—" She stopped cold. "Well, hello, Detective."

Kell stepped between them. "Now isn't a good time. Could we catch up a little later, Simone?"

Lex elbowed him and stepped to the side. "Actually, I was hoping you'd tell me how you knew Trevan Demidov and where he is today."

Simone paled. Her chin lifted. Old wounds glimmered in her eyes, but she met Alexandra's gaze evenly. "For a brief time, Trevan was my lover. Then he kidnapped me and my cousin, as well as Cara Kayrs, Garrett's mum. You've met him, right?"

Lex nodded and ignored the angry tension rolling off Kellach. "Yes."

Simone sniffed, her gaze turning cold. "A vampire killed Trevan, and he's been dead and not missed for decades." She moved toward Lex, her grace somehow threatening. "Why do you ask?"

"Rumor has it he might have something to do with Apollo." Lex held her ground, although she could appreciate how someone might want to stay wary around Simone. The woman promised death in an oddly sensual way. However, hurt glimmered in her eyes.

"Considering he lost his head, I doubt he's behind the current problem." Simone stopped an inch from Lex.

Kellach wrapped a hand around Simone's arm and tugged her toward the open door. "If you don't mind, I'd like a word with my mate."

Lex jumped into gear to follow. "Actually, I'll walk Simone out."

Kellach turned and planted a hand on her chest, moving her back two feet. "I don't think so."

Simone sauntered past him and slammed the door in her wake. The echo vibrated through the suddenly too quiet apartment.

Lex licked her lips and took a discreet step backward.

Kell's hand dropped, and anger swirled in his eyes. "That wasn't necessary."

Sure, it was. "If you'd told me the whole truth, I wouldn't have needed to ask her."

"Trevan nearly devastated Simone, and you just brought the nightmare back." Kell advanced on her, every step a threat. "'Twas unnecessary and cruel, and you won't behave such a way in my flat again."

Her head snapped up. "Then get the hell out of my way, and I'll leave."

"You're not going anywhere." He continued to advance, a pissed-off male.

She snapped. Anger rushed through her, dark in intensity. Out of nowhere, fire crackled on her skin, and she let the fury flow.

He stopped moving and lifted an eyebrow. "You sure you want to play?"

For answer, she closed her hand into a fist and concentrated on creating fire. Heat flared along her palm. Opening her fingers, she allowed a ball to morph into life, just as he'd taught her.

"One warning, Alexandra," he said, his focus on her hand.

Unnecessary. Pivoting, she turned and threw the fire with every ounce of strength she could summon.

The weapon pummeled into the door, spreading out and leaving a scorched circle.

"Feel better?" Kell asked, arrogance cutting lines into his handsome face.

Oh, hell no. She sucked deep and formed another ball of fire. Her aim would be better this time. Concentrating, she drew back and threw for center mass.

The fire reached him, and he captured the ball, rubbing the flame out with his fingers, his gaze remaining on her.

Her breath caught. He held out his palm and formed a glowing, flickering, green ball of flames. Lifting it to his mouth, he blew. The mass gently, slowly, cascaded over oxygen molecules toward her.

She leaned back against the wall, ready to duck.

The flames widened, spreading head to toe, and slid into her.

She cried out, panic shutting her eyes.

The smell of smoke filled her nose, and heat licked her skin. Nothing hurt. Slowly, she opened her eyes and then gasped. Her clothing lay in a smoldering heap at her feet.

Losing any semblance of control, she launched herself at him, hitting him in the gut and plowing them both into the far wall. An original oil of Baffin Cliffs tumbled down, the frame cracking in two.

Kellach encircled her and twisted, rolling her under him while kicking the painting toward the kitchen.

She punched up, furious, the hard tiles chilling her bare ass. "You basta——"

His mouth on hers, hard and angry, shoved the words back down her throat. He kissed her deep, holding her in place, his tongue taming hers. Desire ripped through her with rough claws, awakening her every nerve.

Still, she struggled against him, kissing him back, her hands shoving at his chest, burning his shirt into ragged shreds of silk that fell to the floor.

"Alexandra," he warned against her mouth.

She bit his lip.

His thumb brushed her clit, and heat flared between her legs, flames licking her labia.

She cried out, arching into his hand, even while trying to hold still. The flames, under his control, kissed her thighs. She spread her legs to keep from getting burned, even as need pounded into her sex.

His jeans heated, flashed, and disappeared, leaving him nude.

He fingered her slit.

"No," she gasped, forcing herself to stop moving.

"Yes," he murmured against her lips, his tongue sliding inside just as his finger, dancing with barely-tamed fire, slipped inside her.

Liquid heat filled her with unbearable pleasure. She cried out, her eyes closing. Fear heightened the already out of control desire, and she stopped breathing, her body rioting. He heated her internally to a craving too intense to quench.

It wasn't possible. His ability to harness fire with such accuracy—enough to lick inside her but not damage. The burn, though. God, the burn.

Hot spasms relentlessly took her, crashing through her, throwing her into a climax so intense she screamed his name. The second she wound down, he increased the heat, shoving her high again to ride the edge between pleasure and pain.

"Kellach," she moaned, the warmth from his skin heating hers. His mouth, his hands, his chest . . . all warmed impossibly with the fingers controlling fire inside her.

He removed his fingers and covered her, his cock shoving inside her with one merciless stroke.

Pain and pleasure melded into a sensation beyond both. She expelled a ragged gasp of raw need, any semblance of sanity shattering.

"Alexandra." Both heated hands cupped her face, his fingers threading through her hair. He gave no quarter, gripping her scalp, holding her in place.

Vibrations shook her thighs as they quaked around his hips. His muscles bunched and knotted along his shoulders, and she dug in her fingers, flames dancing between them. There was no way to counter this.

He slid out, all heat and sparks, and powered back into her. With a fierce growl, he twisted one hand to hold her in place and reached down to grab her ass with the other, brushing her brand on the way.

Electricity zinged from the touch, and she moaned.

He lifted her, pounding into her, thrusting hard enough to shake her breasts. The slap of flesh against flesh filled the air, and tension expanded inside her, uncoiling along the way. She blinked, trying to focus. Flames morphed down his back, lighting the hallway. Carnal and savage, his expression hardened into something so masculine and beautiful, he stole her breath.

He pummeled so hard inside her, so far, flames licking the way, she truly lost where she ended and he began. Then there was nothing but climbing, so high and fast, so dangerously free.

A hard thrust, scalding her clit, threw her spiraling over the edge. She cried out, flattening her palms against his chest, riding the waves of fire. They consumed her, wringing every ounce of pleasure from her.

Finally, her legs went boneless and her mind quieted. He stiffened against her, held tight, and came with a hard shudder.

The only sound he made was the hoarse whisper of her name against her neck. "Alexandra." And one more word. *"Mine."*

Chapter 28

Kellach grasped two cups of coffee, his bare feet padding the floor toward the bedroom. Dawn streaked outside in pretty patterns of pink and gold. He'd yanked on an old pair of jeans just in case Simone reappeared.

His woman slept soundlessly in his big bed, her face in a pillow, her arm flung across the mattress. She looked fragile in one of his T-shirts. The blankets had been shoved down, revealing the top of her exquisite ass. If he moved just right, he could make out the Celtic Knot on her hip. His brand.

Satisfaction rumbled through him.

Even so, unease had him drawing in a deep breath. The sex, along with their fire, had been fucking amazing, but they hadn't solved a damn thing. "Alexandra."

She turned around, her eyes already open. "Why do you always use my full name?" Her gaze landed on the coffee cups, and he could swear, she purred. She pushed herself up to sit.

He handed her a cup, enjoying her soft murmur of appreciation when she scented the brew. A pretty pink climbed into her face from the steam. "I like you on my tongue. All of you."

She blinked and then took a big swallow. "The things you say."

"All true." She took another drink and then stopped cold, her eyes widening. "Oh, God. Did I do that?"

He glanced down at the perfect burn marks of her hands on his chest. "Aye."

She gasped. "I'm so sorry. I didn't know——"

He grinned. "Don't worry. Fire takes time to learn to control, and it's amazing you can create so much already." Her hangdog expression hit him hard, so he quickly sent healing cells to the burns. "I liked wearing your mark, but I'll heal the skin."

She sat back and watched, her eyes widening as the burns slowly disappeared. "That's quite a talent."

"You'll have it at some point." But there was no need to rush fire. "While I enjoyed teaching you about fire"—and as to his strength— "we failed to reach an agreement last night."

She sipped her coffee, watching over the rim. "Well, I do concede that perhaps I don't have the control over fire that you do. That other witches may have."

He loved, fucking loved, her sense of fairness.

Why the hell hadn't he taken that approach with her? Oh yeah. He'd been pissed off about her attitude and hurting Simone's feelings. He had to admit, the little lesson in fire had been well worth the anger.

He raised an eyebrow. "And?"

She shrugged. "I guess I can deal with the human scumbags, and you can handle the immortal scumbags."

He smiled, the pressure in his chest finally releasing.

"That is, until I'm immortal. Then all scumbags are free game." She took another drink of coffee.

He didn't exactly agree, but since he had time to deal with that situation, he took the out and nodded. "For now, let's just keep to our own species. Once you're immortal, we'll fight about it." Well, it was fair to give her warning.

She grinned, all imp. "I do like how you fight."

He shook his head. "Fire can keep you from orgasm as easily as licking you to it."

Her eyelids flipped all the way open. "Oh, you wouldn't."

"I certainly would." He set a knee on the bed and sat. "Fair warning."

She lifted an eyebrow. "At some point, I'll be able to control fire as well as you do. So fair warning right back."

Perhaps. Perhaps not. "I'm sure you'll give it your best shot." As she did everything else. Pride filled him, and he let her see it. "I'm pleased with you, Alexandra."

She sipped again. "Does that mean you like me, like me?" Her grin was all sauce.

"Yes." He leaned over and tasted the coffee off her lips. Much better than from his cup. "And you?"

She inhaled, her eyes darkening in a vulnerability that compressed his lungs. "I like you, too." She blew out air. "I trust you, Kellach Dunne." Then she wiggled, a frown marring her perfect lips.

Her trust, probably never given before, cut right into his chest and burrowed deep. "I'm keeping you." The other words, the ones she wasn't quite ready to hear, those would come later. For now, all he could do was show her trust and love . . . and she'd learn to accept both.

His phone buzzed, and he glanced around the room. A quick search found it beneath some socks on the dresser, and he answered the call. "Simone."

Alexandra winced.

Simone cleared her throat over the line. "I'd come talk to you in person, but you sent out enough vibrations last night, I fear your apartment is one big scorched disaster."

He chuckled. "I think the apartment is fine. You may come over."

"No thanks. I've been researching all night, and I think your mate may be on to something."

His mate. Just the words, the acknowledgment of Alexandra as his, shot a masculine satisfaction through him. "Simone, forget about Demidov. The guy was a jackass, and he's dead. Gone and buried."

"He had so many women through the years, the fucking prick, and I think one bore him a kid."

Kell frowned. "He wasn't mated."

"No, but . . . although rare in witches . . . there have been children created without the mating bond." Simone clacked keys in the background. "I've found records from the turn of the century. There may be a child out there."

Kell lifted his head, his thoughts swimming. "If the kid was close to Demidov, he may want revenge for his father's death. Especially against the Nine."

"He or she. Could be a woman." Simone sighed. "Women like revenge just as much as you men, if not more."

"Good point. Keep working that angle and report to Daire." Kell kept his eyes on his mate, wondering if there was a way to get to her father in prison for some more answers.

Simone huffed. "I don't work or take orders from you, Kellach Gideon Dunne." She ended the call.

Alexandra scrunched her nose. "Gideon?"

He sighed. Damn Simone and her loud voice. "My middle name. My cousins all use it when they're irritated with me." Unfortunately, that happened far more than he liked.

"Your cousin is, rather, tough."

Kell smiled. "You remind me of each other."

Alexandra took another sip of her coffee. "Really?"

"Yes. Strong and somewhat sassy with deep loyalty and hidden sweetness." Life had created them both as survivors, but they'd die for those they loved.

"If you say so." Alexandra set her cup on the end table and slid from the bed. "I need to get ready for work."

"What's on the agenda today?" Kell asked, wondering if there was time for some fun in the shower.

She swallowed. "My father's parole hearing is today, and I am scheduled to testify." Standing in her bare feet with only one of his big T-shirts covering her, she appeared young and fragile.

Kell fought the urge to put her back in the luxurious sheets. "What's your testimony?"

She sighed. "He said if I help him get parole, he'll give me all the info on Apollo from the top down."

"Do you trust him?"

"No." Regret shimmered in her eyes, and she twisted the hem of Kell's shirt near her thighs. "I don't want him out or anywhere near my mother."

"I'll keep your mother safe." The promise escaped Kell before he could find a gentler way to make the vow.

Alexandra studied him. "If anything ever happens to me, will you promise to protect her as well as my sister?"

He nodded, touched way out of proportion to the request. "You have my word."

"Thank you."

He cleared his throat. "Did your father ever hurt you or your sister?"

She shrugged. "No. He didn't much care for us, but he didn't hit us. Although he was mean as hell to my mother." Alexandra frowned. "How did you know about him?"

"His name came up as a known associate of Spike Evertol, and we investigated him," Kell said.

"Oh."

"Speaking of your life." Kell strode over to the other end table and opened the drawer to tug out the manila envelope. He tossed it to Alexandra.

She caught it, her hands slapping together. "What's this?"

"Background on you. Considering the king gave it to me, it's probably everything." Kell glanced around for his watch.

"It's not opened."

His gaze landed on her. "No. I figured I'd rather learn everything you want me to hear from you and not the king. The envelope is yours."

She eyed him, a small smile playing with her lips. "That's sweet."

He coughed out a laugh. "Nobody has ever called me sweet."

"Then they don't know you." She skirted the bed, all long legs and smooth skin, and stretched up on her toes to kiss his chin. "Thank you."

Denying his curiosity had been fucking worth it to feel that one touch. "You're welcome." He allowed himself a moment of peace to enjoy her nearness before turning back to business. "Is there any way I can accompany you to the parole hearing today?"

Hope flared in her eyes only to be quickly squelched. "No. As long as you're undercover, we can't be seen together, or I'll lose my job. Plus, you need Titans of Fire to believe you're one of them, right?"

"Right." He rubbed his eyes. "So far, we haven't gotten Pyro to admit his connection to Apollo. I don't think he's high enough on the food chain to know the manufacturer, but he can get us a lot closer."

"What'll make him trust you?" she mused.

"Giving him guns, probably." Kellach held up a hand. "That was the deal. We'd supply guns, and he'd supply Apollo. The trade is supposed to happen tomorrow."

She shook her head. "Tell me you don't have guns."

He pressed his lips together.

"Kellach." She slapped her forehead. "You're kidding me."

"We have the guns, and if we trade, we'll get them back." He shrugged. "We'll do what is necessary to trace the drug to its manufacturer. You know that."

She stretched her neck. "I have to follow rules and the law."

"As do I. They're just different rules and different laws." Someday, she'd see the vastness of the world and realize that humans were only one species with specific laws. The immortal ones had lasted much longer. "For now, you follow yours and I'll follow mine."

She pressed her hands against her hips. "If our laws collide?"

He grinned. "We'll duke it out again."

"Whatever." She stomped toward the shower. "I need to stop by my place for more clothes."

He shoved open a walk-in closet. "I had Simone purchase a full wardrobe for you, considering I keep burning up your clothing."

Alexandra peeked into the spacious room with the abundance of clothes and accessories. "You can't buy me clothing."

"I just did."

She turned, her gaze thoughtful. "Simone seriously went shopping for me?"

Kell snorted. "Well, she had one of her personal shoppers go shopping for you. Take what you want and give the rest to charity." Yeah, he liked providing for Alexandra.

She fingered a teal silk shirt almost with longing. "I'll pay you back."

He tapped her chin. "How about I just burn them off you later?"

A flush covered her pale skin, but she kept glancing around. "So you're loaded, huh?"

"Aye." Most women would be pleased by that fact, but he'd bet his last quid Alexandra wouldn't react like most women.

"Humph."

He tugged her from the closet and toward the shower. "You do no' like money?"

"I do no' like what people will do to keep money." She mimicked his brogue perfectly.

Hmmm. He'd have to change her mind about money because he planned to spend a pile of it on her, cherishing her in a way her father had failed to do for so many years.

For now, he needed to get her into the shower to start the day off right.

Chapter 29

Lex sat on the hard metal chair and tried not to shiver in the freezing environment. She was alone in the waiting room at the prison, waiting to testify at the parole hearing. A guard behind a bulletproof glass window paid her no heed.

The outside door opened, and her heart warmed as her younger sister marched in. "Tori."

Her sister hustled toward her, clipping high-heeled boots across the concrete, and tugged her from the chair for a floral scented hug. "I've missed you."

Lex hugged back, grateful beyond words that her sister had come. "I thought you were going to tour Oregon after California." She leaned back to study her wild child of a sister. Long, curly blond hair streaked with purple cascaded down Tori's back. Her makeup shimmered, and her clothes, a green T-shirt and ripped jeans, somehow sparkled.

Her eyes were a darker blue than Lex's. "We finished the tour, and I knew I needed to be here." Bangles, tons and tons of them, clanged on her left wrist. "You look different."

Yeah. She'd mated a witch, was becoming immortal, and had enjoyed unbelievable sex recently. "We'll talk later."

"Damn straight." Tori rubbed one of Lex's shirtsleeves. "Is this real silk?"

From the corner of her mouth, Lex said, "Later," once more.

Tori nodded and glanced around the dingy room. "Are you ready for this?"

"No. You?"

"Never." Tori sighed. "I stopped by to see Mom before coming here. She wants the bastard to come home."

"I know." Lex shook her head. "It's so sad."

Tori tucked an arm through Lex's. "How's the money holding up?"

"Great," Lex said.

"I'd call you a liar except for that shirt and those amazing boots. You on the take, sis?" Tori chortled.

"No. They were a gift." Lex kept her gaze on the guy behind the glass.

"From whom?" Tori reached down to rub the butter-soft leather. "A man?"

Lex smacked her hand. "What part of *later* don't you understand? For now, the money is fine." Her sister had sold her car and sent most of her last couple paychecks to help out, and unfortunately, she didn't make much.

"Can I stay with you?" Tori asked.

"Of course."

"Good. It's either that or credit, and I'm running low." she sighed.

Lex nodded. "Amen, sister."

A buzz sounded, and the guard gestured them toward the door and ensuing metal detector. Lex led the way, her boots clipping, her shoulders back, her badge perched at her waist.

She walked into the hearing room where five parole officers sat behind a wide wooden table. Their father sat over at a far box, his hands cuffed to the table in front of him.

"There are my girls," he said, smiling as if truly proud to see them.

Tori tripped and Lex slipped an arm through her sister's to help balance her. Trembles quivered through Tori's entire body, and Lex tightened her hold, trying to give her sister strength.

"Come sit down," Lex said, leading Tori to the seats on the other side of the table. "It'll be okay," she whispered.

Tori didn't answer but sat down, her vibrancy dimming.

The head of the board, Miles Stanton, made some announcements and called for testimony. First, their father testified as to how he'd messed up but had found himself in prison and had changed. He stated he wanted nothing more than to get to know his girls again, and he would spend the rest of his life making things up to them.

Miles Stanton, about fifty with graying hair and a bushy beard, nodded at Tori. "The prisoner's daughter, Tori Monzelle, will speak first."

Tori cleared her throat. "I, ah, think parole is a bad idea," she whispered.

Their father clanked his chains. "Tori, baby. Please——"

Stanton shushed him. "Continue, Miss Monzelle."

Lex kept her back straight and took Tori's hand under the table.

Tori gripped her so tightly it hurt. "My father was cruel to my mother, and he sold drugs to our friends, killing one of them. Our life has been a lot better with him out of it." Her voice thickened with tears and shook.

Stanton nodded and focused on Lex. "Alexandra Monzelle will testify next."

Lex kept his gaze. "I'm a detective with the Seattle Police Department, and I know a life-long criminal when I see one. I visited my father a few days ago, and after that conversation, I fully believe he's still involved in the drug trade in Seattle."

Stanton's eyebrows rose. "Do you have any proof?"

"Just our conversation, which is good enough for me." Lex leaned toward the table and eyed each board member in turn. "Parker Monzelle is a bad man who has killed many people. If you let him out, he'll kill more. Keep him here."

A few more people testified, including the warden, who said Parker had been a model prisoner. The testimony floated around Lex, and she held still, her mind fuzzing, until several letters from her mother were read, all begging for Parker to be released.

Nausea filled Lex's stomach as they were read.

Finally, the Board said a decision would be made within the week.

Lex led Tori from the building, feeling nearly suffocated by the concrete and sense of desperation.

Once outside in the chilly air, she looked around for Bernie's borrowed car. A shiny, new, badass black Chevy truck sat in its place. She rolled her eyes and hustled to the truck, opening the passenger side door and jumping in while gesturing for her sister to get in back.

She turned on Kellach, who sat in the driver's seat. "I told you not to come."

He smiled. "I'm not letting you deal with shit like this on your own, Alexandra. Get yourself accustomed to that fact now." He turned and held out a hand. "You must be Victoria."

"I really must be," Tori said, her gaze cutting to Lex. "Uh—"

"I'm Kellach Dunne, of the Dublin Dunnes, and I intend to marry your sister as soon as she realizes I'm in it for the long haul, and I mean the very long haul." He finished shaking hands and turned to start the engine.

Tori sat back. "Boy, do we have some catching up to do," she said slowly to her sister.

Heat filled Lex's face. Her heart thumped hard. He'd said *marry*. Out loud and to her sister. Hell, they were mated, but was she ready to get married? Not that he'd asked. He'd just stated a fact, as if she'd go right along with it and him. At the moment, she couldn't get too pissed about that. Later maybe.

She struggled to contain any emotion. "We'll discuss this later," she murmured to Kellach.

Tori leaned over the back of the seat, her gaze taking in all that was Kell. "You seem like a take charge kind of guy."

He grinned. "I am, but I'm tempering my natural inclinations in a very difficult attempt to woo your sister."

Woo? He actually said *woo*. Lex shook her head. "Put on your seatbelt, Victoria." If her sister was nicely contained farther back, perhaps the conversation would mercifully end.

Tori ignored her, of course. "Usually Lexi goes for dumb jocks she can push around and then dump without a second glance. You don't seem dumb or easily manipulated."

"Thank you," Kell said.

"She has daddy issues, you know," Tori said.

Lex groaned and beat her head against the seat.

"I am aware," Kell agreed, and then, thankfully, turned the full power of his gaze on Tori. "What about you?"

Tori pursed her lips. "Not the same. I mean, Lex chooses poorly and then dumps, while I choose wisely, have some fun, and then move on without getting serious."

Kell lifted an eyebrow. "Sounds like the same animal with different coping mechanisms."

Absolute delight lifted Tori's eyebrows. "Exactly." She reached forward and patted Kell's arm. "I like you."

"I like you, too." He turned back to the road ahead of them.

Lex groaned. "I am in hell."

Tori chuckled. "You don't have a brother or two, do you?"

Kell nodded. "I have two brothers."

"Do they look as good as you?" Tori asked.

"Victoria," Lex snapped. "Knock it off."

"Well, do they?" Tori pressed.

Kell frowned. "Well, we do share similar attributes, but I'd say I'm the fun one. They're both fierce and serious. I'd think twice, because easy and fun don't describe either of my brothers."

"Pity." Tori finally sat back. "Even so, if they look like you, I might make an exception."

And turn into a witch mate? Lex rolled her eyes. "You'd definitely get more than you'd bargained for." She turned toward Kell, the most intense, protective, and possessive man she'd ever met. "And you are not the fun one. I don't know either of your brothers well, but you can't be the fun one."

Kell shot her a look, and she shrugged.

Finally, he pulled up in front of her mother's convalescent home, where another badass on a bike sat next to Kell's waiting Harley. "I thought you might want to see your mother." Kell cut the engine and tossed her the keys. "The truck is yours."

Victoria gaped out the back window. "Tell me that's a brother."

Kellach stretched from the truck and waited until the women had joined him before introducing his brother, Adam. Lex studied him. While Kell was a fast burn, and Daire a smoldering one, this guy? Carefully banked with a hint of turmoil.

Dark eyes, short dark hair, and a jaw angled a bit more than Kell's. Intelligence and something dangerous lurked in his eyes, but his smile was genuine and his hand gentle as they shook. "It's a pleasure," he rumbled.

Tori quite wisely shook his hand and backed away. Quickly.

Smart girl.

Lex turned toward Kell. "I don't need your truck."

"Isn't mine. Is yours." He straddled his bike, and a mini-orgasm shook her womb. He aimed his next comment at Tori. "Your sister is staying at my penthouse, and there's a nice guest suite that's all yours." He rattled off the address. "I'll expect you there tonight, Alexandra."

The Dunne boys took off.

The women watched them leave.

"You might've called me with the news you were dating sex on a stick there," Tori muttered.

Lex shook her head. "He's too much."

"I'd say, he's just enough." Tori slipped her arm through Lex's. "Can't wait to see the penthouse."

"Oh, we're not staying there," Lex said firmly.

Tori bit her lip. "You know? Something tells me we will be staying there."

"Humph." Lex led her sister through the home to their mother's room, and the delight on Jennie's face upon seeing her girls brightened the entire day.

They visited for a while, before Jennie frowned. "Why haven't you brought me all my mail, Lexi?"

Lexi frowned. When she'd been forced from her original apartment and had moved Jennie to the home, she'd opened up a post office box until they found a better place. She'd forgotten the mail. "I'm sorry, I forgot." Her instincts hummed. "Why?"

"Because your father just called and asked about a letter he'd sent." Jennie frowned, her eyes clouding. "Will you bring it to me?"

Lex shared a look with Tori. "Mom, we've talked about this."

"Alexandra, this is my choice, and I want my mail." Her mom's lips firmed.

"Fine." Lex shook her head and then an idea formed. Her father wasn't supposed to contact her mother, and if he had, Lex could report the violation to the parole board. Excellent. She smiled. "I'll get the mail today."

Jennie smiled and patted her hand. "You're a good girl, Lex."

Tori rolled her eyes.

Adam headed off to check on the techs analyzing Apollo and how to counter the darts, while Kell drove on to meet Simone at the cabin. He sensed the vibrations of fury before he cut the engine of his Harley. Tension weighed down the atmosphere around the comfortable cabin.

He took a deep breath. Damn it.

Disembarking, he strode toward the door and shoved it open to find Simone facing off with the demon.

Nicholaj Veis had blond hair and the true black eyes of a purebred demon, giving him a contrasting look of hard angles. Tall and broad, the warrior had fought for more centuries than most demons lived, and he'd once, very long ago, broken Simone's heart.

Or perhaps she'd broken his.

Either way, when the two managed to inhabit the same space, the oxygen disappeared and immortals anywhere close by tensed.

Kell's shoulders tensed so hard, rocks formed.

In contrast, in the small kitchenette, Garrett and Logan wolfed down what appeared to be ham sandwiches.

"Veis?" Kell strode inside, looking for burn marks or scalded wood. None so far. "What the hell are you doing in Seattle?"

"Checking up on me," Logan said around a huge bite of sandwich. He was brother to the demon leader, and Nick his key advisor.

Made sense.

Nick rolled his eyes. "I'm here because Daire requested demon assistance in dealing with Apollo. Checking up on numbnuts here is just a bonus." The mangled vocal chords lowered his tone to a raspy rumble.

Logan grinned. "We're good."

Garrett nodded. "Aunt Simone is taking good care of us."

Simone rolled her eyes. "I am not your aunt, for the zillionth time. My cousin, one I barely like, mated your uncle. That does not make us related."

Kell sighed. Truth be told, Simone adored her cousins and only brought out this bitchy side when Nick was anywhere near. "Is the meeting over?"

"No," Logan added. "Aunt Simone would like it to be, however."

Simone hissed, and steam rose around her. "I'm not even distantly related to you, demon, so stop calling me *aunt*."

Logan grinned again.

"You're playing with fire, buddy," Kell muttered.

Literally. Simone could throw fire better than he could, and she'd have no trouble launching the young demon through a cabin wall with plasma.

"What do you want, Veis?" Kell asked.

"Simone asked for help regarding Trevan Demidov, and I'm here to offer it." Veis drew an envelope from his back pocket.

Simone pressed her hands against her hips, covered by a pencil thin skirt. "I requested help from the king, not you."

Veis turned his focus on her. "The king sent me," he said evenly.

Kell strode forward and took the envelope, yanking free a picture of a young man with dark eyes and brown hair. His bone structure was similar to Trevan's, but his build was bulkier and his coloring not as dark. "So Trevan did have a kid."

"Yes," Veis said. "He's off the radar now, but we're doing a full background as we speak. Between the vampire, demon, and witch nations, we should know what his favorite color is by sundown tonight."

Simone sniffed. "Good. Then your job here is done."

Veis smiled. On a demon, it was more of a warning. "I'm staying in town, little bunny."

Little Bunny? Did the guy want a quick death and right now? Kell didn't know what to say.

Logan and Garrett shared a fast panicked look. As one, they shoved away from the table and all but ran for the door.

"We have to get back to Fire. Pyro is up in arms and wants to rain hell down on the Grizzlies," Garrett said. "If it really looks like he's going to make a move, I'll give you a call."

The boys disappeared.

Smart little bastards. Kell studied his feet, buying time while he thought. Did he really want to get involved? He came to a quick decision and sighed. Simone was family as well as being a member of the Nine, and he couldn't leave her with an irritated demon. "Thank you for this information, Nick. As soon as you hear more, please share. For now, I'm happy to walk you out."

Nick shot him a look. "I'm not quite finished with your cousin."

The double entendre shot a splash of color to Simone's face, turning her even more beautiful. "Take your leave, Kellach. I can handle a lowly demon."

Kell tensed for a fight. *Jesus.* Calling Nicholaj Veis a lowly demon was like calling Daire a puppy.

Instead of taking offense, Nick smiled. Slow and sure . . . and with a shitload of confidence he'd probably earned through the centuries. He said smoothly, "Yes, why don't you handle me, Simone?"

God. The two should just get a hotel room and fuck it out of their systems. Temper tickled the base of Kell's neck, and he had to squelch the urge to start throwing fire at everybody.

A minute stretched into half an hour where Simone sniped, Nick flirted, and Kell held himself back from killing them both.

His phone buzzed finally. "What?" he barked.

"Just got to Fire, and Pyro is mounting up to attack the Grizzlies," Garrett said without preamble. "Just gave me a box of dynamite I'm not quite sure has been stored correctly."

Fuck. All he needed was Bear getting pissed or the king's nephew blowing himself up with faulty explosives.

Kell shot hard warning looks at Simone and Nick. "The witch nation and the demons are allies right now, and we need it to stay that way. Whatever personal shit you two have going on needs to end."

"There's nothing personal between us," Simone said, tossing her head.

"The fuck there isn't," Nick countered. He turned and gave a short, traditional bow. "I give you my word your feisty cousin and I will not unbind the strong treaty between our people, no matter how long it takes me to tame her."

Simone growled low.

Nick grinned. "Demons are notoriously patient, and I am more so than most. However, Simone, I must warn you that my patience is at an end."

Kell lifted his gaze to the ceiling and exhaled heavily. "Would you two just get a room?"

"We have one, if you'd just leave," Nick countered. His phone dinged, and he lifted it to his ear to listen. Then he gave a quick nod. "I have to go." Brushing by Simone, he quickly grabbed her head to smack a kiss on her lips before loping out the door.

Damn but those demons moved fast.

Simone gaped and her eyes widened. "I'm going to blasting kill that demon."

Kell nodded. "Fair enough. Just wait until the current crisis is averted, would you?" If they were going to war with the demons again, he needed some down time first.

Yet seeing Nick finally make a move on Simone had somehow lightened his spirits. Either they'd burn out and explode, or they'd find something worth keeping. It was time to find out, and apparently Nick agreed.

God help the poor bastard. Simone Brightston was not a witch to tangle with, and when pissed, she embodied true female danger.

Good luck, Nick. Kellach whistled until he reached his bike and lifted his phone to his ear to call Bear. Bear answered with a barked hello.

"Bear, it's Kell. Fire is making a move on you."

Bear was silent for a moment. "Good. I'm tired of those pricks. It's time to take them out." He clicked off before Kell could argue.

Holy damn it. The last thing he needed was a club war, especially since Alexandra would be immediately drawn in if the police were called. He swore and kicked his bike into gear. He had to stop the showdown.

Chapter 30

Lex finished showing Tori Kell's penthouse, and finally, her sister dropped onto a leather sofa with a sigh of relief.

"He's hot, smart, and rich? Gee. Any particular reason you're not head over heels?" Tori kicked her boots onto the coffee table.

Lex perched on an armrest. "No, it's just that—"

"What?" Tori shook her head. "It's just that men are assholes who end up in jail and leave you?" She rolled her eyes. "Kellach is not Dad."

"Don't psychoanalyze me." Lex slid down into the chair.

Tori snorted. "Can't help it. I'm good at digging into brains." Actually, although young, she had always read people with intriguing accuracy. "Come on, Lexi. What's going on?"

Lex rested her elbows on her knees and her chin on her hands. "Fine. I like him. Maybe more than like him."

"You lurve him," Tori sang.

"God, you're a moron." Lex chuckled. "But yeah. I mean, maybe." *Okay, yes.* She'd fallen hard for Kellach Dunne. Hmm.

At some point, she'd have to tell her sister about witches and vampires and all of that, but she didn't want to be immortal without Tori. Maybe Tori could find a witch, but definitely not one of the enforcers. No way. "My life has become way too crazy," Lex muttered.

Tori laughed. "That does sound like love."

The front door opened, and Simone Brightston swept inside. "Kellach?" she called, stopping short. "Oh. Hello."

For some reason, Lex jumped to her feet. "Hi, Simone. Ah, this is my sister, Tori. Tori, this is Simone, Kellach's cousin."

Tori lifted her head, her gaze raking Simone. "What a freakin' well of good genes in that family."

Simone blinked. "Thank you."

"Any time." Tori settled more comfortably into the sofa. "Sexy as sin Kellach isn't here, but you're welcome to join us for some dishy girl talk. You in love, avoiding love, or trying not to believe in love right now?"

Simone's lips twitched. "Avoiding love and not quite sure it exists for everybody. You?"

"Oh, I know it exists, but I think it's a force for evil and not good," Tori said cheerfully.

Simone slowly nodded. "I'll change my answer to that one."

Wonderful. Two more unlikely friends Lex couldn't imagine, and yet, in front of her eyes, the stunning Simone Brightston and her wild sister were bonding. She shook her head and focused on Simone. "I'm sorry about yesterday and didn't mean to bring up bad memories."

Simone shrugged. "We're researching into the Demidov connection now, so thanks for the tip."

Lex's instincts started to hum. "Have you found anything?"

Simone studied her and then slowly nodded. "We believe he may have a child out there, but we don't know where or who yet. Once we do, I'm sure Kellach will pass the information on to you."

Lex smiled. Neither of them believed Kell would pass on the information. "Your cousin seems to have a mistaken belief about me."

Simone smiled, turning once again unbelievably beautiful. "Oh, that you're to stay safe and let the big, bad enforcers save the world?"

Lex warmed. "Yeah. That about sums it up."

"Ah, men in, ah, our family seem to have an outdated sense of protectiveness, but I'm sure you'll teach Kell another way. Women have been warriors in my culture, with my people, for centuries." Simone stepped into the room and eyed Victoria. "What do you do?"

"Sing. You?" Tori asked.

Simone folded her hands in her lap. "I work for the family business in Ireland."

Lex lifted an eyebrow, wondering more than ever about the ruling council. "Doing what?" she asked silkily.

Simone grinned. "Management."

Nice save. Lex would find out more, but she had work to do. "I have to get to the station but will be home later. I mean *here* later."

Simone rolled her eyes, while Tori barely bit back a snort. Lex turned for the door, knowing it was probably a bad idea to leave those two alone, but she didn't have much choice. Apollo was killing people, and Bernie had nearly died. She shut the door on Tori chattering to Simone about why men's brains were actually smaller than women's and headed down to borrow Kell's truck again.

If she didn't knock it off, she'd actually start depending on him. *Would that be so bad?*

Man, was this actual love? God. That's all she needed.

The drive to the station started sunny and, in true Seattle fashion, turned cloudy by the time she'd fetched an overflowing basket of mail from the post office. At least it wasn't raining. She hauled the loot in to the station with her, surprised to see Bundt and Masterson huddled over a computer.

"You supposed to be here?" she asked Masterson.

"No." He kept his gaze on the screen. "I'm supposed to wait for the doctor to clear me for duty, but I'm sure he'll get around to it soon enough."

Lex tossed the basket on her desk and skirted Bernie's to reach the duo. "What are you two looking at?"

Bundt fiddled with the controls on the screen. "Video e-mailed anonymously to us about an hour ago, but it's blurry. I'm working on it."

Lex's phone rang, and she stretched to reach it. "Monzelle."

"Hi, Detective. This is Margie from the office of parole," a nasal voice said.

Lex's head snapped up, and her heart kicked against her ribs. "Yes."

"I'm informing all interested parties that Parker Monzelle has been granted parole, mainly because of a batch of letters asking for his release from his ex-wife. He'll be free tomorrow." High-pitched and somehow still sounding bored, Margie gave more details, but Lex had stopped listening.

Holy shit. Parole. Damn it. "Are you sure? Is there an appeals process?" Lex spit out.

"No. Thank you." Margie hung up.

Lex removed the handset from her ear and looked at it. A buzzing started between her ears.

"Lex?" Masterson asked.

She shook her head. "What?"

He lifted his chin toward the phone. "You okay?"

"Yeah." She shook herself out of a near explosion and set the receiver back in the base. "No worries." She'd need to move her mother somewhere else, and she had to warn Tori. But at least the bastard wouldn't get out until the next day. She swallowed. Yeah, she'd figured he'd get out someday, but not yet. And not when things were finally going all right.

Masterson smacked the screen.

"Knock it off," Bundt muttered. He grabbed a folder and held it over his shoulder for Lex. "I finished the research for you and called in a couple favors."

Lex, still fighting brain fog, reached for the file. "What research?"

"Trevan Demidov. The guy had a kid with a woman back east a few decades ago in the states. It's interesting because Demidov was a citizen of Ireland, and the mom one of ours. She died when the kid was five. Kid's name is Yuri. He took his old man's name, so he was easy to find." Bundt's fingers clapped across his keys as he talked. "Had to call in a couple favors to get his juvie record, but I got it."

Lex opened the file and gasped at the photo on top. The witch who had nearly killed Bernie. Light blue eyes, brown hair, fighting shape. He'd been caught early on starting fires. Big fucking surprise. As an adult, Yuri had been a person of interest in a couple investigations involving missing prostitutes, but those cases had gone cold. He'd managed to stay off the radar for at least a decade. Interesting.

"Any news on his father?" she asked.

"Nothing. The guy was all over the social pages years ago, and then one day, poof. Gone." Bundt glanced over his shoulder. "He was tight with some woman name Simone Brightston, who has to be related to the lawyer chick of the guy you thought about banging. They look identical, except the woman in the pictures would be at least fifty or sixty by now."

Masterson rubbed his chin with his healthy arm. "That's weird, though. Having the exact same name."

Lex shrugged, her cheeks heating. "I don't know. A lot of men have sons with the same names. Why not women? Maybe the lawyer is Simone the second. Or third." Or a freaking witch who didn't age. Yeah. She should tell them that. She grinned. "Maybe she's immortal."

Masterson scoffed. "Good one."

Bundt shook his head. "Can you imagine how much tail you'd get with immortality?"

Lex shut her eyes, still reeling from the bad news about her father. "How are you two still upright?" Morons.

"You would like to see me prone, now wouldn't you?" Masterson wiggled his eyebrows.

She laughed.

"Eureka," Bundt bellowed, throwing his hands in the air. "King of the precinct here."

Masterson bent down, and Lex hurried to see the video. She squinted as the picture formed with a body hanging on a tree. Make that spiked to a tree, flesh burned all over.

"Shit. That's Spike," Masterson muttered.

Lex stilled, and her body flushed cold. "Spike Evertol?"

"Yeah." Bundt growled. "What the fuck?"

As she watched, large men stalked toward the victim. The video was blurry, and their faces remained turned away from the camera, but she instantly recognized them as Kellach and Daire Dunne.

Bile rose from her belly, and she shoved it down with cold, hard reality. Spike had been a dealer, a junkie, and a snitch. He'd been killed for one or all three reasons. Kellach had lied to her.

Still watching, she saw Kellach move away and leave Adam and Daire to remove the spikes and let poor Spike's body crumple to the ground. Daire turned toward the camera as if trying to find something.

Bundt swore, and Masterson turned her way. "Shit."

She nodded and continued to watch as the Dunne brothers removed the pieces of corpse, burned skin and all, and disappeared off camera with shovels. She inhaled sharply through her nose. "I'll type up the request for a warrant, and you guys call SWAT. We have enough to raid the entire Titan of Fire compound again." They needed to find that body.

Betrayal swept through her, so much more painful than when she'd been a teenager let down by the father she loved. She'd trusted Kellach, and he'd used her. For whatever purpose, he'd taken her trust and her heart and manipulated her. Man, he was definitely keeping secrets.

Panicked, she fumbled for her cell phone to call Victoria.

"Yep?" Tori answered.

Lex gripped the phone. "Be casual and tell me if Simone is still there."

"Nope. She had to go meet somebody but is coming back for a drink later."

Thank God. Lex breathed out, her shoulders lowering. "Good. Okay, listen to me. Get the hell out of there and go to Mom's. She's close to being released, and she's doing tons better, so I was going to request her release next week, anyway. Get Mom and go to a hotel—any one. I'll figure out how to pay for it later."

Masterson frowned, his gaze on her. "I got you if you need cash."

She nodded and mouthed a thank-you.

Tori sputtered. "What's going on? Lexi—"

"Just do it." Lex lowered her voice to a sharp command. "Trust me, Victoria. Get away from Kell's place, go to Mom, and get to safety. It's urgent." At least until Lex could figure out what was going on.

"Okay." The sound of Tori moving filtered through the line, providing some sense of comfort. "I'll get Mom, but you are so explaining this all later."

"I will. I promise. The doorman will hail you a taxi, but don't tell him where you're going. Wait until the door is shut, then *you* tell the taxi driver Mom's address." Her mind calculated the best way to keep her family safe. If Kellach had burned Spike to death in such a horrific way, he had no soul and wouldn't hesitate to kill again. If he hadn't killed Spike, he'd still had no problem hiding evidence and apparently burying the body, which was criminal and dishonest.

Either way, she was done with him, heartbreak or not. She absolutely wasn't her mother, staying loyal to a man she couldn't trust. To a man who kept such secrets.

"I'll call you later. Stay safe. " She ended the call and sat at Bernie's desk to type an e-mail request for a search warrant as well as arrest warrants for Kellach, Daire, and Adam Dunne. A sharp blade sliced through her heart, so she typed faster. She'd known better. She really had.

Masterson's phone rang, and he answered it to listen and then say a quick thanks. "Fire is making a move on the Grizzlies in a few minutes. Good source."

Lex hunched her shoulders. "I'll make note of that and see if I can get another warrant for the Grizzlies. We do have a duty to keep the peace." She typed faster.

The pain melded into something hotter, forged in pure, raw fury. Oh, Kellach Dunne and his entire family were going to pay.

Chapter 31

Kell straddled his bike, wondering how the hell he was going to keep Bear and his buddies from demolishing all of Titans of Fire. Shit. Did he even care at this point? Unfortunately, until he got a line on the other distributors and the manufacturer of Apollo, he had to keep Pyro and the boys alive.

When he and the other thirty members of Fire roared into Bear's territory, he should've been surprised by the line of Grizzlies and bikes, patiently waiting, but he wasn't. He was Bear, after all.

They stood in front of their bikes, a solid wall of at least forty men. Tough, weathered, and most of them shifters, including Clarke, one of Bear's badass lieutenants. Of course, the Fire gang didn't know they could shift into bears.

The Fire riders, led by Pyro, came to a stop just yards away from Bear.

Bear lifted his head. "You sure you want to do this?"

Several weapons were visible on the Grizzlies, so at least they planned to fight as humans and not shifters.

Kell rolled to a stop next to Pyro. "I strongly suggest we don't do this." Even so, he knew it was too late. If Pyro turned back, it'd be a sign of weakness, and he wouldn't allow that.

"It's a good day to fight," Pyro said.

As if in agreement, thunder rolled, and the skies opened up. The deluge pummeled down.

Kell sighed, making a promise to himself. His next assignment would be somewhere without rain. Maybe on a beach. When this was done, perhaps he'd take Alexandra someplace warm. The idea of her sexy body, bare on sand, almost transported him from the ridiculous fight about to commence.

Pyro lifted his arm and gave a battle cry.

Three helicopters instantly hovered into sight, massive vans screeched to a stop, and human policemen in black combat gear came out of nowhere.

Shit.

One guy grabbed Kellach off his bike, and it took every ounce of control he owned not to fight back and burn the bastard. He found himself face-first on wet asphalt, hands cuffed behind his back, gazing at Bear on his gut. Bear could shift and disembowel the SWAT member who was cuffing him, but instead, he lifted an eyebrow toward Kell.

Kell shrugged. No idea. Had the cops somehow found out about the fight and decided to end it? If so, it could be a good result; he wouldn't have to fake a human fight. Suddenly, his spirits lifted.

Boots, small and sexy, stepped into his line of sight just as a human male tugged him up by his cuffed hands. Alexandra looked at him, raw fury in her eyes. Rain plastered her soft hair to her head and slid in rivulets down her smooth face.

He frowned. "Alexandra?"

She pivoted and cold-cocked him across the left cheekbone. She hit him so hard his head snapped back, and pain flared through his skull.

His mouth dropped open. "What the hell?"

Bear snorted and let out a belly laugh as another SWAT guy pulled him to his feet.

Alexandra stepped back, her boots splashing water. "Kellach Dunne, you're under arrest for the murder of Spike Evertol. You, you fucking bastard, have the right to remain silent . . ." She continued with his Miranda rights, swearing intermittently, her voice cold but so much heat in her eyes, his body responded to the challenge.

Even so, he held back, knowing full well some of the SWAT uniforms had cameras. If they hadn't had witnesses, if he didn't have his own laws to uphold, he'd take her to the ground and show her exactly who he was.

Finally, she wound down.

"You fucking called SWAT on me?" he growled, letting his fury flow.

She looked up at him and snapped, "You bet your ass, dickhead. Enjoy prison." Without another look at him, she turned and walked over to read Adam his rights.

Adam shot him a look. How the hell did she know about Spike? They'd buried the body where it'd never be found.

Kell shook his head and kept his gaze on his woman, who stubbornly ignored him.

Daire, his hands zip-tied behind his back, glared at him. He glared back. What a shit storm.

Vans arrived as techs ripped through the Grizzly garages, throwing things outside, generally making a mess.

Bear looked on, his lids half-lowered, his body relaxed. If anything, he looked so bored as to be sleeping on his feet. Not even the rain pouring down upon his head and soaking his clothing seemed to bother him.

Finally, a tech came out, shaking his head.

Alexandra whistled, and other cops uncuffed Bear and his buddies. "We didn't find anything. This time."

Bear loped toward her, and she faced off with him, no fear on her pretty face. The woman knew exactly what Bear was and how dangerous he could be, and she faced him like she would any perp coming toward her.

Even as pissed off as he was, pride filled Kell. The magnificent creature standing so bravely in the storm belonged to him.

Bear reached her. "I thought we were friends."

She shook her head. "Stay on the right side of the law, and we're friends. Stray an inch, and I'll put you away."

Bear cocked his big head to the side. "You really want me for an enemy?"

"Your choice, Bear." She held his gaze, not budging an inch. "You might want to rethink your friends, anyway."

Bear grinned. "If you end up killing Dunne, give me a call." He turned and shot Kell a smart-ass grin. "Later, Dunne." Turning on his heel, he loped to his garage and began mumbling orders to set things right.

Kell showed his teeth. He might have to burn his old friend, and at the moment, he was fucking okay with that.

Alexandra turned and flashed her teeth at Pyro. "A similar raid at Fire turned up guns in your room as well as those of two prospects who are already heading to the station. Green guns." She cut Kellach a hard look.

Holy fuck. Garrett and Logan had been caught with green laser guns? Those couldn't fall into the hands of humans. His head jerked up.

Alexandra turned away from him again, and he growled.

She stiffened but didn't turn back. "Release all of them except for Pyro, the three murder suspects, and the two prospects. Take them to the station and book them." She began to walk toward a squad car.

"Alexandra," he murmured. He had to get those guns back, She had to know how dangerous it was for humans even to see them. "You're making a mistake."

She turned, her chin lowered. "Oh, I've made plenty of mistakes, but I'm remedying that right now." Pivoting, a stunning warrior in the crashing rain, she walked away from him.

A move she would soon regret.

Lex watched through the two-way mirror of the interrogation room, wanting to be in there so badly her hands shook, but nothing could compromise the case. Her pseudo-relationship, as Bundt thought of it, would get in the way. He and Masterson sat across from Kellach, Daire, Adam, and Simone.

Even so, Kellach's gaze met hers directly through the glass.

She moved to the side.

His gaze followed her.

Shit. Witches could see through the mirror? How? She moved again, just to make sure, and Simone caught her gaze and rolled her eyes.

Fine. They could see.

Kellach kept her gaze, fire flickering in the black depths of his eyes. Even yards away, through glass and a cinder block wall, she could *feel* his fury. Hot enough to burn and a deadly promise of the fight to come once he'd gotten out. He'd been processed already but would remain in a cell until the following morning, when a judge would set bail.

Perhaps with the video, bail would be denied.

What kind of power did the Dunnes have? It'd be interesting to see if international pressure was applied.

Simone tapped a red-tipped fingernail on the table. "We'd prefer to discuss the case with Detective Monzelle."

Bundt snorted, the sound echoing. "Monzelle wants your boys here hung from the nearest tree. Believe me, you don't wanna talk to her." He shifted to face Kellach, his back remaining to Lex. "You wanna work with me. Tell me how you killed Spike, and we'll see what we can do for a deal. Maybe you won't get the death penalty."

Kellach lifted an eyebrow, his gaze not faltering from Lex's.

Bundt slammed a hand on the table. "Stop staring at yourself in the mirror, and look at me. Do you wanna die?"

Kellach didn't flinch.

Masterson sat across from Adam. "You look like the smart one."

Adam stared at him, no expression on his angled face. "I am."

"So make a deal. Tell us what happened with Spike." Masterson flipped open a file in front of him. "These are the stills from a video we have showing you as the killers." His voice lowered to conspiratorial. "We know Spike was a bad guy—a dealer and a junkie. You might've been defending yourself, and things went too far."

Simone tapped the picture. "I'd like to see the video, please."

Masterson shook his head. "Just tell us what happened."

Lex crossed her arms. The Dunnes were too smart to confess, so refusing to reveal the tape was stupid. When Simone calmly explained that fact, Bundt reached for a remote control and showed the video on the far wall.

When it wound down, Simone smiled at the detectives. "That's it?"

"That's enough," Masterson said with confidence. "There's enough there, with the gore and burned flesh, for a jury to conclude your boys here killed poor Spike, who'd had a hard life and had made good by working with the police. Poor, poor, Spike."

Simone scoffed. "I'm sure that video was doctored, and I'll prove it in court if necessary. For now, let me just say that all it appears to show is my clients assisting a poor man, a victim, off a tree after somebody else killed him."

"Oh. How about those shovels?" Masterson leaned toward Simone, and the enforcers tensed instantly.

She waved them back. "Shovels are for yard work."

"Ah." Bundt slapped both hands on the table. "Let's say your clients did help poor Spike down. Where's the body now?"

Simone blinked. "Well, unfortunately, since that video is doctored and those in it couldn't be my clients, they have no knowledge of where poor Spike is now. Where did you obtain this DVD, gentlemen?"

"Doesn't matter," Bundt muttered.

"Oh, but it does." Simone smiled again. "If you can't authenticate the DVD, you can't use it in court, as you must surely know."

Bundt flipped the file closed. "Authentication requires proof that the DVD hasn't been doctored, and we will provide that. Authentication does not require knowing who shot the video."

Lex nodded behind the glass.

Kell's eyes flared.

Thoughts rolled through her brain. Who would want Kellach and Adam shut down? If they'd truly murdered Spike, why wasn't the murder on the video? Only the cleanup had been captured. So . . . if they hadn't murdered Spike, another witch had. Who? And why had the Dunnes cleaned up the mess? Because Spike had obviously been killed by a witch?

She put some of the pieces together. Whoever had killed Spike knew he'd been talking to the police . . . so the warning had been for the police, and Kellach had covered it up.

She lifted her head, looking at Kell. His gaze provided no answers. She turned on her heel. If she couldn't get the answers from him, she'd get them from another source.

Quick steps took her to the adjacent interview room, where Garrett and Logan sat on the other side of a table, hands cuffed to it. The room was more casual and lacked a two-way mirror or recording devices, because she really didn't want their answers recorded right now. She smiled at them and walked inside to sit. "Hello, boys."

Suddenly, they looked like anything but boys. Neither twitched an impressive muscle, and both stared, no expressions on their hardened faces. For the first time, she could see the predators lurking beneath their excellent manners and huge appetites. She wanted to see more and reached across the table, grasping Garrett's light-refracting eyeglasses.

"I wouldn't," Logan rumbled.

She removed the glasses and gasped. Sizzling, metallic gray, almost silver corneas surrounded a black pupil. She leaned closer. Garrett met her gaze without flinching.

"You have beautiful eyes," she murmured.

"That's my line," Garrett deadpanned.

She slid the glasses back on in case anybody came in. "Why don't you wear contacts?"

"I do, but they bug me, so I usually just keep the glasses on when away from home," Garrett said.

She frowned. "Do all vampires have eyes like yours?"

"All vampires have secondary eye colors that are metallic, but most also have a fairly normal eye color. I'm unique." Garrett leaned toward her, and his chain clunked on the table. "You have to get our guns back."

She shook her head. "I can't do that. Sorry."

"You have to." Logan leaned over and lowered his voice. "It's against our laws to let, ah, other people have our guns. You know, proprietary information and all that."

"Having weapons without the proper permits breaks my laws." She folded her hands together.

Garrett cut a look at Logan. "Listen, ma'am. You can't break our laws."

The boys were worrying about her? Man. They had better clue in. "I'm not subject to your laws."

Logan's face cleared. "Ah, I see the problem. Say you're from Washington and you go to California. You're subject to the California laws while there. If you rob a store, you'll face prison time in California, right?"

"Yes." She frowned. Where in the world was he going with this?

He nodded. "Okay. So, you were in one species and subject to human laws. But when you mated Dunne, you became part of another species and are subject to their—our—laws. And giving proprietary weaponry to humans is a big-assed no-no of a law, begging your pardon, ma'am."

"I think you two should worry about yourselves right now and not me." She put on her best cop face.

Garrett's eyebrows lifted to his hairline. "You're in a lot more trouble than we are right now. We can get out of here pretty easily, but there's nowhere you can hide from the Realm or the enforcers."

She tilted her head. "The enforcers?"

"Yeah. The Coven Nine enforcers will be charged with hunting you down for breaking a law." Logan cut Garrett a look. "She has no clue."

Garrett nodded. "Yeah, I'm getting that." He blew out air. "We should probably confiscate the guns for her, don't you think?"

"Maybe. Perhaps the Nine and the Realm will go easy on her. She's new." Logan snapped his fingers. "Wait a sec. Nobody knows about the guns yet, do they? I mean, when will they be tested?"

Lex shook her head, wondering when the hell had she lost control of the conversation. "Probably not until tomorrow or the next day. Guys? I need you to focus here. You're in trouble."

Garrett bit his lip. "So the only people who know about the guns are us, the Dunnes, and the Grizzlies."

"If we don't talk, and the Dunnes don't burn her alive, then she's in the clear." Logan smiled. "Bear thinks you're cute, so he won't rat you out."

Bear thought she was cute? Wait a minute.

"The guns are secured, guys. There's no getting to them," she patiently explained.

Garrett smiled, and Logan laughed outright.

The door flew open, and Dage Kayrs strode inside. Up close, the vampire king was bigger and badder than she'd thought in the diner.

The boys instantly sat at attention.

Lex started to stand, but Dage gestured her back down before flashing a badge and handing over a federal court order. "My apologies, but these two are in federal custody."

Oh, hell no. She shook her head. "Not a chance, King."

He smiled. "I have the badge, the documentation, and the understanding of your chief. So either you know something he doesn't, and you're willing to share such information, or you'll follow this very clear, very legal federal document." He focused on the boys.

"The guns are also part of an international case, and my partner is confiscating them now. With proper documentation of course."

Garrett winced. "Your partner wouldn't be a massive guy with golden eyes, would he?"

Dage shot a hard look at his nephew. "No. Your father is on a mission elsewhere." He smiled at Logan. "I brought a member of your family."

Logan groaned and slumped in his chair. "Which brother?"

Dage's smile held a tinge of evil, and Lex almost felt sorry for the kid.

The door opened, and an incredibly petite blonde walked inside, holding an evidence box.

"Mom!" Logan exclaimed, jumping to his feet along with Garrett. Their chains held tight, and both lurched forward but remained standing. Red colored Logan's face from his neck to his ears.

Mom? The woman was absolutely stunning yet terribly small. No way had she birthed Logan Kyllwood. Lex stood and looked down at someone way too young to be Logan's mom. The woman held out a hand. "Felicity Kyllwood."

"Federal officer," Dage said dryly.

Felicity waved his statement away. "For goodness sake. It's so nice to meet you. Thanks for putting up with the boys." Her voice was unnaturally hoarse to the point of being edgily sexy.

Lex carefully shook a fine-boned hand. Felicity had long, almost white, blond hair and eyes blacker than Kell's. She was fine boned, delicate, and incredibly graceful.

Lex leaned toward her. "Are you a vampire?" she whispered.

Felicity blinked. "Vampires are only male. Well, usually. I'm a demon, Detective." She faced her son. "Am I to understand you boys were caught with our weapons?"

"Yes, ma'am," the boys said in unison, looking down at the table, their shoulders slumping.

Lex frowned. "We raided the place, and I'm sure they weren't planning on that. The guns were well hidden, I heard."

Dage bit his lip. "That's kind of you, Detective."

She couldn't help but defend the poor kids.

"We'll discuss it later," Felicity said with a sweet smile, her voice husky and low.

The kids groaned.

Left without a choice, unless she wanted to challenge Dage's credentials and tell everyone he was actually a vampire, Lex had to release the kids.

Garrett gave her a half-hug, and Logan nudged her with his hip as they passed. He whispered, "Don't be surprised if the entire surveillance system goes down and loses the records of the last few hours. Solar flares and all that."

So, there'd be no record of Dage, Felicity, or the boys. Or any evidence of the Dunne brothers' crime. Where the hell had reality gone?

That left her with a limited time to figure out who'd killed Spike before the Dunne brothers also pulled some international intrigue and disappeared with their knowledge of Apollo and the manufacturer and distributors.

Over her dead body.

Chapter 32

Lex wandered by the other interrogation room to find the interview still going on, with Masterson asking questions and Simone stonewalling him.

Enough of that crap. She walked back into the squad room and punched up Bundt's computer to watch the video again. She slowed it down, watching carefully as Daire and Adam released Spike from the tree with little care but no real anger or intent.

Her stomach began to roll. If either of those men had wanted to kill Spike, they would've done it easily and without exhibiting him on a tree.

She'd been hurt, and she'd been angry because Kellach had lied to her. Now that her mind had cleared, she was still hurt and pissed, but she realized there was no way the Dunne brothers had killed Spike. The question now became how the manufacturer of Apollo had discovered Spike's connection to the police.

Spike wasn't the brightest guy, so the answer could be as simple as he'd been followed. Also, who'd sent the video——and why?

She bit her lip and called the precinct's video and surveillance guru, a woman by the name of Sylvia, and asked her to take a look at the video for . . . well, anything . . . before directing her to put it on the internal server. Sylvia said she'd hurry and get it done, because she'd just received orders that the video and all pictures were part of a federal case, and she had to turn them over.

Lex shook her head. "Do your best," she whispered. Hell. It was just a matter of minutes before Bundt had to release the Dunnes.

Lex's gaze caught on the box of mail on her desk. Lifting her phone, she quickly dialed her sister.

"Lexi? Is everything okay? What's up?" Tori asked, her voice higher than normal.

Lex rubbed her aching eyes. "I think everything's fine, and I may have, ah, overreacted earlier, but I want you to stay where you are and keep Mom safe." She breathed out air, not wanting to say the next words. "Dad got parole."

No sound ticked over the line until Tori spoke. "Fuck."

Yep. That summed it up.

"Where are you?" Lex asked.

"The Ham Motel on the outskirts. It's cheap and out of the way."

Lex sighed. "I'll be there in about an hour, and I'll bring food." She clicked off and started going through her mom's mail, tossing most of it as junk. Finally, she reached the envelope from the penitentiary and had no qualms about opening it up and reading the letter from her father to her mother.

Dearest Jennie,

I miss you so much, and every day, I wish for a chance to make up for my past. To keep you safe and cherish you, as we both know you deserve. I could, once again, be the man I was during the first six months of our marriage, before I began to take drugs. Drugs ruined my life, and I am so very sorry. My kids look at me like I'm a 500 pound gorilla, and I'd give anything to go back to that November we spent in that quaint cottage by the sea. Please send me a letter as soon as you can, as I miss hearing your voice in my head. My friend is waiting for you, and we're still working together to eradicate the poison in this place. He's a warrior, as am I now.

Keep our secret, dear one. We must keep our girls safe.

Also, if there's a way, and I know it's a lot to ask, but please perhaps testify at my parole hearing this time. Or at least ask the girls not to testify against me. I've been successful in my work here, and now I have enemies. It's time to do my work on the outside, where we can be together.

My Love,
Parker

Lex frowned. What the hell was he talking about? What work? What friend? It was time to have a little chat with her mother, apparently. Lex stuffed the letter into her pocket and stomped toward the exit, only to run into Bundt and Masterson, both red faced and furious.

"What's going on?" she asked, already knowing the answer.

"Fucking Dunnes," Masterson spat. "Federal court order, saying they're some sort of international operatives working with fucking Homeland Security. That the video is part of national security, and we have to turn it over."

Lex blinked. "I heard the same thing from records. Damn it."

"Bastards already sauntered out of here like they got away with murder." Masterson punched the empty basket on her desk, and it flew across the room to hit the wall. "Like international cops are hanging with Pyro and Titans of Fire. Sorry about the basket."

"No worries." Nice punch, actually. Her breath heated up, and a panic, purely feminine in nature, began to well through her. Kell was free?

Masterson loped across the room and fetched the basket. "What did you do with all the mail?"

She shrugged. "Mostly junk. I should check the post office box more often."

He dropped into his chair. "I can't believe we had to let them go. A fucking SWAT raid, some decent evidence . . . and they walk out the door." Masterson kicked his desk. "International case, my ass. I bet those fuckers are bringing those green guns over from Ireland and trading them for Apollo. Well, at least we still have those guns."

Lex closed her eyes, once again the bearer of bad news. "Uh—" She gave him the scoop while backing toward the hallway. Finally, she finished just as he launched into a truly creative use of every expletive ever created. She couldn't help the small chuckle when she shoved outside and into the raining night.

Mud puddles, cracked asphalt, and glass lined her way to the truck parked at the rear of the station, under a weak light pole. She halted, water splashing up her legs.

Kellach Dunne leaned back against his truck, his arms crossed, his stance wide. "Good evening, Detective."

* * *

The merest of threads held Kell's control in check, and a low growl rumbled up from his chest upon seeing his mate. He'd hoped the chilled, pouring rain would dampen the temper roaring through him, yet each sharp prick had escalated the emotions boiling in his blood. Now that she was in sight, if she ran, the beast inside him would have no choice but to chase.

His nostrils flared. Yeah, he wanted to chase and take her down.

Her head lifted.

Nope. No running away for his mate.

"Waiting for me?" she asked.

He smiled, the night narrowing in absolute focus to one woman. "Aye," he whispered.

A shudder wracked her body from his low tone but it was not nearly enough to appease him. Not after the night he'd had, not after considering the danger she'd purposely put herself in, by refusing to trust him.

"Some of our scientists have a theory," he said.

She stayed very still, on alert, her gaze on him across the pavement separating them. "Oh?" she breathed.

"Aye. A theory that all immortals share a common ancestor. One that gives us the extra chromosomes, one that makes us . . . more." He pushed off from the truck, and her eyes widened. "A part definitely not human and much more akin to animal. Wild, free, and long-lasting." If the woman didn't learn his nature, how would she ever understand him?

"You're saying you're part animal?" she asked quietly.

"Aye." He took a step toward her.

She dropped, naturally and easily, into a fighting stance. "Animals can be tamed." The challenge in her voice competed with the scent of her arousal.

The beast deep inside him cracked open a link in his chain of control. "Alexandra, you miscalculated today." He struggled to regain control and use logic.

Her chin lowered. "Did I, now?"

In her eyes, he could see the truth. She knew she'd fucked up. But in her stance? In the tilt of her head and the proud carriage of her entire body? A definite *fuck you* challenge from a female mate to her male. Much quicker than he would've expected, she was becoming more than human and was seeking the part of him, the non-human side that had instigated her change.

"I warned you to follow my laws," she murmured.

Intrigue clawed through him along with heated desire. Just how far did she plan to push him?

Another link in the chain split open. "Feeling brave, lass?" he asked.

Her head snapped up, desire spinning red across her face. "I'm always brave, Kellach Gideon Dunne. That's what has you so pissy, isn't it?"

He smiled a flash of teeth, feeling her struggle as the war between desire and pride created an anger-filled lust. "I'm a fair man."

She snorted. "Oh?"

"Aye. So here's your one chance. Come here." Every nerve in his body tensed in anticipation.

She tilted her head, ever so slightly, to the side. Studying him. Uncertainty and curiosity shining bright in her eyes. Even through the rain, the scent of her desire tempted him. She took a deep breath, shuddering out a strong exhale as if embracing the inevitable. "No."

The one word. The simple, absolute, deliberate defiance of his order.

He'd expected it. Hell. He'd *wanted* it.

The beast broke free.

She sensed it.

He knew she did, because against everything she was, she turned to run. He caught her in two steps, lifting her easily, carrying her around the truck to the side shrouded by darkness.

An expert punch landed against his jaw, and he growled low, opening the door and tossing her onto her hands and knees. She tried to scramble across the seat, but he was on her, yanking the door shut as he lunged. She reached for the other door handle, and he ripped off her shirt. Need cascaded from her, but even so, she fought, trying to turn.

He yanked her jeans down to her ankles, and she laughed, the sound low and throaty. Sexy as hell. His fingers found her, wet and hot. So fucking hot.

She moaned and pushed back against his hand, her fingers curling into the seat. "Kellach," she breathed.

He grabbed her hair, yanking back, holding her in place. She gave a whimper, one of need, spreading her knees. He slapped her clit.

She breathed in hard, her ribs compressing, her back bowing. Sensations of raw pleasure shot from her to him, flying under his skin, connecting them.

He slipped a finger inside her, and she tightened around him, trying to hold him in. He slid out, ignoring her groan of protest, and slapped her square on the clit again. She cried out, shock waves ratcheting down her back.

He moved up, his mouth next to her ear. "That's for making me *buy* condoms." Another slap. "That's for making me fucking *wear* condoms."

She moaned, trying to thrash against him.

He held her tight and pinched her swollen bud. "That's for having me arrested."

Mini shocks shuddered through her body. He could feel how close she was, how desperate, so he loosened his hold. She cried out, softly, trying to ride his fingers.

He tightened his hold on her hair, jerking her head up. "Alexandra?"

She shut her eyes. "What?" she gasped.

He angled his hand. "This is for not trusting me." He hit her with the edge of his palm, square on, throwing her into an orgasm that shook her from neck to ass. Then he rubbed her, enjoying the heated wetness, until she mewled.

"Kell, please," she gasped.

He yanked his jeans down. "Please, what?" He covered her, his fingers still playing, his breath on her ear.

"Please."

He pinched. "Not good enough. Say it."

"Fuck me. Please fuck me, Kell," she moaned.

He shoved inside her with one hard thrust, sliding one arm under her to grip the front of her shoulder, and keeping the other tangled in her hair. Without giving her time to adjust, without pausing, he started to pound. With every hard thrust, he yanked her shoulder back, forcing her ass to hit his groin.

She moaned and rocked against him. "More."

He gave her more. For the first time, he held nothing back, pounding into her, going so deep he'd never be free. Her walls gripped him, keeping him in so much heat his blood boiled.

A tremor started inside her, cascading along his shaft. She stiffened and arched her back, crying out his name. He pounded harder, making her take more, making her ride the waves even when she gasped out uncontrollable murmurs. Electricity clawed down his spine to grip his balls. His eyes shut, and white sparks flashed behind his eyelids. He gripped her, holding on, and came hard.

Slowly, he returned to reality and released her hair.

Her head dropped down, and she sighed. The sound of their panting filled the cab of the truck, while steam covered the windows. He withdrew, falling to sit, pulling her damp body around to straddle him. She snuggled her face into his neck, and her body went limp against him.

He rubbed her back, struggling for air. "You are a lot of work, darlin'."

She chortled against his neck before pushing back to face him. Both hands shoved his wet hair away from his face, and she smacked a gentle kiss on his lips. "Sorry I had you arrested. I was hurt you lied to me about Spike."

Just when he'd fucked her silly, definitely had gotten the upper hand, she turned all sweet on him. He sighed. "I'm sorry I didn't tell you about Spike. I figured the less you knew, the safer you'd be." Actually, that turned out to be the exact opposite.

She bit her lip. "How much trouble are we in, immortal world-wise?"

He rolled his eyes. "Much less than we should be, but now I owe the king a favor, which is never a good thing." But he'd pay the piper when the marker came due; it was something to worry about another day. "For now, let's compare research so we can put this fucking case to bed. For good." If they worked together, at least he could keep an eye on her.

She gasped, struggling against him. "Oh, God. There are cameras out here."

"They're down right now and have been since the king was in the vicinity." Kell sighed. "Again, you're a lot of work, Alexandra." He grinned, his heart lighter than it had been since he'd met her. They'd figure it out. All of it.

Chapter 33

After an incredibly good night's sleep, Lex finished dressing, her mind a whirl. She and Kell had reached an agreement to work together, and after they'd picked up her sister and mother, they'd all had a nice dinner together. Her mother had pretty much fallen in love with Kell, and the sentiment appeared to be mutual.

Then Lex had wild witch sex for several hours before jumping into dreamland, only to awaken to find the condo empty. Kell had left to track down a lead, while her mom and sister had gone to a spa with Simone, with Adam Dunne as bodyguard, if the note was to be believed.

Lex grinned and shoved silver earrings through her lobes. Tori could befriend anybody.

Of course, if Kell was correct, Lex and Simone were more alike than Lex had originally thought. Maybe she should make an effort with the stunning witch.

Whistling, Lex strode through the apartment for the kitchen, only to draw up short at Daire glaring at Kell's industrial latte machine. He stood in beyond old jeans, bare feet, and a T-shirt that may have been blue decades ago. "Daire?"

The enforcer turned around. Dark stubble covered his jaw, and the thick hair on his head was ruffled. Lines fanned out from his multi-green colored eyes. "I'll give you a million dollars if you'll make me a cup of coffee. My maker broke, and this one has too many damn buttons. What's wrong with coffee grounds and a bloomin' pot over a fire?"

Her eyebrows rose. "Dude. How old are you?"

He blinked. "Old enough not to be called *dude*." Desperation, the real kind, flitted across his chiseled face. "Please, Alexandra. Coffee."

She bit back a laugh and gestured toward the stools across from the granite kitchen bar. "Sit."

He nodded and crossed around to sit. "Spent the night at Titans of Fire drinking tequila."

Lex shoved a coffee cup under Kell's latte machine, filled the grounds, and quickly pushed buttons to make a quad. "Do you want steamed milk or any of the flavorings?" Several syrups lined the counter.

"God, no. Do I look like I want steamed friggin' milk?" Daire muttered.

She turned around. "Good lord, you're a grouch in the morning."

"It has been said." He nodded, obviously not taking offense.

She quickly handed over the hot quad-shot, watching with wide eyes as he tipped back the entire thing and handed the cup toward her.

"Another."

She lifted her eyebrows and turned back to the machine to push more buttons. "I would've figured you could handle tequila better."

"I usually can, but I haven't slept in about a week, and I needed those guys to loosen up and give me the goods on Apollo." His grateful smile as she turned around to hand him another four shots of espresso seemed almost sweet.

"Did you discover anything?"

He took a deep drink and sighed. "No. Only Pyro seems to have the knowledge, and he wasn't there last night." Daire rubbed his eyes. "I may have to torture him for the info, and that can always backfire."

She put her hands on her hips. "Daire. I'm a cop."

He focused. "Oh yeah. Sorry."

The enforcer didn't sound sorry. "The note on the counter said that Adam would be with my family today at the spa," Lex asked, a little uneasy with her mother being out in public.

"Don't worry. He won't let anything happen to any of them, and I'm sure they checked in under aliases." Daire rolled his neck. Slowly, his eyes began to focus and his body sat straighter.

"That coffee kicks in quick, huh?" She turned to make herself a nice steamed latte with tons of syrup.

"Yeah. Kell's the cheerful one on the morning. Adam and I usually want to shoot somebody."

That was true. Kell had always been cheerful early dawn. And horny. Sipping carefully, she turned back to face Daire. "Is it normal for brothers to become enforcers for your people?" It would seem that they'd want to keep a brother or two safe if one courted danger.

"It's not unusual, to be honest. Family bonds are stronger than any others, and we cover each other's backs well." He took another drink, savoring this time. Then he focused on her. "How are you doing with the mating?"

She coughed and moved the cup away from her mouth. Heat climbed into her cheeks. "Fine."

His cheek creased. "I'm now your brother, Alexandra. You can talk to me."

Brother? "Uh." She took a drink of the sweet brew.

He chuckled. "That disconcerts you."

Yeah. She had enough family to worry about. "I don't know how to have a brother."

Lights glimmered in his odd eyes. "There's that sweetness Kell talks about."

She straightened. "Kell talks about me?"

"Well, sometimes he passes me a note in gym class."

She grinned. "Smartass."

"Aye." Daire downed the rest of his cup. "Here's the deal. You're family, and if you need anything, I'm there as your brother. You're a new mate, so if you need protection, I'm there as a Coven Enforcer."

"My job makes that difficult," she murmured.

"Yes, it does. You're good at your job, and I respect that."

She studied him. "But?"

He lifted a wide shoulder. "We both have our jobs to do."

Right. So his job might interfere with hers at some point. "Don't forget I have no problem arresting you."

He grinned. "I wonna forget that." Then he cleared his throat. "Ah, Kell feels guilty about the mating."

She blinked. "Guilty?"

"Yes. He's a fair guy, probably the most fair guy I've ever met, and he would never have mated you without your consent." Daire snorted. "Probably in writing and with so much 'are you sure questions' you would've changed your mind."

She lifted her chin. "He's all possessive and protective and definitely not acting guilty."

"Well, no. It's done." Daire's eyebrows drew down in the middle. "You're his mate, and that's that."

She shook her head, trying to bite back a smile. "You're all lost in the last century."

"No." Daire sobered. "We know what's out there, and you don't. Not really."

Maybe, but she'd fought any enemy she'd ever had and won. "I like him a lot." Hell, that was an understatement, now wasn't it? She smiled, feeling almost shy. "I love how he calls me *Alexandra* and draws out my name. I never loved my name before I met Kell."

"Good." Daire stood and stretched his back. "Then learn to work with him instead of against him, little sister. I'd hate to see you locked down in Ireland when you want to be here."

Lex blinked. "Are you kidding me?"

"No." Daire padded around the counter to rinse out his cup and set it in the dishwasher.

She put her hand on her hip. "What about you, Dunne?"

"Me?" he turned around.

"Your mate. Do you know who it is?"

He shook his head. "Nope. I'll probably meet her in a couple hundred years, and I guarantee she won't be a cop, enforcer, or soldier."

"Oh really?" Why did some guys just tempt fate like that? Lex shook her head.

"Yeah. I know myself, and I know what I want. It's enough work trying to protect the council and witch nation; I don't need a wild mate out there." Daire patted her shoulder and almost knocked her down. "But I think you're perfect for Kell."

Her heart warmed. The guy was actually kind of sweet. "I hope I'm there when you fall, and don't worry, I'll help you through it."

His lips twitched. "Fair enough. Thanks for the coffee."

She walked him to the door where Kell was just entering, a huge bouquet of red roses in his hand.

Daire snorted and brushed by him.

Kell walked in and handed her the bundle.

She accepted the fragrant bouquet, absurdly touched. "What's this for?"

He looked down over the bundle. "I, ah, was a little rough last night in the truck, and I thought the roses were pretty. I thought maybe you'd like them." His eyes darkened even more.

She smiled, feeling all girly. "They're beautiful." Nobody had ever given her a dozen red roses. "Thank you."

"I like you, Alexandra."

God, she *freakin* loved her name now. She inhaled the scent of fresh flowers. "I like you, too."

He led her into the kitchen and drew down a gorgeous Belleek vase to hold the roses. "I know we agreed to work together last night, and I'm glad we're on the same page. There has to be an *us* outside of this case and this investigation." He turned and pulled her into his arms.

Warmth and male surrounded her. She smiled. "I agree."

"Good." His kiss went deep and left her breathless.

She cleared her throat, wanting to ease his mind. "I, ah, don't blame you for the mating. I mean, for the surprise of it."

He leaned back and studied her. "You don't?"

"No. We both were taken away, and I was just as into the moment as you were." Maybe even more so. It wasn't fair for him to carry that burden alone, even though she hadn't known about matings. The knowledge wouldn't have stopped her that day in the forest, as she had been more than desperate for him. "We need to go on from here."

He dropped a kiss onto her nose. "That fairness of yours takes me away every time. You're a keeper, Alexandra."

"So you've said." They had time to figure out everything. She stretched up on her toes and wandered her mouth along his. Desire flitted through her, warming her head to toe.

He took over the kiss, as she'd known he would, angling her head for better access. When he finally lifted up, they were both panting. The brand at her hip pulsed as if alive, and her heart beat in tune with his——she could just feel it.

The door to the apartment banged open. "Everybody still dressed?" Daire called out.

Kell sighed, his chest moving nicely with the effort. "Aye. We're in the kitchen." He pressed a kiss to her forehead. "Family. Damn it."

Lex stayed in Kell's arms but turned her head on his chest to watch for Daire.

He loped inside, his gaze serious. "We had an attack on the west side of Seattle."

Kell straightened, his body going stiff. "Who?"

"Mel and June Thompson," Daire said.

Lex pushed away from Kell and didn't move an inch. "An attack? Do I need to call it in?"

"No," Kell said softly. "They're ours. What happened?"

Daire rubbed the scruff on his chin, fury darkening his eyes. "Dart attacks with Apollo. Killed both witches."

Lex gasped. "How many darts?"

"At least ten each," Daire said. "Looks like ten is the kill number."

Lex pushed again. "I need to get to the station."

"Keep this to yourself. We have the bodies," Daire said.

She opened her mouth to argue, and Kell squeezed her. "These are ours, baby. We don't know what an autopsy will show yet, and there's no way your people will find the bodies," he said.

"Fine. But keep me informed," she muttered.

Kell planted a hard kiss on her lips. "We will. You stay safe today, mate."

She blinked and then leaned up to kiss him. "You stay safe, too."

Chapter 34

Her heart still thumping a little too hard from the enforcer's kisses, Lex strode into the precinct, ready to kick some ass. Kell hadn't checked in yet about the two downed witches, but there didn't seem to be much to hear. They'd been attacked in their home with darts and had died. That simple.

Lex's life was nothing close to simple right now. She'd told her mother the previous night about Parker gaining parole, and Jennie had been over the moon. Even so, Lex had kept their father's letter to herself. Something was hinky about it. She needed to get all her ducks in a row before confronting her mother, and . . . she had a drug manufacturer to find and shut down.

Police on three continents had been notified and were looking for Yuri Demidov, but she knew the bastard was in Seattle. She just knew it.

She put in a call to Sylvia and left a message about the video. If she could trace the video, she might be able to find the killer, if Sylvia had had the chance before the damn thing was confiscated.

Then she reread her father's letter. Code? The part about a 500 pound gorilla didn't really make sense. Five hundred pounds? Of what? Meth? Was Apollo measured in pounds? Did pounds really mean ounces? And who was his friend on the outside? She rubbed her nose and called the hospital to check on Bernie.

"What?" he bellowed when she was connected to his room.

She grinned. "Just checking in."

"I'm leaving today, but they won't let me leave until the fuckin' doctor signs my form, and he's in surgery." Bernie coughed several times. "But I'm good. I'll be back to work next week."

Somebody, probably his wife, protested loudly in the background.

"Or maybe the week after," Bernie amended.

"Awesome." God, she missed him. "I'll pop by later tonight once you're home." She had to see for herself that he was all right.

"Bring beer," he whispered.

She laughed. "I'll sneak some in." She clicked off.

Her phone rang, and she answered. "Monzelle."

"Hey Lex." Sylvia popped gum loudly. "I took a look at your video, and I think it's in pretty good shape. If I run up at lunch, will you give me the USB or DVD? It'd be easier to take a look at the original, especially since I had to turn over my copy."

Lex kicked back and stretched her neck. "We don't have the original. It was e-mailed to Bundt."

Sylvia popped again. "Nope, couldn't have been. We've been working on the external and larger servers all week, remember? I sent out a notice last Friday?"

Lex shrugged. She rarely paid attention to computer stuff. "I'm sure it was e-mailed."

"Nope. Not a chance. Our e-mail accounts wouldn't have accepted a video the size of that one. Somebody must have had the original in order to deposit it on the internal server like that." More gum crackled. "Drop me a line when you get the scoop." She hung up.

Lex frowned and shoved away from her desk. Her mind clicked facts into gear. Somebody knew Spike had been talking to the cops. Was there a cop involved? She thought about her dad's letter, about his friend, the warrior on the outside who took letters from Jennie. A warrior? Maybe a cop? All those times Mom had dropped by to go to coffee or lunch, had she also been meeting with somebody?

Before her disease had taken a bad turn and she'd stopped visiting?

Bundt strode in from the break room, a cup of coffee in his hand. "This stuff is shit," he muttered.

Lex forced a smile. "Hey, I've been thinking about the video of the Dunne men burying poor Spike. Did the feds confiscate it?"

"Yep." Bundt blew on his coffee and sat, his broad shoulders blocking his computer screen. "Fuckers."

"Definitely." She stretched her neck and tried to look casual.

"Maybe there's a chance we could trace the e-mail account where it came from?"

He shrugged. "We already asked the techs to take a look at it, but they haven't had any luck."

Bullshit. She nodded. "Oh well." All the times her mother had visited ran through her head. Several times Jennie had brought cookies for the gang, and she usually made an extra batch for Bundt and Masterson. Jesus. Had Bundt been part of Masterson being shot? She stood. "It might be shit coffee, but it's all we've got." Acting as if she had all the time in the world, she loped into the break room, where Masterson sat on an orange chair, scarfing down a jelly donut.

Dark circles shadowed his eyes, and lines of pain fanned out by his mouth. "Hey."

She frowned. "You okay?"

"Yeah. Just had physical therapy, but I can't take pain pills and do the job, so I'm sucking it up." He shoveled in pastry. "What's up?"

She poured herself a cup of coffee. "I've been thinking about the e-mail with the video of the Dunnes. Any clue where it came from?"

"Dunno," Masterson said. "Ask Bundt. It came to his address."

Yeah, she'd figured.

"I think we might have a problem." She sat and pulled out her cell phone, quickly dialing her mother.

"Hello, sweetie," her mom said.

Lex lowered her voice, while Masterson looked on, his eyebrows up. "Mom? Right now, I need you to tell me the truth. Who's Dad's warrior on the outside—the one helping him be a warrior on the inside?"

"Oh my," Jennie said, her voice loud enough Masterson could probably hear it. "Oh my."

"*Now*, Mom."

"Lexi, you have to understand. Your dad saw the error of his ways, and he tried to do good. He has been helping a policeman on the outside to get rid of the drug trade on the inside of the prison. He's a hero." A honk sounded in the background.

Lex frowned. "Mom? Where are you?"

"On an errand in a cab. Please don't be mad at your friend," her mom implored.

Heat flushed down Lex to slam into her stomach. "I won't," she lied.

Bundt walked into the break room and headed straight for more coffee. Lex eyed the gun strapped to his hip. He was fast, and he was good. Masterson lifted an eyebrow.

She shook her head. First, she needed confirmation. "Mom? Tell me."

Bundt whistled, poured a gallon of sugar into his coffee, smacked his partner on the shoulder, and sauntered out.

Lex blew out air, her body relaxing. "*Now,* Mom."

"Fine, but you promise you won't be mad. It's that handsome dark-haired man with the pretty eyes. Donny. It's Donny."

Lex's head snapped up.

Donny Masterson sighed and drew his gun. "Hang up."

No way. Betrayal pierced her chest. Lex slowly disengaged the phone to slip it into her pocket. "You're fucking kidding me."

"Leave the phone here," he ordered.

Fuck. She took out her phone and set it on the table. "Why?"

"The money is good, and we've made a fortune selling on the inside at the prisons." Masterson kicked out of his chair and gestured for her to stand. "I'll kill you or Bundt or anybody in my way. You understand?"

"Yeah." She followed his gesture to stand in front of him. "But you got shot."

"Spike, that fucking moron, heard I'd gotten a kill order for him, so he decided to shoot first." Masterson shoved the gun into her ribs. "Prick."

"Why did you have a kill order for Spike?"

Masterson sighed, as if put upon. "After Bundt brought in Spike, we were worried about his connection to you and his connection to your old man. I was concerned about Spike's desperate need to please you, and I figured he might just tell you all. So he needed to die."

"Did you kill him?" she whispered.

"Not personally." Masterson pushed harder with the gun. "Move, Lex."

She winced and started moving toward the squad room. A quick glance around showed Bundt on his phone, several cops working cases, and a couple victims filling out reports. If she screamed, somebody would get shot. She could make a move, but Masterson was good, even with one arm. And his gun was out and ready.

"Keep moving, Lex," he said, pressing harder.

She nodded and acted natural, heading through the throng. When she made her move, it'd have to be without so many civilians around. The guy had one arm and was a moron.

But he'd fooled her.

She reached the exit and stumbled. Masterson shoved the gun harder. "I really don't want to shoot you," he muttered.

Sure, he did.

"I don't see another way out of this, do you?" she asked under her breath.

"Actually, yes." He propelled her along. "Get into my truck and start driving, beautiful. It's time to go see Daddy."

She stumbled. "He's out?"

"Oh yeah. He's out and is looking forward to meeting up with your dumb-ass mama again. She's apparently on her way to see him." Masterson gestured for her to open the passenger side door and scoot over.

She did so, her head roiling. "My mom is on her way there?" Fear trembled through Lex's hands, and she had to fight not to turn on Masterson. Not yet, and not until she knew where her mother was going.

Masterson smiled and sat, the gun pointed levelly at her gut. "Drive. Then maybe you and I can have some fun together."

She rolled her eyes. "One-handed criminals who betray the badge aren't my type, asshole."

He laughed. "What is your type? What exactly is Kellach Dunne? A biker or a true international hero, like those documents said?"

Lex started the car and pulled out into the road, training kicking in and slowing her heart so she could concentrate. "I think he's a hero, and the second he finds out about this, you'd better hope I've already plunked your ass in jail." Heat flared down her torso as adrenaline kicked in and allowed her focus to narrow. "He won't go for jail. He'll cut off your fucking balls." *Yeah, true statement.*

Masterson scoffed. "We'll see about that. I tell ya, the guy has enemies."

Lex shook her head. "Did you kill Spike?"

"No, my partner did." Masterson smiled, the usual charm gone. "Burned the bastard and stuck him to a tree outside Fire to show Spike was working with the cops."

"Why videotape Spike?" she asked, trying to keep him talking.

Masterson chuckled. "To be honest, we figured Pyro would take him down, and we'd have leverage over that asshole. Imagine my surprise when I reclaimed the footage and saw the fucking Irish assholes right where I wanted them."

Her mouth went dry, and she tried to swallow. "Why turn them in?"

"To keep you busy. We know you're fucking one of them." Masterson snorted. "I had no clue they were undercover, however. My partner didn't seem surprised, though."

"Your partner? Yuri Demidov?" she asked, turning down another street when Masterson gestured.

Masterson frowned, both eyebrows going up. "Nice work, Detective."

"Gee, thanks, dickhead." She rolled her eyes. "Wasn't that tough. So how did Demidov find you?"

Masterson rolled his wounded shoulder. "I've been running meth for about ten years, on the streets with Spike and in the prison with Parker. Somehow, Demidov found me and made an offer for me to distribute Apollo. It's been going well."

"That shit kills people," she spat.

"Not if they just take a little."

She turned her head. "You know it's a weapon, right? That he's loading it in darts to kill people."

"I like weapons."

It was difficult to believe that at one time, she'd thought him to be handsome. "I can't wait to slap the cuffs on you," she muttered.

He licked his lips. "I'll be cuffing you, sexy."

Bile rolled around in her stomach and tried to climb up her esophagus. "Ewww."

He directed her toward the docks, and she drove around rusting warehouses until finally parking near a ramshackle warehouse that might have been white at one time. Rust covered the entire side, and damaged boards lined one side.

Lex frowned. "I think you might have structural problems, asshole."

Masterson snorted.

She turned to view him fully. His pupils had dilated, and his face was flushed. "I'm thinking you lied about not taking pain pills."

"Hey. Getting shot hurts." He chuckled, his aim not wavering a whit. "Don't make me shoot you. I promised your dad I wouldn't shoot you until he had a chance for a nice family reunion."

God. Did her dad really want to see her, or did he want to watch her get shot? Her hands trembled, so she set them in her lap.

"There are zip ties in the side of the door. Grab them and zip your hands." Masterson's voice remained clear, a sign that a simple pain pill didn't affect him much.

Lex reached for the ties. "Do you sample all your drugs?"

"Some." He shrugged. "Now, Lex."

She could turn and grab for the gun, but he had the advantage, and she still didn't know where her mother might be. If Jennie was inside with the monster, Lex needed to get in there. Playing the captive would hopefully get her father to let down his guard. She slipped her hands into the tie, using her teeth to pull it closed.

"Tighter," Masterson ordered.

She pulled tighter and then turned to glare at him. "Let's get this over with." For the first time since childhood, she was about to see her father without cuffs or an orange jumpsuit. As she stepped from the car, a chill skittered down her back. She quickly noted several soldiers scattered throughout, on alert. Damn it.

Her boots scraped over cracks in the asphalt as she walked in front of Masterson and into a barely lit warehouse. She blinked several times until her eyes accustomed themselves to the light.

Her father met her at the door. "Alex."

She peered around him to see her mother sitting at the lone table in the massive building, dressed in her Sunday best. Water dripped down the walls, and off to the side, a brand new Mercedes waited quietly. "Are you all right, Mom?"

Jennie nodded and stood, walking toward her with a big smile. Seeing Lex's bound hands, she frowned. "I don't understand."

Parker sighed and slipped an arm over Jennie's shoulders. "Lex isn't quite on board yet, and we needed to get her here."

Jennie shook her head. "No. Let her go." She gasped as Parker squeezed her shoulder.

Lex hissed. "I'm fine, Mom. Just relax. We're all good."

Her father smiled. "Now that's what I want to hear." He pulled Jennie around and pushed her into a chair. "Alex? Come sit."

Jennie frowned and pulled out a chair for Lex.

Lex gave him a look and walked over to sit in the chair, calculating the best way to get out of there alive. Masterson had a gun, and the handle of one poked out of her father's waist.

The front door of the Mercedes opened, and a man stepped out.

She lifted her head. "Yuri Demidov. I've been looking for you." So the pictures of him were current. "I'm supposing you were the one who sent men to my apartment several times. They had, ah, your type of accent." In other words, they were witches, too.

Demidov shut the door and smoothed down very expensive looking silk pants. "Yes. I needed the order from your father, and I figured you'd check your damn mail more often." He shook his head. "I didn't know who was helping you until I saw the video of the Dunnes that Masterson so smartly arranged."

Masterson snorted. "She's fucking Kellach."

Lex stilled.

He rolled his eyes. "I'm not a moron."

She didn't move. The hell he wasn't.

Demidov smiled, his teeth overly white in the dingy building. "This will be easier than I'd hoped." He pulled a gun and pointed it at Jennie's head. "I knew the second I flooded Seattle with Apollo at least one enforcer would show up, but I had no idea they'd send three. I'd like to take them out slowly, one by one. Call your lover."

Chapter 35

Kellach strode out of Fire's conference room after another useless meeting, his instincts humming with an unpleasant energy. The two dead witches had been quiet and law-abiding, and yet somebody had tested Apollo on them without remorse. There were no leads to be found with the dead couple, and a quick autopsy had revealed burned organs and demolished hearts.

Apollo, the mixture of it, was deadlier than the original PK mineral all by itself. Damn it.

Now, at Fire, his gut churned. Something was up. He had to find Alexandra. His phone buzzed. "Alexandra?"

"Ah, no. It's Tori."

"Victoria." He paused near his bike while Daire and Adam emerged from the building, both frowning. "What can I do for you?"

"Well, ah, I can't find either my mother or my sister." She sighed. "I used the gym in the building, and while I was gone, my mother left. So I tried to call Lexi, and she's not answering her phone. Have you talked to her?"

He shot his brothers a look. "I have not. Tell you what? I'll track her down and get right back to you." He clicked off. "Something's wrong."

Daire paused in straddling his bike. "What?"

"Dunno." His phone buzzed again, and he didn't recognize the number. "Hello?"

"Kellach?" Alexandra asked, her voice too calm.

He held up a hand to his brothers. "Where are you?"

A scuffle sounded, and a male cleared his throat. "Kellach Dunne, Enforcer for the Nine. So nice to make your acquaintance."

Kell lifted his head, his body going on full alert. "Yuri Demidov. I'm assuming, of course."

"Good assumption. My friend here brought the lovely Alexandra to me, stating that she's, ah, fucking you. Shall I clue him in to the full extent of your relationship?" Demidov asked, his voice high.

"Let's leave the humans clueless, shall we?" Kell kept his voice level, although he realized that of course, another witch could sense he'd mated Alexandra. "You do know, if you so much as scratch her, I'll take off your head."

Demidov laughed, the sound slightly off. "How about a trade? I'd love to get my hands on Simone Brightston, considering how she betrayed my father. She's one of many I plan to use Apollo on."

Kell tsked. "Sorry, but Simone is out of reach. We've shut down the members of the Nine until we get a handle on Apollo." He lied easily without a hitch in his tone while Daire walked away, phone to his ear, no doubt trying to have somebody trace the call. They did have decent sources in the Realm and those guys, especially Chalton Reese, could perform miracles.

"Well, I'll settle for an enforcer today." Demidov sighed. "After I play a little with your lady, that is."

"She's mated," Kell said flatly. Had the allergy gene kicked in yet? God, he hoped so. "Touch her, and your skin will explode from the contact."

"Then maybe I'll just shoot off parts of her. Or . . . maybe we should see what Apollo does to a newly mated witch." Demidov sniffed.

Kell frowned. "What do you want?" He nodded at Daire's gesture to keep the jackass talking. At least this way, he knew Alexandra wasn't being harmed as he spoke.

"Let's see. How about I trade your bitch here for Daire Dunne? My boss would love to get his hands on Daire," Demidov said.

Kell jerked his head toward Daire to gain his attention. "Your boss wants Daire? Why?"

"I assume that's personal. But I'd go a long way in the organization by turning him in."

"Sorry, but you'll have to deal with me," Kell said. "Daire is out of town."

Daire shook his head vehemently.

Kell held up a hand. Exactly what kind of intel did Demidov have?

"Sorry, but I know he's there because sweet Jennie told me he is. Apparently, she met him last night. Anyway, if you want Alexandra, I want Daire," Demidov said quietly.

Damn it. "Fine. We'll trade Daire for Alexandra. Who's your boss, anyway?" Kell asked.

"Oh, you'll see soon enough." Demidov growled low. "Wait by your phone, and I'll send you instructions." He hung up.

Kell kicked a rock. "Fucking fucktard of a bastard witch." He slid his phone in his pocket. "He's not in charge——there's somebody else." Frankly, the guy sounded half off his nut. "Tell me you got him."

Daire finished listening on the phone and then turned. "We got him."

Alexandra settled into her chair and looked around. Masterson and Yuri had moved over by the Mercedes. They spoke quietly, no doubt planning her death.

She brought her attention closer and stared at her father across the table. "Rumor has it you've been running drugs in prison."

Jennie gasped and turned even paler. "Parker? What about being a warrior?"

Parker shook his head. "You have always been the dumbest bitch around, you know that?" He leaned back, his huge barrel of a chest still significant. "I came out of prison a millionaire. How fucking amazing is that?"

Lex tried to loosen her hands under the table. "You'll go back in the same way, then."

Parker shook his head. "Oh, no, you ungrateful bitch. I'm not going back in. Ever."

Jennie stood, wavering on her new hip. "You lied to me."

"Sit down, or I'll knock you down. " His eyes turned a mean blue Lex remembered well.

"It's okay, Mom. Just sit down," Lex said gently, giving her father a look of warning.

He glared back.

She glanced over at Masterson leaning against the wall and asked him, "How much blood is on your hands?"

He snarled and returned to his discussion with Yuri.

She returned her focus on her father. "What's the plan here? You're really such a bastard you'd watch your own kid get killed?" An ache she'd deny to her grave welled inside her chest.

He shrugged. "We'll trade you for this Daire fellow Yuri wants so badly."

She snarled. "You've always been a shitty liar, you know that?"

He reached out almost casually and cuffed her on the side of the head. Pain flared through her skull, but she didn't flinch.

Jennie jumped up. With almost a happy roar, Parker stood and shoved her back into the chair. She flopped, crying out, trying to catch her balance.

Lex snarled and half-stood. "Touch her again, and I'll fucking kill you."

Jennie huddled closer to her, tears streaking down her face. "Parker? I don't care about me, but you wouldn't let them kill Alexandra, would you? She is your daughter."

Lex shook her head when he didn't bother to answer. "Mom, if they let us go, we'll tell the police. No way are they letting us go." She narrowed her focus to the oxygen molecules around them, beginning to reshape them and draw on fire.

"Stop it, or I'll shoot your mother in the head," Demidov called out. She stilled.

Jennie glanced around, her eyes wild. "Stop what?"

"Nothing." Lex tried to send her a reassuring smile. "Just working on the hand restraints. Unfortunately, they're strong." There had to be a way she could manipulate fire without Demidov knowing.

Kell would move mountains to find her, but she'd left her phone back at the station. Demidov had talked a long time. The enforcers had some pretty damn scary connections. Maybe there was a chance they could've traced the call from Kell's end. Maybe not. Either way, she had to be ready to fight at the first opportunity.

Her mom turned toward her. "I'm so sorry, Lexi. I had no clue."

Lex nodded. "It's all right, Mom. We'll figure this out, I promise."

Parker sat back and patted his big belly. "How's your cunt of a sister? Did she tell you she visited me? Yelled right in my face." He leaned toward her, his gaze narrowing. "I'm looking her up the first second I get."

Jennie gave a soft cry of distress. "You'll leave her alone, you bastard."

Parker turned and half-stood.

Lex coughed, searching desperately for a way to stop his advance. He'd kill her mother if he hit her hard enough, which he appeared more than ready to do. "Where's the money?" she threw out quickly to prevent the assault.

He paused and turned. "Huh?"

"All this money you think you have." Lex glanced around and forced a look of disdain onto her face. "I mean, it's not here. Are you sure they saved you some of the money?"

His chest puffed out, and he sat back down.

Lex relaxed and tried to still her thumping heart.

He nodded. "I have bank accounts, several in my name. I've already checked them." Pride filled his voice before he scowled again, leaning toward her to whisper. "If you hadn't been such a bitch, I would've shared with you. You could've been my connection instead of that grease ball over there."

He smelled like mint and cheap whiskey. She'd forgotten that.

At the memory, her stomach lurched. "I hope you checked the actual accounts and not just what they sent you on the computer. And I hope you changed the passwords immediately, so they couldn't take the money right out after showing the balances to you."

His bushy eyebrows drew down. "What do you mean?"

She leaned toward him and lowered her voice. "If they have the passwords to the accounts, they could've transferred all the money out after showing you the balances. Surely you thought of that."

He rubbed his smooth chin. "Yeah. Yeah, I thought of that and changed the passwords."

Damn idiot. Lex sat back and nodded. "Well, then I guess you have nothing to worry about."

Yet worry fanned out from his eyes all of a sudden. He took out a shiny new smartphone. "I think I can find the accounts on the phone."

Moron. His attention diverted, Lex glanced around. It appeared as if one full wall could open, so there were two exits—the wall-door and the only regular door. Two exits, three armed men to fight, and her mother with unsteady legs to rescue.

As odds went, they sucked.

It was a bad time to deal with her father since she'd just gotten him distracted, but something in her, deep down, had to know. "Will you really let them kill us?" she asked softly.

He looked up from his phone, blinking to focus. Then he shifted his large bulk in the chair, his face turning red. "They're gonna trade you."

"You know that's not true." She shook her head. "Say the words."

"They're trading you." He focused back on the screen.

Hurt exploded into fury inside her. "You're too much of a fucking coward to even say the words." The bastard, her actual father, would just bury his head and then let her murder happen. "You stopped being my father years ago, you fucking loser."

He hunched over his phone.

Minutes ticked by, and then an hour. Yuri and Masterson finished talking, and Yuri spoke on the phone to someone for a while, but Lex couldn't make out the words. She angled her body away from him and imagined the oxygen around her, focusing narrowly on the zip ties around her wrists. Heat flared, and she methodically burned sliver by sliver away.

Finally, Yuri loped her way, a man with a strange glint in his eye, a guy ready to kill. "We have the meeting area almost ready."

Lex raised an eyebrow. "You're really making a show of it, huh?"

He shrugged.

She sucked in air. "You sent soldiers and Duck to my home."

"Yes. I needed the letter from your father with the coded directions of how much product he'd sold and where to deliver it." Yuri almost sounded bored.

She shook her head. "Why did you kill Duck?" Who else could it have been?

"Ah." Yuri tisked his tongue. "Duck had the unfortunate fate of working with Spike, and Spike made the terrible mistake of telling Duck about me. So Duck and then Spike both had to die."

What a complete asshole. She needed to get free and put him away for life. Could witches escape normal prisons? She'd have to find out. One of the bands slipped loose. She was so close. "How are you getting the planekite here from Russia?" she whispered.

Yuri smiled, revealing perfectly white teeth. "Phenakite."

"Whatever." Another sliver loosened.

"Let's just say I have good friends in the Port of Seattle," he said.

Ah. Good tip. As soon as she arrested his ass, she'd trace his contacts at the Port.

The hair on the back of her neck stood up. Awareness hinted in the atmosphere—no breeze, but a sense of home. She stiffened, ready to move.

Yuri stopped moving, and his shoulders rolled back. His gaze darted around the quiet room, and he opened his mouth in a hiss of anger as all hell broke loose.

The massive wall-door burst open and folded in on itself, spiraling smoke and fire up to the rafters. Lex leaped for her mother, knocking her to the ground and covering her as the small door crashed in.

Lex looked to where the door had been. Kell stood there in full combat gear. His gaze caught hers, full and intense.

She shifted to her knees, taking her mother up with her.

Her father roared and grabbed her hair, pulling her to her feet as Yuri ran forward, shooting darts toward Kell. Several found their mark as he pivoted to fire a green laser at Yuri. Jumping toward the bastard, Kell put his body between the shooter and Lex.

A firefight echoed behind her, but she concentrated on her mother. Balancing herself, Lex leaned a hip back into her dad, and dropped to a knee. He flew over her head to land on the pavement. Hard.

Not missing a beat, she grabbed her mom's arms and pulled her to upright. "Run," she hissed.

Jennie, her eyes wide already with shock, hitched on her damaged legs toward the door. Lex covered her mom, shoving her along, until they reached the opening. She glanced frantically around at the quiet area and spotted a truck down the way. "Go get behind that. If you see anybody, find a phone and call 9-1-1." She turned to head back into the warehouse.

Jennie grabbed her arm. "Lexi, wait. Don't—"

Lex turned. "It's my job, Mom. Now go." She turned, and ducking low, ran back into the building.

The Dunne brothers fought the many soldiers across the warehouse, spilling the firefight and hand-to-hand outside. Bear, Garrett, and Logan jumped into the fray, creating pandemonium in an oddly graceful fight to the death.

Kell broke the neck of a witch streaming fire, only to turn and have Yuri plug him in the neck with another dart. His eyes widened, and he went down.

"No!" she screamed, scrambling for him and dropping to her knees.

Garrett roared in fury and tackled Yuri into the Mercedes.

Logan grappled with Masterson, and in front of her eyes, punched through the dirty cop's throat to the wall. Masterson's eyes closed in a harsh death.

"Kell!" She crouched before him, looking for a threat. They went unnoticed as the battle waged on. She grabbed the top of his flak vest and dragged him to a corner.

He groaned, and his body convulsed.

Dropping to her knees, she lifted his head to her lap. "How bad?" she whispered, yanking out the darts. She patted his face. "Don't go. Don't fucking leave me."

His eyes opened. Real flames danced in their depths.

She shook him. God, he couldn't leave her. Not just when she'd found him.

"Stay with me." Her heart expanded with pure terror. "I love you. Please stay."

He winced, and steam rose from his mouth.

She frowned. How much of the drug was in his system?

One of Yuri's soldiers sprang free of the melee and ran toward her, gun out. She grabbed Kell's green gun from his hip, paused, and squeezed off three shots. The soldier's eyes widened, and he dropped face-first to the ground.

Kell groaned, and fire crackled on his arms. "Fuck."

She sucked in air, trying to remember how she'd saved Bernie. Harnessing oxygen, pouring feeling into it, she filled her mouth with fire. Panic hitched her movements, but she pressed her mouth to Kell's and blew.

His chest expanded, and he shuddered.

She did it again, feeling her fire surround the intruding fire in him and quench the burn.

He struggled and then slowly slid his hand around her shoulder.

Then he turned to his side and coughed out fire, much as a drowning victim would water. "Holy fuck." He shook his head.

She smacked him on the back, throwing more fire. "Kell?"

He groaned and stood. "Just a few darts won't kill me." He grinned and rolled to his feet, tugging her up to put her behind him. "Although your breath of fire just saved my liver."

She coughed.

A body slammed into Kell, and they flew into the wall. Lex's gun spiraled away to hit the floor. Kell brought both elbows down on a soldier's shoulders, knocking the guy to the ground.

Lex swept the area, seeing Kell's brothers and their allies finishing off the soldiers. Almost in slow motion, she turned toward the Mercedes, where her father stood, a gun in his hand, aimed at her.

Time truly stopped.

He smiled, his eyes narrowing in that long-ago look. With a snarl she remembered, he pulled the trigger.

Pain burst in her chest. The world quieted. Her eyes widened, and she dropped to the ground.

Chapter 36

"No!" Kellach twisted the neck of the human who'd tackled him and turned to Alexandra, catching her before she hit the ground.

Blood sprayed from her chest. Her eyes widened, her body went slack. She tried to say something, and blood bubbled from her mouth. Kell pivoted to catch the threat just as Adam knocked the gun from Parker Monzelle's hand and punched him out with a hard hit to the temple. He passed out against the Mercedes and plunged to the ground.

Kell laid Alexandra on the cracked concrete, his heart thundering. "No, no, no," he muttered, yanking open her shirt.

The amount of blood made him sway. Panic and fear clutched him hard.

Determination roared through him, animalistic in its nature.

Movement caught his attention from the corner of his eye, and he crouched over his mate to defend. Yuri, dart gun out, started firing. Kell ducked his head and leaped forward, past the point of reason. The scent of his mate's blood filled his senses, darkening his soul.

He reached Yuri and took him all the way to the ground, yanking the gun away and shoving the barrel in Yuri's mouth.

"No," Adam yelled, running toward him.

But Kell was too far gone to listen. He pulled the trigger, shooting at least eight darts down Yuri's throat. The gun emptied, and he flung it away.

Yuri grasped his neck, convulsing, his eyes widening.

Kell slowly stood and backed away.

Fire ripped open Yuri's chest, spraying out with bloody flames. He screamed, the sound high-pitched and evil.

Kell turned and ran back to his mate as she gasped on the ground. "Stay with me, baby." He yanked off his shirt to wipe her chest, to see the damage. Fury tried to take him, and he shoved down the fatalistic desperation. If she left him, he'd go with her. Only Alexandra. Always.

He wiped the blood away from the bullet hole—just above her heart but closer to her shoulder. He pulled her up, wincing at her cry of protest, to see the hole in her back. Through and through.

She reached for him, tears streaking down her face. "Love——"

He brushed her lips. "Love you, too." His heart settled as his mind kicked into gear. "This is gonna hurt a little, baby." Shoving her shirt from her shoulder, he forced oxygen into a fire ball and pressed his palm to her wound.

She shrieked, her body arching in shock.

He winced, his gut roiling. When he turned her, she fought him, but he held strong and cauterized the hole in her back. "'Twas a through and through. Have to stop the bleeding."

Her body went limp, and she nodded, blinking rapidly. His little warrior.

Once the wounds were burned, he placed a palm over the burn and slowly, inextricably, drew the pain into his body. Relieving her.

She gasped, her eyes widening.

He smiled and pressed his lips against hers. "I love you, Alexandra."

She kissed him back, her lips trembling. "I love you more."

He grinned.

Sirens sounded in the distance, and he lifted his head to see his men, some bloody and bruised, all stiffening. The fight was definitely over. Yuri, Masterson, and a slew of their soldiers littered the ground in death.

"Take anybody nonhuman and all evidence of Apollo and go. Now."

Daire nodded and quickly set people to work.

Within minutes, only Kell and Alexandra remained along with Masterson's body, three dead human soldiers, and an unconscious Parker Monzelle. The police burst in, and Kell assisted her to her feet.

"I guess you're undercover for an international police force?" she whispered.

He nodded, hands up. "Aye. As are Garrett and Logan, considering the king wants them to remain here and on the job."

Hopefully, the Seattle PD would let him get his cover story out before trying to kill him once recognizing Masterson's body near the door.

His woman, his mate, his warrior walked toward her people, already issuing orders.

God, he loved her.

Lex settled her mom and sister in the guest room in the penthouse then kicked off her boots in the spacious bedroom, her body aching, her mind fuzzing. Thank goodness her mother had escaped before anybody created fire to throw. "They're still in shock. God, I'm tired."

"Aye." Kell moved in behind her, all warm and delicious male. "I haven't been grilled by the garda like that for some time."

She turned and smiled. "So long as we stick to the story, which is mostly true, we're fine." They'd left out the parts about witches, vampires, and demons. "The brass wasn't happy your fellow soldiers didn't stick around to give reports."

Kell rubbed a bruise near his eye. "They had bodies to dispose of."

Lex grinned. "I like your story of keeping their covers secret better."

"Me too." He frowned and settled his hands at the small of her back, tugging her into safety. "I'm sorry about Masterson."

She frowned, hurt aching down her. "Bundt might not recover. He's devastated." As she would have been if Bernie had turned out to be a low-life drug dealer. "It was hard to explain how somebody hit Masterson hard enough to punch through his throat." She'd claimed she'd been shot by that time and believed the soldier responsible, who'd already left, had some sort of weapon.

Kell dropped a kiss on the top of her head. "Demons fight for the kill, always. Logan was just doing his job."

"I'm not mad at Logan." She leaned back, knowing Kell would keep her upright.

"Good." His eyes glowed that odd green around his iris. "Your chief agreed to keep my cover for me, so hopefully I can continue at Fire. We need to know who the guy above Yuri is and why he wants Daire so badly."

Warmth glided through her. "SWAT raided the port and closed down Yuri's connection."

"That's good, but that's only the beginning," Kell mused.

True. "I guess you're staying in town, huh?"

His upper lip curved. "I'm staying wherever you are."

She caught her breath but didn't dare to hope. "I'm damaged."

"We're all damaged." He brushed a piece of hair from her face, tension of a different sort suggested in his touch.

She shook her head. "My own father shot me." Her voice cracked on the end, and she cleared it. At least she'd put the bastard behind bars again. He wouldn't get out this time. "I don't trust well."

"You'll learn." Kell leaned down and brushed her lips with his. "I'll keep you safe, Alexandra." Slowly, he drew her shirt off.

"I trust *you*." Her words went deeper than love. "Completely."

He stiffened and then gathered her closer. "I love you, little warrior."

She laughed. "I'm keeping my job as a cop, you badass enforcer."

He grinned. "I'm aware, and so long as you keep to the deal of you fighting humans and me fighting immortals, we're good."

"I don't remember actually agreeing to that deal," she murmured, sliding up on her tiptoes to nip his whiskered chin.

"Well then." His voice deepened. "Let's negotiate, shall we?" Bunching his shoulders, he lifted her and then tossed her onto the bed.

She rolled and came up laughing. No matter what happened, she could trust that they'd be together. When he'd been hurt, she'd had a vision of her life without him, and it was cold and empty. He brought warmth to her, and she wanted to keep him. "I love you, Dunne."

He grinned and stalked toward her, all male animal. "I love you more, Alexandra." Then he was on her. "Let's negotiate now."

Don't miss the start of a pulse-pounding new post-apocalyptic series by Rebecca Zanetti, *The Scorpius Syndrome*, available in print and e-book next February!

Despair hungered in the darkness, not lingering, not languishing . . . but waiting to bite. No longer the little brother of rage, despair had taken over the night, ever present, an actor instead of an afterthought.

Lynne picked her way along the deserted twelve-lane interstate, allowing the weak light from the moon to guide her. An unnatural silence hung heavy over the empty land. A few rusted carcasses of cars lined the sides, otherwise, the once vibrant 405 was dead . . . yet she trod carefully.

Her months of hiding had taught her stealth. Prey needed stealth, as did the hunter.

She was both.

The tennis shoes she'd stolen from an abandoned thrift store protected her feet from the cracked asphalt. A click echoed in the darkness.

About time.

She'd made it closer to Los Angeles . . . well, what used to be Los Angeles . . . than she'd hoped.

A strobe light hit her full on, rendering sight useless. She closed her eyes. They'd either kill her or not. Either way, no need to go blind. "I want to see Mercury."

Silence. Then several more clicks. Guns of some type.

She forced strength into her voice. "You don't want to kill me without taking me to Mercury first." Jax Mercury, to be exact. If he really existed. If not, she was screwed anyway.

"Why would we do that?" A voice from the darkness, angry and near.

She opened her eyes, allowing light to narrow her pupils. "I'm Lynne Harmony."

Gasps, low and male, echoed around her. They'd closed in silently, just as well trained as she'd heard. As she'd hoped.

"Bullshit," a voice hissed from her left.

She tilted her head toward the voice, then slowly, so slowly they wouldn't be spooked, she unbuttoned her shirt. No cat calls, no suggestive responses followed. Shrugging her shoulders, she dropped the cotton to the ground, facing the light.

She hadn't worn a bra, but she doubted the echoing exhales of shock were from her size Bs. More likely, the shimmering blue outline of her heart caught their attention. Yeah, she was a freak. Typhoid Mary in the body of a woman who'd made a mistake. A big one. But she might be able to save the men surrounding her. "So. Jax Mercury. Now."

One man stepped closer. Gang tattoos lined his face, inked tears showing his kills. He might have been thirty, he might have been sixty. Regardless, he was dangerous. Eyeing her chest, he quickly crossed himself. "Holy Mary, Mother of God."

"Not even close." Wearily, she reached down and grabbed her shirt, shrugging it back on. She figured the *take me to your leader* line would get her shot and didn't say it. "Do you want to live or not?"

He met her gaze, hope and fear twisting his scarred upper lip. "Yes."

It was the most sincere sound she'd heard in months. "We're running out of time." Time had deserted them long ago, but she needed to get a move on. "Please." The sound shocked her, the civility of it, a word she'd forgotten how to use. The slightest of hopes warmed that blue organ in her chest, reminding her of who she used to be. Who she'd lost.

Another figure stepped forward, big and silent. Deadly power vibrated in the shift of muscle as light illuminated him from behind, keeping his features shrouded. "I didn't tell you to put your shirt back on." No emotion, no hint of humanity echoed in the deep rumble.

The lack of emotion twittered anxiety through her abdomen. Without missing a beat, she secured each button, keeping the movements slow and sure. "I take it you're Mercury." Regardless of name, there was no doubt the guy was in charge.

"If I am?" Soft, his voice promised death.

The promise she'd make him keep. Someday. The breeze picked up, tumbling weeds across the deserted 405. She fought a shiver. Any weakness shown might get her killed. "You know who I am."

"I know who you say you are." His overwhelming form blocked out the light, reminding her of her smaller size. "Take off your shirt."

Something about the way he said it gave her pause. Before, she hadn't cared. But with him so close she could smell *male*, an awareness of her femininity brought fresh fear. Nevertheless, she unbuttoned her shirt.

Her hands trembled.

Straightening her spine, she squared her shoulders and left the shirt on, the worn material gaping in the front.

He waited.

She lifted her chin, trying to meet his eyes, although she couldn't see them. The men around them remained silent, yet alertness carried on the breeze. How many guns were trained on her? She wanted to tell them it would only take one. While she'd been through hell, she'd never really learned to fight.

The wind whipped into action, lifting her long hair away from her face. Her arms tightened against her ribcage. Goose bumps rose along her skin.

Swearing softly, the man stepped in, long tapered fingers drawing her shirt apart. He shifted to the side, allowing light to blast her front. Neon blue glowed over her flesh.

"Jesus." He pressed his palm against her breastbone—directly above her heart.

Shock tightened her muscles, her eyes widening, heart ripping into a gallop. Her nipples pebbled from the breeze. Warmth cascaded from his hand when he spread his fingers over the odd blue of her skin. When was the last time someone had touched her gently?

And gentle, he was.

The touch had her looking down at his damaged hand. Faded white scars slashed across his knuckles, above the veins, past his wrist. The bizarre glow from her heart filtered through his long fingers. Her entire chest was blue from within. The veins closest to her heart, which glowed neon blue, shone strong enough to be seen through her ribs and sternum.

He exhaled loudly, removing his touch.

An odd sense of loss filtered down her spine. Then surprise came as he quickly buttoned her shirt to the top.

He clasped her by the elbow. "Cut the light." His voice didn't rise, but instantly, the light extinguished. "I'm Mercury. What do you want?"

What a question. What she wanted, nobody could provide. Yet she struggled to find the right words. Night after night, traveling under darkness to reach him, she'd planned for this moment. But the words wouldn't come. She wanted to breathe. To rest. To hide. "Help. I need your help." The truth tumbled out too fast to stop.

He stiffened and then tightened his hold on her arm. "That, darlin', you're gonna have to earn."

New York Times and *USA Today* bestselling author REBECCA ZANETTI has worked as an art curator, Senate aide, lawyer, college professor, and a hearing examiner—only to culminate it all in stories about alpha males and the women who claim them. She writes contemporary romances, dark paranormal romances, and romantic suspense novels.

Growing up amid the glorious backdrops and winter wonderlands of the Pacific Northwest has given Rebecca fantastic scenery and adventures to weave into her stories. She resides in the wild north with her husband, children, and extended family who inspire her every day—or at the very least give her plenty of characters to write about.

Please visit Rebecca at: www.rebeccazanetti.com/
www.facebook.com/RebeccaZanetti.Author.FanPage
twitter.com/RebeccaZanetti

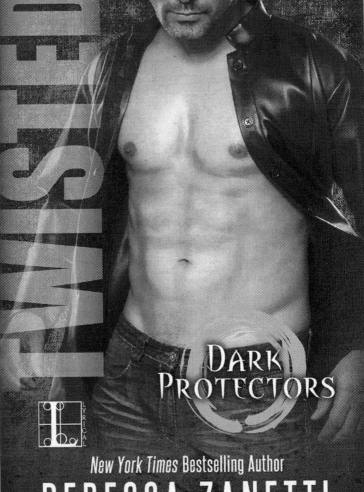

TWISTED

DARK
PROTECTORS

New York Times Bestselling Author
REBECCA ZANETTI

SHADOWED

DARK PROTECTORS

New York Times Bestselling Author

REBECCA ZANETTI

DARK PROTECTORS

New York Times Bestselling Author

REBECCA ZANETTI

MARKED

DARK PROTECTORS

New York Times Bestselling Author

REBECCA ZANETTI

Printed in the United States
by Baker & Taylor Publisher Services